# LOVE AND RESISTANCE

## THE TRILOGY

MARION KUMMEROW

Love and Resistance, The Trilogy

Marion Kummerow

ISBN Paperback version: 978-3-948865-13-9

All Rights Reserved

Copyright © 2018 Marion Kummerow

This story is based on actual events. The main characters Q and Hilde have existed in real life under a different name. The author has tried to keep as close to real events as possible, but incidents, characters and timelines have been changed for dramatic purposes. Side characters may be composites, or entirely fictitious.

# CONTENTS

# PART I: UNRELENTING

# CHAPTER 1

Dr. Wilhelm Quedlin didn't know it, but today, the course of his life was about to change.

Q, as his family and friends called him, was on his way to work on this sunny October morning in 1932. Oranienburg was lovely this time of year, with trees flaming their fall colors along the banks of the Havel River.

Strolling through the gates of Auer-Gesellschaft, he quickly headed to his labs. Then stopped. The door to his office stood open, which was peculiar, but he entered nonetheless. He stopped just inside, surprise freezing him in his tracks. Two police officers were waiting for him. He recovered quickly and removed his hat, nodding to the men congenially as he placed it on the rack.

"Good day, gentlemen. What can I do for you?" he asked, trying to mask his surprise and worry with a polite welcome. An unexpected visit from the police was almost never a good thing. The political climate in Germany had grown increasingly tense, and everyone knew it was much better to keep a low profile these days.

"Doctor Quedlin, we need you to accompany us down to the police station," the older officer said, unashamedly eying Q with blank, dark eyes.

"Is there a problem?" Q asked, trying to remain calm even as his mind raced to identify anything he could have done wrong. And who might have been around to witness his error and report it. Telling on one's fellow man was no longer taboo like before, but actually encouraged by the government.

"You need to come with us now," the older officer repeated, stepping forward, his expression brooking no argument.

Q nodded and retrieved his hat from the rack he'd just hung it on. "Of course, officer." He stepped out of the office, keeping his eyes straight ahead and his hands in his pockets as he walked from the building, followed by the two police officers. On his way out, the eyes of his fellow workers watched him surreptitiously. Of course, they wanted to know what was going on, but without drawing attention to themselves, lest the police decided they too needed to be questioned.

The policemen ushered him from the building, past a seemingly perplexed gatekeeper and placed him in the back seat of a black DKW2. The motorized vehicle took off just as soon as everyone was inside. Q was squeezed between two officers, the seating very tight and uncomfortable from his point of view, but then again, the police were rarely concerned with anyone's comfort.

He looked straight ahead, seeing the people hurrying along the streets, turning their heads to avoid the passing police automobile. No one seemed to even notice the beautiful sunny autumn day. Their minds were focused on getting to their destination and minding their own business. Even in his current predicament, or maybe because of it, he thought it sad that most people didn't share so much as a passing smile or warm greeting to the people they encountered along the street.

On their way to the police station, they passed the Oranienburg Palace, with its white stucco walls and red tiled roof as well as several brick and stone buildings housing churches and schools. As they approached the last intersection before the police station, Q noticed a small group of men wearing the SS *Schutzstaffel* uniform standing on the street corner.

Unlike the police officers currently riding in the vehicle with him, those men wore all black uniforms. Their caps were adorned with the *Totenkopf* skull and bones symbol, indicating they were loyal followers of the National Socialist German Worker's Party.

Nazis.

The late July elections had seen many parliament seats go to both the Nazis and the Communists, and political unrest was growing stronger with each passing day. Q sighed inwardly as he pondered on the reasons for the growing tensions.

With the crash of the United States Stock Market three years earlier, and the tremendous financial burden placed upon the German people by the Versailles Treaty to make reparations for Germany's actions in the Great War, the economy and people were suffering greatly.

Banks had collapsed, factories and entire industries were in jeopardy of closing, and people were ripe for some sort of change. This was evidenced when Adolf Hitler's Nazi party won an overwhelming thirty-seven percent of the popular vote in the most recent election.

Q looked at the younger police officer sitting next to him and asked, "Can you tell me what the problem is?" He understood very well that people didn't get taken to the police station for a minor transgression and wanted to know what he was facing.

"Doctor Quedlin, we–"

"Silence!" the older officer stated from the front seat. "He will find out soon enough."

Q bit his tongue so that he wouldn't make a pointed remark and incite the rude policeman any further. The trickle of fear he'd felt since seeing the police officers in his office had increased during the automobile ride. It now crept up his spine and made his neck hair stand on end.

Finally, the police vehicle stopped in front of the three story brick building, and he was ushered into the station that had most definitely seen better days. The wooden furniture was worn and very sparse. Only two wooden chairs stood against the far wall, the only accommodations being made for visitors, of which Q was almost positive were few and far between. The climate didn't allow for people to bring themselves to the police station unless the circumstances were dire and no other options existed.

He lowered his eyes and noticed the dirty and cracked tiles on the floor, which fit perfectly into the threatening and tense atmosphere of the entire place. Q's fear escalated, but he did his best to regulate his breathing and stay calm.

*Do not let them sense your fear. You've done nothing wrong. Remember that.*

But his self-talk did little to quell his nervousness when a ranking officer approached. "Doctor Quedlin?"

"Yes. Could someone please explain why I've been brought here?"

"Of course. Take him to the interrogation room," the ranking officer demanded, his voice harsh and intimidating. Another officer grabbed Q's elbow and led him down the hallway, pushing him into a sparsely furnished room featuring a large, bare bulb light hanging over a well-worn wooden table and three chairs.

"Sit!" the man barked, pushing on Q's shoulder until he took a seat.

The ranking officer entered the room and waited until the other one had left before he seated himself across from the table. When the metal door snapped shut, Q felt a sudden surge of panic. He was trapped, and nobody could come to his rescue. The officer stared into Q's eyes, and Q tried not to fidget. "Oberkommissar Strobel," he said by way of introduction. "You know why you're here?"

"No, Herr Oberkommissar, if you would please let me know what this is about?" Q hoped the other man didn't hear the panic in his cracking voice.

Oberkommissar Strobel sent him a stern glance, "You are Dr. Wilhelm Quedlin?"

"Yes."

"What were you doing at Auer-Gesellschaft?"

Q took a deep breath. The police probably knew all of that already, but he would play their little game. "I work there as chief engineer in the chemical laboratory and supervise a team of scientists."

"Since when?"

"I started working for Auer-Gesellschaft four years ago after I received my PhD in chemical engineering from the Technical University of Berlin."

"What exactly did you work on?"

A puzzled look crossed Q's face. He had no intention of going into detail about his scientific research. After all, that was classified material. "Herr Oberkommissar, I wrote my dissertation about the thermal decay of nitrous oxide, and at Auer-Gesellschaft, this expertise served handy in researching and investigating new ways of finding a method to de-stabilize..."

Oberkommissar Strobel cut him off. "Enough." He paused for effect and added, "Doctor Quedlin, you have been accused of industrial espionage."

# CHAPTER 2

Q looked at the police officer, letting the words register, and barely contained his laugh. *Industrial espionage? Me? That's ridiculous!*

He had collaborated with fellow scientists on many projects but stealing and selling that knowledge to someone else was not something he would ever do. No, he knew how hard it was and how much effort and dedication it cost to work in research. Never would his ethics allow him to even contemplate stealing the intellectual property of another scientist.

Oberkommissar Strobel apparently had some kind of evidence against him, and Q searched his brain to find something – anything – he could have done wrong but drew a blank. It would be best to wait until the Oberkommissar presented him with concrete accusations and compiled evidence.

That is, if he actually had any. It wasn't unheard of for the police to act upon rumors and accusations without any proof whatsoever. Just the hint of impropriety was enough to be punished these days.

He held the Oberkommissar's stare and said, "Industrial spying? Of what?"

The officer stood up, slammed his palms against the table and leaned forward until his breath wafted into Q's face. "What you have done constitutes high treason."

High treason? That was quite ridiculous. Q didn't flinch and kept his voice calm. "Again, what evidence do you have to support those accusations?"

Q might be afraid, but he still was a scientist who dealt with cold facts and analysis on a daily basis, not with generalized assumptions. If the police didn't put facts on the table, they probably didn't have anything solid against him.

The officer looked at him. "Do you deny these accusations?"

For everything he knew, Q had a clean slate, and this knowledge gave him the strength not to succumb to the threatening atmosphere. He kept his poker face in place, looking into the officer's eyes. "You haven't actually made any. You've yet to tell me what exactly I have supposedly done wrong."

"How about working with the enemy?"

That's when it hit him, and Q had a sneaky suspicion that his only wrongdoing might be in his political opinions. Since the Russian October revolution when he was a teenager, Q had made no secret of the fact that he was rather fond of the ideas behind the Bolsheviks and Vladimir Lenin's idea of government. As a young and idealistic student, he applauded the actions of the peasants and working class who, in 1917, overthrew first the Tsarist autocracy of Russia and then the provisional government.

He still recalled the joy he'd felt on behalf of the Soviet people when the peasants and workers fought back against the stringent punishments and seized control of their government.

Communism seemed like the perfect ideology – hand over the power to the people. Under that rule, there would be free and open elections, where representatives of the workers and peasants were elected to lead the country, rather than some autocratic monarchy ruling and serving only themselves. The idea that all people were created equal and that no one was worth more than anyone else agreed with Q's engrained sense of fairness.

Many of his compatriots felt the same way, believing communism was the only way to prevent war between nations and help the people live in peace with one another.

Q raised a brow in question. "Do you have evidence to support your accusation?"

Rather than respond, Oberkommissar Strobel turned on his heel and left the room without a word, slamming the door shut behind him. The sound of metal on metal caused Q to hunch his shoulders. He knew this was an attempt to make him nervous, and it worked, despite his best intentions to remain calm.

His mind wandered back to his time at university and how he had worked with a bunch of Russian scientists while doing the research for his PhD about the thermal decay of nitrous oxide.

"Q, your hypothesis seems plausible," Vladimir, one of the Russian master students, had stated.

Q had nodded. "By my calculations, the unwanted reaction of the nitrous oxide converting back to nitrogen gas can be minimized by reducing the amount of time the gaseous mixtures are in contact with the catalyst."

"That may be so, but what about the temperature as a controlling factor?"

Q had gone back to his lab and run some additional tests while the other scientists had done the same. Three weeks later, they'd made the breakthrough they'd been striving for. They were one step closer to manufacturing nitrates using industrial nitrogen fixation techniques.

The sound of steps passing the door to his room brought his mind back to the present. Was it possible that news of that collaboration was what had landed him in this interrogation room? He and the Russian researchers had shared many ideas, helping solve one another's setbacks as they all strove to discover *the next big thing,* the one detail that would change the course of science forever.

They all wanted to leave a legacy in the world. To become part of history. Like Albert Einstein, a man Q admired immensely and who had received the Nobel Prize in Physics for his vast work in the field of theoretical physics.

Einstein was a professor at Humboldt University of Berlin and Q had been given the rare opportunity to sit in on several lectures where Einstein discussed his newly discovered photoelectric effect and the quantum theory.

Now, years later, Q would always remember the privilege of listening to such a brilliant man and had striven to make his own marks upon science. Collaboration and the exchanging of research material was a part of that, and as long as the intellectual property being shared and exchanged was his, it wasn't illegal. At least not yet.

So what exactly did the police hold against him? What evidence could they possibly have to support their accusations of high treason and industrial espionage?

He decided it was best not to offer anything they might not already know about, but rather stand firm and make them produce the evidence. In these uncertain times, one never knew who was listening or what information might be interpreted incorrectly and out of context.

Accidently or on purpose.

# CHAPTER 3

Before long, Oberkommissar Strobel returned to the interrogation room. "Tell us what we want to know."

Q shook his head, lifting his hands in question. "I've done nothing wrong. Tell me what it is I'm being accused of."

"Don't play stupid." You're an intelligent man if we can believe your biography. Trust me, this will all go better for you if you simply tell us the truth."

Q clasped his hands beneath the table to still their shaking. "I've done nothing."

Oberkommissar Strobel muttered a curse and once again left the room. Q sat there, his nervousness giving way to impatience as one hour became two and three. The more time that went by, the more worried he grew. His stomach growled and reminded him painfully it was already past lunch time, and he hadn't eaten in more than twelve hours.

*They can't keep me here forever. They have to produce some evidence or let me go.*

Just when he was about to knock on the door and demand to be released, the door opened again, and Oberkommissar Strobel entered the room with another policeman in tow.

The second officer held a piece of paper in his hands. Q recognized the paper; it was an article he had written about gas masks.

*They must have searched my flat looking for evidence while I was detained here. That's why this is taking so long.*

Q closed his eyes for a moment to keep the relief from showing in them. If the article was the only thing they had found to hold against him, he was out of trouble.

The police officer put the article on the table, shoving it towards him. "Explain this."

Q forced himself to keep a straight face. This was not the moment for mirth or to give any indication of his sense of superiority. That would not go over well for him. No, he strove to appear daunted by the authorities, but cooperative and honest. A good citizen, willing to help the police.

"This is an article about gas masks. Where did you get this?" Q asked.

"In your flat. Amongst thousands of useless pieces of paper." The officer rolled his eyes and turned to his superior. "Herr Oberkommissar, his entire desk is covered knee-deep with notes, sheets of papers, magazines, and newspapers."

Q's mind formed the image of the carefully maintained disorder on his desk, and he groaned inwardly at the thought of how long it would take him to put everything back into its place. "For my research, I must collect all sorts of information and tend to retain every piece of paper I come across."

"That does not explain why you had this particular piece of paper, now does it?"

"No, sir. It doesn't because I didn't find that piece of paper. I wrote the article." Q pointed to his name on the upper right hand of the page. "See. That's me."

"Why did you write such an article?" the Oberkommissar demanded.

"Because I was asked to by my employer. I was tasked to research alternative and more economical ways of producing gas masks for the general population. To make them more affordable so all Germans could protect themselves. The article was published in Auer-Gesellschaft's technical magazine, which is printed on a regular basis. It provides an update on the progress and developments made by our research team."

The officers looked at each other, and Q felt the tension in the room easing. "So, your work was designed to keep Germans safe?"

Q nodded. "Yes."

"That is a very honorable and noble task. Were you successful?" the second officer asked, admiration now evident in his voice rather than accusation.

"Yes. I believe so. With so much talk about war and our enemies, my company wanted to give the German people a sense of security."

The officers both nodded. Since chemical warfare in the form of hazardous gases had first been used in the Great War, the general population had become almost manic about protecting themselves. With the general sense of hatred the German people felt from the rest of the world, owning a personal gas mask had become not only a recommended safety precaution but also all the rage.

The Oberkommissar gave him a smile, and Q nearly sagged in his seat. "Wait here."

Both officers stepped outside the door, and Q listened to their muted conversation.

"Is that article all you found at his flat?"

"Yes."

"No evidence of spying activity or communication with our enemies?"

"None. We found no signs that he's particularly active with any political party."

"Well then, he can leave. Let him go, but remind him that he can't leave town as he's still under suspicion."

Q tried to act as if he'd not overheard their entire conversation when the second officer stepped back into the room. "Did you have more questions?"

"Not at this time. You're free to go, but you must remain in Oranienburg until further notice. We will drive you home."

He could just imagine the face of his curious old landlady should he arrive home courtesy of a police car. He shook his head, stood up, and walked towards the door. "Thank you, but I prefer to walk."

The officer shrugged. "Very well. Your choice. Remember, don't leave town."

"I won't." Q left the police station and stepped back out into the now diminishing sunshine.

His flat was on the other side of town, and he found himself carefully observing the people he met as he embarked on the thirty-minute walk. He looked at every face, wondering what thoughts lurked behind their eyes. How did the police get suspicious? Had someone denounced him? And if so, who? Mentally, he examined each of his neighbors and colleagues, wondering who had informed on him. Whom could he still trust? Anyone?

The answer was no one. He could no longer trust anyone.

Gloom was in the air, and Q believed Germany was on the verge of something major happening. The mood on the streets was restless, as if everyone was just waiting for the signal to act. Since the July elections, Hitler had been stirring the masses against the current government, and people were growing increasingly agitated. Q was hopeful that change for the better was coming soon, but today's events had him wondering.

He arrived at his apartment to find it torn apart, books and papers strewn everywhere. A deep sigh escaped him as he found emptied bookshelves, dumped out drawers and clothing scattered on the floor. Even his mattress had been tipped over in the police's futile search for compromising material.

Q held his breath before venturing into his small study, his *sacred space*. Here, nobody was allowed in out of fear of upsetting the fragile ordering system.

A pang hit him in the stomach, and he all but doubled over when he saw the devastation in his office. Every thematically sorted stack of paper had been turned upside down, and hundreds – no, thousands – of pieces of paper lay scattered across the floor.

*It'll take me weeks to organize everything in here.*

Sighing, he returned to the bedroom and began to put things back where they belonged. For the next few hours, he folded clothes and placed them back in the dresser drawers. He remade the bed and hung his business clothes in the closet.

The kitchen was next, and he was pleasantly surprised to find only one broken glass from the search. He tidied up the area and then headed for his study, where he gathered up the piles of paper filled with formulas, sketches, and calculations into several big boxes. He replaced the books on the shelves and arranged the chemistry magazines back into a pile.

Once he was satisfied that the room at least looked tidy again, he opened the hall closet and used a bread knife to pry loose the floorboard at the back. He took out a handful of *Reichsmark* notes.

His breath whooshed out of him, and he pressed his hand to his forehead. Thank God. They hadn't discovered the hidey-hole where he'd stashed money, not completely trusting banks since their collapse a few years back. Each week, he added a few more marks to his stash. He didn't know what he was saving it for, but he knew there would come a day when it would not only be welcome but necessary for his survival. He wanted to be prepared.

# CHAPTER 4

H ilde Dremmer glanced at her watch and groaned. *Two hours left.*
Today had been a boring and tedious workday at the insurance
company where she processed insurance claims.

She got up and walked over to the small kitchen, smiling at two of
her friends and colleagues, who were brewing coffee and making plans
for the upcoming weekend.

"Hey, Hilde. Are you sure you won't join us?" Erika, a pretty, curvy
brunette asked, a pleading note in her voice and a pout upon her lips.

Hilde wrinkled her nose. "I moved to Berlin to have fun, not attend
some boring political discussion."

"It won't be boring," Gertrud promised with a nod that made her
ponytail hop up and down. Gertrud was the proverbial German girl with
her sandy hair, blue eyes, and healthy pink cheeks. While Hilde herself
had blue eyes, her hair was darker; long light brown strands she usually
wore in a bun.

"So you say. I really have no interest in politics," Hilde answered.
Her father had planted that seed in her head as a young girl, and it had
stayed.

*Politics are not for women, and you'd be wise to remember that.
Keep your hands as far away from politics as you can, and you'll do fine.*

"Don't you want to know what people are saying?" Erika asked, cocking her head to the side.

"Not really. There are things more fun to do for twenty-year-olds like us, don't you think? Let's go to the moving pictures instead."

"We went to the pictures last weekend, remember?" Gertrud reminded her, then wiggled her eyebrows up and down. "We might meet some cute fellows at the debate," she added, as if that was reason enough to be bored for hours.

"Some of the politicians are really handsome," Erika said, a pleading look on her face.

"Handsome? Like who?" Hilde asked, her interest mildly piqued.

Her friends shared a look before Erika answered, "Like Adolf Hitler and some of his party members."

She had heard the name before. "Isn't he that politician with the National Socialist German Worker's Party?"

"Yes, the Nazis," Gertrud said. "And you really should come listen to him. He has so many great plans for Germany."

"And he's handsome," Erika added.

Hilde snorted, recalling a picture she'd seen of him in the local news-paper. "He's not at all my type. And that ridiculous mustache of his. Come on, girls, you can do better than him."

She didn't add that she'd read about some of Hitler's ideas and was appalled by his ideas about racism. How could one even think about penalizing someone because of his or her race or ethnicity? Shouldn't every person have the chance to be acknowledged for her character and not for her ancestors?

Changing the subject, she asked, "There are so many entertaining and exciting things to do here, not like that boring suburb of Hamburg where I grew up. Why don't we go out and have fun?"

"There's a new picture playing. We could go see that," Gertrud offered as an alternative.

"Sounds good," Hilde agreed, warming to the idea. "And we can go to a dance afterward?"

"I'd love to," Erika agreed, worrying her bottom lip. "I guess I can hear Hitler speak another time, but I'll have to make sure it's okay with my parents first."

Hilde was torn between relief and sadness as she thought about her friends needing permission. She no longer had to deal with her overprotective father and step-mother. She'd left them behind, along with her two half-sisters when she'd come to Berlin to live with her mother two years ago. Her mother, Marianne "Annie" Klein, cared little for what her daughter did or how long she stayed out each night. She never asked about Hilde's friends, where she was going, or what she would do once she got there.

"Do that tonight," Hilde suggested.

"I will."

"If they don't agree, we could always find something else to do. There's so much going on here in Berlin. Culture and concerts, and museums…"

Erika and Gertrud shook their heads, "Yes, but it's not like it used to be," Gertrud said, pitching her voice low. "Everything was a lot more carefree years ago, but now it seems everyone is so tense. Almost depressed." She lowered her voice further. "And there are police everywhere."

"My father says Berlin is filling up with bad people," Erika added, keeping her voice low too. "Everyone has to watch everyone else."

Gertrud nodded. "I can remember when the idea of a political meeting was unheard of. Now, there's a meeting of some sort almost every night."

"That's because people are scared. No jobs. No money. And the democratic parties currently in power don't seem to be helping." Erika's voice was just above a whisper. "The Nazis and the Communists are the ones bringing us hope. A new government that's not afraid to speak out for our nation and willing to turn the economy around."

The three women sipped their coffee, growing quiet as they reflected upon the changes Germany had already seen in the last year. The government had changed leadership twice now, yet unemployment was still on the rise, with a staggering six million people or thirty percent without a job. As a result, poverty could be seen everywhere, and even those employed had difficulties making ends meet in this declining economy.

"Well, enough of this depressing talk. I need to get back to work and so do you two," Hilde said. They grinned and returned to their desks.

Hilde had no desire to join the ever-growing army of the jobless, desperate people they'd just been discussing and got back to processing the claim in front of her.

# CHAPTER 5

The next morning, Q arrived at his office, rested and in a good mood, considering how poorly his day had gone yesterday. He had a smile on his face as he approached the gatekeeper and gave the man a small wave.

"Good morning, Herr Schmidt."

The guard looked perplexed for a moment and then his face turned sad. "Doctor Quedlin. I'm afraid I can't let you inside the building. I've been instructed to escort you to the director's office should you turn up."

His smile fell. "What are you talking about?" Panic gripped him as dread crept up his spine.

"I'm very sorry, Doctor Quedlin. I don't have a choice in the matter." The poor man wasn't able to meet Q's eyes. "I've always liked you, sir, and I can't tell you how much it has meant to me that you always treated me like a valued person."

Most of the scientists looked down upon anyone less educated. Q felt ashamed for the way his colleagues treated the guard like a non-person. "You are a valued person, Herr Schmidt, and never forget that. Any idea what the director wants to see me about?"

The guard shook his head. "No, but I was instructed to take you directly to his office if you arrived or lose my job."

Q raised a brow. "Well, I wouldn't want you getting into trouble on my account." He allowed the guard time to lock up the guard shack and then walked beside the man as they headed for the director's office, located in the administration building. On the way, they didn't talk, and Q wondered what had happened. After the police let him go yesterday, he was sure everything was okay.

As they entered the administration office, he passed numerous co-workers. Not one of them would greet him or meet his eyes. They all looked the other way or pretended to be too busy doing something else to notice him. So everyone knew he'd been accused of industrial espionage.

The behavior of his co-workers stabbed his heart. He'd been working at Auer-Gesellschaft for four years now and been promoted to chief engineer three years ago. And while he wasn't a close friend with anyone at work, he'd considered them good colleagues. He hadn't done anything wrong, and yet everyone apparently judged him on the mere accusation and shunned him.

Herr Schmidt stopped outside Director Hoffmann's office and tapped on the door. "Doctor Quedlin has arrived."

"Thank you. Send him in and wait outside."

Q didn't like the sound of that but entered the office anyway. He and Director Hoffmann had never been the close friends the rumors about his quick promotion alluded to, but they shared a mutual respect for one another.

"You asked to see me, Director Hoffmann?"

"Doctor Quedlin, I'm going to get right to the point."

The director had never been a man of many words, and today was no different. Yet, Q sensed there was an underlying fear to his brusque words. "Effective immediately, you are no longer employed with Auer-Gesellschaft. The gatekeeper will escort you to your office where you can retrieve your personal effects. Your notebooks and research belong to the company, and they are not to leave the premises. You will then leave and not return."

Q's heartbeat thumped in his ears. "Sir, I don't understand. If this is about yesterday, the police let me go after realizing they had made a mistake." Q couldn't believe the words of his superior. His work was his passion and he was about to lose everything, because of…what? A false accusation?

22

Director Hoffmann looked torn but stuck with his decision. "I cannot risk my own career and well-standing with the authorities by continuing to employ men who have been accused of espionage."

"But the accusations are false. They searched my apartment and found nothing. I have never done anything wrong!" Q raised his voice, trying to get some sense into the man who was about to fire him on a whim. "You should know that I'd never steal from my co-workers or our company. Haven't I proven time and again in the last four years that I always have the best of Auer-Gesellschaft in my mind?"

"That may be, but the suspicion has been cast, and I cannot have myself or this company under suspicion as well." Director Hoffmann turned around, effectively dismissing Q.

"There is nothing I can say to change your mind?" Q asked in one final attempt to salvage his job.

"No. I'm sorry."

Q shrugged and stepped out of the office, looking at Herr Schmidt. "Let's go. I'm fired."

The gatekeeper looked at the ground and shuffled his feet, murmuring some unintelligible words. They made their way back to the laboratory building and Q's now ex-office. His mind worked overtime as he acknowledged he was simply a victim of the fear that seemed to drive everyone these days. Fear of losing their jobs. Fear of being under suspicion. Fear of the police. *Fear of being alive*, he thought bitterly.

He didn't blame the director for making sure his notebooks stayed in the lab. As things had become more politically tense in Germany, the government had started classifying all research. In fact, his work had been considered so critical to national defense in the case of an upcoming war, he'd been forced to sign a confidentiality agreement. Which he'd adhered to. So much so, that he hadn't even mentioned it or his work to the police yesterday while being interrogated.

He took one final look around, to the desk and worktable where he'd done some of his best work the last few years, then glanced through the window to the adjacent lab. Sadness swept through him at his loss. He would no longer have access to the research equipment and fruitful cooperation he and his colleagues had shared.

He turned away, focusing his attention back on the framed picture of his mother, Ingrid, and a coffee mug she'd given him for his birthday. He opened his briefcase and placed both items inside.

As his glance fell to an open notebook on his desk that featured the same chaotic order as his desk at home, he traced a finger over the formulas on the open page, his heart growing weary.

For the last several months, Q had been working tirelessly on new methods to analyze organic arsenic compounds. While methods for detecting other chemical weapons, including chlorine, phosgene, and mustard gas were in existence, none had been fully developed to detect arsenic compounds.

Prior to the Royal Air Force of Great Britain intervening in the Russian Civil War in 1919, the detection method had been unnecessary. Not anymore. The chemical lewisite, an organic arsenic compound, was not only a lung irritant but also a vesicant, causing blisters to form on those exposed to it.

Since the compound was both odorless and colorless, the only indication of exposure occurred when it was already too late, and those affected began to feel the stinging pain on their skin, in their respiratory tract, or in their eyes. Being able to detect this potential chemical weapon was a critical improvement in the defense of Germans against chemical warfare.

Q had been on the verge of making a breakthrough discovery, but now it would be up to his co-workers to find the last piece of the puzzle. One of them stepped into the lab and Q reached for one of his notebooks. He just had to make sure his latest discoveries wouldn't be forgotten.

He turned to the gatekeeper. "Just let me give my notes to my colleague and I'll be ready to leave."

Herr Schmidt looked slightly hesitant about allowing this, but before he could say a word, Q sauntered into the lab. "Arnold, my latest notes are in there. They'll be helpful in finding the detection method."

His colleague jumped at the words, apparently not aware that Q had entered the lab. "I...you...thanks." He took the notebook in a hurry and appeared to want to back out of the laboratory. Q's heart broke a little bit more. Why did everyone treat him like a leper?

"Wait. I believe we've ruled out the possibility of using water as the method of detection. While using a pH indicator to detect the formation of hydrochloric acid is plausible, the resulting secondary reaction is only slightly less dangerous."

"I have to go."

Q's shoulders sagged as he watched the man he'd so closely work with for years flee as if retreating from a monster. Dejected, he returned to his office and left, not allowing himself to look back as Herr Schmidt escorted him to the front gate. There he shook the guard's hand. "Thank you."

"Doctor Quedlin, I'm so sorry this is happening to you."

"Take care," Q said and headed off down the street. Since all his personal belongings had fit inside his briefcase, he didn't bother to go home. He would enjoy the unexpected day off, he decided, maybe visit a café. He took the suburban train, to Berlin Friedrichstrasse, and from there made his way to the main thoroughfare where people liked to congregate and socialize, Unter den Linden.

He chose a vacant table at a small café and ordered a coffee while he contemplated his next move. Many people passed by on this morning in October, a few very well off society ladies, but also a large number of poor people. Beggars. Most of them coming and going to one of the labor bureaus in the hope of securing some sort of meager employment, even if just for this one day.

The longer he sat there, the angrier he became. *First, I'm accused of a crime I haven't committed, and then I'm fired for the same crime I haven't committed. What kind of world am I living in? Since when is an accusation all it takes to stigmatize a person?*

Q was a scientist right to his bone, always had been. He throve on facts. Numbers. Formulas. But there were no facts involved at his layoff. Just empty accusations and fear. He brought the cup to his lips, inhaling the sweet yet bitter aroma of his coffee before he took another sip. The hot liquid filled his mouth, bringing a sense of warmth and comfort.

It was time to stop commiserating and start analyzing his options. To be truthful, he hadn't been happy at his job for quite some time. Not since his work had been classified as "important to the war." Maybe Director Hoffmann had done him a favor by firing him? At least now he was free to pursue his true passion – inventions for the good of humanity, not in the service of a government preparing to go to war.

25

War was horrible. He'd been a teenager during the last war, too young to understand, but old enough to wear the scars on his soul. He hated what it did to people and the destruction it left behind. He hated what the mere threat of another war was doing to people now. And he hated the capriciousness that seemed to rule the decisions nowadays. Like getting fired on an untenable accusation.

Still, he couldn't get rid of the nagging feeling in his gut that things in Germany were going to become much worse.

# CHAPTER 6

One week after his first visit to the police station, Q awoke to a pounding on his door and voices demanding he open it up.

He scrubbed the sleep from his eyes and opened the door to see the same policemen standing there. "Doctor Quedlin, you must come with us now."

"What's this about? We've already been–"

"Now." They stepped forward as if to grab him.

Still sleepy, he said, "Let me get dressed and put on shoes first."

"Very well. Make it quick," the older officer said.

Q nodded and retreated to his bedroom, where he quickly donned his clothing and his shoes. He also grabbed a jacket as the weather had turned cold and blustery, and November mornings could be very chilly.

"Come along," one of the officers said, turning to leave.

Q followed them to the waiting black DKW2 police car and then into the station, where he didn't believe his eyes. Klara Haller, a former colleague, paced the hallway, taking quick puffs on her cigarette. Her pacing increased when she saw him, but she butted out her cigarette in an ashtray and followed in their course as the two policemen ushered him into the interrogation room.

Still without a clue as to why she was here, or why he was here for that matter, he took a calming breath and decided to wait and listen.

"Why haven't you arrested him? He's a dissenter and a traitor," Klara said in a high-pitched voice.

"*Fräulein*, if you could just–"

"This man has been working against the German government and must be stopped."

"Please stick to the facts. Now, would you please tell Doctor Quedlin what you told us?"

Klara struggled to get control of her emotions, then gave Q a scathing look. "He's been talking about Russia and how perfect the ideas of communism are."

"You've heard him say such things?"

She nodded. "He spoke of some Russians he once worked with."

"When was this?" the older officer asked, making notes on the paper in front of him.

"I don't remember," she said, lifting her chin.

"Did you see him talking to these Russians?"

"Well...no, but he likes the idea of communism. Ask him." She pointed a finger at Q.

The officers turned their attention to Q, the older one asking, "Is Fräulein Haller correct? Do you sympathize with the Communist Party?"

Being a member of the Communist Party wasn't illegal, but in the opinions of these police officers, it was apparently akin to being an industrial spy. Q shook his head and carefully chose his words. "I'm a scientist, not a politician. I've never engaged in any sort of political activity, not even while I was at university."

"So you deny being a Communist?"

"Don't you think inventions and progress should benefit all people? Not just a few rich elite factions?" Q faked a calmness he didn't feel.

"What's he talking about?" Klara demanded to know.

Q had seen the flicker of doubt in the eyes of the policemen and knew he could win them over if he tailored his arguments to agree with their set of attitudes, even if only in part. He decided to appeal to their sense of justice, but even more so to their need of safety for themselves and their families.

"Remember that article you found in my apartment last week?" He waited until the police officers nodded. "That gas mask was intended to be affordable to everyone. Wouldn't it be better if any citizen, including the police and their families, had a gas mask available to them and not just military, high ranking government officials, and rich people? Wouldn't you feel better knowing your families were protected while you were at work?"

Klara glared as the police officers nodded, accepting Q's argument, and she interrupted with a high-pitched voice. "Don't let him fool you. He has connections to the Communist Party."

The officers looked torn for a moment. The Communist Party was not something anyone readily admitted to, not when faced with the local authorities. They were seen as radicals and troublemakers.

"Fräulein Haller, do you have proof of these associations?" the younger policeman asked, and Q mentally congratulated himself. Finally, the discussion had been steered back on grounds based on *hard facts*, not nebulous suspicions.

Klara looked uncertain for a moment and then shook her head. "No."

Confidence surged in Q, and he instinctively puffed out his chest. "I think my colleague may have misunderstood some of my comments. I may have mentioned Russia in a conversation about some new advancement or invention that had been brought to my attention, but no more so than I have mentioned America or England."

The older officer looked at Klara. "Is that true?"

She scowled at Q and slowly nodded, "I guess. But he belongs–"

The officer held up his hand. "Doctor Quedlin, which political party do you belong to?"

Q shook his head. "None of them. I've never joined a political party."

The police officers had reached their level of tolerance for Klara's accusations. "Fräulein Haller, it seems you have no facts to back up your claims that Doctor Quedlin is a sympathizer with the Communists."

Then he turned toward Q and asked, "Doctor Quedlin, under what context would you have discussed America or England?"

Q smiled as a wave of relief coursed through his veins. "Four years ago, in the final stages of finishing my PhD thesis, I was privileged to spend six weeks visiting England. While I took some time for vacation, I was also allowed to attend a scientific conference in the field of organic chemistry. The attendees were renowned scientists from many countries, but I especially liked the British and American colleagues. They have some of the most advanced methodologies in the world, and it was a pleasure to exchange new approaches to research and minor break-throughs with them."

"So you returned home after six weeks?"

"No, officer. I was also privileged to attend the 1928 Summer Olympics in Amsterdam while travelling, where I cheered for the German athletes to win medals for our Fatherland. In fact, I witnessed Ingrid Mayer win the female floret, and Georg Lammers gain the bronze medal in the 100-meter sprints. Both were sublime moments of national pride. If you wish to see my official accreditation, I can present it to you later today."

The officers shook their heads. "That won't be necessary."

The younger officer spoke up. "Doctor Quedlin, can you explain why one of your colleagues had reported you saying, and I quote, 'Everything that has to do with the Nazis is ridiculous.' It was also reported that, on more than one occasion, you made fun of them."

Q frowned, and a queasy feeling settled in his stomach; the conversation was steering into dangerous territory. He made a mental note to be more careful in the future and never openly ridicule the Nazis again. Apparently, in these days, it was better to duck his head and keep his mouth shut – just like everyone else.

Thinking feverishly, he once again stated, "I may have said this, trying to be funny. Apparently it wasn't a good joke. And what do I know of politics? I'm a scientist. Everyone in this room," he looked from one officer to the other, before he continued, "is surely better prepared to judge whether the Nazis are a veritable party or not."

His heart beat in his throat, and he prayed they wouldn't delve deeper into the Nazi issue. This might have the potential to get him into serious trouble.

Thankfully, the police officers seemed to get tired of the fruitless conversation. "Fräulein Haller, this man is no threat to the German Nation or a Communist Party sympathizer. Be more careful in your accusations from now on." The officer gave her a warning glare before turning to Q. "You're free to go."

On the way back to the exit, the policeman lowered his voice and spoke to Q. "This gas mask you've been working on? Is it already being sold?"

Q had to swallow down a chuckle and answered in the most serious voice he was capable of. "Officer, Auer-Gesellschaft has not put it on the market yet, and unfortunately, I was released from the company after the interrogation last week."

When he saw the man's disappointed face, he was reminded that policemen were only fellow humans following their orders. Since they hadn't been rough or mean with him, he added, "I believe if you ask Director Hoffmann for a prototype of the gas mask to conclude your investigation, you'll receive one."

He bid his goodbyes and followed Klara Haller from the building. Once out on the street, he grabbed her arm and turned her to face him. "Why did you do that?"

Klara gave him a disbelieving look, pulling her arm from his grasp. "You of all people should know!"

Puzzled, he observed her for a moment and then shook his head. "So, this is your revenge? To get me arrested for high treason?"

He felt his voice rise and strove for calm. Klara had fallen for him since she joined the company a year ago and had pursued him relentlessly. She was a beautiful woman, but nothing about her attracted him. So he'd turned her down many times, declining her invitations to dinner or the moving pictures, and requests to be his date at company socials.

She shuffled awkwardly and mumbled, "I was just doing my civilian duty to keep my eyes open."

He shook his head and left her standing without a further word. Women like her were one of the reasons he was still a bachelor at the age of twenty-nine. That and the fact that he just hadn't met a woman he was interested in. His first love was science and women were only a distraction. No woman alive would appreciate him spending yet another night in his lab because he was so close to finding the missing link. He could do without the headaches having a girlfriend brought with it.

Q walked down the sidewalk, pondering on the economic and political climate in Germany. *Things are going to get a lot worse.* His country was in trouble, and if something didn't change, it was headed directly into doom.

On the walk home, a growing urgency to do something arose in his mind. But he couldn't even begin to fathom what that would be. What could a single scientist do to save his country from war and destruction? To save it from itself?

# CHAPTER 7

Hilde and her girlfriends entered the theater foyer. Thanks to Hilde's step-father, Robert Klein, they'd secured tickets for the highly coveted opening night of the opera *The Marriage of Figaro* by Wolfgang Amadeus Mozart. They patiently waited their turn at the concession counter, wanting to purchase a soda before the performance began.

"Look at those fellows over there," Erika pointed out in a whisper.

Gertrud and Hilde dutifully turned their heads. "Where?"

"The fellows lounging against the wall."

The three girls looked at the men, and Gertrud mused, "They look like they're seated in one of the private theater boxes." Even before she'd finished speaking, three women, dressed in the latest fashion gowns and adorned with expensive jewelry, exited the bathroom and looped their arms with the men.

"Look at their clothes." Gertrud sighed. "I'd love to be able to dress like that."

"Why don't you?" Hilde asked.

Gertrud looked at her long, mid-calf length navy blue skirt and sighed. "Apart from not being able to afford a designer gown, my mother would kill me before allowing me to leave the house showing even a tiny bit of cleavage."

Erika nodded. "My parents would dress me in a sack if they could." She pointed to where her skirt ended and her silk stockings began. "My father doesn't like men being able to see my ankles. He says it's not ladylike."

Hilde laughed and glanced down at her own clothing. An elegant yet comfortable and warm pants suit. "You girls and your sheer stockings. I don't know why you insist on wearing them during winter. You're always getting runs in them and going to the seamstress to get them repaired."

"That's because they're expensive."

"And cold. Not only do I not have to spend my money on getting my stockings fixed, but my legs stay warm. It's much more practical in this weather."

Berlin in November could get frigid, and this evening was a perfect example. The air temperature was near freezing, and while no snow had fallen yet, the potential was strong given the clouds that had been gathering all day.

"My mother would never allow it," Erika said, pouting. "Pants are for men, she insists."

That comment stabbed at Hilde's heart. Yes, she loved wearing pant suits in winter, but she didn't love her own mother's lack of caring. As far as her mother was concerned, Hilde could leave the house stark naked and she wouldn't oppose it.

"Hey, those fellows are awfully cute." Erika nudged Hilde's arm.

Hilde turned her head and made a face. "Those are boys, not men."

"What are you talking about, Hilde?"

"They're way too young and immature."

"They're about our ages," Gertrud said.

"Precisely. Too young." Hilde turned to enter the theater.

Erika giggled and asked, "So what are you looking for in a man?"

Hilde thought for a moment and then ticked the list off on her fingers. "Well, to begin with, he should be older and more mature than me. He should be self-confident enough to love me just the way I am. And most importantly, he should be willing to stick around and not leave me at the first hint of trouble."

Where did that come from? Hilde was surprised at her own words. Why did she instantly assume someone would leave her?

"Is that all you're looking for?" Erika teased.

Hilde shook her head. "No. He has to have strong principles. He needs to believe in what he does and be willing to stand up for it. I don't want a man who bends at the first sign of adversity."

Gertrude rolled her eyes and Erika giggled.

Hilde ignored them and went on. "I want someone who believes in the good of humanity and seeks to change the world to be a better place. A man with intelligence. Good looking. And a heart-melting smile."

Erika and Gertrud burst out laughing. "You forgot broad shoulders and big biceps. Hilde, you need to accept reality. The man you're looking for doesn't exist."

"What are you saying?" Hilde asked, looking between her two friends.

"There you go again, being naïve and idealistic." Erika smiled at her and then confided, "I would unquestionably settle for a handsome man. Like your step-father, if he were twenty years younger. I'm so excited to see him on stage."

The girls found their seats and Hilde's smile faded as she listened to Gertrud echo Erika's fascination with her step-father, Robert.

"He has such a fabulous voice, and he's quite the charmer. Your mother is lucky to be married to such a handsome and glamorous man. His voice is to die for. Have you thanked him for the tickets?"

"Of course I did," Hilde said. "He told me it was a pleasure for him, but unfortunately, he won't be able to meet us after the performance, because he and Mother have to rush off to the premiere party."

Her friends pouted, and the disappointment on their faces was obvious. Erika was the first one to talk again. "You're such a lucky girl. Your step-father is a famous opera singer and your mother is one of the most modern moms around. She lets you do anything you want."

*Yes, she's modern all right.* So modern that she abandoned her baby girl to marry an opera singer. Hilde had never told either of her friends about her mother abandoning her when she was two years old. How she'd never felt her mother loved her. Or how she was jealous of Robert, because her mother obviously cared more for him than she did for her own daughter.

"The performance is about to start," she said instead. Their conversation came to an end as the lights in the theater dimmed. Hilde kept her eyes trained on the stage, but her mind was caught up in memories.

She'd been two years old, and her father had been fighting at the frontlines of the Great War when her mother had met the famous opera singer and started an affair with him. Apparently the task of raising a two-year-old child was too much of a burden for her mother, because soon after moving in with Robert, she'd dropped Hilde off at her grandmother's house.

Hilde had loved her grandmother dearly, but even living with a woman who'd showered her with love and acceptance hadn't been able to dull the pain her mother had caused by abandoning her.

It wasn't something a little girl could easily forget, and Hilde had made herself a solemn promise to never treat her own little ones so callously. She would never abandon them. *I will always be there for my own children. They won't have to grow up with their grandmother. And they'll never doubt, not for an instant, my love for them.*

That thought almost had her bursting out laughing. Just the thought of Marianne – or Annie, the name her mother preferred to be called nowadays – raising grandkids was ludicrous. And Emma? Her stepmom? They didn't even talk to one another. Not since Hilde had left her father's house after a row and moved in with her mother in Berlin two years ago. She'd burned her bridges and any hope of ever returning home to her father and his family.

She sighed, wishing she could do things over. Not leave in a fight. Experience the feeling of being loved again.

Thankfully, Erika grabbed her arm when young Figaro appeared on stage and brought Hilde's mind back to more pleasurable things.

# CHAPTER 8

Q took the tram into Berlin where he had rented a room in a friend's apartment a few months ago. He was a frequent visitor to Berlin on the weekends and found staying there much easier than making the hour-long journey back to his place in Oranienburg after attending a cultural event or going out at night.

He'd known Jakob Goldmann since his days at university, when he had been a tutor for one of Jakob's chemical engineering classes. Despite the age difference of six years, they had become fast friends.

After his PhD, Q had started working for Auer-Gesellschaft and moved to Oranienburg while Jakob was offered a job as a chemical engineer in a big company inside Berlin that produced synthetic materials. His friend was a bright young man and after just a few months on the job, he'd been moved up the ranks and now supervised a team of four workers.

Q pondered whether to use his key, but given it was a weekday and he usually only showed up on weekends, he knocked on the door instead. It was early evening and he smiled when Jakob opened the door. "Q! What are you doing here in the middle of the week?"

"Well, since I'm without a job, I decided to come talk to you about our idea," he said while shaking his friend's hand.

Jakob stepped back, ushering Q inside. "What do you mean you're without a job?"

Q briefly filled his friend in and asked, "Are you still serious about starting up a chemical laboratory? About being self-employed?"

Jakob didn't even hesitate. "I certainly am. Are you thinking we should finally stop talking and start doing things?"

Q grinned. "I can't think of a better time. I have a lot of free time on my hands right now."

"Coming here on a weekday certainly sounds like you have nothing else to do."

"Come on." Q boxed his friend's shoulder. "You want it as much as I do."

They both laughed. They'd been talking about their big plans for years, but due to the bad economic situation in Germany, it had never seemed the right time. Now might be perfect.

"How would we get started?" Jakob asked, gesturing for Q to have a seat on the couch.

Q plopped down and said, "Well, we'd need a laboratory space. And equipment."

"There are some vacant buildings just past where I work. We could check there."

"That sounds like a good idea. We'll need two office rooms and a big lab. Or better, two. To separate different lines of experiments."

"Yes. And I already know a few people who might give us work." Jakob hopped up and down. They continued talking themselves into a state of excitement and Q could see the laboratory come to life in his mind. State of the art equipment, newest technology, enough space to do whatever was required to find new solutions to old problems.

After a while, he disappeared into his room and came back with pen and paper to jot down their ideas.

"We can't afford that," Jakob murmured with sagging shoulders as he summed up the numbers Q had written down.

Staring at the staggering number at the bottom of the paper, Q swallowed hard and admitted, "Even if we use all of our combined savings, we don't have enough to get started."

Neither man was rich, but they had both lived well below their means while earning an excellent income from their jobs. Even without the benefit of a paycheck, Q's royalties for having sold the commercial rights to several of his patents in the field of chemistry were more than enough to support him.

"Why don't I visit my bank tomorrow morning and ask for a small-business loan?"

Jakob nodded. "It's worth a try."

~

"Doctor Quedlin, I'm sorry, but we're unable to give you a loan at this time," the bank employee said.

"What? Why? I have more than enough collateral to secure the loan…"

"It has nothing to do with that, I'm afraid."

Q raised an eyebrow. "I don't follow. Would you please explain why you are refusing my request?"

The bank employee looked uncomfortable and squirmed in his seat. "Doctor Quedlin, you are a valued client of our bank, but as you said yourself, you have recently quit your employment and are now depending solely on your royalty checks."

"Which are more than enough to sustain me for the time being." Q pointed to the business plan he'd drafted together with Jakob last night. "Then, with the income the laboratory will generate after an initial start-up phase of three months–"

"Doctor Quedlin, a new enterprise is risky and given the current economic situation in Germany, it's not guaranteed you'll be able to meet the credit payments."

Q rolled his eyes. This wasn't going the way he wanted it. "*Mein Herr*, the items we've already discussed as collateral more than meet the value of the money I'm seeking to borrow."

"And several years ago, I would have been happy to finish the paper-work, but the policies of our bank have changed. We now need almost double the security for these types of loans."

"I'll visit another bank."

"You're free to do so, but they will give you the same answer. Due to the declining economy, no bank in Germany is in a position to take huge risks right now."

*Huge risks?* He was asking for a modest loan of less than one year of Jakob's and his combined income. But this bullheaded bank employee just didn't understand. Taking a deep breath, he said, "If you need more securities, my business partner, Jakob Goldmann, should have more than enough."

The bank employee thinned his lips. "I don't believe that would be a wise call on your part at all."

"And why is that?" Q folded his hands on his lap in an attempt to keep his calm.

"We prefer to do business with Germans."

"Jakob is German."

"Well, he may have acquired a German passport, but he is of Jewish descent."

"You cannot be serious." He all but jumped out of his seat and had the greatest urge to drag the arrogant man across the desk by his tie.

"I am very serious. In fact, I must warn you that continued association with those persons could lead to the seizure of your own accounts."

"You would discriminate against a good citizen because of his race? That is a stupid policy. Awful in fact. All humans were created..."

Q stopped himself before he started a monologue about how ridiculous anti-Semitism was and how he truly believed that communism was a superior ideology. All people deserved to be valued the same and have the same rights, regardless of their race, ancestry, or even gender. No exceptions. But Q realized that those ideas weren't very popular with the bank employee – or the police, he reminded himself – and kept his mouth shut.

"Doctor Quedlin, are you affiliated with the Communist Party?"

Q shook his head. "No. I'm not affiliated with anyone."

"Then I would strongly advise you to be careful about your statements. If Hitler becomes chancellor, as everyone here hopes, he will make Germany a better and stronger country. He has some very progressive ideas."

"If one wants to believe that, then that is one's prerogative."

The bank employee gave him a hard look. "Might I remind you that I have the ability to freeze your account if you insist on supporting the wrong side of the law."

Q closed his eyes for a moment, seeking patience and calm. It was better to keep silent for the moment. He thanked the bank employee and returned to Jakob's apartment.

"How did it go?" his friend asked the moment he walked in the door that evening.

"Not good. I don't have enough security for the loan, and when I mentioned you, I was basically threatened with having my accounts seized."

Jakob turned his face away, but Q knew his friend well enough to feel his pain when he answered, "Well, maybe we should wait until the economy bounces back."

"Maybe." Q sank down onto the couch, a frown marring his brow. "There's more to it than our plans to become self-employed."

"What else has you worried, my friend?"

"You."

"Me?" Jakob finally turned around, and Q didn't like what he read in his friend's eyes. Fear. Shame. Denial.

"Yes. The bank employee's attitude reminded me of how much anti-Semitism is growing in this country. I'm afraid it's going to get much worse."

"I think you're overdramatizing the situation. People are rational beings. *Homo economicus.* They will never follow Hitler's outrageous ideas. This is just a temporary situation."

"You and I we both know the homo economicus is a myth, an idea that works in theory, but not in real life. People flock to Hitler's ideas of renewed grandeur, and they will use anyone and anything as scapegoats if it helps them escape their own misery." Q jumped up and paced the room, running his hand through his short blond curls.

Suddenly, he stopped and planted himself an arm's-length distance from Jakob. "Leave the country!" He nearly shouted the words.

His friend stared wide-eyed at him. "Leave my home?"

"Yes. Leave now. You're twenty-three and have your entire life before you. You're young, bright, and graduated in chemistry. You speak fluent Polish, English, and German. You should have no trouble finding a job anywhere in Europe or abroad."

"Now, you're overreacting, Q. I don't want to leave Berlin. My parents love it here. And with my mother's heart condition, I don't think she can handle another relocation." The entire Goldmann family had emigrated to Germany from Poland sixteen years ago during the Great War.

"Your parents don't have to go."

Jakob's mouth fell open. "I don't want to leave them alone. Things will get better. You'll see."

Q shook his head. "Perhaps. If the economy gets better soon and this great depression doesn't worsen, it might get better."

"I hope it happens sooner than later," Jakob replied.

Q admired the hope his friend espoused, but his gut feeling told him otherwise. A better economy wouldn't be enough. Nor would it come soon enough. Not by a long shot.

# CHAPTER 9

After realizing that his own laboratory wasn't a possibility right then, Q spent many hours thinking about how to best make his stand for peace and a livable future.

He'd been fond of Russia since the October Revolution in 1917. More than once, he'd admired the benefits the Russian people gained once Lenin and the Bolsheviks took over from the autocratic Tsarist regime. But since then little progress had happened. Russia was still mostly rural and needed help to industrialize the country in an effort to make it a power for peace in the future.

Giving all his technical knowledge to the Russian people would be a first step in empowering them to become an industrialized nation. But he had to be careful. During the last years, Germany had become a place where fear and suspicion reigned. Everyone kept to themselves these days, and conversations about the future or viewpoints opposing the mainstream were held exclusively behind closed doors, rather than on the street corners. And in very select company.

One day, he met with a few former fellow students he knew to be fond of the ideas of communism. They were congregating under the guise of a literature club, and everyone had to bring a book to each meeting. Today's topic was the literature of Leopold Tolstoy.

After everyone had arrived, the doors to the classroom were shut, and they soon started a heated discussion about current politics and the threat the Nazis posed to life as they knew it.

"But how can we help Mother Russia?"

Q raised his voice. "The best place to start would be in helping Russia defend herself. It's essential to industrialize and militarize Russia in an effort to protect the country from the evil invasions of neighboring countries."

"That is true. With Russia's vast natural resources and land, many other countries are jealous and would love nothing more than to take some of it for themselves."

"Like Japan," said Kurt, a man with bushy black brows.

"And Hungary or Poland," added Reinhard, a man old enough to be Q's grandfather.

Wilfried held out a hand. "Don't forget Turkey and Austria."

"And Germany," Q said, and everyone stared at him. "Come on, fellows. Our country is not beyond taking land during a war. Haven't we started war after war for land and resources?"

"You're right," Kurt agreed. "In the past, everyone who wanted land took it by force. And whoever owned land had to protect it with the blood of its people to keep it. But communism will change this. Humans will realize that they can live in peace, and everyone can still own enough to eat one's fill and be happy."

Everyone nodded, and a slender blonde girl named Johanna stood up, "Yes. The Russian people are good people. They have shown us how to get rid of a regime of injustice. They carry the right *Weltanschauung*. They just don't have the technicians and engineers to carry it out. Now it's our turn to help them."

All of the scientists in the classroom were ready to help and transfer the knowledge and information Russia needed to modernize and keep up with their potential enemies. If tensions in the region increased, it was vital that Russia withstand an invasion from any country that looked upon them as easy prey.

Q liked the idea, but a little warning voice in his head made him raise his concern. "That is all fine and well. But how do we make sure this knowledge is never used against peaceful countries or their own people?"

Everyone started talking at once. When the noise ebbed away, Johanna spoke up again. "They won't. In communism, the people are the government. And they wouldn't do anything to harm themselves."

That sounded like a very rational response. If the true power of a nation was in the hands of its very people, they would look out for the best for everyone. Everyone agreed the first stage of enabling the Russian people to develop was to help them defend themselves.

"Maybe we should emigrate to Russia and oversee the implementation of our work," Michael suggested.

Q shook his head. "No, that's not the best idea. We are more useful if we remain here in Germany to facilitate and promote a lifestyle of peace in both countries. Part of Russia's problem is that it has been cut off from the rest of the world. They need a voice on the outside."

Everyone present agreed, but one question still remained to be answered. "How do we get in touch with the Soviets?"

It was quiet for a moment before Michael said, "There's a Soviet trade mission in Berlin."

"A trade mission?"

"Yes. The official mission is to promote the trade between Germany and Russia." Michael lowered his voice before he continued, "But, the Russian government uses this mission as a way to recruit spies and sell military goods to Germany."

"That is strictly forbidden by the Versailles Treaty," Kurt chimed in.

"Yes. But Germany and Russia signed the Rapallo Treaty in 1922. Two diplomatically isolated and outlawed countries joining forces to help each other."

"That is just a ruse to allow both countries to gain military strength," Johanna cautioned.

"We need more information on the subject," Q suggested.

"I agree," Michael said. "I suggest we ask a volunteer to try and gain access to the trade mission and their secret purpose of existence."

Q immediately raised his hand. "I'll do it."

"Are you sure?" Wilfried asked.

"I am. If Germany is buying weapons from Russia, we need to know about it."

The meeting adjourned a few minutes later, and everyone left the classroom in a hurry. He picked up his copy of *Anna Karenina* and followed the others out of the university building.

He decided to sleep in Berlin instead of returning to Oranienburg. Tomorrow morning, he'd embark on the adventure to reach the secret inner circles of the Soviet trade mission in Berlin.

⟅

Early the next morning, Q left his apartment. After what happened at Auer-Gesellschaft, he decided some precautions couldn't hurt. He searched the apartment for a disguise and stuffed it into a bag before leaving. Taking a detour to the Berlin Zoo train station, he entered the public restrooms to change his clothing. A stale smell of pee reached his nostrils, and he quickly scanned the toilets for one that was acceptably clean.

He locked the door behind himself and changed into his disguise, black heavy-duty pants and an oversized jacket he'd borrowed from Jakob. His friend might be younger than he was, but his shoulders were much broader. He was also about two inches taller. The dark brown jacket hung on Q's shoulders, making him look like a craftsman who didn't care much about his looks and not like the scientist he was.

Before emerging as, he hoped, an unrecognizable man, he pulled his hat low over his brow, covering his signature curls.

Half an hour and several detours later, he entered the Soviet trade mission at Unter den Linden and asked to speak with the commercial attaché. He pretended to be the owner of a craftsman's workshop seeking opportunities to trade goods with Russia.

The receptionist noted his name and request before she instructed him to seat himself in the waiting area. Almost an hour went by before a man in his fifties approached him. "Herr Quedlin?"

Q stood up and surveyed the man in front of him. "Yes. I am Wilhelm Quedlin. Herr Handelsattaché?"

The man didn't answer but gestured for Q to follow him. They took seats in an office, and the other man asked, "How may I help you?"

"I was hoping to speak to whomever is in charge of scientific operations and exchange of knowledge."

46

The commercial attaché raised his brows. "What does the owner of a craftsman's workshop know about science?"

"Sir, I'm actually not a craftsman."

"I thought so. Your outfit is actually rather ridiculous."

Q sucked in a breath. He'd hoped to be convincing in his role. "I didn't want to be seen coming here."

Now the other man seemed to be interested and leaned back in his seat. He lit a cigar and puffed out a few smoke circles while he scrutinized Q. After a while, he finally said, "So what do you really want?"

"I'm a chemical engineer and would like to offer my knowledge and my inventions to the Russian people."

The commercial attaché narrowed his eyes and shook his head. "That could be a trick. Who tells me you're sincere?"

Q thought quickly and answered, "I worked with several Russian scientists while at university. One of them was Dmitry Zelinsky. He's now a professor at the Moscow State University. He will vouch for me." *I hope he remembers me.*

The man stared into Q's eyes, apparently debating whether he should believe him or not. Then he spoke up, "Come back next month. In the meantime, we will verify your credentials."

"That's fair." He handed the man a copy of the article he'd written about the gas masks. "Here's a small offering for you to see that I'm serious."

The man took the paper and bid him leave. "Thank you."

# CHAPTER 10

H ilde finished the file in front of her and stacked it on top of the others she'd processed that morning on the corner of her desk. She stretched her arms above her head and glanced at the large clock at the head of the room. Almost lunch time.

She cleared away the pens on her desk and reached for the sack lunch she normally brought along before heading for the small break room, waving at Erika and Gertrud to join her. Her company was too small to have a canteen and eating out was expensive.

Gertrud sat down next to her, disgruntled. "They're threatening to fire some employees at the end of the month."

"I know. I heard. In this bad economy, the company is having a hard time staying afloat. People prefer to save the insurance fee and count on their luck," Hilde answered, opening her lunch box.

"The entire country is sinking. The unemployment rate is now nearing forty percent. Forty percent! Can you even believe such a thing has been allowed to happen?" Erika asked, shaking her head in disgust.

Every evening on her way home from work, Hilde passed the lines of people standing outside the soup kitchens and the job centers. The lines were growing, and the people standing in them were looking more desperate each day that passed. Hilde always felt a pang of empathy for them and thanked God every day that she still held a job. Not a great one, but one that allowed her to contribute her share to the household expenses. While she would love to move out on her own, it wouldn't happen anytime soon. It was just too expensive.

"Something needs to be done, or we'll soon be a nation of beggars," a woman from the sales force said in a loud voice. She'd joined their table together with two older men Hilde had seen several times, but didn't remember their names.

"The Allied Powers are to blame for this," one of the men said, and suddenly, everyone in the room looked at their table, and you could hear a pin drop.

"Yes, yes," several people said in agreement.

The man spoke up again. "What gives them the right to choke the very life from the German people? Their reparations are outright dehumanizing."

The head of the sales force had entered the room, and his big bulging face turned a deep shade of purple when he heard his subordinates talking like this. Hilde feared for a moment they'd have to face his disapproval, but he chimed right in on the conversation. "The Versailles Treaty is crippling our country. I was a young lad during the last war, and yet I'll have to work my entire life to pay back a debt I didn't incur."

"I agree. Why don't the French, British, and Russians try to exist under such harsh conditions and see what happens?"

"We need a strong leader to stand up for Germany and stop this madness."

Hilde instinctively ducked her head and stayed out of the conversation. This wouldn't go anywhere reasonable.

"Only a strong chancellor can bring our nation back to her former strength and glory. The war is long over. It's about time for someone to step in and send the Entente Alliance back to where they came from."

"With their tails between their legs," Erika added, and the others applauded.

"One of our customers told me the Allied Powers want more money. What was agreed is not enough for them and they're mounting an attack against Germany to extract even more. They want us reduced to nothing more than slaves," the head of the sales force said.

Another man chimed in. "We need to stop this now before it cannot be undone."

Hilde ate her lunch, questioning how much of this talk was actually based on facts and how much was pure street talk. She vaguely remembered having read somewhere that payment of reparations had been stopped the year before.

"Hitler is our man." This came from a gentleman at the end of the table. "He's not a puppy of the Allied Forces, and he's promising employment for everyone. His first step is to build Autobahns all over Germany, to increase mobility of people and goods."

"Can you imagine how it would be to drive a car from Berlin all the way to Stuttgart on a road that actually deserves that name? Without potholes, curves or intersections?" one of the men said with shining eyes and the conversation turned towards cars and the promise of affordable cars for everyone.

The girls shook their heads, quickly finished their lunch, and left the break room. As soon as they were out of earshot, Erika lowered her voice to a whisper. "I heard that the British want to take over Germany because their island is slowly sinking into the North Sea."

Hilde gasped.

"And did you know the French soldiers eat little kids? We certainly don't want them in our country," Gertrud added with a shudder.

Those statements of her friends were so bizarre and far-fetched she figured they must be joking, but both of them showed only seriousness on their faces. What if they told the truth? Could it be?

Erika and Gertrud seemed well informed and invested in their opinions, whereas Hilde herself had no opinion whatsoever. Her father, a very politically oriented individual, had always taught her politics was no place for a woman.

*But he's miles away and being ignorant isn't getting you anywhere. Maybe you need to become better informed.*

"See you girls after work," Erika said, drawing her from her mental meanderings.

"See you. Have a lovely afternoon," Gertrud said and headed back to her desk.

Hilde was left alone, her mind spinning with everything she'd just heard. What was truth and what was just a fantastic story devised to play upon the fears of the people?

In this instance, she decided to learn about politics. After work, she stopped at the newspaper vendor stationed on the corner and purchased the *Berliner Morgenpost* and a big notebook. As soon as she arrived home, she read the paper from cover to cover, paying special attention to everything about current politics.

Organized as she was, she began a meticulous study of the different political parties, making a chart with the programs and beliefs each one stood for and cutting out pictures of key people to put on her new "learning wall." The more she read about politics, the more interested she became and the more she wanted to know.

Her notebook became her canvas, and like an artist, she began to paint a picture with words of the political environment in Germany over the next weeks. Beneath the picture of Hindenburg, she wrote the words *Weimarer Republic*. He represented the current and ineffective government of Germany. Summarizing his achievements was easy. *Failure* was all she needed. The current government was failing in every aspect she could see. A change was needed. But who could offer a change for the better?

Three main players competed for votes: Adolf Hitler, head of the NSDAP – Nazi Party; Otto Wels, head of the SPD – Socialist Democrat Party; and Ernst Thälmann, leader of the KPD – Communist Party.

To the picture of each of the three men, she added a small statement that summed up each party's core beliefs. This took some effort, and she honed the statement several times over the next days and weeks, whenever she collected new information.

Beneath the picture of Hitler, she wrote the words: *Führerprinzip* – Strong Leadership. Nationalistic. Economy directed by industry. Strong military. Superiority of the Aryan race.

Under the picture of Wels, she added the words: Reform. Opponent of Anti-Semitism. Egalitarian for economy and industry.

That left only the Communist Party picture of Thälmann, under which she wrote: Dictatorship of the proletariat. Equality of men and women, but against the Republic and Democracy.

Hilde sighed. Germany was going under, and as far as she was concerned, none of the popular parties would be her salvation. It was much more possible either the left or the right would lead her into complete destruction.

Still, she eyed her work in progress and felt a small sense of accomplishment. At least she now understood the political climate around her and was determined to keep abreast of what was happening and hopefully make an educated decision if the time came to do so.

# CHAPTER 11

Q stared at his desk covered in papers with scribbled formulas and sketches of devices not yet in existence. *Somewhere must be the missing link! I just haven't found it yet.* Not able to focus anymore, he decided to take a break and go for a short walk to freshen up his mind.

While he was still angry with Director Hoffmann for treating him unjustly and firing him without reason, he couldn't deny that he felt better than he had in years. The burden of holding down a demanding job and having to subordinate his research to commercial interests had fallen like a stone from his shoulder.

Finally, he had all the time in the world to follow his passion and work exclusively on his own research, making inventions in the field of electronics, chemistry, and radio-transmission. And while he was thankful for that, the memory of the arbitrary treatment was a constant thorn in his side. A thorn that spurred him on to work harder and devote his time to inventing as many useful things as possible to help foster peace in Europe while also helping his Russian friends to make the Soviet Union a power that could combat Germany in the upcoming war.

War hadn't been announced, and everybody around him seemed to believe the Great War had been the last one, but Q feared his country was headed for another war sooner or later. And the wise thing to do was to prepare for that day. One could never be too prepared.

That knowledge fueled his determination, and he decided not to look for another job. As his royalties were still coming in regularly, with more hopefully being added, he was in the comfortable position of not having to work for his living. Instead, he used all his time and energy for research and made some major advancement into the usage of the oxides of nitrogen.

It was already dark on this winter afternoon, and he shuffled his feet in the freshly fallen snow as he considered his options. Recently, he'd diversified his research work and experimented with the possibility of using radio to operate devices or machines by remote control. Another of his ideas was to use sound waves and radio transmissions to detect obstacles. But something was missing.

Then he heard it.

"Who-o-o, who-o-o."

Q squinted his eyes in an effort to see the owl, but it was too dark, and the bird probably was sitting in a tree blocked from his view. As a youngster, when he'd lived with his parents in the countryside near Magdeburg, he'd seen many owls and bats.

*Bats! That's it!*

He turned around and hurried home.

A few years back, an American physicist had proven that bats used ultrasound to orient themselves. As he hurried, his scientist mind envisioned a means to locate things like airplanes, ships and even vehicles using a system of echoes similar to the one bats used, but viable for long range detection. Radio waves.

He was itching to go over his formulas and set up some experiments, but as soon as he entered the building, his landlady appeared out of nowhere. *I'll bet she has some kind of tenant detection system.*

"Doctor Quedlin, do you have one moment?"

No, he didn't. "Surely, ma'am."

She entered her flat and returned with a large envelope in hand. "This came with the daily post."

"Thank you, ma'am." He reached for the envelope containing an official-looking seal and wanted to sprint up the stairs to his own apartment. But he hadn't taken into account the supreme curiosity of his land-lady, who held onto the envelope, asking, "What is it?"

Q had no interest in divulging the contents to his landlady, so he answered nonchalantly, "Technical papers I need for my work."

"Oh," she said, her curiosity obviously not yet satisfied. "Did you notice we had another power outage today? This is happening a lot lately. Would you have any idea why?"

He tried his best to look worried and dispel her suspicion. "Yes, ma'am, I noticed. It's quite a nuisance. The power company must be having a problem somewhere along the line. Hopefully, they will get it fixed sooner than later. Good evening, ma'am."

With a nod, he snapped up the envelope and turned on his heel before his grin could give him away. Then he rushed up the stairs, taking three steps at a time.

If his landlady had the faintest idea the frequent outages were a direct result of his electrical experiments, he'd be out on the street in no time at all. She was suspicious enough since he'd lost his job, and he was sure she would be anything but happy if she ever found out he used his apart-ment to conduct scientific research that sometimes involved explosive substances or caused minor hiccups like electrical outages.

Inside his flat, he tore the envelope open. It was from the patent office, and he laughed as he looked over the paper inside.

Q gathered up his most recent studies and stuffed them into his briefcase. Glancing at his watch, he smiled. In half an hour he would meet his friends Jakob, Otto, and Leopold. With his recent acquisition of a Ford Köln automobile, the journey from Oranienburg to Berlin took less than twenty minutes.

Just in time, he parked his automobile at the curb next to the bar where his friends already waited for him. They'd known each other since university and had since met in irregular intervals to discuss the newest developments in science. Jokingly, they'd given themselves the name *Tüftlerclub* as the four of them liked to invent, research, and tinker.

After he proudly presented his new car and enjoyed the admiration of his friends, they stepped inside and ordered Schnitzel with potato salad. When everyone had a beer in hand, Otto addressed the one topic that everyone in Germany seemed to talk about today: Hitler's *Machtergreifung* – seizure of power.

"Did you see the headlines?" Otto asked excitedly.

"Everyone has," Leopold answered. "Hitler has seized control of the government."

Since the radio broke the news last night that Hitler had proclaimed himself the new chancellor of Germany along with his NSDAP party acquiring several high-ranking cabinet posts, an unusual excitement had captured every person in Germany. Q had perceived that people seemed to be one of two persuasions: happily excited or very upset with the Nazi party.

"Can you believe that within a few hours, Swastika flags have appeared on just about every building?" Q asked.

"Now everything will change for the better," Otto said. "Hitler will get us out of the unjust Versailles Treaty and make us a proud and powerful nation once again."

Leopold nodded eagerly. "You're right. The reparations imposed upon Germany after the Great War were nothing more than a way to humiliate our nation. It's time to stop that."

"Come on, fellows. The reparations were ended last year during the Lausanne Conference. You can't blame them for the bad economy." Jakob tried to bring the discussion back to the facts, but neither Leopold nor Otto wanted to hear them right now.

"They certainly didn't help. I hope Hitler can do everything he's promised."

"Everything?" Q asked, looking around the table. "What about his racism and anti-Semitism?"

Leopold and Otto looked at Jakob and sobered a bit. "Neither of us agree on that part of his ideas, but it's nothing to be afraid of. Things are never as bad as they look. Besides, I think that type of thing was just talk."

Q's gut twisted, and he shrugged, "I certainly hope so. But only time will tell."

His friends had always been more carefree than he was, and they'd teased him time after time for overthinking. Even Jakob seemed fairly nonchalant about the situation, although there was a new tension about him that Q hadn't noticed months earlier.

Deep down, Q knew Hitler was a fanatic, willing to go to extremes to make his beliefs come true. Much like Q himself, who would sacrifice almost anything for his science. But while Q always intended to serve humankind, he doubted that Hitler acted on the same maxim.

Their conversation switched from politics to science and after the second beer, they started reciting funny rhymes and spoonerisms.

*"Es klapperten die Klapperschlangen*
*bis ihre Klappern schlapper klangen."*

Q stood up, "I have another one." Then he recited:

"She sells sea shells;

It's sea shells she sells."

When Q drove home, he had thoroughly enjoyed the evening with his friends, but for some reason, he couldn't get rid of the feeling that the events yesterday had irreparably changed the course of history. But even he couldn't imagine that this day would, decades later, be named the most fateful day of the century.

~

The next week, Q visited the Soviet trade mission again. This time, the commercial attaché was happy to see him and introduced himself with the name Herr Iwanov.

"Doctor Quedlin, what a pleasure to see you. Please take a seat."

Two more men were already sitting at the small table in the middle of the room and gave him a friendly nod. After some small talk, Herr Iwanov said, "We have made contact with Mr. Zelinksy, and he confirmed to us that you are a loyal believer in the ideals of the October Revolution and Communism. Our scientists also double-checked the information you provided in regards to the gas mask. It is of high quality and very useful to the Russian people. Therefore, we would like to suggest an 'official' cooperation, if that is what you were after."

Q nodded. "Thank you, Herr Iwanov. That is indeed high praise."

"We are unable to offer you much money, but…"

Q shook his head. "You misunderstand my reason for being here. I don't want money."

Everyone in the room looked at him, and it was so quiet you could hear a pin drop. "You don't?"

"No, I am doing this for the greater good." He missed the looks the Soviet men shared with one another. "I want to help humanity, and hopefully, prevent another devastating war."

"You feel war is a possibility?" one of the men inquired.

Q nodded. "Yes. I believe the new government in Germany is headed directly there. Every day, Hitler is keeping a tighter rein on things and getting rid of unwanted opposition. I'm very sure he will do everything in his power to make his dreams come true."

The other man scrutinized Q for a moment. "If you believe Hitler is here to stay and is as dangerous as you say, you must be aware that working with us will make you a traitor and put you in grave danger."

A shiver ran down Q's spine. He hadn't given that aspect much thought when he'd decided to gather intelligence for the Russians, but after the *Machtergreifung* last week, he'd had to re-think his decision. Even though it wasn't technically illegal to give his own work to other nations, the current powers wouldn't forgive anyone working against them.

He squared his shoulders before he answered, "I have given this possibility some thought, and have come to the conclusion that the greater good is more important than my own well-being."

The three men nodded with admiration, and Herr Iwanov said, "That is a very rare and courageous attitude you're showing. But why bring your information and skills to us? Why Russia and not another country? After all, our countries were enemies in the last war."

A grin spread over Q's face. "I believe Germany has been enemies with every other country around. But to answer your question, I've thoroughly studied the other European nations, and I believe Russia is the only country that will use my inventions and expertise with the good of the people in mind. I wish for my discoveries to be used to help my fellow man in a peaceful manner."

The men exchanged incredulous glances. "Your answer shows that

58

you're a scientist and not a politician. Given the chance, men will always act against one another."

Q looked around the room and asked, "Will they? Hasn't Bolshevism abolished the selfish egoism of a few and replaced it with a government of the people?" He shook his head, answering his own rhetorical question. "I merely want the best for myself and others, and there are many more men and women who think the same way."

# CHAPTER 12

During one of Q's meetings with his Russian contact, whom he only knew by the name Pavel, the agent asked him, "Would you be willing to travel to Paris on a mission?"

"Paris?" Q raised an eyebrow. "That's in France."

"Yes, it is, Q. As you suggested yourself, the Nazi government is problematic, to say the least. They are an unknown force in the equilibrium of powers and seem to care little for maintaining peace in the region."

"And what does that have to do with Paris?" Q asked.

"Our government has taken up negotiations with the French – absolutely confidentially and unofficially, of course. We are seeking to exchange knowledge to better prepare all neighboring European countries for war against Germany."

Q nodded. "That makes sense, but what role do I play in that?"

Pavel leaned across the table in the crowded café and lowered his voice. "We have received a request for help from a group of French chemical engineers who are working closely with gas warfare. With your experience and expertise, we believe you can help them solve the problem."

A flattered smile curled Q's lips, and a tingle of excitement rushed through his veins. This would be his first important mission and to

France no less. He'd learned French at school but was in no way fluent in the language.

"I would be honored to help."

The Russian agent explained the details of the trip, and when he had finished, Q asked, "How should I explain my trip? I can't tell the authorities I'm going to help some French scientists to find ways to detect and counteract gas warfare. Can I?"

The thought of what might happen if he was caught and the authorities learned his true reason for going to Paris froze his blood.

Pavel grinned and then asked, "Do you know how to ski?"

"Ski? Yes. Why?"

"To hide the true reason for your trip."

Q was so nervous he had difficulties following the words of his counterpart. *Skiing in Paris? Don't they have a better plan?*

"We have arranged for a hotel in Klosters. You'll take a weeklong skiing holiday. Switzerland has always remained neutral in every conflict and nobody will suspect any political motives if you travel there. Go skiing, have fun, and then continue your trip to Paris without telling anyone. You'll find all the details in here."

The agent handed him an envelope. "Apart from travel documents and instructions, there are enough Swiss francs and French francs in there to cover your travel expenses for this trip."

Q eyed the envelope suspiciously. Being paid for his trip didn't mesh with his idealistic motifs of working for the greater good. "I don't want to be paid for my help."

The agent pushed the envelope into Q's hands. "Take it. Use the money with our thanks."

Q argued with the man a few more minutes and then capitulated. "Very well, but I'll only use the money to travel to Paris to meet with these engineers and will return the rest at our next meeting. I will pay for the skiing holiday myself."

"As you wish." The agent smiled and disappeared, while Q sat in the café trying to fully process what just happened. He didn't dare open the envelope in there, and stuffed it into his briefcase before he paid and left.

As soon as Q returned to his apartment in Oranienburg, he tore the envelope open and rushed to read the details of his trip. He was to leave in a few days, and his mind was buzzing with the plans he needed to make. And the excuses he needed to have ready.

Because he'd never heard from the police again about the investigation against him for industrial espionage, he was fairly certain it had been closed, but a small doubt remained. He didn't want to poke the sleeping lion, but not knowing the outcome made him uncomfortable. Thus, he sat down to write a letter to the police asking about the official outcome of his investigation.

He cringed as he imagined how different an interrogation by the SA Brownshirts or the SS Schutzstaffel might look from what he had experienced with the police were they to discover his true reason for travelling to Paris. Those paramilitary wings of the Nazi Party were known to punch first and ask questions later, and Q was certain he didn't want to be the subject of their attention. In any form.

Q tried his best to enjoy his two days of skiing vacation in Klosters but was too nervous. His mission occupied his mind every waking moment. His trip to Paris on the night train went smoothly, and the next morning, he met with the French scientists.

They were all friendly and intelligent men, but unfortunately, their English was a lot worse than he'd hoped for – and their German nonexistent – causing several minor hiccups in the course of the next days. But what drove him nearly insane were the work habits of his French colleagues. Every little detail required an hour-long discussion before it could be implemented.

*If they start another fruitless discussion, I'll start screaming. Have those Frenchmen never heard of efficiency?*

At home, people got right to the heart of the problem and fixing it. Name the problem. Think of a solution. Test it. If it didn't work, repeat. There was no need to discuss all the possible solutions when one could just go and test them out. But the French worked the opposite way.

When presented with a new problem, they talked about it. A lot. Usually, about ten minutes into the discussion, his colleagues forgot about his presence and switched to their mother tongue. Back at home, he'd thought his understanding of the French language was passable, but now he knew better.

As soon as his colleagues inevitably started talking at the same time and sped up their speaking, he lost track of the conversation, and his understanding was reduced to mumbo-jumbo.

He leaned back, observed the three chemical engineers and found himself staring in amazement at their heated discussion. It seemed perfectly normal for them to raise their voices at each other, shouting for hours without apparent reason about a problem, just to later congratulate each other for coming up with a solution. It was peculiar, but it apparently worked.

Their methods were so much less efficient than those he was used to, but to his utter surprise, they managed to come up with solutions anyway. Sometimes amazing solutions he wouldn't have thought of.

The one part of their day Q truly enjoyed was lunch. From the first day, he fell in love with the French cuisine and the wine. Rather than a hurried half an hour or even a respectable hour for lunch, the Frenchmen took a full two hours, sometimes more. Every time they ate, it was a celebration and Q fully participated. It was such an amazing experience to savor the food instead of gulping it down without thinking. His colleagues even urged him to join them in drinking a glass of wine during lunch because it was good for the health.

This was another peculiar French habit. In Germany, you could be fired for drinking at work, but here? They'd probably fire you if you didn't have a glass of wine with your meal. Suspicious at first, Q soon started to like this habit. One small glass of wine – not more – stimulated his brain and loosened his inhibitions enough to give his colleagues a taste of his not-so-perfect French language skills.

"*Vous parlez français!*" Antoine Dubois said, and Q nodded proudly. From that moment on, the ice was broken and Q was accepted as a friend. "*Je suis Antoine,*" his colleague offered, introducing himself. In response, Q answered, "*Mon nom suis Wilhelm, mais m'apelle Q.*"

Everyone laughed at his faulty usage of French grammar, but it didn't matter. From now on, he was part of their team, and they did their best to make him feel welcome in Paris.

The next day they invited him to dinner after work and as always, they talked about anything and everything under the sun. Soon, the discussion turned to politics and Antoine asked him, "Your new chancellor, Hitler, he is temporary?"

Q thought for a moment and then shook his head. "At this point, I'm afraid not. He has a lot of support from the military and the people."

"But his seizure of power...there was nothing democratic about it. Won't he be called to account?"

"In the old Germany, yes, but we have a new Germany now." Q could see the worry on their faces; one he secretly shared.

"Just last week the news said books are being burned, and opponents hunted down. *Gleichschaltung* they call it," another of his colleagues said.

Q nodded. "The word literally means to synchronize or bring into line. I believe the Nazi Party is trying to bring about a specific doctrine and way of thinking. They want more control."

"There have been reports of people being arrested who openly criticized the Nazi form of government."

Q hadn't heard such reports but wasn't surprised. "Many of my fellow compatriots don't take Hitler and what he's trying to do seriously. Most seem to think he is all talk and exaggeration just for show."

"But you don't?" Antoine asked.

"I wouldn't be here if I did." He grinned. "I believe he is very dangerous. He's talked about expelling all thirty political parties out of Germany. He's after absolute power and authority over my country."

"And what happens when he gets it?"

"May God prevent this." Q didn't have an answer for that question, but he feared the man's lust for power would send Germany and the whole of Europe into an inferno.

His colleagues seemed to have filled their need for information about German politics and changed the topic to the latest shows and events in Paris. Their conversation was a mishmash of French and English, and Q had difficulty keeping up. His mind started to wander as someone in the restaurant shouted, "Turn the radio louder. The German Parliament building was destroyed today."

Everyone in the room stopped talking, and Q listened in growing horror at how quickly the political situation in his country was coming unraveled.

*Today, Monday, February 27, 1933, the Reichstag building in Berlin, the capital of Germany, was set ablaze in an event that is being deemed arson.*

*Our reporter in Berlin confirms that a mentally ill Dutchman has been arrested. He was found hiding inside the burning building.*

*The main chamber of the building was completely engulfed in flames when authorities arrived. No word yet on what was used to start the fire.*

*Our man in Berlin has forwarded the following statement by Hermann Göring, the second most powerful man in the current Nazi regime, regarding today's events.*

*"This is the beginning of a Communist upheaval. They will start a revolution now. We cannot miss one minute to strike back!"*

*German President Paul von Hindenburg, at the urging of Chancellor Hitler, has been asked to issue an emergency decree suspending all civil liberties in order to counter the illegal and horrific actions of the Communist Party.*

*Chancellor Hitler himself spoke to the people shortly after several additional arrests were made. "Now, there will be no mercy. Whoever is against us will be slaughtered. The German nation will not understand if we are kind. Every Communist will be shot, wherever we find him. The Communist members of parliament have to be hanged tonight. Everyone will be arrested who works for the Communists."*

*We will keep you apprised of the situation, but it appears that Germany is getting ready to declare war on its own citizens. I'm sure I'm not alone in asking how they have come to a conclusion about who set this fire so quickly. Maybe because this event was orchestrated by the Nazi Party to gain support and legitimize their dictatorship and uncon-stitutional takeover of the government last month.*

*This is another setback in the French-German relations, and I'm sure our government will pass a statement soon.*

Q's colleagues stared at him, eyes wide open, waiting for his reac-tion. "Well...it seems our mutual concerns about Hitler and the Nazis have come to pass."

Despite the horrific news, he found it amusing at how differently the news had been presented to the French people. In Germany, the virtues of the government to take fast and decisive actions would have been celebrated, the perpetrators of this crime painted as monsters.

And it seemed that the rest of the world wasn't quite sure if the rhetoric coming out of the Nazi leadership was to be believed. The radio speaker had even insinuated a plot by the Nazis.

"How could Göring and Hitler accuse the Communist Party of this act? What was the evidence? What about the Dutchman?" Everyone had questions to ask.

"Because it benefits them to do so," Q replied, still reeling from the impact of what he just learned.

Later in his hotel room, he thought a long time about the implications and what would come next.

The shocks continued the next day when the *Reichstagsbrandverordnung* was passed. Hitler had succeeded in getting the civil liberties and all constitutional rights of the German citizens revoked.

"What does this mean for your countrymen?" Antoine asked the next morning over coffee as the report came in.

"Basically, it means that the SA now has the right to arrest anyone without giving a reason. There will be no legal protection or any chance of defending oneself against false accusations." A shiver ran down his spine as Q remembered when he'd been accused of high treason last fall. Under these new laws, he would have been shot on sight, or worse.

"So, the authorities will arrest everyone they suspect has ties to a political party other than the Nazis?" another colleague asked in horror.

Q nodded. "That's what it sounds like."

"But where will they imprison that many people?"

Q was wondering that himself, but he didn't have an answer.

The next day he was due to leave Paris, but his colleagues didn't want to let him go. They generously offered for him to stay and said they'd help him find a job in Paris.

"Although your French is awful," Antoine grinned, "I'm sure any company involved in nitrogen research would gladly employ you if you come recommended by anyone of our group."

"I appreciate your offer, I really do, but my place is in Berlin."

"It's too dangerous for you to return to Germany. I'm sure your stay here would be considered as opposing the government."

Q had weighed the risks most of the night. He was worried that his past accusations might come back to haunt him. Everyone and anyone suspected of supporting the Communist Party would now be open to prosecution.

But in the end, he knew he could be of the most use to his friends in Russia, and for peace, if he returned to Berlin. As much as he wanted to stay safe in Paris, he wanted to do his bit to help overthrow the Nazi regime. And he could not do that from inside France.

"Thank you, my friend, but I must return home." He left in the evening to return to Klosters, once again thankful the Russian agent had arranged to disguise his trip as a skiing vacation. No one would suspect him of engaging in any subversive activity in Switzerland.

When he boarded the train two days later to return to Berlin, he passed the time by reviewing his accomplishments the last few days. He'd been able to help the French scientists with their problem detecting a rare nitrogen gas, and he knew they'd prepare their country to defend itself in the upcoming war. A war that was inevitable at this point. In exchange, he'd learned many things he could use for his current projects.

Q leaned back in the empty train compartment and watched the beautiful countryside passing by. The train was driving north alongside the Rhine River, passing breathtaking scenery. Steamships traveled the brownish river, fast ships going downstream and slowly trudging ships going upstream. Green, forest-covered hills rose to both sides of the river, and every now and then, they passed a marvelous castle high up on the mountains.

The cradle of German culture. He remembered the legend of the beautiful siren Lorelei sitting on the cliff high above the Rhine and combing her golden hair. With her strikingly beautiful voice, she attracted shipmen and caused them to crash on the rocks.

The lyrics to the legend had become a well-known folk song, and he whistled its melody.

*Die schönste Jungfrau sitzet*
*dort oben wunderbar;*
*ihr gold'nes Geschmeide blitzet,*
*sie kämmt ihr goldnes Haar;*

. . .

*sie kämmt es mit goldenem Kamme*
*und singt ein Lied dabei,*
*das hat eine wundersame,*
*gewaltige Melodei.*


*Den Schiffer im kleinen Schiffe*
*ergreift es mit wildem Weh;*
*er schaut nicht die Felsenriffe,*
*er schaut nur hinauf in die Höh'.*


*Ich glaube, die Wellen verschlingen*
*am ende noch Schiffer und Kahn;*
*und das hat mit ihrem Singen*
*die Lorelei gethan.*

(find the English translation in the <u>Acknowledgements</u>)

He sneered. The NSDAP party was like a siren, distracting everyone with her alluring song and ultimately causing the whole country to crash. After witnessing firsthand how the news reports were being twisted by the German leadership, he feared things were about to get much worse.

Any sense of morality was stripped away by the unconstitutional revoking of the German constitution. The government was no longer lawful, nor did they have any restrictions being placed upon them.

A sense of freedom flooded Q in recognizing that fact. He had always prided himself on being a man of ethics and high morals. But faced with a lawless government intent on stripping all rights and liberties from the people who might oppose them, he no longer felt morally bound to act within their law.

Before this day, he had only given his own intellectual property to his Russian friends, but now...he was actively thinking about engaging in what any intelligent person would deem industrial espionage. And he didn't feel the least bit guilty. The Nazi regime had to be stopped. At any cost.

# CHAPTER 13

Hilde sat at her desk, wondering why all of the employees had been called to attend a meeting. Since January, the threat of firings had increased every day, driving tensions high and creating an atmosphere of fear.

Every morning, she entered her office with a knotted stomach from the sheer amount of negativity inside the company. People didn't smile and greet anymore. Instead, they ducked their heads and silently walked by. Nobody stopped longer than necessary at the water cooler or gathered beside the coffee urn for a little chat. No, everyone seemed to be frozen by fear, trying to work as hard as possible to impress their superiors.

She glanced at the clock, and her stomach tightened as she saw it was only a few minutes until the meeting was to start. Taking a deep breath, she left her desk to join the other employees as they gathered in the large meeting hall.

No one dared to talk aloud, but the nervous whispers told Hilde everyone was afraid they were about to be fired in one large group. She was quite confident. She processed the insurance claims, and her department was swamped with work. They surely wouldn't fire her. She bit her lip. Surely.

Erika waved her over. She worked in the accounting department and had often mentioned that the company wasn't doing as poorly as the managers made it seem. At least the company managed to still make a small profit every month.

A few minutes later, the director greeted them somberly and started his speech: "As most of you know, times have been hard, and while we have done our best to cut back on expenses, we have now come to the point where we are forced to prune the company of dead wood. We have spent a considerable amount of time looking over our current employees, and I'm proud to say that we will be continuing with the right people in place to be successful in the coming months and years."

Hilde was stunned. The director was speaking about firing people and seemed to be happy about that fact. Her stomach churned as his words replayed in her head, but before she could wonder about whether or not she'd done enough to keep her job, the director continued his speech.

"I know this decision means some extra work for the remaining employees, but I'm sure every one of you will proudly make this small sacrifice for our nation and our *Führer*."

*The devil! What is this man talking about?*

"We have decided to free our company of the heavy burden of all employees who don't belong to the superior Aryan race. You are to retrieve your personal effects and pick up your final paycheck at the recruitment office within the hour."

A cacophony of voices arose, but the director had already stepped down from the podium and disappeared. Hilde glanced around at the stunned faces of her co-workers. Some wore smug sneers. Others – the fired ones – wore a look of desperation that clawed at her heart. The majority looked shell-shocked. They avoided her eyes and looked down to the floor. Head ducking seemed to be the new ability to master.

Hilde whispered to Gertrud, "Can you believe this? They fired everyone independent of their job title or their tenure with the company. Just because of their race."

Erika didn't seem to mind. She had some exciting news to share. She found Hilde and Gertrud amidst the multitude of people and joined them. "Girls, we have to celebrate! You're looking at the new head of the accounting department."

Gertrud raised a brow. "How's that?"

"Everyone else except me and the two interns have been laid off, so it was only natural I'd get the promotion." She beamed with pride, and her happiness would have been contagious if it weren't for the dire circumstances.

Hilde couldn't hide the disgusted grimace she knew was settled on her face. "What's wrong with you? How can you be happy now?"

Erika merely shrugged. "You have to take the opportunities when they appear. I can't do anything about the company's decision, so I do myself a favor by going along with it. I would never have been promoted so fast if it weren't for this lucky serendipity."

"Lucky?" Hilde hissed, unable to hide the emotion seizing her system. "Don't you even care that the people you've worked with have lost their jobs? And for no other reason than being Jews?"

"Certainly, I feel badly, but I'm also being practical here. I have to think about myself. Besides, the company doesn't want them. They should go somewhere else. Someplace where no one will care they're Jews. The *Führer* says we're better off without them."

Gertrud put a hand on Hilde's shoulder and sent her a better-keep-your-mouth-shut look. She swallowed down her sharp answer and merely scowled at Erika, who was unconcerned by her friend's disapproval and advised, "You should be thankful you weren't fired. Stop whining over the fate of other people. Everyone needs to be looking after themselves these days."

Then she turned and walked away, already practicing the determined walk of a head of accounting. Gertrud grabbed Hilde's elbow and dragged her toward the stairs. "I'm not happy about this any more than you are, but Erika is partly right. Don't talk about your disapproval or make waves. Not one word. You don't want to appear as a *Judenfreund* who sides with the Jews, or you could end up getting hauled away by the SA. Most of us are shocked at what just occurred, but we're also glad we got to keep our jobs. Look around you. Many of these people have families to provide for."

Hilde nodded, following Gertrud as everyone filed back to his or her desk. She listened half-heartedly to the whispers, frustrated and feeling powerless as she heard more than one person mentioning it was the Jews' fault that Germany ached under the grip of the Great Depression.

"The Jews have been stealing our jobs for years now. We didn't ask for them to come here. We've been too nice, allowing them to take German jobs. It's time for us to rise up and take back our country. They should all go back to where they came from."

Hilde tried to keep her silence, but her colleagues were talking such nonsense, she couldn't resist trying to reason with them. "You're not being fair. The Jews have helped Germany in many ways."

"Really? By taking our jobs?"

"We welcomed them with open arms at one point," she argued.

"Well, now we want them to leave us alone. Instead of destroying our country, they need to go home and fix theirs."

"Most of them don't have a home to go back to. Their families have lived in Germany for many generations, or has that completely skipped your minds?" She was growing agitated at the absurdity of what was coming out of her colleagues' mouths.

She entered her department, and her heart broke a little when she passed the glass door to the treasury department and saw Adam Eppstein standing in front of his desk with sagging shoulders. The normally cheerful man was a picture of misery, and hatred for the Nazis rose up inside of her. Adam Eppstein had been the one to train her when she first joined the company. He'd soon been promoted to head of treasury, and Hilde had always valued him as a fellow employee, boss, and human. His only fault was being a Jew.

"Herr Eppstein, can I help you collect your things?"

He said nothing, still in shock, staring blankly into the air. When he didn't answer or move, Hilde located a box and collected his personal effects from his office and desk. She glanced around and asked, "Anything else?"

He shook his head and finally seemed to wake from his state of shock. "Fräulein Dremmer, what am I supposed to do now?" he asked, fear and uncertainty on his face.

Hilde's heart went out to him. She knew he and his wife had three small children, the youngest one just two months old. With everything else going on in the country, he was unlikely to get a new job soon. What could she tell him?

"Herr Eppstein, I'm sorry, but maybe you should use this as an opportunity to get out of the country. See this as a silver lining and take your family someplace else." She lowered her voice. "Someplace safe."

"Where?" he asked brokenly, fighting back tears.

"How about Switzerland? The Swiss never get involved in these wars. There are lots of banks, and with your treasury experience, you should have no trouble finding a job."

Adam Eppstein gave her a sad smile and then shook his head. "I wish that were possible, but my oldest son just started school. He is the best in his class. It was difficult enough to find a school that would take him."

"I understand your concern for your family, but how will you feel when you can't feed them? Maybe uprooting them is the lesser evil in this situation."

As he closed the door to his office for the last time, Hilde walked with him down the hallway. "Do you really want to stay in a country where they treat you like horse dung?"

"Fräulein Dremmer, this is my home. I was born here. My parents were born here, my wife and her parents…my children. I have nowhere else to go."

# CHAPTER 14

Q visited his mother, Ingrid. He had avoided visiting her before his trip to Klosters and Paris because she had a way of knowing what went on in his head. Since he was a child, she'd always known when he lied or even when he'd attempted to avoid certain topics. And his intelligence work was definitely a topic he wanted to avoid. It was better if she knew nothing about it.

Today was no exception, and his plan to recount only the skiing portion of the trip failed miserably. Over a cup of freshly brewed coffee, she stared at him and asked, "What are you *not* telling me, son?"

"Mother, there's nothing else."

She squinted her eyes and responded, "You're touching your earlobe, Wilhelm. You do that when you try to hide something from me."

Why did he blush like a schoolboy? He was a grown man and didn't have to report to his mother anymore. But because he loved her dearly, he didn't want to lie to her. "Mother. You're right. But I can't tell you. It's better if you don't know."

She stared at him for several long moments, then seemed to come to some internal decision. "Don't get yourself into trouble, Wilhelm." She patted his hand and changed the topic. "What inventions are you currently working on?"

His mother didn't understand much of science, but she always showed interest in his research and even though he was sure she didn't understand most of what he explained, she always remembered the details and proudly told all of her friends about her genius son.

"I'm working on a new type of mist filter that can be built into the gas masks used by soldiers fighting on the front lines of a war."

"Haven't you done that already at the Auer-Gesellschaft?" She seemed surprised.

"Yes, Mother, but the commercial rights to those inventions belong to them, and I want to find a new and better solution that doesn't infringe on the patents I filed while I was an employee there. Then I can sell the rights to other companies and more persons, soldiers as well as civilians, can profit from an affordable gas mask." He didn't mention he would give the rights free of charge to his Russian friends.

"*Liebling*, do you really think there will be another war? Haven't we suffered enough in the Great War?"

"I certainly hope there won't be another war, but that doesn't stop me from preparing for one."

They talked a while longer before he stood up and kissed his mother on the cheek. "I have to leave. Take care, Mother."

Back in Oranienburg, he found a letter from the police on his doorstep and tore it open with trembling fingers. Once he'd read the note, a sigh of relief left his lungs.

The letter stated the investigation against him, alleging espionage, had been closed for lack of evidence. They'd enclosed the confiscated article and even apologized for the inconvenience. At least from this quarter he was free and clear.

As autumn approached, Q became increasingly unhappy with his working environment. Working all on his own was fine and well, but not having a well-equipped laboratory was frustrating and hindered his research.

During one of the regular meetings with his friends, Otto said, "You seem unhappy, my friend."

"It's just that I'm sick and tired of working from my apartment. I need to get my hands on a fully-equipped laboratory."

Jakob laughed. "It's about time, don't you think?"

"Yes, you need a change of scenery," Leopold said and added, "I happen to have connections at the Biological Reich Institute for Agriculture and Forestry. Why don't I make a call and set up a meeting between you and the director?"

Hope fluttered in his chest. "You'd do that?"

"Sure, if you want."

Q thought for a moment before he replied, "I guess I'm ready to join the ranks of common employees again. I'd love to meet with your acquaintance. You're sure it's not a bother?"

"Come on, that's what friends are for. And with your reputation, they'd be the lucky ones to employ you."

"They probably have never heard of me..."

Jakob chuckled. "As always, you're being modest, Q. Berlin is such a small place, I'm sure everyone working in the scientific world has heard of you or read one of your articles. You have such a good standing in the scientific community and your dissertation on nitrous oxide was widely recognized as an important contribution to the advancement of chemistry."

Q nodded, feeling more light-hearted at the prospect. "Okay. Okay. Thank you, Leopold. Meeting the director of the Biological Reich Institute sounds like a fine idea."

A few days later, Q met with the director, who unfortunately wasn't as excited as Q or his friends. "Doctor Quedlin, I have to tell you that the investigation involving you, alleging industrial spying, gives me some pause for concern."

Q couldn't hide his surprise. "How did you even come to hear about that? There was no evidence that I had done anything untoward. In fact, the accusations came from a woman who thought herself romantically inclined towards me. When I didn't return her affection, she fabricated those accusations out of revenge."

The director raised a brow. "Director Hoffmann from the Auer-Gesellschaft never mentioned that part. As for the accusations being false, do you have anything to back that up?"

Q had come prepared and pulled from his briefcase the letter stating the investigation had been closed for lack of evidence. "That letter is from the court."

The director read it from top to bottom before handing it back. "You are surely aware of the new political powers at work. I would hate to fall under any suspicion with them. Are you by chance a member of the NSDAP, the Nazi Party?"

Q shook his head. "I am a member of no political party. I'm a scientist and have no interest in politics. Joining a party should be for people who are interested in working in politics."

"So, it's true then?" The director squinted his eyes and scrutinized Q's face.

"What's true?" Q asked.

"That you don't like the Nazis?"

For a split-second, Q's breath hitched in his lungs, but he schooled his face before the director could notice anything but mild surprise in his expression. In the future, he had to be more careful about sharing his true feelings for the Nazis. Because he didn't want to start a prospective working relation with a lie, he decided to go with a half-truth, hoping to delude the director. "I did not say that, and my not joining the NSDAP is in no way an indication that I do not support them."

He paused, pondering whether that was enough. The director extended the silence for at least another thirty seconds before he smiled. "Very good, then. I can offer you a position as a freelancer. Would that be acceptable to you?"

Q stood up and shook the director's hand. "That would be fine."

On his way home, Q toyed with the idea of joining the Nazi Party as a way of providing better cover for his actions. But his stomach clenched at the mere thought of it. It was one thing to lie by omission, but acting out a lie day in, day out by joining the Nazi Party? No, he wasn't made for acting and pretending.

Leopold visited him in the evening to ask about the interview. "How did it go?"

"I'm not sure," Q answered. "He held me to account on the investigation about industrial espionage and wouldn't employ me because I'm not a member of the Nazi Party. But he offered me a freelancer's job instead."

"I understand how you feel. The government has already suggested I give preference to party members for jobs overseeing the research and development area for my company."

Q pursed his lips and shrugged.

"Look at it this way, being a freelancer is much better than being on staff. You will have more control of your schedule and can travel and do research on your own without permission."

"And I will have that great big laboratory at my disposal. I haven't worked with plant care and protection, but I'm excited about this new area of study."

"I'm sure you'll do fine."

"I just hope this new kind of work won't be used for military purposes. I'm sick and tired of having my inventions used to militarize a country instead of serving the human race and the goal of peace."

Most of his later work at Auer-Gesellschaft had been geared toward military usage, and his inventions had been exploited for use against other human beings. Like his work with the arsenic compounds and other gases. He'd seen the reports and heard the rumors. Instead of using his discoveries to protect people, they were now being twisted and used to kill via gas attack. It sickened him to know he'd been a part in making those weapons possible.

"Plant protection will keep you out of the military focus," Leopold said.

"Let's hope so, by goodness. Because I'm fairly certain Hitler's ultimate goal is world domination, which will push Germany into another war, even more destructive than the last one. And I don't want to be part of that!"

Leopold tried to calm down his friend. "Q, you're so pessimistic. People learned their lessons from the last war and they won't repeat the past. You just have to trust them. The Great War was the war to end all wars."

Q shook his head. "I'm not so sure about that. Communism is the only form of government able to provide a peaceful co-existence of all nations because the core value of communism is the philosophy that all humans are created equal."

Leopold laughed at his naïve take on communism. "Where on earth did you get that idea?"

Q frowned. "*Decline of the West* by Oswald Spengler."

Leopold merely grinned at him and asked, "So, you've never actually read the theories about communism and Marxism?"

"No."

"Then you should. I think you might be in for a surprise."

"Why is that?" Q asked, not really paying attention to the discussion anymore. He knew what he knew. Listening to Leopold or reading some books wouldn't change that.

"Because your idealized version of communism doesn't exist. It's not the way you think it is."

Q shook his head. "I know enough." In his scientific mind, communism sounded perfect. All humans were created as equals. Everyone working for the best of the community. One for all and all for one. "I don't need to read about Marxism. Those are just political theories. I have important scientific research to do."

Leopold raised a brow and shook his head. "You should make time."

That statement continued to roll around in his head, long after he and Leopold parted ways. Had he gotten it all wrong?

No, not him.

# CHAPTER 15

Spring came to 1934 and things in Germany had slowly deteriorated, but Q had managed to carve out an existence he could live with. At least for the time being.

A few weeks ago, he'd left his flat in Oranienburg with the nosy landlady to move into a slightly bigger two-bedroom flat in the center of Berlin that suited his bachelor needs quite nicely. Partly nostalgic and partly satisfied to turn over a new leaf in his life, he also stopped subletting the room at Jakob's place.

One evening in April, he and Leopold headed to the moving pictures. With the current political situation creating stress for everyone, they needed a distraction. Stan Laurel and Oliver Hardy, commonly referred to as "*Dick und Doof*" had released a new short film, *Going Bye-Bye*. Their slapstick comedy was the perfect way to end a week of hard work, at least in Q's opinion.

Leopold wasn't as fond of their humor but tagged along because he'd get to choose the next picture. They sat in the dark theater and Q elbowed Leopold several times because he kept quiet during some of the most hilarious scenes. "Come on, this is funny."

His friend growled. "Somewhat."

During the first reel, a group of women a few rows in front of them caught his attention because one of them laughed loudly at every punch line, even when everyone else didn't seem to get it.

Q couldn't make out which of the three girls it was, but her sense of humor and her unconcerned laughter intrigued him. For some reason, this unknown woman sparked his interest, and he hadn't actually seen her yet.

This attraction puzzled him. He hadn't been this intrigued by a woman in – forever. Yes, he'd gone out with a few, but sooner or later, he'd always become bored and preferred to dedicate his time to his research than to a woman. His friends had begun teasing him about how he was married to science and might as well become a Catholic priest. And their teasing had only intensified now that he'd turned thirty-one. All of his friends were happily married or at least engaged at this age.

*I don't need a woman to be happy. She'll only distract me from my inventions. She'd never understand.*

But when he saw the three girls standing in the vast lobby of the theater during the small fifteen-minute break between reels, he couldn't resist approaching them. The three of them looked like a commercial for German girls: sandy, dark blonde, and brunette. All of them with bright blue eyes, and the sandy blonde wore her hair in traditional pretzel braids.

Then she spoke, and the sound of her soft feminine voice drew him near like a siren. When he finally distinguished her, he had to swallow back a lump in his throat. *Oh my god, she's so beautiful.* Her dark blonde hair fell in soft waves around her shoulders and against her neck. She had it tied back with a ribbon, and he wondered if it was as soft as it looked.

His eyes wandered down her body, and he was struck by her appearance. Instead of wearing a dress and stockings like most of the other girls, she clothed herself in a short-sleeved white blouse and long, wide-legged pants. She stood proudly, her back straight and he was reminded of a picture of Marlene Dietrich in a similar pose.

While he'd never seen the actress in person, he admired her for her strong character, the way she always said what she thought, and her audacity in wearing pants suits in public. No woman had ever dared that before. Except maybe for the beauty standing in front of him.

81

"Good evening, ladies. May we join you for a moment?"

When they nodded in unison, suppressing their giggles, he continued, "I'm Wilhelm Quedlin, but my friends call me Q. This is my friend Leopold Stieber."

He watched the blonde blush as she introduced herself. "Good evening. I'm Hildegard Dremmer, but my friends call me Hilde. These are my friends Erika and Gertrud."

While Leopold engaged in small talk with her girlfriends, Q took a step closer to Hilde and complimented her on her choice of attire. "You look like Marlene Dietrich in that outfit."

She flashed the cutest blush. "You think so?"

"I do. But I like the color of your hair much better."

"Hmm, thanks," was all she said.

Q was enthralled with the way Hilde seemed tongue-tied around him. She kept glancing up at him from beneath her long dark lashes, and when she spoke to him, she sounded almost out of breath. He wanted nothing more than to touch her silky hair, but that would, of course, be inappropriate. Instead, he said, "I noticed how much you laughed at *Dick und Doof*; they're my favorite actors."

She blushed a shade darker. "Ahem...yes...was I laughing too loud?"

By any normal standard, her laughter had been way too loud, but he shook his head. "Not at all. I loved it. It's a rare occasion to hear someone laugh unconcernedly in these days."

A shadow crossed her face before she nodded. "Times are difficult, aren't they?"

Q had no intention of going down the sorry road of the overall economic and political situation in Germany and looked for a better topic to discuss when the first bell interrupted his train of thought. They'd have to go inside the theater in a minute, and this was perhaps his only chance. "Would you allow me to invite you for afternoon coffee one day?"

She side-glanced at her friends before answering, "I'd love to."

Q's heart jumped, and he smiled at her. "Perfect. How about next Saturday? Three p.m. at the Café Potsdamer Platz?"

Hilde nodded. "Yes."

Moments later, the bell rang again and the lights dimmed, indicating the second reel was loaded and ready to begin. Q took Hilde's hand and kissed the back of it. "Until next Saturday, beautiful. I shall meet you at Potsdamer Platz."

Leopold stood next to him and watched Hilde and her girlfriends disappear inside. "You do realize she's much too young for an old man like you?"

Q tore his eyes away from the girl who'd conquered him like a whirlwind and looked straight into the face of his friend. "No. She's just right."

"Come on, she can't be much older than twenty."

"Twenty-two. I asked." Q grinned at him. "Leopold, congratulate me."

"On what? Robbing the cradle?"

"No. You've just been the first person to meet my future wife."

# CHAPTER 16

Hilde returned to the moving-picture theater with Erika and Gertrude, but her mind wasn't on the second half of the film. It was on the handsome stranger who'd just asked her out. Q was tall and slim, and even though his blond hair had been cut very short, she believed it would be curly if left to grow.

His narrow, long face featured a very pronounced chin and dark eyebrows behind his rimless glasses. She actually liked the glasses; they gave him a very intellectual look. And the way he spoke showed he was a man of education. Maybe a teacher? She cursed herself for not asking some questions about him. Like what he did for a living. She'd have to ask more questions when they met again.

*Next Saturday!* Part of her already longed to see him again, to get to know him better, but another part of her was horribly scared and made plans to balk.

Her heart was still beating faster, and she hoped she hadn't made a complete fool of herself while he flirted with her. Apparently, he hadn't been completely deterred by her tongue-tied behavior because he'd asked her out. And she was still shocked that she'd agreed. *Haven't you vowed to never fall in love? This man has the power to hurt you.*

After the picture ended, Erika and Gertrud started their inquisition. "I can't believe you agreed to go out with that man. You don't even know him," Erika said while they left the building.

"He's not exactly the type who'd make the cover of a magazine. And he wears glasses," Gertrud added.

"The glasses give him a serene and intellectual look. I liked it." Hilde tried to defend her admirer.

"You can't be serious. And he was so skinny. He probably doesn't exercise ever."

Hilde heard her friends tearing Q apart, but she let their comments flow over her. "What's wrong with tall and slim? I don't need a muscle man. I want someone I can look up to. An intelligent man."

"Where does he work?" Gertrud asked as they rounded the corner.

"Probably a teacher. He has that look about him," Erika surmised.

"Not at all. He's not that smart. He's probably a clerk in a clothing store or something boring like that."

"How old do you think he is?" Erika asked Gertrud as if Hilde wasn't present.

"Too old for Hilde to be going out with him."

Hilde made a face at them. "Maybe for you, but I think he's just right. Not like those silly boys our age." Behind his serious appearance, she'd spotted a hidden glint of mischief in his amazing blue eyes. No, he wasn't some dreadfully boring clerk. She could feel it. His eyes had captured her with their meaningfulness. And a man whose favorite actors were Stan and Ollie must have a sense of humor.

As they passed their favorite restaurant, Hilde asked, "Girls, want a soda before we head home?"

"Certainly, but I have to be back before midnight," Erika reminded her.

"Me too. Say, does your mother never give you a curfew?" Gertrud asked.

Hilde shrugged. "No."

Her mother did not care what time she came home each night. One of the reasons she'd moved to Berlin had been to get away from her over-protective father and step-mother. So why did she feel stabbed in her heart every time her friends complained about their well-meaning and concerned parents? *I should be happy about my freedom. Wasn't that what I wanted?*

She pushed those thoughts aside before hurt and guilt could settle in her soul. Thinking about how she'd left her father after that terrible fight was the surest way to ruin the evening.

As they entered the small diner and placed their orders, she turned her thoughts away from her parents and back to the man who called himself Q. *Now, he's worth thinking about.*

# CHAPTER 17

Q looked forward to meeting the beautiful Hilde again all week long. In fact, she occupied so much space in his brain, he even made a mistake in one of his calculations and ended up having to throw away two days of work to start the experiment again.

That was such an unusual behavior for him that he almost decided to forget about her. She was becoming the thing he feared. A distraction.

But after giving it some consideration, he found she intrigued him enough to risk his focus to meet with her. Apart from her obvious beauty, it was more than her looks that drew him to her. The way she dressed and the self-confidence she exuded made him want to get to know the woman underneath.

He sensed she owned an inner strength that was at odds with the way she'd been so tongue-tied at their last meeting. Her shyness had been cute, but he wondered how the real Hilde would behave.

Saturday arrived, and Q made sure to arrive with plenty of time to spare. He parked his car where several roads converged at the big public square in the center of Berlin. Entering the square from the south, he passed the Brandenburg Gate and the Reichstag building, which had been in flames one year before, causing the government to suspend the basic human rights granted in the *Weimarer Verfassung*.

Q watched the Reichstag and fought down a bitter taste, while he recited a verse from *The Sorcerer's Apprentice* by Johann Wolfgang von Goethe:

*Sir, my need is sore.*
*Spirits that I've cited*
*My commands ignore.*

People would soon find out that this was only the first of many stages leading Germany straight into a National Socialist dictatorship. Hopefully, it wouldn't be too late by then.

Hilde arrived at the Café Potsdamer Platz a few minutes later from the north. He spotted her buoyant stride long before he could distinguish her face and met her halfway, greeting her with a huge grin. "*Guten Tag.* How are you, lovely Hilde, on this wonderful afternoon?"

Her cheeks stained with a deep purple blush, and she cast her eyes down as she answered, "I'm fine, thank you."

Q mused about her adorable shyness and decided to redeem her. "Would you like to get something to drink or eat?"

"Why don't we have some coffee and possibly a pastry?" she suggested.

Q led her towards one of the tables in the outdoor area, and they placed their order with the waitress. "I've been looking forward to meeting you, Hilde. Tell me something about yourself. Do you work?"

She gave him an indignant look. "Of course I work. I finished business school several years ago and was lucky to get a job processing client claims for an insurance company."

*So she doesn't buy into the Nazi ideology of being solely a housewife and mother.* "Were you born in Berlin?" he asked, sipping his coffee as it arrived.

"No, I was born in Hamburg. I lived there until I was eighteen and then I moved here to live with my mother, step-father, and half-brother."

Q nodded and tabled his questions for later because her voice clearly indicated she didn't wish to talk about her family. "Well, I'm glad you moved to Berlin. Otherwise, I would have missed meeting the most beautiful woman in the world."

Hilde blushed and dedicated her attention to her fingernails. When Q watched her in silence, she soon regained her composure and raised her head. He looked into the most beautiful blue eyes he'd ever seen, and his heart warmed.

"So what about you?" she asked.

Q trailed a finger down her hand that lay on the table top. "I was born in Magdeburg. My parents moved to Berlin when I was fifteen, and I, naturally, came with them."

"So, what do you do for a living?" she asked, her eyes dilating with what he hoped was excitement when he slipped her fingers into his hand.

"I'm a scientist. I studied chemistry at university and have a PhD in engineering. Right now, I'm working for the Biological Reich Institute of Agriculture and Forestry as a freelancer."

"That sounds very interesting." She glanced at him with the sweetest expression possible and his heart melted.

"It is, but working with plants is not my passion."

"What is?" she asked, and he became acutely aware of her warm, soft fingers in his hand.

"Research. Inventions. Making discoveries that can be used for the good of mankind."

"Like what?" Her eyes lit up with genuine interest, and he felt encouraged to tell her about his passion. Not a single woman he'd gone out with had ever wanted to know more about his inventions. But Hilde did.

He recounted some of his findings, and soon their discussion turned into a light-hearted banter, where they discovered each other's likes and dislikes. Q enjoyed the conversation and time flew by. Both of them looked surprised when the waitress politely informed them several hours later that the Café was about to close.

"May I drive you home?"

"That would be nice."

Q walked by her side, leading the way to his automobile, and after going several yards, he reached over and took her hand in his own. He opened the door for her, and she gave him directions to her house. Once there, he asked, "May I ask you out again?"

Hilde nodded. "I would like that."

"Me too. I had such a wonderful time today."

89

"So did I." She led him up to the front door of the five-story apartment building, suddenly acting more nervous than she had all day long.

Q watched her carefully, trying to decide whether he should kiss her or not. He really wanted to, but her nervousness had him deciding to place a brief kiss on her cheek. When he pulled away, he was glad for his decision. She seemed distraught, biting her bottom lip.

Moments later, he walked away, feeling happier than he could remember. *She's definitely going to be my wife.*

# CHAPTER 18

A few days later, Q picked her up from her place of work and took her out to dinner at a local restaurant. It was a lovely spring evening, and they were able to sit outside at a table near the back of the garden area.

The nicely arranged garden, with lush green bushes and beautiful flower beds boasting pink peonies, blue clematis, and white lily of the valley, smelled of the coming summer and lightheartedness. A feeling so many citizens of Berlin had almost forgotten existed.

Hilde was clearly as enchanted by the peaceful surroundings as he was and they relaxed into their seats, enjoying their dinner and each other's company. When a flower girl came by their table, he purchased a red rose for Hilde, smelling it before handing it to her with a wink. "For you, my dear."

"Thank you," she said as she took the rose and touched his hand in a caring gesture.

Q watched her for a moment and on an impulse, he asked, "Would you like to come with me to visit my brother Gunther? He lives in a small town about two hours from Berlin by car. You'll love the peaceful atmosphere there."

"Now?" she asked with a twinkle in her eyes.

"Of course not." He grinned. "In two or three weeks from now. We'll leave early on a Sunday morning. Make a full day of it."

She made a face as if she was pondering his question before she burst out laughing. "I'd love to."

Q smiled back and thought what a lucky man he was. Later, he escorted her from the restaurant and drove her home. He walked her up to the doorstep, and this time, he didn't hesitate to kiss her. They shared a passionate kiss and were still locked in one another's arms when the sound of a female chuckle came from behind them.

He quickly released Hilde and stepped away, watching the older woman as she came forward and eyed him with blue eyes so similar to Hilde's. "Don't stop on my account."

Hilde was clearly embarrassed as he could see by the chagrin that crept onto her face. He stepped in front of her and addressed the woman. "Good evening. I'm very sorry for the disturbance. My name is Wilhelm Quedlin."

"I'm Marianne, Hilde's mother." She started to unlock the door and then turned back and noticed his black Ford sitting on the curb. "You came here by automobile?"

Q nodded and wanted to leave, but Marianne touched his arm. "Why don't you come on in, Wilhelm?" she asked before turning to her daughter. "Hilde, no need to keep your beau outside."

She led the way into the staircase and up to the third floor. Q followed her, not exactly sure what to think. He'd expected Hilde's mother to reprimand him for kissing her daughter on the doorstep, but inviting him in? That was pretty unusual.

Marianne unlocked the apartment door and seated him on the big couch in the tiny living room, and Q took a look around. It was sparsely furnished. An antique wooden bureau adorned the wall opposite the sofa and to the left was a beautiful cupboard holding the good china. The centerpiece of the room was a glass coffee table surrounded by a dark leather couch and two matching chairs. Every piece was of timeless beauty. Hilde's mother obviously had good, and expensive, taste.

When Hilde went to sit down at the far end of the couch, her mother tsked at her. "Go sit next to your man. For goodness' sake, he's going to think you're a prude."

92

Q looked from mother to daughter, feeling the tension between them, and it dawned on him why Hilde never wanted to talk about her family. It was so different from the way he and his mother treated each other.

Hilde reluctantly moved closer to him, careful to leave enough space between them to avoid any accidental touch. Her awkwardness was visible on her face, and he could sense it in the tension she emitted.

Her mother didn't seem to notice. "It's so lovely to have you here, Wilhelm. Hilde hasn't talked much about you. Tell me, what is it you do for a living?"

"I'm a scientist."

"Oh, how interesting. You're a professor at the university?"

"Not quite. I work at the Biological Reich Institute for Agriculture and Forestry in the field of plant protection."

"You work for the government. Now that is promising. Tell me more."

"The Reich Institute is funded by the state, but we're not actually working for the government. We're an independent scientific institution." *At least for the time being.*

Marianne went on to ask questions about his background, his automobile, his flat, and he couldn't help but compare his current situation with the interview he'd had with the bank clerk when he'd applied for the loan. Biting back a laugh, he waited for her to ask to see his bank account statements.

But one look at Hilde's agonized expression sobered him up. "It's been a lovely discussion, *Gnädige Frau*, but I should probably head home now."

"Nonsense, and please call me Annie." She looked at her daughter. "Wilhelm can come by whenever he wants. He–"

"Annie," Q interrupted and stood up, "I'm very thankful for your generous welcome, but I'm afraid I have to get up very early tomorrow morning and should bid goodbye."

Hilde's mother stretched out her hand, "I hope to see you again soon. And don't worry about bringing my daughter home late. I won't even mind if you drop her off in the morning."

Startled, he looked down at Hilde, who was looking down at her wringing hands. "I'll see you on Saturday, my dear."

Q left the apartment and walked back to his car, trying to process what Annie had said. He'd never been in such a strange situation. *Did she just invite me to sleep with her daughter? What kind of weird, twisted relationship is this?*

～

Hilde wished the floor would open up and swallow her whole. Q hadn't shown any sign of annoyance, considering her mother had been almost vulgar. But then again, Q was always nice to everyone, regardless of who they were.

But now he probably wouldn't want to see her ever again. She hid her face behind her hands and wanted to scream.

When her mother returned from walking Q to the door, Hilde couldn't take it anymore and shouted at her, "What was that all about? Do you want him to believe I'm a tramp?"

Annie waved away her daughter's concern. "Oh, don't be that way. That's what young people do. You should be enjoying life."

Hilde shook her head in disgust. She wasn't fooled at all by her mother's acceptance of Q. The minute she'd seen his automobile parked at the curb, Hilde had seen the *Deutsche Mark* symbols in her mother's eyes. "You're unbelievable. The only reason you like him is because you think he has money."

"Well, doesn't he?"

"Maybe or maybe not. I don't care." Hilde fought the urge to grab her mother by the neck and shake her until her brains rattled.

"You should," her mother said, straightening the pillows on the couch.

"You're always looking out for yourself."

"What's wrong with that? When you're older, you will understand having a husband to provide for you is important. And in these troubling times, it's doubly important that he has enough money and a safe job."

"I don't need a man to take care of me." Hilde stomped her foot.

"Whoever put those silly ideas in your head, it wasn't me. I tried to teach you the right things. A good woman stays at home and raises her children. She does the laundry, has a warm meal on the table for her husband when he comes home from work, and makes sure her children behave in a way she and the *Führer* can be proud of."

"And what if that isn't the life I want? What if I want to provide for myself?" Hilde growled, her eyes squinting in fury.

Annie raised her head for a moment to look at her daughter before she busied herself dusting the coffee table. "My dear daughter, you need to start paying attention. This is what we women are meant to do. It doesn't do you any good to rebel against God and your Fatherland."

Hilde opened up her mouth to respond, but her mother bulldozed over her.

"In this dire economy, everyone has to make a sacrifice, and when good men are out of work, it's selfish and anti-German for a married woman not to voluntarily give up her job so a man can work and provide for his family."

Hilde had heard of women being fired from their jobs for exactly that reason. She knew everything about the Nazi ideal of a "good German woman" and she disagreed with almost every single point of it. "I want to be free and independent. But you wouldn't understand that, would you, Mother? You haven't worked a single day in your entire life."

"You don't know how difficult raising two children is," her mother answered.

It was the first time she'd acted this rude against her mother, and while she knew she was crossing the line, she couldn't hold back anymore. The bottled-up emotions of twenty years had reached the boiling point, and the words left her mouth like an explosion.

"Raising children? I don't remember you being around when I was young. You didn't raise me; you never even loved me! You dumped me off at Granny's house to go traipsing around with your new lover. And I seriously doubt you had much to do with raising my half-brother."

"You ungrateful little tramp!"

Hilde caught her breath and stared her mother down before she stalked towards her bedroom. "That's right. I'm ungrateful. I don't appreciate how you abandoned your two-year-old daughter while my father was at war. I'd rather be ungrateful, thank you very much."

She slammed the door to the bedroom and sank down onto the bed in desolation. But instead of the tears she'd expected, her eyes stayed dry, and a sense of relief washed over her. There, she'd said it. She'd told her mother how much she'd suffered from being abandoned as a child.

# CHAPTER 19

H ilde was early for work because she'd hurried out of the house, wanting to avoid her mother. The entrance door was still closed, so she took off for a walk around the block. Her eyes cast to the ground, her shoulders hunched, she shuffled along and shrieked when she bumped into someone and felt herself embraced by two strong arms.

"I called out to you, but you were in your own world," Q's familiar voice said before he pressed a kiss on her lips.

She gave in to his kiss and let him hold her a few moments longer before she broke free and straightened her summer dress. "You still want to see me?"

"Why wouldn't I want to see you, sweetest of all women?" he asked, stroking a finger down her cheek.

"Because, you know, yesterday...my mother...she was... I mean..."

He took her chin into his hands and gently forced her to look at him. "*Liebste,* Hilde. I will only judge you on your own actions, never on those of other persons. So, shall we still meet on Saturday?"

She nodded and sent him a happy smile. "Thanks for coming. I was worried you'd never want to see me again."

"I know. That's why I came to look for you. Now let me walk you to your work. You wouldn't want to give them a reason to fire you, right?"

~

Three weeks later, Hilde and Q were officially going together and were seeing each other almost every other day. As promised, they drove out of Berlin to visit his brother Gunther and his family in a small village by the Baltic.

"Tell me about your brother's family," she said as she watched him drive and thought how lucky she was to have a man like him in her life.

"Gunther has been married to a wonderful woman named Katrin for twenty years, and they have four children. The youngest is nine years old."

"Twenty years? How old is he?"

Q chuckled before he answered. "He's ancient. Fifteen years older than me."

"That explains a lot. What does he do?" she asked while looking out the window. They had left the city of Berlin behind and drove now through the countryside. Fewer and fewer buildings lined the street and even those gave way to vast open areas with wheat and potato fields.

"He's a lawyer."

"Oh," Hilde murmured.

"Yes, oh. So, how was your work?"

"Boring."

"And your mother?"

Hilde made a face at him. "You know perfectly well that I don't want to discuss my mother."

Q chuckled. "Yes, I know."

"I'm thinking about moving out. She probably wouldn't even notice."

He glanced at her for a moment and reached over to take her hand. "If I can help you with anything, let me know. Just don't get into too big a hurry."

"I won't. How do you do it?" she asked.

"Do what?"

"Whenever I'm with you, I feel so safe and...loved. Being with you is comfortable and never awkward."

"Never?" he asked with a mischievous grin that told her he was thinking back to their first couple of dates when she hadn't done much more than blush and mumble.

"Well, maybe the first couple of times we went out, but not now. You accept me just as I am, and you let me speak my mind."

"That's because it's such a beautiful mind." He lifted their joined hands and kissed the back of hers.

Hilde settled back into the seat, enjoying the ride in the small black Ford. "Q, this trip was a good idea."

"I'm an inventor. Having good ideas is my job."

She giggled. "I'll try to remember next time."

After driving a while in silence, she asked him, "Why doesn't your brother live in Berlin? Wouldn't there be more work for a lawyer?"

"That's a long story."

"I'm all ears."

He squeezed her fingers and seemed to think about his words. "Gunther worked as head of the department in the education ministry in Berlin, where he was responsible for the legal affairs of all German State Universities – until the Nazis suspended him almost one year ago."

She glanced over at Q's seemingly calm face. "But why? Did he do anything wrong?"

Q coughed out a bitter laugh. "The only wrong he did was to be a registered member of the Social Democratic Party. They suspended him because he wouldn't cancel his party membership and join the Nazi Party, NSDAP. He was suspended, and a short time later, they forced him to retire with a minimal pension at the age of forty-six."

"I'm so sorry."

"Yes, I am too. Without a job and four kids to provide for he had to move out here because the costs of living in Berlin were just too high."

"Couldn't he get a new job?" she asked.

"He never took the final exams required to work as a lawyer at court. As far as I know, he's done that now and is waiting for approval from some ministry to be admitted as a lawyer."

Hilde clenched her fists and wanted to punch someone. How could Q stay so calm witnessing this kind of injustice? She shouted out, "The Nazis have ruined so many things for so many people. I hate them!"

Q reached over and squeezed her hand. "Hilde, you mustn't ever say those things in public. It's not safe."

"The last time I checked, we still had freedom of speech," she said through gritted teeth.

Without Hilde noticing, Q had stopped the car at the curb and turned towards her. "Hildelein, it's not safe. One wrong word might get you into trouble nowadays. You never know whom you can trust."

The concern on his face was so intense, her heart squeezed. *He must know a lot more about the current situation than I do.* She sighed. "I wish everyone would shout out their hate at the top of their lungs. As loud as they can."

"I wish that too sometimes, but the time isn't right. The Nazis have eyes and ears everywhere. It's better to blend in and not fall under any suspicion than to have them openly watching you."

"I hate them," she repeated like a stubborn little girl. "How can I pretend to like them? Since I was small, I've started discussions and fights about things I thought wrong."

"You'll have to change. You're an adult now. You can do that."

"I guess I can." She sighed, deep and loud.

Q squeezed her hand a bit harder. "I don't want anything bad happening to you," he said, his voice hard and demanding, his eyes piercing into hers. "Promise me!"

His genuine concern for her safety warmed her heart. If this was how it felt to be loved, then maybe she should reconsider her vow not to love anymore? She leaned over to kiss him on the cheek. "I promise. I'll keep all of my hate speech about the Nazis for your ears alone."

Q tapped her nose. "Thank you. I look forward to hearing it."

He started the engine again and headed towards their destination. As they entered the small town where Gunther lived, Hilde had the strange feeling something was missing. But what? It took her a few moments to realize that this cute little town looked like it must have in the old days. No sign of the Nazi reign. No uniformed SA or SS patrolled the streets, and no Nazi flags hung from prominent buildings, probably for the lack of ostentatious buildings.

They passed a few people, and her mouth hung open when Q waved a greeting, and the people waved back.

"Close your mouth, Hilde. You'll catch flies."

She snapped it closed, then opened it again to say, "They waved at you and smiled."

"Yes. Feels good, doesn't it?"

"This is so different than Berlin. It seems like a different planet. Nice and quiet."

"It is." He parked the car in front of a modest two-story red-brick family home. "We've arrived."

# CHAPTER 20

Gunther opened the door and rushed out, hugging Q and giving Hilde a handshake. "Welcome in my modest exile."

Q clapped him on the back. "Good to see you. Where's Katrin?"

"She left yesterday evening with the little ones to visit her parents. Her mother is very sick."

"Maybe next time," Q suggested and followed his brother inside the house. He recognized the furniture in the hall and living room from his brother's former flat in Berlin. They showed the wear of four children having mistreated them, and for a moment, the image of Hilde's and his children climbing over the sofa and chasing each other around the coffee table flashed through his mind. He grabbed her hand and couldn't hide his huge smile.

Gunther asked them to wait in the living room while he prepared coffee and served the cake Katrin had baked for their guests. When they'd settled around the table and sipped their coffee, Hilde complimented Gunther on the beautiful garden and the cute little house.

"It's nice, yes, but we might move back to Berlin soon."

"How's that?" Q asked.

"I took the exam I'd missed and received approval by the court of first instance to start working as a lawyer."

"They approved you? Just like that?" Q asked. "When the Nazis dismissed you from your role in the education ministry, I feared they wouldn't approve you as a common lawyer either."

Gunther gave his brother a tight smile with a side-glance at Hilde. "Even the current government sees the need for competent lawyers."

"Yes," Q agreed. "But wouldn't you be working for Nazis? I know you hate them and what they stand for."

"I may not agree with everything our current government does, but as an attorney, my sole guidance is the law, which is the same for everyone." He eyed Hilde with a suspicious look that clearly conveyed that Q was speaking too much.

Laughing, Q nodded in her direction. "Don't worry, brother. She's trustworthy."

"How can you be so sure?" Gunther asked.

"I know her."

"You just can't be too sure these days. I don't know whom to trust right now."

Gunther glared at them, and Q felt the need to defend Hilde. He could understand where his brother was coming from, but it had to stop where his girlfriend was concerned. "Well, you trust me, and I trust Hilde. That must be enough."

"But what do you really know about her? Or her parents for that matter? Isn't her step-father the celebrated opera singer Robert Klein?"

"Yes, he is. I haven't met him though."

Gunther snorted rudely. "For heaven's sake! He's still on the stage performing."

"So what?"

"Q, you know as well as I do that every artist who has in any form criticized the regime has been punished with stage ban. If he's still performing, he must be a supporter of the Nazis."

"Maybe. Or maybe he's just part of the silent masses. Keeping his mouth shut to hold on to his job? And what does that have to do with Hilde?"

"Like father, like son."

"Gunther, you're being unfair. He's her step-father."

"She lives with them, doesn't she? You can't trust her. What if she says the wrong thing and they turn her in? Or you? Or me?"

Q was getting annoyed at his brother. Gunther could be so bull-headed. He wanted to give a sharp response when Hilde raised her voice. "Excuse me, but I'm sitting right here. There is no need to talk about me as if I weren't."

She glared at Gunther. "You don't have to trust me, but believe me when I tell you I hate the Nazis and everything they stand for."

"Why? What did they do to you? What do your parents believe?" Gunther fired off one question after another without giving Hilde time to answer. "What is your political conviction? Are you an NSDAP member? Are your parents? What are their loyalties?"

Hilde shook her head and finally interrupted him. "I'm not a member of any party, and I don't know whether my mother or Robert is. Politics was never a topic of discussion at either my father's or my mother's house."

"And yet you want me to believe you hate the Nazis and wouldn't go off denouncing anyone at the first chance you get?" he said with a derisive grin.

"I do."

"If politics were never discussed at your home, how do you know anything about it? What have the Nazis done to you that justifies your hatred?"

"Nothing. But I could ask you the same questions."

Gunther gave a harsh laugh. "They fired me, and that's enough for me."

Hilde jumped up, and Q put a calming hand on her leg, urging her to sit down again. "Why don't we just agree that none of us here like the Nazis and talk about something else? The weather? Or the peaceful town?"

Gunther and Hilde stared at each other like two boxers in the ring, but then Hilde relaxed and said, "Truce?"

"Truce," Gunther agreed, the smile not quite reaching his eyes.

Their visit didn't last much longer, and they soon sat in Q's Ford returning home. Hilde had become quiet after arguing with his brother, and he was worried about her. "I'm sorry. He's not usually like that."

Hilde didn't hold back. "I don't like him at all. He's unfair and self-righteous. He honestly thinks he's the only one entitled to hate the Nazis."

"Yes, he does, but keep in mind he is a good man. I know he doesn't come across as very friendly, but he's changed during the last year. Losing his prestigious job and having to move his family away from Berlin has left so much bitterness and hurt in his soul. But he'll come around. You two will get along better the more you get to know him."

"Do you have any more brothers or sisters?" she asked after a while.

Instead of answering her right away, he fixated his eyes on the street and grew very quiet. Even though she had to see how his knuckles turned white grabbing the steering wheel, she didn't pressure him, just waited patiently for him to speak. *That's why I love her so much.* His voice was shaky when he finally answered her question.

"I'm the youngest of four brothers. You just met Gunther, the oldest. He's fifteen years my senior. Then came Knut and Albert, thirteen and eleven years older than me."

"You were the baby of the family," she said with a teasing tone. "The nestling. Not like me; I'm the oldest sibling."

He kept quiet, hoping she'd let go of the topic, but no such luck.

"When will I get to meet your other brothers?"

Q debated not answering her. Talking about his family always dredged up bad memories.

"Q?" she asked, concern evident in her voice, "You don't have to tell me if you don't want to."

He glanced at her, and his heart softened at the view of her sweet face. It wasn't right to keep this part of his story from her. She was the woman he wanted to spend the rest of his life with, and she had a right to know. He shook his head. "No. They are dead."

She blew out a breath and reached for his hand. "I'm sorry. What happened?"

He gripped the steering wheel even harder. "Albert was a very intelligent young man. A mathematician. Some called him brilliant. During the last war, he joined up, even though his profession was exempt. He wanted to do his duty, serve his country. You know, all this stupid talk about national honor? Well, he became a pilot and went down over France."

"How awful." She slapped a hand over her mouth and for a tiny moment, she thought about her father and how grateful she was that he had made it back alive from the frontlines of the Great War.

"Yes. It was. He was shot down. Other planes in the area didn't see him get out. According to their eye-witness reports, his plane nose-dived into the ground and exploded. He must have died instantly."

"I'm very sorry."

"Life wasn't the same after we got the notice. Albert had just turned twenty-three and had a beautiful girlfriend waiting for him at home. It was a horrible waste of a young and promising life. I was ten back then, and he'd been my hero since I can remember." Q paused for a moment and then murmured, "This is why I hate war so much. It takes so many lives – causes so much grief. We humans should be wiser than to start another war."

Hilde left him alone with his thoughts for a while before she asked in a soft voice, "And your other brother? Knut?"

Q sighed. "We don't know. He disappeared in Norway."

"Disappeared? I don't understand."

He gave her a rueful smile. "Neither does my mother. Knut was an adventurer. He was always on the move, traveling somewhere. Exploring, he called it. He never contented himself taking the beaten path. No, he always had to go where nobody else had been before. Since he left for his trip to Norway five years ago, we haven't heard from him again."

"Oh, the not knowing…" she trailed off.

He nodded. "My mother, Ingrid, still holds out hope that one day he will show up on her doorstep with a bag full of stories to tell. But Gunther and I are almost certain he's dead."

He could see Hilde was fighting tears when she talked again. "That must be horrible for your mother. I mean, losing a child is probably the worst thing that can happen to you. But the insecurity, not knowing for certain your son is indeed dead and not knowing if he needs your help… that is even worse."

Q nodded. "1929 was a very hard year for my family. Knut went missing, and a few weeks later, my father died unexpectedly from the aftermath of pneumonia. He was showing signs of recovery when, overnight, an embolism in his lung finished him off."

"Your poor mother," Hilde murmured. "Does she live in Berlin?"

"Yes." Q was quiet for a while and then added. "Now, maybe you can understand why Gunther was so harsh about talking in front of you. Neither my brother nor myself have any intentions of adding to the list of deceased children. My mother has had enough sorrow in her life."

Q let his thoughts drift to his missing brother. It had been so long. Knut definitely had his flaws, but he wouldn't just disappear without trying to get some kind of word to his mother that he was well and alive. Knut was dead.

This conversation was a good reminder that he needed to take more precautions about his intelligence work for the Russians. He didn't want to give the German authorities any reason to look in his direction. His mother shouldn't have to lose another son.

# CHAPTER 21

Hilde enjoyed the drive back to Berlin until Q turned the tables and asked about her family. She made a face at him, but he insisted, "Now that I've told you my sad story, it's only fair you do the same."

"Well, I live with my mother, whom you've had the misfortune to meet."

Q chuckled "She is…different."

"You could definitely say that. All my girlfriends envy me because she's so easygoing and never gives me a curfew or opposes my choice of clothing, but sometimes I'd rather…"

"…fight with her about how long you're allowed to stay out?" He completed her sentence.

Now that he'd voiced it, it sounded strange, and she had to laugh. "I know, it sounds strange, but sometimes I think she doesn't care about me. She probably wouldn't even notice if I didn't come home at all." A lump formed in her throat. Why did she still *want* her mother to care for her? Wasn't she grown up and self-reliant by now?

Q stroked her leg. "I would notice."

*That's because you love me. She doesn't.*

"What about your step-father, Robert Klein? He's quite a celebrity. But how is he in real life?"

"He's nice, but we don't have a close relationship." She didn't say that while Robert was always polite, he'd never talked to her on a personal level. By the way he sometimes looked at her with puppy eyes, she suspected he felt guilty to be the reason her mother had abandoned her way back then.

"I've even been to several of his performances – he truly is a great tenor. His voice is outstanding."

Hilde nodded. "When did you last see him perform?"

"Earlier this year. I saw him sing in *Rheingold* by Richard Wagner and *Iphigenia in Tauris* by Christoph Willibald Gluck."

"You like music?"

"I do. A lot."

"What's your favorite instrument?"

"That's easy. The transverse flute."

Hilde cocked her head. "That's a strange instrument for a man to like."

"Not at all. There is something so soothing about the smooth notes. I should play for you some day."

"I'd love that," Hilde agreed. "I used to like going to the opera and even musical concerts, but since the Nazis have instituted their *Gleichschaltung*, they're destroying even the classic operas. Have you noticed how they changed certain characters and some lyrics in *Rheingold* to adapt it to the Nazi philosophy?"

"I'm afraid I haven't. It was the first time I've seen this opera." He glanced over to her. "But I'm not surprised. National Socialism is slowly taking over every aspect of our lives. Whether we want it or not."

"Isn't there something we can do?" she asked, but Q only shook his head and changed the subject. "What about your father?"

"I don't talk to him anymore. Not since I left. He's married to my step-mother, Emma. They have two daughters, my half-sisters, Sophie and Julia."

"How long have you been gone?"

"Four years."

"That's a long time." He reached for her hand to squeeze it before he let it go and grabbed the steering wheel again. "Why did you leave?"

She sighed. *Why?* It had seemed like a good decision, but she wasn't so sure anymore. "We had a fight. I don't even remember the reason. We always fought. My step-mother is the complete opposite of my mother. She was very strict and never let me go out, or do any of the enjoyable things teenagers like to do."

Q chuckled. "You probably fought about something stupid and completely irrelevant for anyone but a teenager. I do remember those days."

Hilde sent him a surprised glance. "I thought you and your mother always got along well?"

"We did. But we still fought when she wouldn't allow me to do things that I wanted to do. Isn't that normal?"

Maybe it was, but to her, it had meant a great deal. She'd felt like Emma was out to ruin all her fun, to show her how bad a person Hilde was and how much she disturbed their little family. *How much I wasn't wanted.*

"How old are your sisters?" Q asked.

Hilde had to calculate their ages. "Julia is nine years younger than me and Sophie thirteen. That would make them thirteen and nine by now. It's been such a long time."

"Don't you miss them?"

She crunched her nose. "I'm not sure. You see, I was eight years old when my father married Emma and took me to live with them. One year later, Julia was born. I felt so dispensable. I hated her. I envied her for having a mother who cared for her. When Sophie arrived, things got worse. Emma didn't have that much time anymore. She was always occupied with the two little ones and I..." Tears sprang to her eyes.

"*Liebling*, please don't cry. That was a long time ago, and I'm sure she loves you."

"Well, if she did, she hid that part very well," Hilde said stubbornly. "We fought all the time. About everything. And my father always took her side. After one particularly nasty fight, I packed my bags and moved to Berlin to live with my mother."

"Does your mother still talk to your father?"

"Talk? Not that I know of. She hates him with all her heart. I've never heard her say anything nice about him. I guess that's why I haven't spoken to him again. She would make my life hell."

"She may have her reasons," said Q. "We don't know what happened between them and whether she still has hurt feelings about their separation."

Hilde snorted. "Hurt feelings? You don't know her. And it was she who left him. He was fighting on the front lines of the Great War when she left him."

"She took you while he was off fighting for his country?" Q asked, unable to hide the surprise in his voice.

"Oh, no. She didn't take me. I was an inconvenience. She dumped me on my grandmother's doorstep and took off with Robert."

"I'm so sorry, *Liebling*. That must have been an awful experience for you."

"It was. My grandmother was the sweetest person around, but I still waited year after year for my mother to come back for me. Or my father."

He grew silent for a few minutes before he asked, "Don't you think it's time to talk to your father and his family again?"

Hilde violently shook her head. "No."

"Hilde, family is important. Don't you want to know if they're doing well?"

She pressed her lips together. "He knows where I am and hasn't made an effort to contact me. Why should I contact him?"

"It's always difficult to make the first step. Perhaps he's as hurt as you are. Will you at least keep that idea in your head?"

Hilde looked at him and saw the love in his face. Contrary to everyone else in the world, Q indeed cared for her and wanted to help. She gave him credit for his concern, but she wasn't ready to revisit the past and fight her demons. "Fine. But I won't promise anything."

"Fair enough. Just think about it."

# CHAPTER 22

One year turned into another, and Hilde finally got her chance to meet Q's mother, Ingrid. She lived in Berlin, but up till now, the timing had never worked for Hilde to accompany him to see her.

Hilde had been on edge for days, wanting to make the best possible impression. She stood in front of her closet and eyed her entire wardrobe for hours, choosing an outfit only to discard it the next moment. She heard the clock ticking in the background. *I'm running out of time. If I don't choose something soon, I'll have to go in the nude.* She giggled at the thought. That would definitely make an impression.

Finally, she put on a cream-white starched blouse with short sleeves and a tiny vee-neck. The dark green woolen skirt dropped to mid-calf, and she pulled on the matching jacket to finish off her look. She then entered the bathroom to put on some makeup and pinned her shoulder-length hair into an elegant roll on top of her head. She glanced into the mirror, satisfied with her efforts. *Exactly the image I want to convey to his mother. She just has to like me!*

Less than a minute later, the doorbell rang; Q waited for her outside with two flower bouquets in his hands. "For the two women I love," he said and held the bigger one out to her. Hilde's heart melted, and her nervousness was all but gone.

"Thank you so much." She sniffed at the beautiful orange, yellow, and red flowers and rushed to put the bouquet into a vase before she returned to the door and Q.

They drove more than half an hour until he parked the car in front of a building on the other side of Berlin. The building had definitely seen better days, but that was true for most of the capital.

Q opened the car door for her and helped her out. He pulled a touch harder than necessary, and she flew into his arms. With a mischievous grin, he took the chance to hold her tight for a moment and kiss her neck.

"You did that on purpose," she said once he released her.

"Who? Me? You really think I could do something so unashamed?"

She broke out in laughter and took his hand. Q had the ability to make her feel secure and joyous at the same time. And the more she got to know him, the more she wanted to spend the rest of her life with him.

Q knocked on the door, and a few moments later, an old lady with brilliant white hair and a dark brown skirt and sweater combination opened the door.

"Wilhelm! Come in, come in. And you must be Hildegard." She pulled both of them into the small apartment and hugged first her son and then Hilde.

"Please, just Hilde, *Frau* Quedlin," she said.

"Don't be silly, dear. Call me Ingrid." The older woman released her and glanced her over before turning to Q. "She's beautiful, son."

He winked and nodded. "I know."

Ingrid chuckled and then led the way to the kitchen. "I'm sorry, but this is the only table I have. The place is just too small. Do you want tea?"

"Yes. Please. May I help you with something?" Hilde asked.

"No, dear. My Wilhelm can help. You sit and enjoy." Hilde watched as Q hurried around the small kitchen to do his mother's bidding.

"Hilde, this is such a treat for me. Wilhelm has never brought a girl-friend with him."

Hilde's ears started burning, and she wished she'd worn her hair down. "He hasn't? Well, he shall bring me from now on."

Ingrid smiled at her and reached up to press the cross around her neck between her thumb and forefinger. Hilde's eyes followed the gesture and she commented, "That's a beautiful necklace."

"Thank you, dear. It helps me to cope with all the worries and hardships."

Hilde saw the eyes of Q's mother water and she bit her lip. But just a moment later, Ingrid had gathered her composure and asked, "Now, tell me about you, my dear."

"I work at an insurance company."

"That's good. So many people are out of work nowadays. The government does its best to generate jobs, but it's just not enough. They even had to release long-time government employees like my son, Gunther."

Hilde's eyes widened, and Q sent her a warning glare before he nodded. "Yes, it's such a shame he and his family had to move so far away." Turning to Hilde, he added, "Mother is besotted with her grand-children."

Ingrid cocked her head and scrutinized Q as if she was expecting him to add something, but she looked at Hilde again and asked, "Have you met Gunther and his family?"

Hilde dutifully responded, "I met him several months ago, but his wife and sons were absent that day." She didn't add that he hadn't liked her at all – a feeling that was mutual.

"Well, since he's not here, I can tell you Wilhelm was always my favorite son." Ingrid patted his arm and smiled. "Probably because he was born when the others were already half grown. He got all the atten-tion, almost like a single child. I was afraid I spoiled him too much because he never showed interest in marrying and having children."

Q rolled his eyes. "Mother..."

"Come on, Wilhelm. You do have honorable intentions with this lovely girl, don't you?" It was refreshing to notice that, for once, he was the one blushing and squirming. Who'd have thought his mother held that kind of power?

Q turned towards Hilde and said, "Have I told you my mother is a follower of Rudolf Steiner and his theory of anthroposophy?"

Ingrid was quick to explain. "Through meditation, you can control your thinking, your will, and create an atmosphere of impartiality and positivity. It helps to understand the greater picture and calm down your own grief and negativity."

Hilde smiled and nodded, not sure she quite understood. Q must have seen the look of confusion on her face and added, "I like some of Steiner's ideas. Especially his take on organic or biodynamic agriculture. Since I've started working for the Reich Institute, I've studied many of his essays, pointing out the dangers of synthetic fertilizers for the ecosystem as a whole. He promotes the idea that a farm as the smallest agricultural unit thrives through diversity, and the integration of livestock and crops into a closed loop of cross-fertilization."

"Oh, Wilhelm. That's marvelous."

Ingrid's eyes lit up, and Hilde watched as she and her son discussed the benefits and drawbacks of Rudolf Steiner's philosophy. While Q argued from the scientific angle, his mother understood anthroposophy from a more intuitive and spiritual angle.

Both of them had all but forgotten about Hilde, and she sensed a stab to her heart as she witnessed how much love those two held for each other. Their relationship was so much closer than she'd ever had with her mother or her step-mother. Even when they didn't agree on a point, they never became angry or irritated with the other person.

The more she observed Q's interaction with his mother, the more pensive she became. Since her mother had first left her at the age of two, she'd felt homeless. Unloved. Not even when her father had finally taken her to live with him and his new wife six years later had she felt like she belonged.

Now, in hindsight, she understood Emma was a good woman and had tried to give Hilde a home. But the little girl carried so much hurt with her, she didn't want to accept Emma as a mother. She'd wanted her birth mother to love her!

In fact, her whole life had been a quest for love – to be loved by the one person who wasn't able to give her the love she longed for. At the same time, she'd put up walls around her heart to keep away any other person. Afraid to experience the same rejection and hurt again.

She'd vowed to never love again. To keep her heart safe and sound. Q had been the first person to dig a hole into her wall of defense. He made her feel safe. Loved. The center of his world. She never had any doubts that he might one day abandon her.

"Everything all right?" he asked as they drove back home.

"Just thinking. You have such a good relationship with your mother. Something I never had with either of my parents."

"It doesn't have to be like that. You still have time to reconcile with your father."

She grew quiet, and when they were almost back to their destination, she nodded. "It might be worth trying. Should I write him a letter?"

"A letter sounds like a great first step."

"I'll do it. I'll write the letter tonight and send it off in the morning before work."

Q's eyes showed how proud he was of her. When he dropped her off at her front door, he kissed her lingeringly and said, "I love you."

Her heart stopped. There it was. That dreaded love word. She'd known it all along, since she met him, but today was the first time he'd said it. Her whole body tensed as the meaning of his words settled in her soul. *I love you.* She wanted to repeat those words, but her throat was dry as a sand dune and no words would come out.

As always, Q seemed to know exactly what was going on inside her, because he put a finger to her lips and whispered, "You don't have to say anything, Hildelein. I loved you from the first moment I saw you – no, from the first moment I heard you laugh – in the moving-picture theater, and every day since then my love for you has grown stronger and deeper." Then he took her tense hands into his and added, "I promise, I will never abandon you. I will love you until I draw my last breath."

Tears pooled in her eyes and she pressed her body against his, embracing him with all her strength, as if she could keep them joined like this forever. And finally – finally – the wall around her heart came crumbling down with a force that almost blew her away. "I love you, too. I love you so much, it almost hurts."

He kissed her cheek and then removed himself from her grip to hold her at arm's length. "Is this why you're weeping?"

She couldn't do anything but nod, and Q wiped away her tears with his finger. "Don't cry, my love."

Hilde kissed him one last time and then slipped inside. She had a letter to write.

Writing the letter was easier than she'd thought it would be. Maybe it was because the ice that had surrounded her heart for so long had finally thawed.

The next morning, she left for work a few minutes early, sticking the letter into the post box. When she turned around with a feeling of satisfaction and pride, reality set in.

A man dressed in nothing but rags shoved a woman waiting at the tram station and ran off with her handbag. Hilde gasped as the woman started screaming, *"Hilfe, ein Dieb!"* pointing to the running man with her handbag.

Within moments, SS policemen were chasing the thief down. He didn't even get two buildings away before he was surrounded. But rather than arresting him, Hilde witnessed how the SS officers began beating him with their wooden bats.

She wanted to puke at the awful spectacle and looked around to see if anyone else had noticed. But all the other passersby continued as if nothing had happened; nobody even raised their head to watch. A man was being beaten to death in front of her eyes, and nobody did anything to stop this barbaric behavior. "He's stolen a purse, for God's sake. That's not a capital crime," she murmured to herself.

Her head whirled with emotions, and she took a step forward, driven by the need to stop the horrific scene, only to have her shoulder grabbed harshly. She turned her head and glared into the eyes of a stranger. He dragged her away from the scene, growling at her, "Are you crazy, woman? Do you want to die too? Move along."

Hilde stared at the man, following him like a puppet around the corner. Only then did he release her, and she came back to reality with a jolt. "Thank you. I was…I'm sorry."

He glanced at her. "Be more careful from now on. It would be a shame. You're such a beautiful young woman."

In a daze, she nodded and turned on her heel to walk to work, not looking at anyone or stopping for anything. But the picture of the SS officers beating a handbag thief to death had been deeply ingrained into her mind.

# CHAPTER 23

Q impatiently waited for Hilde to get off work. When she left the building, he waved over and shouted, "Darling, come here. I want to show you something."

Hilde grinned at him. "You're hopping up and down like a small child. Is it already Christmas?"

"No. Better. You'll see."

When they arrived at his place, he said, "Look what I bought."

"A radio? This is the big surprise?" She'd grown accustomed to his excitement about anything technical, but a simple radio?

"It's one of the most technologically advanced radios in existence. A *Volksempfänger*. You know, the one they've been advertising in newspapers and on advertising columns?"

"I've seen the advertisements," she smiled at him, "but I'm sure there's more to it than meets the eye."

"How did you know?"

Hilde giggled, because after their going out more than one year, he still seemed surprised when she knew he was hiding something.

He kissed her and said, "You know me too well. Of course there's more. The little *Goebbelsschnauze* here could only receive middle and long wave, which let us listen to German stations. I've tinkered with the inner life of our little baby and installed a trap circuit so we can distinguish the weaker signals as well. Want to listen?"

Q turned the knob, and a French voice sounded from the radio, and they both listened to the broken words. "There's too much interference. This is the problem with middle and long waves. I'll have to think of something better. If I could adapt the *Volksempfänger* to receive short waves as well..."

He had all but forgotten about Hilde and strode over into his office where he searched for a screwdriver on his desk. Hilde followed him and asked, "What are you doing?"

"Here, I found it." He looked up into her confused face. "Sorry, darling, but I just had a great idea. Why don't you make us some coffee, and I'll show you in a few minutes?"

Hilde just rolled her eyes and trotted off. When she came back a while later with two mugs of coffee in her hands, he was sitting at his desk amidst heaps of paper with scribbled sketches, several tools, and wires lying around the brand new radio disassembled into its components. Her voice startled him. "Where should I put the coffee?"

"Coffee? Sure!" He pointed to a corner, and she actually found a spot to set down the mugs. A moment later, she stood at his side and pointed to his desk. "Q, this place is a mess. Let me help you straighten–"

"Don't you touch anything. Everything is right where it belongs."

She glanced around. "There's no way that's true. I could help you build some files and–"

"No! I like things just like they are. If you straighten it up, I won't be able to find anything."

Hilde rolled her eyes at him again. "I don't know how you find anything now."

He winked at her. "I have my own system. Now, see this." He showed her one of his sketches and explained, "With a smaller reel and copper wires and a few adjustments here and there, our radio can receive short waves."

"And?"

"Hilde, this means we'll be able to hear foreign radio stations as well. Italian operas. French chansons. British history programs. Isn't that great?" *And the real news, not the propaganda our government wants us to believe.*

She put her hands on his shoulders. "Did you see this sticker on the radio? The one that says, 'Listening to foreign radio stations is a crime against national security and will be punished with imprisonment.'"

He stood up and wrapped an arm around her waist. "Don't worry so much. Think of all the possibilities."

Hilde kissed him on the nose. "Please promise me you'll be careful. Don't let anyone know what you're doing."

"Duly noted." He stood and kissed her chin, then her cheek, then the top of her head. He pulled away, not daring to go any further. "And now let's have our coffee. I can finish this tomorrow."

In his free time, Q worked relentlessly on several new inventions. One of them was refining the mist filters for gas masks, the same thing he'd researched while still at Auer-Gesellschaft a few years back. It still bothered him a great deal that he hadn't been able to complete that specific task.

He made sure to stay away from the old technology, and finally found a completely different method. A better and cheaper method, no less. He tweaked the end results some more to make sure he wouldn't violate any of the patents he'd filed as an employee of the Auer-Gesellschaft.

As soon as he'd filed for and been granted the patent of *Anordnung zur Richtungsbestimmung,* he scouted for companies willing to buy the commercial rights from him. Soon enough, he found a serious prospect.

Drägerwerke was Germany's leading manufacturer of medical equipment, and once he'd sent them a copy of his patent, the head of production had been very anxious to meet with him. A few days later, Q traveled to their headquarters in Lübeck.

During the meeting, it soon became clear why they so badly wanted to buy the commercial rights to his patent. They were after a big military contract from the German government. Apparently, the contract would only be granted if they could provide medical equipment as well as gas masks. And up until now, Auer-Gesellschaft effectively held a monopoly on them, thanks to Q's earlier patents.

Q knew his new method of folding and applying the adhesive was superior to the old one, and that the performance of the gas filters would be greatly enhanced when using it. Drägerwerke was a good company, but Q still had a nagging feeling in his stomach because the head of production was more interested in crushing the competition – Q's former employer – and making big money with the government contract than in providing the cheapest and best possible protection for the general public. Once again, his invention would be used mainly for military purposes.

But when the procurement manager named a staggering figure they were willing to pay for the exclusive commercial rights in Germany, he pushed the nagging feeling away and agreed. After all, he would need a nest egg if he were to marry Hilde and have a family with her, and the amount they offered was equivalent to a three-years' salary.

On his way home, he was disheartened. Why didn't anyone under-stand his wishes that his inventions should be used for the people and not against them? Why was everyone so keen on Germany's re-militariza-tion? Didn't they see this would inevitably lead to war and complete destruction?

After pondering the situation, he decided not to search for a buyer of the commercial rights for Italy, where he'd already filed for and been granted the patent as well. Any Italian company would only follow the example of Drägerwerke.

Instead, he set up a meeting with his Russian contacts at the Soviet trade mission, confident the communists would use his technology for the protection of the general public and not for profit.

Pavel was surprised to see him after Q hadn't contacted him in quite a while. "Hello, Q, what brings you here?" the agent asked.

"I've been working on improvements for the gas mask filters I showed you earlier."

"Oh, yes, I remember. Your technical knowledge has served our comrades well, but unfortunately, the production process is tedious and cost-intensive."

Q nodded. "I know. But my new folding and adhesive technology will solve those problems. I want gas masks to be accessible to every last person in case a new war breaks out."

After some discussion back and forth with Moscow, Pavel produced a very generous offer. "I have good news for you. Your technology is worth quite a lot, and we're very interested in acquiring the commercial rights outside of Germany." He named the exact amount of money Q had already received from Drägerwerke.

Q shook his head. "No. No. I couldn't possibly accept that kind of money. Consider this my contribution to a peaceful coexistence of our nations."

Pavel tried to convince him to take the money, but Q adamantly refused to. Some of his friends probably thought him naïve to pass up so much money, but wasn't it a worthy cause? Giving back to mankind and doing his bit for peace.

He left the Soviet trade mission at Unter den Linden with a whistle on his lips and the feeling of having done the right thing.

# CHAPTER 24

H ilde looked out of the window of her mother's kitchen for the
hundredth time. *Why doesn't he come already?* She paced back to
the living room, eyeing the letter on the bureau as if it could suddenly
spring to life and attack her. Her fingers trembled as she reached for it
and touched the soft white paper with her hands. The letter was lightweight and slim, probably only one sheet of paper.

Her name and address were written with a typewriter. No sender. But
the postage stamp indicated it came from Hamburg. *It's from my father. It
must be.*

She looked at the clock on top of the bureau and then paced back to
the kitchen with the letter in hand, looking out of the window once again.
*He should be here by now. Why isn't he coming?*

Her first intention had been to tear open the letter in the privacy of
her bedroom, but then she couldn't. She'd stood there staring at it, unable
to move. What if it contained bad news? If her father didn't want to see
her? Or if her mother walked in and caught her opening the letter written
by the man she still hated so much? What if Annie destroyed her father's
note before she could read the contents? It wasn't safe, Hilde tried to
rationalize. She'd wait for Q to arrive. He would know what to do.

She returned to the living room and looked around the place. On the
corner of the couch she spied one of her half-brother's *Hitlerjugend*

uniforms lying there, together with the ever-present swastika arm band and several swastika flags in different sizes. A lump formed in her throat and she had the urgent need to breathe air. Fresh air.

The Nazis had long ago invaded even her most private space. Since her half-brother had joined the NS youth organization, *Hitlerjugend,* there was no escaping the constant propaganda. Not even in the safety of her home. *I have to leave this place. Soon. I feel like I'm drowning.*

With a bitterness that surprised her, she thought that at least on that account her mother shared the same opinion. More than once, she'd told Hilde it was time for her to get married and move out.

Finally, she heard a car approach and saw Q pull up out front. She rushed from the house and climbed into the vehicle, all before he could turn off the engine or even think about coming to get her.

"Happy to see me?" he asked with a wink.

She pulled the envelope from her pocket and thrust it at him. "This came today." Now that he'd finally arrived, the words came tumbling out of her mouth faster than lightning. "It's from Hamburg. It must be from my father, but I was afraid Mother would come home and see it, so I hid it in my pocket. I was afraid to open it because I wasn't sure–"

Q chuckled and placed a finger over her lips, effectively silencing her for a moment. "Easy, Hilde. Take a deep breath for me and then start again."

She nodded, swallowing hard. "Can we drive to your place and open it there?"

"I think I can do that. You don't want Annie to know about the letter?"

"No, I don't. She still hates my father so much. She would disapprove of my contacting him in the first place."

Q drove her to his building and escorted her up the stairs to the little apartment. "Sit down, then open the letter and see what he has to say."

Hilde sat down, and he placed the letter in her lap. She looked around the room, thinking once again how nicely it was decorated considering it belonged to a bachelor. The wooden floors were covered by a large rug, and the couch she sat on had obviously not been used by many people. Two side chairs sat on either side of the couch, stacked high with papers. Q and his penchant for collecting everything.

She took a steadying breath and attempted to open the letter, but her fingers were shaking too badly to manage the task.

"Here, let me open it for you." He produced a letter opener and slit the top of the envelope before handing it back to her.

She took a nervous breath and unfolded the paper. The letters sprang around on the paper, but somehow she managed to read the note.

*Dear Hilde,*

*I was so happy to hear from you. All of us have missed you. You are welcome to visit anytime. This is still your home.*

*Please bring your young man with you. I would love to make his acquaintance.*

*Love,*

*Your father*

"He sounds happy," Hilde murmured, almost unable to believe her eyes. A huge weight lifted from her chest as she carefully stroked the paper and imagined her father in his office, smoking a cigar while writing the letter.

"Do you want to visit him? I could drive us to Hamburg for a week-end," Q offered.

She nodded, wanting to see her father and yet afraid her happiness would disappear once she got there.

Q produced some paper, a pen, inkwell, and envelope. "Why don't you write him back and give him your phone number as well? That way he can contact you sooner and we can make arrangements to go visit him right away."

She blankly stared at him. "I can't do that. What if he calls and my mother answers the line?"

"True, that could cause a problem." Q furrowed his brow. "Why don't you give him my phone number?"

"You would do that for me?" she asked, lifting the pen up and preparing to start the letter.

He grabbed her around the waist and pressed a kiss to her neck. "I would do anything for you, Hildelein. I love you. Go ahead. Write him with my phone number and then I'll take you out to dinner to celebrate."

"I don't know what to say," Hilde said.

"Then bring those things with us and I'll help you write the letter while we wait for our food to arrive. I'm starving."

Hilde smiled and gathered up the writing supplies. Dinner was wonderful, and in no time at all, they had a letter to her father composed.

On the way back to her mother's house, Hilde grew nervous once again. She couldn't purchase a stamp or mail the letter until the morning. Q walked her up to the third floor, but before she could ask him about mailing the letter for her, Annie opened the door. She glanced at them, her eyes locking on the envelope in her daughter's hand.

"What's that? Did the postman leave a piece of mail on the front step?" Annie reached for the envelope, yanking it out of her hands before Hilde could pull it away.

Her mother looked like she'd sucked on a lemon, blatant disgust on her face. "This is for Carl. What on earth do you have to say to your father?"

Q snatched the letter from Annie's fingers and said to Hilde, "I'll mail it in the morning."

"Show me the letter!" Hilde's mother demanded. "I hope you're not complaining about me to this…disgraceful person. Since the day I married him, he's caused nothing but trouble. A man who leaves his wife and baby daughter alone to go sauntering around the world isn't worth the cost of the paper and ink to write him. I refuse to permit you further contact with him."

"Saunter around the world? He was a soldier, fighting at the front, for God's sake!" Hilde replied, but her mother only gave her a cold stare.

"Others stayed at home to care for their wives. He chose not to."

"I'll see you tomorrow," Q whispered and kissed Hilde's cheek before he quietly backed out of the corridor and stormed down the stairs as if the devil incarnate was chasing him.

Hilde didn't blame him, knowing another nasty argument with her mother was on its way. She took a steadying breath and attempted to brush past her mother and into the house. If she could reach the safety of her bedroom and close the door before her mother caught up, she might be able to hold onto the happiness she'd felt earlier.

But she had no such luck. Annie drew level with her a few feet from her room. "You'd better start looking for another place to stay. In fact, if you insist on having contact with Carl, why don't you go and move back in with him?"

Hilde didn't bother to turn around or respond. She put one foot in front of the other until she reached her room and sank down onto the bed. *I wish I had someplace else to live. I hate this house. I hate her.*

"Nervous?" Q asked Hilde as they passed the Brandenburger Tor on their way to Hamburg.

"Why would I be nervous? We're only visiting the father I left after a row five years ago and haven't talked to since." She tried a joke but shuddered inwardly. She closed her eyes to take a deep breath. Without Q, she wouldn't be here. He'd nudged her to take the first step and had even offered to accompany her and drive her to Hamburg in his little Ford. Otherwise, she'd have taken the train and probably have jumped off at the first stop and run back.

A wave of reassurance washed over her as she observed his slim, long fingers grasping the steering wheel. He drove the car like he did anything in his life: with meticulous attention to detail and great authority. She loved that man so much, it occupied every last corner of her body and soul.

Q glanced at her. "Don't overthink it. Everything will be fine."

Hilde nodded and they drove in silence until they reached the new Autobahn to Hamburg.

"With the Autobahn we'll be in Hamburg in no time at all," Q said.

Hilde giggled. "At work that's just about everything they talk about. The wonderful new highways, better and faster mobility for everyone. The Nazis should rename themselves to *The Autoparty*."

Q reached out for her hand. "I know. And it may be the only good thing Hitler has done for our country. But then, it's a big show, just like everything else that has happened since the *Machtergreifung*."

Just a few days ago, Berlin had seen another huge deployment of soldiers, with colorful parades and thousands of people cheering and celebrating the *Führer* and his farseeing politics.

"The people are celebrating this man as if he was Jesus Christ personally, God-sent to redeem the German Nation," Hilde said with disgust and turned on the radio, just to hear the newest propaganda by Minister Goebbels himself.

"*...another great success in the efforts for betterment of our Fatherland. The jobless rate is down from over thirty percent to ten percent in less than three years, since our Führer Adolf Hitler took over...*"

She turned off the radio again. "I'll vomit if I have to hear more of this. They claim all the credit for the good things, while they forget to mention how they achieved it." She talked herself into a heated rage. "Do you know why the unemployment rate is dropping so fast? I've seen it with my own eyes. They're firing all the Jews, and taking them out of the statistics. And they've fired many married women who have a working husband. Fine way to decrease unemployment!"

"And don't forget the additional five hundred thousand men they've put into the military," Q added with an amused voice.

Hilde glared at him. "How can you take this so lightly? That's not funny."

"It isn't. But it won't help to get all enraged. On the contrary, it will make us vulnerable. Remember, it's best to keep a low profile. I wouldn't want you to make the acquaintance of a Gestapo officer."

An icy chill traveled down her spine. While nothing official was known, there had been rumors about what kind of things happened during a Gestapo interrogation. Things she didn't even want to imagine, much less experience.

"You're right," she said and fell into silence. "But I still don't get it."

"What don't you get?" Q asked.

"Why the French and British don't mind that Hitler reunified the Saar Basin with the Reich."

"They mind, but they're trying to appease Hitler at this time. They're hoping that by giving him what he wants, he won't ask for more."

"Do you think their strategy will work?"

Q shook his head, "No. I think that decision is going to come back to haunt everyone in Europe and prove to be a huge mistake in years to come."

Hilde lapsed into silence and worried about her own problems. She hadn't seen her father in almost five years. How different would he look? And her sisters?

Her thoughts wandered back in time to the day when he'd returned from the last war and had found his daughter living with his mother while his wife was sharing bed and table with another man. The humiliation and anger on his face had been deeply ingrained into her soul.

Back then, she'd mistaken it for disapproval of herself. And for most of her life she'd encased this hurt, grief, and guilt in her heart. Even though her grandmother had many times explained it wasn't Hilde's fault, she hadn't believed one word the good woman said. It was her fault – and hers only – that both her mother and her father had abandoned her. She just wasn't worthy of being loved.

Tears sprang to her eyes at the memory. Even when he'd come back from war, she hadn't understood why he'd left her with her grandmother. She loved her grandmother dearly, but she'd longed to live with her parents. Like any five-year-old girl would.

It wasn't until much later that she understood he hadn't been able to care for her and leaving her with his mother had been his only option. There was no way a single man recently returned from the cruelties of war and working all day could take care of a child on his own.

It wasn't until 1920 when her father married Emma that he brought eight-year-old Hilde home to live with them. She'd suddenly had a family again, but it wasn't the family she wanted. To give her step-mother credit, the woman had tried her best to be a mother to Hilde. But she'd been hurt and refused to give even a little bit.

Things worsened with the birth of her first half-sister, because the baby reminded her every day that Emma was only her step-mother and her own mother had gotten rid of her.

That was the toughest time she'd faced in her life and she shuddered at the memory. She vowed to never abandon her own children, should she be blessed with any.

Hilde sighed, and Q reached over to touch her thigh. "Hildelein, don't worry. Everything will work out."

She turned her head and gave him a smile. "Yes, it will. I love you." *I am so deeply, crazily in love with you, it's almost frightening.* It was a feeling she'd never had before and it consumed every part of her. She wanted to belong to him. She wanted him to be her family and longed to experience the blisses of marriage.

"I love you too." He kissed his forefinger and then tapped it on her lips. "You're going to be just fine. Remember, I'm here with you all the time."

Hilde sighed in relief. Since she had started going with Q, she had become so accustomed to having his reassurance and loving presence in her life. He was her family. Her best friend. Her love. He was everything she could ever have wished for in a man. Q would never hurt her. Or abandon her.

# CHAPTER 26

Q grew increasingly worried about Hilde the farther they traveled from Berlin. Since leaving the city, she'd been unusually quiet and pale. Now, he asked himself if he'd pressured her too much into reconciling with her father and she wasn't emotionally ready.

Her inner turmoil was palpable inside the confinement of his small car, and all he wanted was to make her pain go away. Just how?

When Hilde sighed again, looking out the window, he glanced over and noticed her trembling hands. At the next recreation area, he left the Autobahn.

"Still nervous?" Q asked as he pulled the car to a stop.

A single tear slid down her cheek and he brushed it away with his thumb before he exited the automobile and helped her out. "Come here," he said and embraced her in his arms. They stood still for a long time until he sensed the tension in her body easing.

"Are you all right?" Q asked.

"I guess I am. Just very nervous." Hilde tried a small smile.

"Everything will be fine. If your father was still angry or resentful, he wouldn't have sent such a joyful and welcoming letter."

"I keep telling myself that."

"Well, start believing it."

She laughed. "You make it sound so simple."

He kissed her nose. "It can be, if you'll allow it."

Pulling him close, she listened to his heart under her ear. "How do you always know the right words to say?"

"Because my heart is connected to yours, and it hears what you need."

She melted. Simply melted against him. Yes, she could do this, with him by her side.

After a while, Q led Hilde back into the automobile and started the engine. "Ready to tackle the dragon?"

Hilde giggled. "Well, yes."

Q leaned over for a kiss and said, "That's much better." Then they continued their journey to Hamburg. A short while later, they stopped in front of a modest single-family house in the suburbs.

Two teenage girls were sitting on the front porch, rushing into the house before Q and Hilde managed to get out of the car. "Papa. Mama. They're here!"

"I guess someone has been waiting anxiously." Q chuckled.

"Sophie and Julia. They've grown so much."

As soon as Q opened the car door for Hilde, her father appeared in the door. He was a handsome man with greying hair at his temples and bushy grey eyebrows. Q instantly liked the man.

"Hilde, I'm so happy to see you!" He strode towards them, pulled her into his chest and hugged her tight for several long moments. Q could see Hilde's eyes watering and when her father released her, he squeezed her hand in a reassuring gesture.

Hilde made the introductions, "Father, this is Wilhelm Quedlin."

Her father shook Q's hand. "It's a pleasure to meet you, Herr Quedlin."

"Herr Dremmer, the pleasure is all mine, but please call me Q."

Carl Dremmer looked from Q to his daughter and said, "I see. Q it is then. Please come inside."

Her sisters rushed forward to greet them and Q had to hide a grin when they seemed to remember they were supposed to behave and slowed down at the last moment to shake his and Hilde's hands with a curtsy.

Only then did he notice a woman in the background, who'd patiently waited her turn to greet their guests. "Welcome home, Hilde." She stepped forward, smiling away the slight tension he noticed between the two women. Sophie and Julie came to the rescue, cutting the welcome short by grabbing Hilde's hands and pulling her with them back into the house.

"Please excuse the manners of my girls, but they've been anxiously waiting since the day we received Hilde's letter. But you must be hungry, please come in."

Q retrieved their luggage, and soon, the whole family was sitting around the table drinking coffee and eating homemade strawberry cake. After coffee the women disappeared into the kitchen to wash the dishes and prepare dinner.

"Want a drink?" Carl Dremmer asked Q, escorting him into his office.

"Yes, please, Herr Dremmer."

"Nonsense. Please call me Carl."

"Thank you for the warm welcome, Carl."

"No, it's I who should be thanking you for being such a positive influence on my daughter." His voice showed no trace of emotion, but the tic in his eyelid revealed how much the man had suffered by being estranged from his oldest daughter.

"You've met my ex-wife?" Carl asked.

Q chuckled. "Yes. She's interesting, to say the least."

Carl made a face. "That's a nice way of saying…well, enough about her. I hope I never have to cope with her again. But please tell me something about yourself."

The two men chatted for a while until Q cleared his throat. "Since we're alone, there is another reason I wanted Hilde to reconcile with you."

"Oh?" Carl asked, looking interested.

"Yes. I want to ask for your daughter's hand."

"Yes! A thousand times yes," Carl agreed with obvious joy and winked at Q, "under one condition."

Q swallowed hard. "Condition?"

"You have to promise to visit more often."

"I can promise that."

They left the office, Q's heart beating fast at the prospect of a future with Hilde by his side.

# CHAPTER 27

Hilde enjoyed getting to know her sisters again, and when Emma appeared in the doorway, she was humbled by her step-mother's capacity for forgiveness. She hadn't thought it would be so easy to catch up, but it had been, even though she'd hurt Emma a great deal when she was a teenager.

"I can't believe how much the girls have changed," she told Emma as she helped put dinner on the table. So many things had changed in the last five years, but the house was still very much the same.

Her father was beaming from ear to ear when he and Q stepped out of his office, and Hilde wondered what those two had talked about. Emma apparently had also noticed his good mood and pulled her aside before everyone sat down to dinner. "Hilde, please don't leave your father again. It nearly broke his heart when you left after the quarrel. He hasn't been the same man since then."

Hilde's eyes filled with tears. Everything had suddenly become too much. "I can't stay, but I can promise to keep in touch and visit more often." She met Emma's eyes. "Thank you for putting up with me and for taking such good care of my father."

Emma hugged her. "You're very welcome."

"I'm sorry I was such a brat."

"You were a hurting teenager. But let's not talk about the past."

Hilde laughed, feeling her heart ease even more, and they joined the rest of the family in the dining room. Later that night, Q was assigned Julia's room while Hilde joined her sisters in Sophie's room. The three girls giggled and chatted until very late that night, and Hilde felt as if she was on a sleepover with her girlfriends. Except that her younger sisters peppered her with questions about Berlin and her life in the capital.

"What's the city like?" Julia asked, her eyes bright with excitement.

"Are there lots of cute boys?" Sophie chimed in.

"What do you know about boys?" Hilde asked with a chuckle and tried to recall what she'd been like at this age. She felt sure boys hadn't even been on her mind.

"Tell us what it's like," they begged.

"Well, the city is big. There are motion-picture theaters and the opera. Concerts and parades."

"That sounds so exciting. Can we come visit you?"

Hilde started to give an immediate "yes" but paused before saying more cautiously, "I'll speak with Father about it. Maybe you could all come for a visit?"

Much later, when her sisters had fallen asleep, she lay awake. The girls were young and naturally assumed that everything was bigger and more exciting in the capital. She'd thought the same thing at their age, but in reality, her life was rather normal.

Work. Going out with Q. Motion pictures or the theater. Once in a while a trip to the Baltic Sea. Those were the most exciting things she could think of.

The next day, Hilde's heart warmed at the way Q interacted with her youngest sister, Sophie. They were becoming best friends. When Sophie came running over to her, Hilde smiled, "You and Wilhelm are getting along."

"Wilhelm?" She wrinkled her nose. "He said I could call him Q."

"That's what all of his friends call him."

"You're so lucky, Hilde. He's so handsome and intelligent, and he has an answer to all of my questions."

"Don't be a bother, all right?" Hilde warned her, worried Q might become annoyed with all of her questions.

"Your sister is so cute and very curious," Q told Hilde a while later.

"She informed me you are very intelligent." Hilde grinned.

Q chuckled. "It's not hard to appear intelligent to an eleven-year-old. But she's so interested in everything going on, I have to keep reminding myself not to say anything political. She's much too young to be involved with those things."

"I agree. Thank you for watching out for her." She slung an arm around his waist. "She should have a carefree childhood and not be bothered with those things."

Later that day, she and Q were talking with her parents about the changes the Nazis had made to the education system. "It's not really about learning anymore. The education nowadays consists mainly of drilling in the National Socialist philosophy. And they added a new subject. *Rassenkunde*."

"Ethnogency? As in theory of the races?" Q asked with raised eyebrows. "In school?"

Carl nodded. "Yes. They come home with all kinds of bullshit ideas planted in their heads. And I can't do anything about it. I can't complain or correct them, because if they were to say the wrong thing to their teacher, they would get in trouble."

Emma sent her husband a stern look. "It is as it is. We should be grateful they are such good girls."

"I'm still worried about them. Since Julia has joined the *Bund Deutscher Mädel*, which is Hitler's version of a girl's club, she's talking all the time about how important sports are to prepare young men and women for war. At least Sophie is too young, so I've been able to keep her out of the BDM for at least another year."

Hilde swallowed and pressed her fingertips to her temples. "They're preparing the children for war?"

"All signs are pointing to war," Q confirmed.

Carl made a face as if he'd swallowed a lemon. "I'm afraid sooner rather than later. Thank God, I'm too old for that. My experiences in the last war are more than enough for a lifetime."

Emma interrupted the discussion. "The girls should be home any minute. Have you heard Sophie sing?"

Carl beamed with pride. "She's very talented and has a great voice."

"Father, Q plays the transverse flute. Doesn't Sophie have one as well? Maybe the two of them could play some music for us?"

"That's a wonderful idea. Q, do you mind?"

"Not at all." Q headed indoors to find the flute and his musical partner, who had just arrived home. Fifteen minutes later, Q and Sophie were making beautiful music together while the rest of the family listened.

Hilde fell more in love with him as each moment passed. *My father likes him. Emma and my sisters like him. Even my mother likes him, even though her reasons have nothing to do with his character and everything with his material worth.*

The weekend passed far too quickly, and soon, she and Q were headed back to Berlin. In the car, they recounted the past two days, laughing over her sisters' antics. Q squeezed her hand. "Hilde, I really liked your family. From now on we should visit them more often."

"Yes, we should do that. This weekend was fun."

Q was silent for a few minutes and then spoke, "I enjoyed getting to know your father, and I asked him for your hand in marriage when we were in his office the day we arrived. He said yes, so I was wondering if you would marry me?"

Hilde's eyes widened as she looked at him and then laughed. Q had just asked her to marry him in the most un-romantic way she could imagine. But this was him. Practical. Result-oriented. She wasn't surprised at all, or disappointed that he had proposed to her while driving his automobile.

She squeezed his thigh. "Yes."

Q smiled at her and said, "We can start making plans as soon as we get back to Berlin. First of all, we need to find a flat that is big enough for both of us."

"That sounds wonderful. What about our honeymoon?" she joked, but Q furrowed his brows and answered, absolutely serious.

"I've thought about that, too. What do you think, if we take a sabbatical to travel across Europe? Three months shouldn't be a problem. I've saved some money and you could ask for unpaid vacation–"

"Q, don't you think we should actually get married first?" She laughed at him.

He glanced over at her. "If you insist. But I've never been happier. I want to live life to the fullest with you. The sooner, the better. You never know how long it will last."

# CHAPTER 28

L ife picked right back up and Hilde and Q started making a list of the things they needed to do before they could get married. Find an apartment. Apply for a marriage license. Organize the reception. Prepare for the honeymoon.

Even after they settled on a date, the list continued to grow, but their need to relax didn't.

It was increasingly difficult to find entertaining things to do, because the National Socialists had usurped every last part of German day-to-day life. Even the first-ever color picture, *Becky Sharp,* which Q invited Hilde to watch, was embedded with short propaganda films.

Which reminded Q that he'd not given his Russian contact any information lately. But now, with more than himself at stake, Q didn't dare to visit the Soviet trade mission again. Instead, he sent Pavel a note and from then on, they met regularly at ever-changing public places. The Berlin Zoo park, the Wannsee Lake, an art exhibition.

About one month after his proposal, Hilde waved a piece of paper at him when he arrived to pick her up. "You won't believe what this is," she said with a sour face.

"Don't I at least get a kiss?" he asked.

She gave him a half-hearted kiss before she blurted out with a high-pitched voice, "The Reichstag has passed another racial law."

"Let me see," he said and took the paper from her shaking hands. According to the piece of paper, all couples eager to marry must now abide with the *Law for the Protection of German Blood and German Honor* that forbade marriages and extramarital intercourse between Jews and Germans. "Neither of us is Jewish, so this won't hinder us from getting married."

Hilde pierced him with angry eyes. "You haven't heard all of it. You now have to prove you're Aryan to get permission to marry. The man at the civil registry explained that we both have to present a *Lesser Aryan Certificate.*"

Looking into her worried eyes, it dawned on him that this might mean a delay in their wedding plans. He sighed. "What do we need to get this certificate?"

She shoved another paper into his hand that indicated the requirements. "Here."

The document explained that seven birth or baptism certificates were required – the person wanting to get married, his parents, as well as maternal and paternal grandparents. Additionally, three marriage certificates, one for each set of parents and grandparents. In lieu of the original documents, they could submit certified proofs.

"Oh my, we better start gathering the documents right away." He sighed and reached out to embrace her. "Don't worry."

She pressed her cheek against his chest. "We can't apply for the license and fix a date before we have the required certificate. And the man at the civil registry warned me that there is already a long waiting time, because since the law was passed a few days ago, no more weddings have been scheduled."

Hilde's father and her mother helped gather the needed documents, and as 1936 arrived, she held her Lesser Aryan Certificate in her hands. But they faced unforeseen problems on Q's side.

His maternal grandmother had been born in Temesvar, Hungary and thus was suspected to be non-Aryan by descent. After several letters back and forth to the authorities in Temesvar, it became clear that they couldn't produce a birth certificate of Q's grandmother. Despite his mistrust for Hilde, Q's brother Gunther offered to help and send an official letter in his position as lawyer.

Many a time Hilde confided in her friends Erika and Gertrud that she was beginning to lose hope of ever getting married. Every time they got close to fixing a date, they were forced to postpone it. Again and again and again.

On one occasion, she told her friends, "I'm so fed up with all of this, I'm going to cancel the wedding and break up with Q."

Gertrud laughed at her. "As if you could do that, Hilde. You love that man so much."

Hilde dropped her face into her hands. "It's true. If I didn't know he's the one, I would have given up on the idea of marriage months ago. I hate those stupid racial laws and what they make us go through."

Gertrud patted her arm. "I agree. They're a pain, and we certainly could do without them."

"Don't say that," Erika chimed in. "Those racial laws may be inconvenient at times, but they do serve a purpose. We may not understand them, but the people who made them are much wiser than we are."

Hilde and Gertrud exchanged eye rolls behind Erika's back but let their friend continue to sing the praise of racial segregation.

By mid-year, as they were still attempting to prove Q's Aryan heritage, it became hard to ignore the signs of a totally different kind of trouble. Germany was preparing for war. The neighboring European countries were preparing for war. Even the Russians were preparing for war.

"England is preparing for war," Q told Hilde one evening after listening to BBC radio on his enhanced *Volksempfänger*.

She nodded. "You said this day was coming. Isn't there anything that can be done to prevent it?"

"I'm afraid not. And there's more troubling news. I heard they're building a new super-prison in Oranienburg. Apparently, it will be at the same location currently housing a small concentration camp for political prisoners."

"How do you know all of this?" She snuggled up to him.

He tapped her nose. "Oranienburg is a small place. When I lived there, I knew some of the guards. Most of them have been replaced by SS men because they haven't been strict enough with the prisoners."

Hilde shuddered and didn't ask what *strict* meant. If it was anything similar to the rumors she'd heard about the way suspects were treated at the Gestapo headquarters in Prinz-Albrecht-Strasse, then she didn't want to know.

Q continued, "Apparently all persons considered a political danger to the Nazi regime can end up there without judicial review or the right to a lawyer. Communists, Social Democrats, critics, and everyone who dares raise his voice against the Nazi system. Well, those, and everyone who's deemed undesirable, including the homeless, beggars, criminals, homosexuals and even Jehovah's Witnesses."

"Oh my God, that's pretty much everyone! You say one wrong word and you end up in one of those camps? That can't be true."

"I'm afraid it is." Q pressed Hilde against his body and kissed her. "This is why you have to be careful. Don't ever criticize the government."

Hilde's palms broke out into a cold sweat and she turned uncomfortably in his arms, "I didn't tell you…"

His brows furrowed. "Didn't tell me what?"

"The day I mailed my father that first letter, there was a man. He stole a woman's purse. She started screaming and SS officers came from everywhere. They caught up with him and beat him to death in the street."

She swallowed, knowing he wouldn't like the next part. "I was so upset, I wasn't thinking straight. I took a small step forward, trying to keep them from killing him, but some stranger grabbed my shoulder, pulled me away, and lectured me."

Q hugged her close, a long sigh of relief exiting his lungs. "Thank God he did. They probably would've killed you too. Please promise to be more careful."

"I promise, but I can't get the picture of that man out of my head."

He kissed her hair. "It will remind you to be careful."

~

Eight months after Q's proposal, Hilde had almost lost all hope. "We'll never be able to get married," she sobbed into his shoulder.

"Hilde, sweetheart. I love you so much. What difference does a wedding certificate make?"

She looked at him with questions in her eyes, and he continued, "I don't care whether or not we're officially married, we could still live together."

"But that would be very unusual and inappropriate."

"I know," Q said against her lips. "But what other choice do we have? I hate seeing you so upset by all of this."

"I'll be fine. Maybe we should even travel to Temesvar to take things into our hands?"

Q hugged her tight. "That's my girl. And if Gunther's last letter to the former priest in Temesvar doesn't produce anything, we'll do just that."

A knock on the door startled them, and Hilde wondered who it could be. An unexpected knock on the door was almost never a good thing. Q opened the door and Hilde saw his curious neighbor peering into the flat.

"Doctor Quedlin, the postman left this registered letter earlier in the afternoon."

Q took the letter from her hand, and when he didn't offer an explanation, the neighbor added, "It's from Hungary. Does it contain documents pertaining to your marriage?"

Hilde saw the amused smile on Q's face as he answered the woman, "Thank you very much for accepting the letter and taking the trouble to bring it over."

The eyes of the neighbor were glued to the letter. "Don't you want to open it?"

"I certainly do. I'll need to go to my office for the letter opener. Thank you so much again." With these words, he closed the door and Hilde grinned from ear to ear.

"That woman certainly is nosy. Now let's see what it says."

"Hm. I believe someone else is nosy too," he teased.

"Come on, we've been waiting such a long time. Open it before I tear it apart."

"But only because it's you asking." Q fetched the letter opener and Hilde's heart stood still while he fingered a document from the envelope.

"A baptism certificate from the Catholic Church in Temesvar." He dropped the document onto the table and spun Hilde around. "We can get married now."

"Finally," she cried, holding onto him with all her strength. "I almost stopped believing it would ever happen."

He kissed her hard. "I'll apply for the Aryan certificate first thing tomorrow morning."

The next day, when Q picked her up at work, he had to report yet another obstacle. "I'm sorry, sweetheart, but the official at the wedding bureau informed me that in addition to the Aryan certificate, we now need a health certificate as well."

"A health certificate? Why that?" Hilde frowned.

"Apparently, another law was passed a while ago, the Marital Health Law. It requires all engaged couples to present a recent medical document proving they are free of a long list of hereditary diseases. This is supposed to keep the German race 'clean and healthy.'"

Hilde stomped her foot. "All of these stupid laws! When will they end?"

"I don't know. I agree they're ridiculous, but there's nothing we can do. Except maybe run away and get married in some other country."

She cocked her head. "That sounds like a good idea, and if there's anything else they require us to do, we should contemplate that option."

Q took his hand in hers. "But then you can't have the reception we've planned with all our friends and family celebrating with us."

She pouted. "All right, we'll go to the doctor and get that damned certificate. Compared to compiling the paperwork, it sounds easy."

While they waited for the blood samples to be analyzed and the certificate mailed to them, life continued as usual.

Q worked on new inventions in his free time, always with the goal of protecting lives in an upcoming war. One of his best ideas was the improvement on the existing echo-sound system that would work for both ships and airplanes. He even offered the commercial rights to the United Kingdom Admiralty, but they were satisfied with their current systems.

The Royal Air Force, though, was very interested in a workable echo-sounder for their airplanes and asked him to deliver a working prototype, not just theories on paper. This unfortunately proved to be impossible because Q didn't have the means to produce a prototype on his own. Plus, if the German authorities ever found out, they'd confiscate his work and declare them "important war property of the Reich."

He continued to meet with the Russian agent and gave all of his knowledge away for free to Russia. It humored him that he could sell one and the same thing to the rich and give it for free to the poor. One day, an intermediary even connected him with the United States War Department, who were very interested in some of Q's inventions. Apart from an extensive questionnaire, nothing ever came out of it.

Exactly one year after the day Q proposed to Hilde, both of them received their health certificates in the mail. But when they finally held their marriage license in hand, it was late July 1936 and all of Berlin was in a flurry of activities to host the Summer Olympic Games. There was no way they could get married and have a reception until after the games.

Everything in the capital revolved around the upcoming Olympics. Last-minute work was done on the new track and field stadium, the gymnasiums, and other arenas. To help assuage the IOC's concerns over the anti-Semitism prevalent in Nazi Germany, Hitler added a token participant with a Jewish father to the German team. The Nazis even "cleaned up" the entire city of Berlin in preparation for the arrival of the world.

Q watched with wonder as the city of Berlin changed before his eyes. The party removed signs stating "Jews not wanted" from the city and the main tourist attractions. All beggars, invalids, street urchins and Romany – gypsies – were removed from the city and contained in a special camp during the Olympic Games.

But what struck Q most were the non-obvious changes. People

148

seemed friendlier and all of a sudden the oppressive, bleak atmosphere gave way to a tolerant, friendly, and cosmopolitan one, the way Berlin had been a decade ago. Everyone smiled and people went out of their way to help the arriving foreign tourists and athletes.

The Nazi propaganda newspaper *Der Stürmer* was ordered to be sold below the counter. The visitors shouldn't witness any visible evidence of the everyday cruelties.

When walking around the center, Q got the impression things in Berlin weren't all that bad. Was Hitler changing for the better? Would things finally return to normal? Q was willing to give the government the benefit of the doubt.

When the big day of the opening ceremony came, Q surprised Hilde with tickets to witness the spectacular event. Apart from the thousands of people filling the stadium, the eyes of the entire world lay on Berlin because the games were broadcast on television for the first time.

For weeks, everyone had been talking about the historic Olympic Torch Relay and how everyone would always remember the games held in Berlin because it was the first time the torch was relayed all the way from Olympia in Greece to the Olympic Village in Berlin.

"Here he comes," Q said to Hilde over the roar of the crowd when the last torchbearer ran out of the tunnel and into the stadium. Hitler himself was seated in his special box that overshadowed everyone else's, gracefully accepting the cheers and screams of the crowd begging him to step out and show himself to the masses.

But the moment Fritz Schilgen entered the stadium and carried the torch up the stairs to the cauldron, all eyes followed the torch in his hand until he lit the eternal Olympic Flame.

The organizing committee around *Reichssportführer* Hans von Tschammer had pulled out all the stops to choreograph a glorious ceremony and had arranged for twenty-five thousand pigeons to be released just after the cauldron was lit. Like everyone else, Q felt the enchantment of the white pigeons flying high in the sky and put his arm around Hilde's shoulders.

*Peace doves. Maybe that's a sign to the rest of Europe that Hitler is willing to negotiate in peace.*

But the beautiful spectacle ended the moment the cannon was shot off. The sound literally scared the poop out of the pigeons, and Q could hear the pitter patter of pigeon poop landing on the spectators all around him. He turned to look at Hilde, whose straw hat was specked with rather unpleasant droppings.

She grinned at him from beneath the brim of her hat, her nose wrinkled up as she helped wipe the pigeon poop from his hair.

"Thank you," he said after the nasty business was complete.

"No problem. I wonder who came up with the idea of the pigeons?"

"I wonder if they're still walking around freely?" Q added.

"Let's hope they are. I'm looking forward to watching the competitions. The entire city feels different."

Q agreed. "Let's hope it continues."

But their hopes became thinner as the games wore on. The black US American athlete, Jesse Owens, soon became the darling of the public and the crowd never missed an opportunity to cheer him on. Owens could have been the perfect hero of the games, winning four gold medals, if it wasn't for Hitler's refusal to congratulate him at each medal ceremony.

Hilde and Q witnessed more than one otherwise true-to-party-lines Nazi criticizing the *Führer* for his refusal to acknowledge Owens' outstanding achievement. After Owens won the one-hundred-meter race, Hitler stood up, tossed his chair back, and rushed from the stadium in a fit of fury.

Q almost couldn't believe his eyes. Not only were one hundred thousand visitors in the stadium privy to a glimpse of the real Hitler, but the whole world on television were witnesses as well. "This is the end of Berlin's Midsummer Night's Dream."

And the following weeks proved him correct. After the tourists left and the television cameras were turned off, terror and despotism took over. Nazi Germany was back in full force, even worse than before the games. And the German people had nowhere to go for help. The world had been at their door, but the image they had taken away was only a mirage, hiding true evil inside.

# CHAPTER 30

Once the dust had settled, Q and Hilde made quick plans to get married. They were both fed up with making wedding preparations only to have to cancel them, and decided on a clandestine wedding.

"I don't want to jinx it by making a lot of plans again," Hilde said.

"Then we won't."

"I'm afraid if we wait too long, someone will pass another stupid law or somehow sabotage our wedding another way. I just want to be your wife."

Q grinned. He'd never been the advocate for a big wedding, but he'd agreed because Hilde wanted it. "Your wish is my command. We'll take the earliest date available at the registry office and won't tell anyone about it. Just you and me."

But the closer the date came, the more he grew quiet and withdrawn. Hilde had asked him several times if he was nervous, and each time, he nodded and changed the topic. Because the truth was, he felt guilty. He was torn...between his love for her and his need to protect her.

In the two years they'd been together, Q had never once mentioned his "other" activities, because he thought the less she knew, the better it was for her. He had become overly careful in his intelligence work, but if he were found out, he'd be hauled away without a trace. And Hilde would have no idea what had happened. She might even believe he'd abandoned her.

The thought tore him apart. His deception was tearing him apart. The lying had to stop. He couldn't base his marriage on a lie.

Two days before the settled date, he decided to come clean with her and said, "Hilde, let's go for a walk."

She nodded and he took her hand, walking with her until they reached the park. "Q, what's wrong?" she said, her face a mask of fear and uncertainty.

*God help me. I hope I'm doing the right thing.*

"I need to tell you something. Please, listen to all of it, and then, if you don't want to marry me, I'll understand. But I love you so much, I cannot base our marriage on a lie."

The panic on her face sent shock waves of pain through his body and he hurried to explain himself.

"I've been secretly working with the Russians by giving them technical knowledge and gathering intelligence for the last several years."

~

"What did you just say?" Hilde's veins filled with ice. As he repeated the statement, she studied his handsome face, and suddenly, his behavior over the last weeks made sense. She'd suspected there was more to his unusual withdrawal than nerves, but never in her wildest imagination had she imagined he was actively working against the Hitler regime.

"Q...I...what?"

"Hilde, I didn't want to tell you. I thought I was protecting you, but then I realized I had to trust you enough to tell you my biggest secret."

Hilde looked at him, but instead of the tall, thin man she'd fallen in love with, she now saw him being hauled off by the Gestapo. Tortured. Humiliated. Locked away in one of the camps for political prisoners. A place from which no one returned.

Her eyes filled with tears. "Why?"

"I had to do something. This was my way of fighting back. At first, I thought I could help prevent war, but now I just hope to make it as short as possible."

"You know what will happen…"

Q squeezed her hands. "I do know. It's a risk I'm willing to take, but not one I expect you to shoulder without having time to consider it." He released her hands and stepped back. "I understand if you want to break our engagement. It would break my heart, but I love you so much, I don't want to put you in danger."

"Q…"

He looked deeply into her eyes and she could see all his love for her, and deep down, she saw the unrelenting spirit, the drive to do the right thing. That was why she'd fallen in love with him, but would she be able to withstand the constant threat? Could she be as unrelenting as he was?

Q watched her closely. "Hildelein, if you want me to, I could stop my scouting work. For you."

A million thoughts and feelings attacked her mind and body. The minutes passed and she still wasn't able to form a coherent thought. "My love, I need to sleep on this. It's too much to take in right now."

He nodded. "I understand. Let me take you home."

Hilde stopped him. "Q, I love you, I really do, but I need to be alone right now." She kissed him goodbye and walked away without looking back.

Hilde tossed and turned most of the night, knowing he'd expect an answer the next day. Her love for this man was overwhelming, more than she'd thought she was capable of. But what he was doing was dangerous. And not just to him. If she married him, the Gestapo would never believe she wasn't at least passively involved in his illegal activities.

Should she still marry him or not? Was he worth risking her life for? As she headed to work the next morning, she still didn't know the answer.

# CHAPTER 31

After Hilde left, Q wandered aimlessly through the park. The leaves on the trees had turned into the most beautiful shades of yellow, orange, and red. The last rays of sunshine bathed the landscape in a golden glow, but he couldn't enjoy this beautiful October day.

He'd dropped a bombshell on his beloved Hilde by telling her his secret, and now all he could do was wait for her to make the most difficult decision in her life. *Alea iacta est.* The die is cast. Now it was her turn and there was nothing he could do about it. Her decision might break his heart or change the course of his life.

A few hours later, his mind was still in turmoil. On the one hand, he felt relieved that she knew the truth and he didn't have to lie anymore, but on the other hand, his words had caused Hilde so much pain. Even though the image of the agony in her eyes when he'd come clean about his subversive activities haunted his mind, he would do it all again.

He loved Hilde so much, and if she decided she couldn't go through with their wedding now that she knew, he would understand. It would break his heart, but he would understand. The image of a future without Hilde in his life made him groan, but that wasn't his choice to make.

With nothing else to do than wait, he returned home, but didn't manage to stay there for long before he walked out again into the clear and cold October night. A perfect half-moon rode the sky and dampened the shine of the stars. The golden moonlight shone bright and clear onto the quiet capital while he wandered around most of the night, thinking about what was important in his life.

The answer to that question had changed over the last few years. Before meeting Hilde, it was his personal mission to try and prevent the war from occurring. But Hilde had taken up so much space in his heart and his life that his priorities had changed. He had to keep the love of his life safe. Even if that meant protecting her from himself.

As he passed an immense chestnut tree – the chestnuts already fallen to the ground and the leaves about to follow them soon – his mind recognized the inevitable end to all life. *Why am I living in this place and at this time? Why not thirty years ago? Or thirty years in the future? What is the reason of my being? What will be my legacy?*

Questions only time could answer. Time that was moving all too slowly today.

When the sun rose over the morning mist, he finally went home and climbed into his bed. In the afternoon, he headed to the insurance office, anxious to see Hilde and find out her decision.

When she came out and walked toward him, his heart jumped with joy only to miss a beat the next moment when he noticed a furrow between her brows. Hilde greeted him with the same full-blown smile and passionate kiss as always, which he took as a good sign.

"Feel like taking a walk?" he asked.

"Yes. Let's go to the Zoo," Hilde suggested and he grinned. The immense Berlin Zoo park had become one of their favorite places in the city to take it easy and relax.

Q clasped her hand in his own. The park was only a few blocks away and soon they were strolling under chestnut and linden trees. She eventually pulled him to a stop, glancing around to make sure they didn't have unwelcome listeners.

"Hilde…"

"Q…"

They both chuckled at having spoken at the same time. She bit her lip and tried again, and it took all of his self-control to stay quiet and listen.

"Yesterday, what you told me was shocking. Not because I don't approve of your doing those things but because I could only see the potential threat." She raised a hand and cupped his cheek. "It was a difficult decision and I'm well aware of the implications, even for my own life. But try as I might, I cannot get around the fact that I love you and don't want to live one minute of my life without you."

Q waited, holding his breath as she tried to finish. "And I do want you to continue fighting the Hitler regime, because it's the right thing to do and I'm actually proud of you."

She smiled at him and relief flooded his system.

"We will marry tomorrow," she continued," and stay together until death do us part. Come hell or high water. The rest we'll figure out. Together."

Q was so relieved, deliriously happy and stunned into a momentary silence. When that moment passed, he swept her up into his arms and kissed her passionately. He swirled her around, lifting her up, and making her giggle in response.

"You've just made me the happiest man in the world," he said, setting her back onto her feet and kissing her once more.

Hilde looked at him with love shining in her eyes, "I love you, Wilhelm Quedlin."

"And I love you, Hilde Dremmer. I promise to always love you, no matter what."

Hilde leaned up on her tiptoes and kissed his lips. "So, are you ready to get married tomorrow?"

Q nodded. By tomorrow at this time, they would be Mr. and Mrs. Wilhelm Quedlin. They were finally getting married and all his dreams would come true.

# PART II: UNYIELDING

# CHAPTER 1

*October 24, 1936*

D o you, Wilhelm Quedlin, want to take the here present Hildegard
Dremmer as your legal wife? Then answer with 'Yes.'"

Hilde looked striking in her knee-length dress, the accentuated waist-
line hugging her figure to perfection. The red fabric with the white polka
dots contrasted nicely with her bright blue eyes, while her light brown
hair gently brushed her shoulders. But Q didn't have much time to
admire the woman he loved.

"Yes, I do," he said, his firm voice underscoring his certainty.

The marriage registrar turned to look at Hilde and asked the same
question, "Do you, Hildegard Dremmer, want to take the here present
Wilhelm Quedlin as your legal husband? Then answer with 'Yes.'"

"Yes, I do," she responded, absolutely glowing as she smiled at the
man she loved. In her smile, he could see the tension of the last year
resolve. Sometimes it had seemed they'd never succeed, but they did it.
They were seconds away from being married.

"Herewith I declare you husband and wife according to German law.
You may exchange the rings now."

Erika stood from her seat and delivered the rings. Q had bought matching wedding bands, but unlike his own, Hilde's ring sported a beautiful princess cut diamond.

After the exchange of the rings, the official congratulated them and smiled. "You may now kiss your bride."

Who could resist such a proposal? Q took Hilde into his arms and kissed her lips until she squirmed in his embrace and the witnesses, Erika and Gertrud, clapped their hands.

Q and Hilde, as well as the two witnesses, signed the marriage register, and less than fifteen minutes after they walked into the sober room, the ceremony was over.

Apart from the two obligatory witnesses, no other guests were present. While Q himself was actually glad that the civil marriage ceremony had taken place without foolish emotionalism and pathos, he knew Hilde had wanted something more personal.

He leaned over to whisper into Hilde's ear. "I'm sorry you didn't get the big wedding you originally planned."

Hilde shook her head, a soft smile appearing on her face. "I don't need a big wedding. I just need to be your wife."

Q laughed. "That has been a problem, hasn't it?"

They'd been trying to make this day happen for more than a year, hunting down the paperwork and wading through a sea of red tape in order to receive a marriage license.

Hilde's friends congratulated them, and Q nodded in their direction. "Shall we, ladies?"

He helped all of them into their coats, and once more, his eyes rested on Hilde, who looked absolutely stunning in her pale green woolen coat with three huge wooden buttons.

Hilde and her two friends had chosen everyday clothing. Once they'd decided on a clandestine wedding, they wanted to make it as low-key as possible. Part of the plan was to evade the bevy of photographers waiting outside the registry office to take – and sell – pictures of the bridal couples and the wedding parties.

"Ready?" Q asked, and when they all nodded, he held the door open for the three women, following them outside. It was a nice day with blue skies and just a bite of impending winter in the air.

The photographers immediately gathered around them, raising their cameras, but looked confused when they couldn't make out which woman was the bride. Q reached out and slipped his arms through both Erika's and Gertrud's, and the three of them made silly faces. Moments later, Hilde took Erika's place.

They continued to work their way past the photographers asking them to stop and pose. Q couldn't resist taunting them and asked, "No pictures, boys?"

"Who's the bride?" one of them shot back.

"Wouldn't you like to know?" Q answered with a chuckle. He knew the photographers were there to earn money, but too often, their pictures appeared in the gossip column of the local newspaper. Q shuddered at the thought of being so blatantly displayed. Long ago, he and Hilde decided to keep a low profile, and that included not showing up in the papers.

The photographers finally gave up, moving out of their way and continuing to the next, more willing, bridal party.

Hilde and Q waved goodbye to Erika and Gertrud, who needed to get back to work.

"We'll see you tonight at the restaurant," Hilde added before slipping her arm around Q.

"Mrs. Quedlin," he said, giving her a little wink. "I need a coffee and a pastry to recover from the stress of getting married. What about you?"

She giggled in response and let him lead her the fifteen-minute walk to a pastry shop near their new apartment.

They ordered freshly brewed coffee and two sinfully sweet cream cakes: Hilde's with egg liqueur, Q's with chocolate.

"Aren't you sad that your mother and your friends couldn't attend the ceremony?" Hilde asked him.

Q frowned for a moment before answering, "Certainly. I wish Mother could have been present, but she's so fragile lately, I didn't want to make her travel across Berlin for such a short ceremony. We'll visit her next week and take some nice pastry to celebrate." He squeezed Hilde's hand. "For me, the ceremony in itself wasn't important. It was an administrative deed – nothing more. I'm just glad it's over, and you're mine now."

He grinned at her and lifted her hand to his lips, kissing his way up to her elbow. Hilde's cheeks took on a rosy hue, and she quickly removed her hand from his grasp. "Yes, the preparations were tedious, and more than once I thought we'd never be allowed to get married."

"I'm still at a loss at how Gunther managed to finally receive our grandmother's baptism certificate from the priest in Hungary," Q said, smiling at the memory of how hard his brother worked to get that precious slip of paper.

"He really went above and beyond the call of duty to help us, " she agreed.

"I have a surprise for you," Q said as they finished their coffee and pastry.

"What is it?" Hilde's eyes glowed as she asked, glancing once more at the precious ring on her right hand.

"Jakob asked one of his friends, who is an interior decorator, to open up his warehouse for us this afternoon. He has a new shipment of furniture that we can look at."

Hilde pouted, but there was amusement in the gesture. "I still have to get used to your idea of being romantic, but it's a great idea. A comfortable couch would be rather nice."

While Q had moved into their new apartment in the district of Charlottenburg a while ago, Hilde had done so only this morning before going to the registry office.

"Let's go then," he said, once again surprised at her different way of thinking. Hadn't she always complained that the apartment wasn't properly furnished, and the front room contained nothing more than two wooden chairs, borrowed from the kitchen table? So what could be more appropriate than buying furniture on their wedding day?

They had a lot of fun looking at and testing the feel of the selection and after an hour, they purchased two couches and arranged to have them delivered the next day. Jakob's friend congratulated them on their choice of the studio couches. "Well done, my friends. Those are the last high-quality cover fabrics our Fatherland used to make."

Q raised an eyebrow. "How so?"

"Nowadays, all we get are second-grade quality fabrics. The good ones are reserved for military purposes."

Hilde wrinkled her nose. Nobody wanted to believe in the imminence of another war, but the signs became more prominent with every passing day.

Q thanked Jakob's friend once again for the generous offer to buy the couches at a nice discount, and then he and Hilde walked back to their apartment.

Hilde had visited the market first thing that morning. Now she removed plates containing cold meats and cheese from the icebox. She retrieved the rolls she had purchased as well as some mustard and a small plate of sliced vegetables, while Q set the table for two.

It was a sight to behold, his beautiful *wife* in the kitchen of the apartment that was now their common home.

"I still can't believe we're finally married, Mrs. Quedlin," he said and kissed her lips. They sat at the kitchen table and ate a cold lunch, feeding one another small bites from time to time. They'd meet a few of their best friends later for a celebratory dinner, but that wasn't for hours yet.

And Q already had plans on how to spend those hours. Once it looked like Hilde had eaten her fill, he scooted his chair back and swept her up into his arms.

"Q! What are you doing?" she asked with a laughing shriek.

He paused for a moment and looked down into her blue eyes. "Are we, or are we not, now legally married?"

She looped her arms around his neck. "We are."

Q nodded and carried her towards the bedroom, pushing the door shut behind them with his foot. "Good. Let's act like it then."

Several hours later and long into the afternoon, Q blinked his eyes open, stretching his arms above his head. Then he turned his head, kissing the tousled hair of a soundly sleeping Hilde. *I'm a married man.* The mere thought constricted his heart, and he wondered if any man on earth could be happier than he was. He'd known he loved her since the first moment he met her two years ago, but actually being married felt different.

She smiled in her sleep, and he couldn't resist stroking her light brown hair and her bare white shoulders, and then he trailed a finger down her back. Hilde stirred, but wouldn't wake. When he kissed her on the lips, she murmured something, but still wouldn't open her eyes. A warm feeling took possession of him. *She's mine. And she's the best life's companion I could have wished for.*

"Time to wake up, love."

Hilde's eyes fluttered open, a cute blush covering her cheeks as reality settled in. "Hmm, this is how married couples spend their days?" she asked, returning his kiss.

Q grinned. "Since this is the first time I've been married, I tend to believe it is."

"Isn't it wonderful?" She asked and snuggled up closer.

"You are wonderful, my love. I have loved you before, but now it feels like you took total possession of my life, body, and soul."

Hilde giggled. "My, that's an unusual statement for a scientist."

Q shifted slightly, furrowing his brows. "I can't explain it. The mere act of signing a paper shouldn't have made any difference to my emotional state, but it did. For some odd reason, I love you even more now, Mrs. Quedlin."

"And I like the sound of Mrs. Quedlin," she said and turned in his arms. Through the window, they saw the sun standing low behind a tree, painting like an artist highlights in the most spectacular forms and colors on the white wall opposite the window. Circles in yellow hues alternated with oval-shaped grey shadows and bright orange patterns that resembled an abstract painting.

"What time is it?" Hilde asked after watching the spectacle for a few minutes.

Q took a look at his watch on the nightstand. "Five-thirty. We probably should hurry up, or we'll miss our own wedding celebration."

Hilde sat up, the sheet slipping down her body. "Five-thirty! We slept all afternoon?"

"Hmm, I remember we did more than just sleep." The fine blonde hairs on her arms stood on end, and he almost regretted that they needed to attend their own wedding celebration. He kissed her bare back. "Go get dressed. I'll use the bathroom after you."

Forty-five minutes later, she stepped into the front room, wearing the same figure-hugging red dress with white polka dots she'd donned earlier that morning, but with matching red five-inch heels, the uppers seemingly nothing but straps, instead of the flat ballerinas. Her tousled hair was carefully combed back into a banana updo, and her face was primped with matching red lipstick while blue eye shadow lit up her bright blue eyes. Q whistled low. "My love, you look absolutely stunning."

Hilde ran her eyes up and down his body and returned the compliment. "You look rather handsome today as well. And happy."

"That's because I am," he said and placed a careful kiss on her painted lips.

# CHAPTER 2

$A$s they arrived at the Chinese restaurant near the famous department store *Kaufhaus des Westens*, Hilde asked, "Do you think your friends suspect something?"

Q shrugged. "Let's go in and find out."

Erika and Gertrud were already waiting for them, together with Q's best friends, Jakob, Otto, and Leopold with his wife, Dörthe. They exchanged hugs with everyone, making the introductions, and went to sit at the reserved table when Leopold eyed Hilde suspiciously. "So, what's the occasion for this get-together?"

Gertrud and Erika started giggling, and Hilde shot them an evil look. "Occasion?" She drawled out the word, squeezing Q's hand under the table.

Leopold cocked his head, looking from Hilde to Q and back. "You two are up to something. You look different."

Another fit of giggles came from the girls, and Jakob busied himself with the menu. All three of them had been sworn to secrecy.

"Different?" Hilde parroted his words and clasped her hand over her mouth to retain the violent giggle forming inside.

Dörthe's eyes went wide, and she shouted, "Look at the ring. She's wearing a ring!"

Q whispered into Hilde's ear, "Next time use the other hand," before he announced in a loud voice, "Hilde and I got married this morning."

Hilde managed to whisper back, "There won't be a next clandestine wedding for me," before everyone got up to congratulate them.

The waiter appeared as soon as everyone had settled down again and suggested they order the special five-course house menu for the eight of them. Everyone agreed, and he soon returned with a plum brandy on the house for the newlyweds and their guests.

The first course was egg drop soup, and the chatter at the table slowed down while eight hungry mouths dug into the delicious soup. Next, the waiter brought out a platter containing small egg rolls, lobster spring rolls, and pot stickers.

Hilde laughed out loud at the faces of her girlfriends searching for cutlery and pointed at the wooden chopsticks lying beside each plate. Erika gave her a startled glance. "You expect me to use…that?"

Q nodded and showed both Erika and Gertrud, who'd never eaten Chinese food before, how to use the chopsticks. The rest of the group merrily laughed at their clumsy efforts, and Hilde was glad she'd secretly perfected her mastery of those treacherous sticks during the last week.

While Gertrud mastered the technique rather quickly, Erika gave up. The waiter apparently noticed her desperation and silently slid a fork beside her plate.

The dinner continued with lots of chatter and idle gossip by everyone, for once forgetting the difficult times. The main course consisted of sweet and sour chicken, fried rice, and a spicy beef and vegetable dish.

When the waiter finally removed their plates, Hilde leaned against Q. "There's no way I can eat even a single morsel of food more."

Q kissed her temple and smirked. "That's too bad for you. But I'll gladly eat your dessert."

"Eat my dessert? You'd better not! That might be grounds to ask for a divorce," she joked and giggled at his pouty face.

Q narrowed his eyes. "But you said you were full."

The waiter brought out a platter of desserts: fried bananas in honey, dumplings filled with poppy seeds and little pink, green, and white slimy balls Hilde couldn't identify. She licked her lips and armed herself with the chopsticks, saying, "If you didn't know it, I have one stomach for food and an entirely different one for dessert. And that one is still empty."

Everyone around the table laughed and deferred to the bride, letting her take the first serving. Once both stomachs were full, her head whirled with the lively conversation, and she couldn't imagine a better way to end the day.

Jakob and Otto, though, could. They had discovered a new bar just a few short blocks away that served the most delicious Hungarian wines. The walk felt good. Hilde loved the way Q tenderly and possessively wrapped his arm around her shoulders. But even more, she loved the knowledge that from now on, they'd be going home together at the end of the night.

After more than one round of sweet Hungarian wine, Q leaned over to Leopold and reminded his friend of the first night he'd seen Hilde at the moving-picture theater. "Told you she was going to be my wife."

Leopold sipped his wine. "Yes, you did. And I didn't believe it."

"You did what?" Hilde asked, but before she could say more, Erika produced a small package and gave it to the bridal couple.

Hilde opened the wrapping to reveal a book titled *1000 Spoonerisms and Shuffle Rhymes*.

After thanking Erika for the gift, Q took the book from Hilde's hand and said with a serious voice, "Let's see what we find in here." Then he opened the book to page twenty-four and recited the first verse:

> *Ich hoff', dass diese heile Welt*
> *noch eine ganze Weile hält.*
> *(I hope this perfect world*
> *Will stay perfect for another while)*

Hilde leaned against Q, tears of emotion filling her eyes. The outer world had stopped being perfect a long while ago, but her personal world had fallen into place like a puzzle. Admiring the ring on her finger, she thought, *Yes. It's a perfect world with Q, and I hope it'll last a lifetime.*

Then she opened the booklet to page twenty-seven, his birthday, and recited:

*It is kisstomary to cuss the bride.*

Everyone laughed as Q mockingly cursed her before taking her in his arms and kissing her. Hilde felt slightly tipsy, and she had no idea if it was the slaphappy atmosphere, the wine, or both.

Jakob took the book from her hand, and everyone took turns reciting verses, amidst much laughter and fun.

*Do you see the butterfly, flutter by?*

The Hungarian owners of the bar, as well as some of their countrymen, became curious about those hilarious Germans and joined them with more wine and their own funny rhymes until a dark-haired, bearded fellow with the physique of a bull produced a guitar and started playing energetic melodies with passionate gypsy sounds.

After listening to the first song, Q asked the man if he could play the "Hungarian Dance No. 5" by Johannes Brahms for them. The man nodded. "Certainly I can."

Q looked at Hilde with a mischievous grin.

"What?" she asked.

"I believe this is our traditional bridal waltz."

The man had started to play the captivating yet simple melody, and Q dragged Hilde to the makeshift dance floor beside the bar. "But this is not a waltz..." she protested faintly.

"And this wedding is not traditional," Q answered and captured her in his arms, leaving her no other recourse than to hold on for dear life and follow his steps. Soon everyone joined them, dancing, singing, and having fun.

Shortly before midnight, the group bid their new Hungarian friends goodbye, and the owner of the bar said, "I never thought Germans could be so funny. Keep this joy in your hearts, and your marriage will always prosper."

Back at home – their mutual home – they slipped into bed, tired after a long and exciting day. Q stroked her hair. "Did you have a good day?"

Hilde nodded. "The best. How about you?"

"Spectacular." He grew silent for a moment and then asked, "Are you terribly upset that we cannot embark on our honeymoon right away?"

She thought for a moment and then shook her head. "No. I like the idea of traipsing around Europe in the springtime much better than in the winter."

"Good. Oh, I forgot something." Q slipped from the bed and returned moments later with a leather-clad box in his hands. "This was delivered yesterday. It's from Carl and Emma."

Hilde sat up on the bed and took the box, opening it to reveal an elegant yet simple silver cutlery set. She trailed a finger over the smooth material that quickly warmed under her touch.

"It's not engraved…" he said.

She shook her head. "I wouldn't want it to be. My father would have known that. It's perfect."

"So are you."

Hilde returned the spoon to the leather box. "I love you, Dr. Wilhelm Quedlin. Thank you for this wonderful day."

# CHAPTER 3

Q and Hilde paid a visit to his mother, recounting the happenings of their wedding day.

Ingrid greeted them with hot tea and home-baked gingerbread cookies. Her entire apartment smelled of cinnamon, ginger, and clove. It was early December, but in Q's opinion, it was never too early to eat Christmas cookies. He inhaled deeply, his mouth watering as he sat at the small kitchen table.

"When will you go on your honeymoon?" his mother asked.

Q glanced at Hilde in her simple midnight-blue turtleneck sweater and black pants. It was still a miracle to him that they were finally married. "Not before springtime. We want to travel across Europe for at least three months."

"Three months? That's a rather long time. How did you get that much vacation, Hilde?"

Q was a freelancer at the Biological Reich Institute and had both the possibility and the means to take extended time off, but Hilde was employed at an insurance company, processing claims.

Hilde's face lit up. "I've requested an unpaid leave of absence from my work, and the company agreed."

*Because the Nazi ideology doesn't want married women working, Q* thought bitterly.

For once, the Nazi ideology actually worked in their favor, which might be the part that angered him most. He'd come to hate the Nazis so much, he just couldn't enjoy Hilde's vacation the way she did.

His mother, perceptive as ever, took his hand and searched his eyes. "Darling, you should be thankful for this opportunity. Leaving Berlin for a bit will be a relief for you both, I would imagine."

A shiver ran down his spine, and he wondered how much his mother really knew or suspected of his subversive work.

"Yes, Momma, we're looking forward to it, aren't we?" Q said, reaching over and squeezing Hilde's hand.

She all but hopped up and down on her chair. "I'm so excited. We've planned a Grand Tour starting in Spain and then working our way back through France, Switzerland, and Italy. We'll get to see all those fantastic places like the Alhambra, Madrid, Barcelona, Paris, the Pyrenees, the Alps, and the Mediterranean of course..."

Ingrid smiled at the obvious enthusiasm Hilde showed. "You've had such a hard time getting married. Enjoy yourselves while you still can. Soon enough, you'll have the patter of little feet demanding your attention, which will make trips like this much more difficult."

*Children? Me?* Prior to meeting Hilde, he'd never given it much thought, but now Q imagined a sweet little girl with Hilde's blue eyes and the same enthusiasm. Sounds of laughter. The smell of baby.

Before they left, Ingrid gave each of them a wedding gift.

"Momma, you shouldn't have," Q protested, but his mother would hear nothing of it.

"Open it!"

Hilde unwrapped her small parcel and found a beautiful red jasper pendant with a golden necklace inside. Ingrid helped her to put it on and explained, "This is the lucky stone for your zodiac sign. And God knows we all are in need of some luck during these difficult times."

Then it was Q's turn to open his present. He found a letter opener adorned with a purple amethyst and grinned. He hated the way most people opened their letters. It left rugged edges. "Thank you so much, Momma. It's beautiful. And practical."

∾

For a while, everything returned to normal. But preparing for an extended trip outside the country had proved to be almost as troublesome as obtaining their marriage license.

Once again, they made the trip to various offices and embassies to request passports, visas, and travel permissions. Q's previous trips to other European countries – including the last one four years ago to Paris, helping French warfare chemists – had been a piece of cake in comparison.

All those little obstacles showed Q just how much the Nazis had already tightened their grip around Germany and her citizens, and how much the neighboring countries were in alarm. His mother was right; they should see the world while they still could, but the real threat to their freedom of travel was war, not children.

One day, Q attended one of the conspiratorial meetings with like-minded people who supported the idea of communism. It was disguised as a literature club, and he left the laboratory with *The Robbers* by Friedrich Schiller in his briefcase.

The walk to the Technical University of Berlin was short, and as always, they shut the doors tightly after everyone had arrived. For today, *everyone* meant Q himself, old Reinhard, and Johanna, a blonde of twenty or so years.

Q asked them, "Where's everyone else?"

Reinhard shook his head, but Johanna offered some information. "Kurt and Wilfried were arrested earlier this week."

"Arrested? What for?" Q asked, feeling the shock spread through his body.

Johanna scoffed. "For reading the wrong kind of books."

"You're joking with me," he said, but the sad shake of her head told him otherwise.

"The Gestapo found several books of Erich Maria Remarque and other banned authors in their possession and hauled them away. We haven't heard anything about their fates in three days."

Q swallowed a lump in his throat. Vivid images of bloody flesh and the rancid smell of mortal fear entered his mind. He shivered. "And the rest...?"

Reinhard answered, "It's not safe anymore to come here. We should stop meeting."

Johanna nodded.

"You can't just give up. Not now, when we're needed the most. It's no longer just about helping Russia, it's about tearing Germany from the clutches of evil and destruction." Q ran a hand through his curls, pacing up and down the small study room in the University building.

"It's just the three of us. The others have already decided not to attend anymore." Reinhard's was the knowing voice of someone who'd seen unimaginable terrors in the Great War that made Q realize the extent of the decision being discussed. "I'm nearing eighty," Reinhard continued, "and Johanna is just a young girl. And you – you're recently married. We're not the material heroes are made of."

"You're serious..." Q whispered.

Johanna cast her eyes to the ground, unable to meet Q's. "I'm sorry. It's just...I want to live." Then she picked up her volume of *The Robbers* and left.

Q looked into the knowing eyes of Reinhard, who took his cane and prepared to leave as well. Before he reached the door, he turned once more to stare at Q and said, "I'm not of much use for our cause anymore, but you, my son, you go ahead and do what you must."

When the door closed behind the old man, Q closed his eyes to keep tears from falling. Suddenly, he felt desolate.

The last man standing.

# CHAPTER 4

L ate in April 1937, Hilde and Q finally finished their preparations and were set to travel when another escalation in the Spanish Civil War – the bombing of Guernica – caused them to change their plans at the last minute. Q even asked his Russian contact about the situation. The agent had enough background information to advise strongly against visiting Spain or France at that time.

Hilde looked out the window as the train pulled into the station at Breuil-Cervinia ski resort in northwestern Italy, her eyes going wide at the sight of the majestic mountains rising up from the valley floor. Lush greens at the bottom gave way to rugged grey escarpment topped by white dollops of whipped cream.

During the long hours of their two-day journey, she amused herself by looking out the window and cataloging the things she saw. Breathtaking scenery with rolling hills, dark forests, and small villages. Fields of daffodils and roadside poppies announcing spring. Quaint little lakes and fields that looked so perfect, it was hard to place them as existing only a few hundred miles from Berlin. where dread and terror lurked behind every corner.

Far away from the capital, the only shadows obscuring her lighthearted mind had been the occasional stops along the way where police officers would board the train to ask the passengers for a brief inspection of paperwork.

Each time Q handed over their papers, she involuntarily held her breath, not relaxing until the officer handed them back and left their compartment.

As they crossed the Swiss border, Hilde finally relaxed. But now, after being cooped up inside the train for so many hours, she longed to breathe fresh air once again.

The train stopped.

"We're here!" Hilde exclaimed and grabbed her bag to jump off the train in a hurry.

"I can see that," Q answered with a grin. He slowed her down by placing a hand upon her lower back and together they made their way off the train.

Q collected their suitcases from the luggage wagon and then gestured for her to join him as they went in search of their hotel. The valley floor was showing signs of spring, but despite the blinding sun, the air carried a definite chill.

"Look, the mountains are still covered with snow," she said with a glance at the breathtaking scenery surrounding them. "Doesn't it look exactly like the pictures we've seen?"

"That's good, isn't it?" he asked good-naturedly.

Hilde laughed and skipped ahead a bit. "I want to go skiing."

"Skiing will have to wait until tomorrow. It's way past lunchtime already."

"Oh," she said with a pout, but then brightened, determined to only see the bright side of things. "That's all right, we'll be much more rested tomorrow."

They arrived at the hotel, and while not a grand structure, it impressed with sand-colored stone walls that had weathered over the centuries and flower boxes at the windows filled with blossoming geraniums in orange and red hues.

"Isn't that lovely?" Hilde exclaimed as they entered the cozy building and the receptionist led them upstairs to their room.

"I hope this room will be satisfactory?" the young man inquired as he opened the door to let them inside.

Q nodded. "I'm sure it will be fine." But Hilde rushed inside and plopped onto the queen-sized bed, stretching out her limbs. "I love the place."

Their host nodded and helped Q carry in the rest of their luggage before bowing his head and leaving them to explore the room by themselves. Hilde stood again, wandered over to the closest window and pushed the curtains wide, gasping at the sight before her.

"Q, you have to see this, the Matterhorn is right over there," she said, pointing to the large mountain peak framed by the wooden window. While Breuil-Cervinia lay in Italy, the impressive mountain range in the Northeast belonged to Switzerland.

He joined her at the window to appreciate the panorama, giving her a smile before returning to unpack their belongings.

Hilde let her eyes wander over the small village spread out below her, and a sense of excitement and adventure made her giggle like a schoolgirl.

"What's so funny?" Q asked, setting a pair of shoes just inside the armoire tucked in the corner of the room.

"I can't believe we're finally here," Hilde answered, spreading her arms wide and spinning in a small circle.

Q grinned at her, catching her around the waist and dancing her across the room. "Believe it."

She nodded, dizzy with joy and spinning in circles. This was paradise. Unpacking could wait – she had to explore first, and walked towards the other window of their corner room. The mountain chain that spread out before her now wasn't nearly as magnificent, but Hilde had read in the travel guide that the highest peaks were nearly eleven thousand feet above sea level and were covered with glacier ice year round.

Great fissures and treacherous slopes awaited those foolish enough to climb outside of the groomed areas, but she didn't feel afraid to venture up the mountain. Instead, she felt a sense of freedom she hadn't experienced since learning about Q's subversive intelligence activities.

In Berlin, she lived with a constant fear that he would be found out. Every time she spied an SS or Gestapo officer on the streets, she felt a chill run down her spine, always terrified she'd hear the dreaded words, "Stop. You're traitors working against the Führer and Fatherland."

More than once, she'd stopped breathing until they had walked on by, just to come up breathless with a red face. *What a way to act unsuspicious.* Those moments had become a common occurrence, and it wasn't until now that she realized how tense her life had become.

She hadn't heard Q's steps, and started when he laid a hand on her shoulder. "Love, you can watch that panorama all you want in the next days, but I'm starving. Why don't you unpack, and we'll go in search of dinner? Our host suggested a little Italian place in the village that serves excellent pasta."

*Did he? When?* Hilde turned in Q's arms and kissed him. "Hmm. Pasta sounds perfect. I'm hungry, too." She made short work of emptying her suitcase. She set her shoes alongside Q's, hung up her dresses, skirts, blouses, and slacks, and used the top drawer of the bureau with the large oval mirror attached to stash her unmentionables.

"Ready," she said a few minutes later.

Q nodded approvingly and placed both of their suitcases beneath the bed. "We won't be needing these for a while." He headed for the door, grabbing his coat and hat, suggesting she do the same. "It will be cold once the sun goes down."

Hilde had already grabbed her coat and added a hat and a pair of gloves as well. "I'm already having fun."

Q led her down the staircase, then stopped to speak with their host for a moment to ask for directions to the recommended restaurant. Ten minutes later, they were stepping inside the small establishment, smiles on their faces as they were greeted with enthusiasm.

A well-fed man directed them to a table for two. *"Benvenuti, Signori!"*

Q helped Hilde take off her coat and handed it to the man. The menu, though, was a surprise. As it was written exclusively in Italian, they had difficulties choosing what to eat. Instead of deciphering the meaning of words like *salsiccia, pisello,* or *melanzana*, they decided to put their choice into the hands of the waiter and upon his return, Q asked him to surprise two ravenous travelers with the best food he had.

Hilde laughed as the corpulent man clapped his hands and bustled away. "He seems happy with your decision."

Before Q could reply, the waiter returned with an opened bottle of

178

red wine. He poured them both a glass and said in his broken German, "Wine of the house."

Hilde admired the deep red tone of the liquid and raised the glass to sniff the wine. A rich, flowery yet sweet scent wafted to her nostrils, and she smiled in appreciation. When she took a sip, the rich, tangy flavor burst upon her tongue, leaving a trace of nut as she swallowed.

"Excellent wine," she murmured, taking another sip.

"Definitely," Q responded. "I guess the Italian wine is famous for a reason."

The *primo piatto*, first course, arrived, and Hilde stared at the delicacies brought to them. Noodles covered in a seasoned tomato sauce, meatballs that exploded with flavor, and slices of homemade bread with melted butter dripping from them.

Hilde was almost full when the waiter arrived with their *secondo piatto*, the main dish, with the most tender meat and crisp, steamed vegetables. And just when she thought her belly would burst, the waiter returned with more food: ice cream and then cheese.

As they finished their meal, she slipped onto the bench beside Q and leaned against him, sipping her wine and listening as the locals celebrated…what, she didn't know, but it was obvious there was a celebration of some sort going on. Toasts were made. Songs were sung. Couples laughed together, and as the evening wore on, she felt so very blessed to be sharing this moment with Q.

It was the happiest she'd been since the moment she said, "Yes, I do" in front of the magistrate many months ago. For once, she didn't have to look over her shoulder or be careful what she said. She was blissfully happy in this moment, and as her eyes met Q's and he caressed her arm, his eyes echoed her sentiment. Pure happiness.

# CHAPTER 5

T he next morning, Q awoke with the sun tickling his eyes as it crept
through their window. For a moment, he had no idea where he
was. He'd slept so peacefully and better than he had in a long time. *Italy.*
He blinked against the sunlight and rolled over to kiss Hilde awake. Her
soft shoulders smelled of wine and roses. He inhaled her unique scent,
remembering the evening before. "Good morning, sleeping beauty, ready
to go skiing?"

Her eyes fluttered open, and a bright smile lit her face when she
nodded. "Yes."

"Good. Let's get dressed and have breakfast downstairs before we
embark upon our adventure."

Q kissed her forehead, and they both hurried through their morning
ablutions, dressing warmly for their excursion up the mountain, excited
about the day ahead.

They settled in the hotel's breakfast room, and while eating, Q asked
the receptionist for directions. First, they headed towards a small shop to
rent ski equipment. Despite the language barrier, they got everything
they needed and soon enough took the gondola up to the top of the
mountain, from where they planned to ski back down to the village.

From the valley floor, it seemed like an excellent plan, and neither Q nor Hilde gave a thought to how difficult skiing down from the top might be.

The gondola ride up the mountain was magical, and Q watched in amusement as Hilde tried to see everything at once. Her gaze kept straying to the massive mountains that rose up in the distance.

"It's so beautiful," she repeated over and over. If she'd loved watching nature on their train journey, then she was now utterly enthralled by the majestic mountain panorama. Far away, the Matterhorn rose above the other peaks, but the much lower and closer mountains on the Italian side weren't any less impressive.

Q closed his eyes for a moment and felt the stress they'd been living under slowly fade away. He knew when they returned to Berlin, it would come rushing back quicker than they would have preferred, but for these next weeks and months, he didn't want to think about threats and danger.

Meanwhile, the gondola had reached the top and slowed to a crawl. An attendant, dressed warmly in hat, coat, and mittens, assisted them off the lift car with their skiing equipment. Q shivered as they made their way out to the open slope. It was fairly flat near the gondola station, and he and Hilde took their time putting on their skis, making sure everything was buckled up correctly.

Donning his cap and watching as she did the same, he asked, "Ready?" A sign at the top had indicated several paths to choose from, but not understanding fully what the symbols and colors meant, he elected to ignore it and followed the route most of the other skiers were taking.

Hilde nodded, and he pushed off, gliding along the pleasantly graded slope with a feeling of relief and freedom. But his smile quickly gave way to concern and then a shadow of foreboding as the slope narrowed and steepened drastically. *What did that sign mean? I should have asked someone.*

He managed to keep himself upright, zigzagging back and forth across the steep hill, glancing back every few seconds to make sure Hilde was managing to do the same. He'd not even made it a third of the way down when her anguished cry reached him.

Q dug the side of his skis into the snow and came to a stop, using his poles to keep his balance while he looked up to see Hilde lying in the snow, her legs tangled, one ski lying several feet away from her.

"Darling, are you hurt?" he shouted up to her, swallowing down the rising panic as he released his own skis and made his way up to her.

"I fell," she whimpered.

"I can see that. Are you injured?"

Hilde tried to get up. "My knee…it hurts."

Q squatted down next to her and removed her other ski, helping her sit up. Then he gently probed around her knee, observing how she scrunched her nose with discomfort. He shook his head. "You can't ski down in this condition. We'll walk back up to the lift and ride it down."

"No!" she said, shaking her head vehemently. "I didn't come all this way to ride in the gondola. I want to ski down."

"I don't think it's wise to risk further injury to your knee…" Q sighed. Her face had taken on that mulish look he'd come to know so well. Her mind was made up, and there was nothing in the world that would convince her otherwise.

"I'll take my time and be more cautious. I can do this." She gave him a watery smile, putting on her brave face. In response, all he could do was nod.

"Are you sure? This hill is much steeper than it looked at the beginning. What if it gets harder?"

"I'm going to enjoy myself," she answered, using her poles to push herself to a standing position. "Could you bring me the other ski, please?"

Against his better judgment, Q retrieved her other ski and held her arm for balance as he secured it to her foot. "Are you sure you don't want to walk back to the gondola?" He tried one last time to convince her. The village was a long way down from here.

"I'm sure." She tested her weight on the injured knee, and to her credit, he didn't even see her flinch. "See, I'm fine. Why don't I go first, since I'll probably be slower than you?"

Q nodded and made his way back down to where he'd left his skis. Putting them on, he then followed behind Hilde, his eyes never wavering from her as she attempted to stay upright. They reached the bottom of the first hill, and Q skied up next to her. "How are you doing?"

Hilde tried to smile, but it didn't reach her eyes. "This is much harder than I remembered."

"I could try…"

She pursed her lips. "No, let's keep going."

Q watched her push off again. If he weren't so worried, he'd be proud of her. Hilde fought her way down the slope, unyielding in her determination to master it. But she fell repeatedly, and by the time they reached the next small landing, she was breathing heavily and having trouble regaining her feet again.

The sun had reached its zenith and mercilessly burnt down on them. Q felt the sting of its rays on his pale winter skin. At least it was warm. When he spotted a flat patch, he convinced Hilde to sit down and take a rest. They ate and drank their meager provisions, and while the mountain range lay still and peaceful as before, Q now felt an overwhelming respect for the power it represented.

Coming from the flats of Northern Germany, they'd both severely underestimated the hazards of the mountain area. At the moment, he worried about the unforgiving rays of the sun, but that would soon change.

"Hilde, darling…"

"Q, don't look so worried," she said, looking refreshed after their break. He traced his fingers down her red cheeks, and she winced at the touch.

"You're getting burned."

Hilde gave a rueful laugh. "That's amazing, since I'm freezing. My feet are so cold, I can barely feel my toes."

"We need to keep moving, Hilde. Can you make it?"

Yes, she could. She had to – it was the only way out. Hilde cursed her own stupidity and murmured under her breath, "I should have listened to you. This is much too difficult for a beginner like me."

She fell again into the harsh white snow. Getting up proved more difficult each time, and by now, not only was her knee screaming with pain, but her entire body wanted her to stop moving.

Earlier, the sun had burnt her tender face, but now as they skied into the shadow of the peaks towering over them, and the cold breeze kicked up, her teeth were chattering and her fingers barely able to clutch her poles.

The biting cold wind whipped right through her woolen sweater and the layers beneath. With the number of times Hilde had fallen, her clothing had become encrusted with snow and was now soaking. The icy moisture seeped through her other layers, and with every move, the wet cotton disgustingly clung to her body, intensifying the bone chills.

*I'm a fool. I wanted to prove I could do this, but why?*

Q cheered her on and encouraged her to get up after each fall, but he couldn't fool her. His eyes indicated he was worried beyond measure.

"I'm sorry, I should have listened to you," she said the next time he helped her up.

"Don't worry, my love, we'll make it," Q said as they rounded the top of the next hill and gestured at the village lying directly ahead of them, separated only by a broad and flat hill. From there it was only a few minutes' walk to their hotel, but Hilde was so exhausted, she could barely remain upright, let alone carry her own skis.

He noticed before she could say a word and carried both sets of skis, using his free arm to steady her as she limped along beside him. Q left the skis outside the front lobby and then Hilde closed her eyes as he scooped her up in his arms and carried her up the stairs to their room.

What had started out as a wonderfully exciting day had turned into a skiing nightmare. She collapsed onto the bed, sinking onto the edge of the mattress, near to tears with relief. Her body demanded sleep.

"Hilde! Wake up!"

Why didn't he let her sleep? "I'm so tired."

Q's voice reached her through the fog of exhaustion, but she couldn't make much sense of it. "You need to get out of your wet clothing and then I'll have a look at your knee."

Whatever it was he wanted to do to her, she didn't care. Like a puppet on a string, she rolled from side to side, lifted her legs and arms whenever he requested it, all with the intention of making him go away and let her sleep.

"Hildelein, darling, you're shivering."

Strange. She wasn't cold. In fact, she didn't *feel* anything. Not even the sheets beneath her or his hands on her body as he pushed the flannel nightgown down her torso.

"Into bed with you now," Q urged her, plumping up the pillows behind her back and tucking the quilt around her shoulders. "I'll see if I can round up some hot tea for you. Stay in bed and get warm."

"Q?" she called after him when he started to leave the room.

"Yes?" he turned, giving her a quizzical look.

"I'm tired."

"I know, darling. Sleep, I'll be right back." As she gave in to her exhaustion, her eyes must have fluttered shut, because she didn't see him leave the room, nor did she notice his return bearing a tray with hot water, cups, sugar, cream, and tea. He woke her, holding a cup of steaming tea to her lips, forcing her to take careful sips.

The hot liquid ran down her throat, and for a short moment, everything got worse. She became painfully aware of the congealment in her limbs, and as her feet and hands thawed, pins and needles tortured her. Her hands shivered so badly, Q took the cup from her and held it himself, feeding her more tiny sips of heat.

Delicious heat.

With the warmth, life returned to her limbs and her brain. "I'm sorry for ruining our first honeymoon day."

"Don't be sorry, my love. I'm just glad we made it back to the hotel. I called a doctor for you."

"I don't need a doctor. I just need to rest…" But the distressed look in his bright blue eyes made her stop midsentence. If Q needed her to be seen by a doctor to stop worrying, so be it.

"I want a doctor to look at your knee and your sunburn, just to make sure," he said, stroking her hair. "You're still shivering."

"I don't know if I'll ever feel warm again," she murmured and slumped back into the pillows.

"Drink some more tea, then I'll see about finding you another blanket."

Hilde dutifully drank the hot liquid he held to her lips, each sip bringing back sensation to her body. When he prepared to leave to fetch another blanket, she found the strength to reach for his arm. "Don't leave again."

"You're still cold."

"Snuggle with me. That would warm me up." Hilde tried a small smile, and he gave in to her request, slipped off his shoes, and climbed onto the other side of the bed to gather her in his arms, tucking the quilt around her body like a cocoon.

Hilde dozed off in the security of the thought that the man she loved watched over her, until a brisk knocking on the door announced the arrival of the doctor. Q invited him in and then paced at the end of the bed while the doctor examined her injured knee.

"Signora Quedlin, it appears you've pulled a tendon and strained the muscles from your knee down your calf and across the top of your foot. How did you say this injury occurred?"

"Well, I fell when we attempted to ski down from the top of the mountain…"

"What? Are you experienced skiers?" the doctor inquired, looking between Q and Hilde.

She shook her head. "I've been once before…"

The doctor muttered something in Italian that sounded like a curse word and looked angry. "You tourists are so irresponsible at times. These mountains are not for beginners. Did you not see the warning sign at the top?"

Q nodded. "I did, but I have to confess the colors and symbols didn't mean anything to me."

"You're lucky one of you wasn't seriously injured. Next time, stay on the blue slopes close to the village."

"We will," Q answered, feeling the sting of the chastisement.

"Good," the doctor replied, seeming somewhat mollified by Q's response. "Your wife will need to rest her knee for several days before she can try skiing again." He packed up his supplies and Q escorted him to the door.

Hilde's eyelids closed and she was already half asleep when she heard Q's voice, "Are you hungry?"

"No. Just tired."

"Then sleep." A kiss on her nose was the last thing she felt before the land of dreams claimed her.

∾

She woke the next morning and attempted to roll over in the bed, only to gasp as a sharp pain rushed from her ankle to her knee. "Ouch!"

"Hilde?" Q's voice came from the other side of the room. He was already up and fully dressed.

"My knee hurts." She carefully sat up and stared at the swollen joint. It was easily double the size of the other knee, and the skin featured all colors of the rainbow, from a light yellow, to greens and blues, to dark black bruises on the bones.

"You're a piece of art," Q said, following her gaze and obviously thinking the same. "And the red colors are up here." He gestured at her sunburnt face. "Let me get some lotion."

The cool liquid he rubbed into her face soothed the tight stinging sensation on her cheekbones, and she sighed. "Much better."

"Yes, we both got a little too much sun yesterday. I already bought sunscreen."

Hilde looked at Q's bright red face and reached for the lotion to rub the cool liquid on his stubbly face.

A loud growl came from her stomach, and she pushed herself to a sitting position before asking, "Could you help me get dressed?"

"Why?"

She pressed her hand to her rumbling belly. "I'm hungry. We should go to breakfast."

Q grinned. "Well, breakfast sounds like a wonderful idea. Can you manage the stairs, or should I throw you over my shoulder like a flour sack?"

Hilde slapped his shoulder. "Don't you dare!"

He grinned some more, assisted her in getting dressed, then helped her downstairs to the breakfast room.

They spent several lazy days talking with other travelers and getting a feel for the small village's amenities, soaking in the wild and rugged yet peaceful atmosphere of the Alps. Nothing here resembled the

187

frightful life in Berlin, and Hilde couldn't remember a time in her life she'd enjoyed more, even hampered as she was by her injury.

The threats in Breuil-Cervinia didn't come from humans, but from nature, like the frequent snow slides crashing down the scarps on the other side of the valley; their thunderous noise often tore up the silence in the village, echoing manifold back and forth between the mountain walls.

But in contrast to the hidden yet omnipresent danger in their hometown, it was much easier to avoid the threats of nature.

A week later, they attempted to ski again, with much more success this time. They stuck to the blue beginners' slopes, and after a day or two, neither of them were even falling all that much.

Their honeymoon in Italy was turning out to be perfect. No problems. No worries. No watching what one said and to whom they were talking. Freedom. Something neither of them – especially Q – had experienced in so many years.

# CHAPTER 6

A s June arrived, so did their time to leave the Alps. They boarded the train, bound for Sicily, and Q was more in love now than ever before.

They finally arrived in Naples just as the sun was rising above the horizon, and even though they'd only gotten a few hours of sleep, they were more than ready to play tourist once again.

Hilde had disappeared behind the retractable changing screen to put on one of the summer dresses she'd bought for the trip. When she didn't come out again, Q asked anxiously, "Are you ready to explore the city?"

"Almost," she answered, and Q continued to gather their things. The train had already slowed to a crawl as it moved through the outskirts of the city, passing historic ruins of times gone by.

But as Hilde stepped out from behind the screen, he all but dropped the things in his hands, whistling low and long as he stared at her. She looked stunning in her lightweight dress in an A-line cut with flared skirts, puffed sleeves, and a gathered bodice that rested just below her bustline. The bright colors flattered her and brought out the glimmer in her blue eyes.

He ran his fingers down the patterned fabric of the dress that was perfect for a warm summer day. "Hilde, you are gorgeous. By far the most beautiful woman in all of Italy. No, in all of Europe."

Hilde blushed and giggled. "Thank you."

"I shall have to beat the men off with a stick," Q murmured as they exited the train. They'd stay in the port city a few days until they'd secured a ferry to Palermo on the island of Sicily.

Naples was a mixture of history, some of it dating back over several thousand years. Castles, churches, and testaments to the great Roman Empire, and in the distance, the imposing silhouette of Mount Vesuvius towered like a silent guardian.

"Can you see it?" Hilde asked him as they explored the center of the city.

"See what?" he asked, letting his gaze wander around.

"What it must have been like to live during the time of the Romans? I can almost hear the chariots coming down the street." She inhaled deeply.

Q grinned and imitated her, smelling the scent of oranges and jasmine strong in the air. "And I can smell rotten fish, human waste, and the remains of victims of the plague."

"You're so...so...unromantic," she sputtered.

"You're right. I'm sorry," he answered and gathered her in his arms.

"Wouldn't it be nice to actually *experience* how life was back then?" Hilde asked.

Q thought for a moment and frowned. "I should invent a time machine so you can go back and become a Roman lady." He laughed at the hopeful gleam in her eyes. Tweaking her nose, he chuckled, "I'm not sure that's even possible, so allow your fertile imagination to run wild."

Hilde giggled. "My imagination will work just fine. Besides, I'm not at all sure you'd look good in a tunic."

He raised a brow at her and then shook his head. "I'm sure I would not enjoy being dressed like that. My knees are knobby."

She giggled some more, happy and carefree. As they wandered farther into the city, Hilde was shocked by the conditions she and Q encountered. The amount of poverty displayed was appalling. Children and adults alike dressed in nothing but tattered and dirty rags. Shanty houses with only one room served as living, cooking, and sleeping quarters for the entire family. Most of the homes had no doors, merely rags or sheets partially covering the doorframes.

"Q, how can these people live like this?" she asked in a whispered voice that no one but he could hear.

He shook his head. "I truly don't know. Things are bad in Germany, but not this bad. I didn't believe I would ever say this, but the living conditions in Germany are much better than here."

And they were, but then he noticed something else. Even though the people of Naples were poverty-stricken, most of them had friendly smiles on their faces. He commented on this to Hilde. "Look at their faces."

Hilde did and scrunched her nose in thought. "They're happy. Much happier than the people in Berlin."

~

A few days later, they took the ferry to Palermo, which was as noisy, dirty, and poor as Naples. They quickly embarked on the next train along the coast until they got off in a lovely seaside village to find a place to stay.

It was already early evening when they found the perfect small hotel with hot spas supplied with boiling water from a nearby inactive volcano. They were both tired and hungry. Q tipped the man at the reception desk to help cart their luggage to their room, then he arranged for a light meal to be brought to them by the host of the small restaurant next to the hotel, who was more than happy to earn a few extra lire for his effort."

Hilde made use of the washroom to rinse the dirt of the trip from her feet, and then she washed her exposed arms, neck, and face. She was just blotting the excess moisture from her skin when Q stepped into the small space, having the same idea.

"I can't believe how crowded and dirty Palermo was," she said.

"Yes, it was even worse than Naples, but this village is cute and clean," he answered as he washed his hands and arms.

Q finished rinsing his face and then the receptionist arrived with the dinner he'd requested. They ate in relative silence, letting the happenings of the past days replay in their minds.

Later Hilde was gazing out the window when he sat down next to her, pulling her into the crook of his arm. "Have I told you today how much I adore you?" He placed a kiss on her hair, just above her ear.

Hilde turned and met his gaze. "No."

"Well, I do. You're the best thing that has ever happened to me in my entire life. If I had to die now, I'd die content and with a smile on my face, because I'd known you and loved you."

She kissed him. "You're not to talk about dying, at least not anytime soon. We don't have to be afraid here. This is our blissful time to just enjoy being together. Without a care in the world."

Q nodded. "That is true. For the first time in years, I'm not constantly looking over my shoulder. I'm so thankful for our time here together."

"I too am thankful. I know Naples wasn't what we expected, but I cannot help contrasting the differences between the citizens of Naples and those of Berlin. These people have so little, and yet they can find a reason to smile and laugh. In Germany, people are afraid to laugh."

"Let's not talk about home. Let's get some sleep," he said and undressed to go to bed.

The tiny village and the hotel turned out to be a small paradise, and they met many foreign tourists from Russia, Sweden, England, France, and several other places. Just the day before, an English couple had joined their table at a small café and upon learning that he and Hilde hailed from Germany, a discussion concerning the Nazis had ensued. Q had been on tenterhooks afraid Hilde might say too much and give away their secret. It was one thing to admit that they weren't very fond of the Nazis, but an entirely different one to be actively involved in the resistance.

They were sitting in the lounge of the hotel drinking an afternoon coffee when Q cautioned Hilde, "Even though most people here are friendly and probably share our opinion, we can't let them know about… you know."

"I would never commit that mistake," Hilde assured him, lowering her voice. "Even though Germany is many miles away from here, the Nazis have eyes and ears all over." And they did. The Nazis had an extensive reach across Europe.

She continued to talk about something, but Q had stopped listening and groaned.

"What's wrong?" she asked, concerned.

He gestured briefly towards the other side of the lobby. "You'll never believe who just arrived here."

# CHAPTER 7

H ilde followed Q's gaze and gasped.

The well-built man with the military-cut grey hair and the piercing green eyes looked a lot younger than his almost sixty years. His impressive presence filled the lobby, and all chatter had died down to a whisper upon his arrival.

He wore the dress uniform of the Deutsche Wehrmacht, the German Army, and though neither Hilde nor Q had met him before, she instantly recognized the handsome man as Generalfeldmarschall Werner von Blomberg, Commander-in-Chief of the Armed Forces and Minister of War.

A chill rushed down her spine. She'd felt so safe in Italy and now this.

"Q?"

Q shook his head, indicating this was not the time for her questions. Despite his nonchalant behavior, she could feel the anxiety radiating off of him, and a dull suspicion crossed her mind. He'd behaved oddly all day, and he'd insisted they take their coffee in the lounge and wait... for...the Minister of War?

Hilde's chest constricted. *No, that's not possible. Or is it?*

"What haven't you told me, Wilhelm Quedlin?" she asked him in a stern whisper.

Q squirmed under her stare. "I thought von Blomberg was a widower. So who's the woman clinging to his arm?"

*Woman?* Glancing back, Hilde noticed the curvaceous brunette standing beside von Blomberg and casting loving glances at him. "That woman can't be older than twenty-five; she must be his daughter."

"Looking at him like a love-sick puppy? Not likely." Q smirked.

"Are you going to answer my question?" Hilde pressed him.

Q sighed. "I'm supposed to be meeting with a Russian agent assigned to Italy."

Hilde's eyes opened wide. "Why didn't you tell me?"

"I just did."

She leaned closer. "That wasn't what I meant."

"I know. I was hoping to avoid this altogether." A flurry of activity was now taking place in the foyer of the hotel as every available employee rushed to make the Generalfeldmarschall and his guest comfortable.

Q was sitting sideways at the table, and Hilde watched him as he continued to drink his coffee, his face shuttered and without expression. That is, until von Blomberg took notice of them and approached their table.

He greeted them with a "Heil Hitler" and Hilde watched the brief moment of disgust flash in Q's eyes. Meeting her gaze briefly, he stood to his feet and returned the greeting, raising his hand and offering a *Hitlergruss* to von Blomberg.

Hilde took her cue from Q and followed suit, not wanting to draw undue attention to them.

"I can recognize a good Aryan when I see him. Where are you from?" von Blomberg explained and waved an employee over to bring two more chairs and coffee. Without asking, he and his companion sat at Q's and Hilde's table.

Hilde's throat was dry as the desert at noon, and for the life of her, she couldn't say a word. With her heart thundering in her throat, she grabbed onto Q's hand like a lifeline.

Thankfully, Q was more composed and dutifully answered von Blomberg's question. "My wife and I are from Berlin. It's an honor to meet you, Herr Generalfeldmarschall."

"None of those formalities. Luise and I are here exclusively on personal business," he said with a doting look at the young woman.

While he and Q exchanged pleasantries, Hilde gave the younger woman a tight smile. "I'm Hilde. Pleased to meet you."

Luise obviously came from a humble background and felt slightly uncomfortable in the limelight. Hilde's heart warmed, and she pitied the girl – almost.

"It's so nice meeting some other people from Germany here. I hope you don't mind our joining you? The travel was tiring."

*Isn't it a bit late to ask? Now that you're already sitting at our table?* But Hilde bit down her remark, and as she couldn't think of a way to politely refuse, she nodded. "Not at all."

Coffee arrived and with each sip of the aromatic liquid, Luise came out of her shell and chatted away. Hilde wanted to jump up and rush from the room. Instead, she patiently conversed about the weather, dresses, and all of the exciting things they'd seen and done while on their travels.

She glanced over to Q for help, but he wasn't in any better situation than she was.

~

Q surreptitiously glanced at the clock hanging on the wall, worried his Russian contact was going to show up at any minute and run straight into the Generalfeldmarschall.

Von Blomberg updated him on the glorious Nazi progress in several areas, and Q did his best to pretend interest and joy. Apparently with success, because von Blomberg leaned back in his chair and pierced Q with his alert green eyes. "You're a man after my liking. What's your contribution to the *Reich*?"

Q swallowed hard. *Do everything in my might to shorten its lifespan.* "I'm a chemical engineer, working for the Biological Reich Institute."

"A scientist." Von Blomberg seemed delighted and asked more questions about the kind of work Q was involved in.

Q put up a brave front and answered all his questions, while anxiety corroded his insides. He turned his head to Hilde, but she was deep in conversation with Luise. From her side, he couldn't hope for a rescue.

"We could use someone with your talents in the Wehrmacht," von Blomberg said, and Q almost doubled over. *He can't be serious, can he?*

"Sir, I'm afraid I'm much too old to be of any worth as a soldier," he protested faintly and then paled. A man who could only be the Russian agent had arrived and was heading straight for him, oblivious to the man sitting at his table.

Q shook his head violently, not so much as an answer to the Generalfeldmarschall, but with the intent to scare the agent away.

Von Blomberg laughed heartily. "Not as a soldier. The Ministry of War has a lot to offer a good scientist. In fact, we are in need of someone with your brilliant mind to head our research department. We're always working to find better and more efficient weapons."

*To kill more people. I would rather kill myself than work for you.*

The Russian approached closer, a searching look in his eyes. *He can't recognize von Blomberg because he sees only his back. If he says one wrong word, we're all in deep trouble.* Q could only hope the agent was experienced enough not to give them away with a silly action.

"...I believe you would do a credible job in that position," Von Blomberg continued, and Q felt as if someone was tightening a rope around his neck. Beads of sweat formed on his forehead and worked their way down his temples. The agent was now mere yards from them.

Q wiped the sweat from his face with a kerchief and said louder than necessary, "I'm sorry. It's hot in here, Herr Generalfeldmarschall von Blomberg."

The man approaching him hesitated almost imperceptibly and made a beeline for the stairs leading to the floors with the guest rooms.

"None of those formalities. Please call me Werner," Von Blomberg said with a jovial grin. "We have a lot to discuss."

"Thank you, Herr…Werner. My name is Wilhelm," Q answered shakily. "That is a very generous offer, and I will certainly take it into consideration."

Out of the corner of his eye, he saw a hotel employee chasing behind the Russian who'd disappeared upstairs. Afraid of the tumult that might ensue and inform von Blomberg who the Russian was and why he was here, Q decided it was best to keep Werner's attention on what was happening at their table.

"Right now, I'm enjoying my honeymoon with my wife." He reached across the table and squeezed Hilde's thigh, causing her to blush prettily.

Werner glanced at her and laughed. "Young love. Isn't it adorable? But I must insist. We need men of your talent. Enjoy your honeymoon, and once you return to Berlin, report to my office."

Q started to respond, but the hotel director who'd been summoned from his office came to his rescue, greeting the Generalfeldmarschall and his companion: "Welcome to our hotel, sir, it's an honor to have you staying with us. I've personally seen that our best suite is prepared for you, if you'll follow me, please?"

Werner stood up and held a hand out to Luise before addressing Q, "I expect to converse some more with you during our stay here." He nodded at Hilde and walked off with the hotel director leading the way.

With a deep sigh, Q ushered Hilde towards the exit and out onto the sidewalk. His pulse drummed as if he'd been running a sprint and Hilde seemed to feel the same anxiety. He could smell the fear rolling off of her in waves.

In silence, they walked hand in hand until they ended on the nearby beach. Hilde stopped to remove her shoes and stockings to dip her feet into the cool water as it flowed back and forth across the packed sand.

The sound of the waves lapping on the beach had a calming effect, and he followed suit. Taking his shoes off, he tied their laces together and slung them around his neck, taking Hilde's hand in his own as they walked in silence.

He had to think – to ponder the consequences of meeting Werner von Blomberg. The reality of his dangerous life in Berlin had come crashing into the blissful enjoyment of the last few weeks. No matter how much he wished it were not so, they were never going to be completely safe.

Not in this world. Not as long as the Nazis were in power. Not even on their honeymoon.

# CHAPTER 8

H ilde could tell that the events of the last hour had shaken Q to the core. Despite his calm exterior, it took only one look into his eyes to recognize the turmoil boiling inside him.

Without speaking a single word, they walked along the beach, his pace increasing until she could barely keep up with him. Hilde slipped her hand out of his and stopped, unsure if he'd even noticed, because he kept on walking. A smile flickered on her lips. He'd come back when he was done thinking.

She sat down on the beach and patiently waited for his return while looking out at the horizon. Fleecy clouds floated across the deep blue sky, bringing a pattern of light and shadow to the ocean. Doubts and fears overshadowed the joy in her heart, dimming what should have been another wonderful day on the beach in the Mediterranean.

Q returned half an hour later, took her hand, and pulled her up against his chest. They held tight onto each other for a minute and even before he voiced the first word, she sensed his inner struggle.

"That was close. Too close." Q's voice could barely be heard above the waves.

"It was close, but everything turned out all right." She paused and took his hand, dragging him along the beach. Some thoughts demanded movement to be worked through. "We had a few weeks to pretend life was blissful, but we both know that danger is a constant part of our lives. Even here."

Q shook his head. "I feel so guilty for dragging you into this mess. We're supposed to be on our honeymoon–"

"Shush." She stopped. "*Liebling*, don't get so worked up. It wasn't your fault, and," she tilted her head to the side, "I love you, and I cannot imagine my life without you. I would rather die by your side than live without you."

Q turned her into his arms and kissed her with as much passion as desperation. They were both breathless when their lips parted and he said, "I want to get out."

"Get out?" Her heart constricted, and a shiver ran down her spine as she leaned back in his arms to explore his blue eyes.

"The intelligence work. I want to stop."

Hilde breathed again.

After considering his words for a moment, she asked, "Would you be able to look me in the eyes every single day, or – more importantly – be able to look at yourself in the mirror, if you stopped?"

Q rubbed his chin, considering her question for a long moment. "Probably not." He looked out to sea and then asked quietly, "But what do I do about the Generalfeldmarschall? I certainly don't want to work for the Ministry of War, but I don't see any way out."

Hilde nodded. "You probably don't have a choice. You'll have to go and at least talk to the man once we're back in Berlin."

"But I don't want to work for him," Q insisted.

"I know." She reached up and caressed his cheek. Q had a tendency to overthink things. "You'll go and meet with the man and then see how to continue from there."

"But–"

"No buts. In this case, it's best to take things day by day. We don't know what the future brings, and by the time we're back in Berlin, he may already have forgotten about the job offer." She didn't believe in her own words.

"You're right, my love. What would I do without you?"

She grinned. "Sit in some laboratory working on some important invention?"

"You know me too well."

～

The next morning, they woke up to a grey sky. Dark stormy clouds loomed on the horizon. It was their first day of bad weather since they'd left the Alps. But Q was determined to not let anything ruin their honeymoon – not the meeting with the Generalfeldmarschall and certainly not a thunderstorm.

He suggested spending the day at the most luxurious hot spa in town. While their hotel also offered a small pool, the town spa boasted several basins with different temperatures.

They entered the establishment through an ancient portal, and once inside, Hilde gasped at the sight. The original Roman architecture had been lovingly reconstructed. The main bath was surrounded by a walkabout covered in colorful tiles. While the pool was open-air, the walkabout featured a richly decorated roof, resting on sturdy columns with the heads of Roman gods overlooking the area.

From the walkabout, several openings led to smaller private baths in different sizes and shapes, each one more elaborate than the next. The boiling hot thermal-spring water bubbled through a set of open channels, flowing into the stone pools. The farther the water had to travel, the colder the receiving bath was.

Q and Hilde climbed into a heart-shaped pool. She reclined in the bath, tipped her head back, and waved a hand towards Q. "Where is the slave girl that is supposed to wash my hair?"

Q looked around the small area with a frown upon his face. "What are you talking about?"

Hilde giggled as she explained herself. "This looks so real, I was envisioning what life must have been like during the Roman and Greek empires. I'm a Roman lady with a multitude of servants at my beck and call."

Q laughed at these silly romantic and sentimental games. "You do have a vivid imagination."

"Right now I'm waiting for my servant to help me get ready to receive my lover because my husband is always traveling to countries far away."

"That I cannot accept," he said and tickled her in response.

Before Hilde could reply, Luise and Werner appeared in the entrance. Luise spotted them and came over, sliding into the hot water beside them. "Ahhh, aren't these Roman baths wonderful?"

Q and Hilde exchanged a look, and he said dryly, "Yes, they were." *Until you arrived.*

As Werner entered the pool, Q breathed against a constricting wall around his chest. Werner, though, grinned jovially at him. "The Roman Empire perished, but the Third Reich will prevail a thousand years. Our legacy will be even more glorious than those of the Greeks and the Romans."

Q nodded and added with a serious voice. "I believe generations to come will remember Hitler and his doings." He glanced over to Hilde, who'd been hogged by a chatty Luise. She rolled her eyes in his direction, and he raised his voice, "My love, your cheeks are reddening. We'll have to get you out of the hot water." With an apologetic glance to Werner and Luise, he added, "My wife is very susceptible to the heat."

As pleasantly as possible, they said their goodbyes, then hurried to the changing rooms and left the town spa. Back at the hotel, Hilde said, "We need to leave. Soon."

"Luise seems quite taken with you."

"And Werner likewise with you. If we remain a few more days, we could all become best friends," Hilde said with a twist to her mouth.

Q chuckled. "I can see how eager you are for that to happen." He exhaled a long breath, going through all the possibilities before finally nodding. "We'll leave first thing in the morning."

While it was the wise thing to do, Q also wanted to stay until he was able to meet with the Russian contact. Unfortunately, he had no means to let him know where they were headed.

# CHAPTER 9

Hilde and Q left the next morning, taking a bus inland to a small village located at the bottom of Mount Etna, a volcano on the east coast of Sicily. It was a tiny and peaceful place in the mountains and soon enough they returned to their blissful honeymoon state.

The Generalfeldmarschall was as quickly forgotten as the danger of Q's clandestine intelligence work. Some days later, they decided to walk up to the crater of the volcano. It was a very strenuous hike, and yet so beautiful.

After every turn, another beautiful view greeted them, each one more breathtaking than the one before. Below them lay green fields with blooming yellow bushes, and in the distance, the dark blue Mediterranean with a few white boats bobbing on the waves. The blue sky was a shade lighter than the ocean and cotton-ball clouds flocked to the horizon.

As they neared the top of the volcano, a strong smell of sulfur greeted them and Hilde covered her mouth and nose with the thin scarf she'd tied over her hair before leaving that morning. "We must be almost to the top."

"I believe so," Q said.

Ten minutes later, they were gingerly peering over the edge of a cliff at the red, glowing lava several hundred feet below. The view from that height was amazing, and after glimpsing their fill of the bubbling guts of the mountain, they retreated a short distance away to enjoy the view of the valley below.

The mountain rumbled like a man with an empty stomach and Hilde jerked up. "Please, Q, let's hike down."

Q chuckled but obeyed when he saw the fear in her eyes. "Okay, let's go. I don't think it'll erupt anytime soon, though. The last big eruption occurred nine years ago and a smaller one in 1931. Geologists believe the volcano is in recess for at least another five years."

On their hike up, she'd only had eyes for the beautiful land and seascape, but on their way down, Hilde noticed the evidence of the big eruption in 1928. Lava had spilled from the mouth of the volcano and flowed down the mountainside on its way to the ocean – swallowing an entire village.

Hilde shuddered, and Q paused to wrap his arms around her. "There's no need to worry."

She wasn't so sure about that but tried a brave smile and pointed at the path of destruction the now cooled lava had left in its inky path. "I think everyone is wrong. The earth is rumbling like an angry bear, ready to spit out a load of death and destruction."

"You're exaggerating." Q tried to appease her.

"I'm not, and you know it," she insisted. "We're sitting on a barrel of explosives, just waiting for someone to ignite the fuse."

Q looked at her in confusion. "You're not talking about the volcano, are you?"

Tears wetted her eyes as she shook her head, trying to keep her voice steady. "War is coming. It's inevitable."

"Sadly, I believe you're right." He took her hand as they continued their hike down.

"Look at the desolate landscapes the lava left behind. Much like a moonscape." Not that any human had set foot on the moon outside of the imaginations of H. G. Wells or Fritz Lang.

Q helped her down a steep part of the mountain before he answered, "A war will be worse than this." She knew he was fifteen when the Great War ended.

After a pause, he continued, "While I've never been on the battlefield, I've heard enough stories from my older brothers to imagine the destruction. And with all the newly invented weapons, the coming war will be even more destructive."

Hilde shuddered at the thought that her entire country or maybe all of Europe might look like this stretch of devastated land on the slopes of Mount Etna. It was best not to go down that road, but to concentrate on the present.

Climbing up had been hard, but going down wasn't proving to be much easier. Two hours later, they reached the road again and stopped to rest their strained knees.

She took a big gulp from their water bottle, then leaned against Q. "I couldn't possibly have wished for a better life's companion than you."

He kissed her nose. "I love you, Hildelein. I've loved you from the first moment I saw you in the motion-picture theatre, and after three years, I'm still amazed that every day my love for you has grown even more."

She hugged him tight, lost in her thoughts. She didn't regret her decision to marry him, even if it meant exposing herself to danger. His intelligence work was honorable, and with every passing day, she was more convinced that the Nazis were out to destroy the entire world. Someone had to stop them. And if Q could be a small spoke in the wheel, she'd be proud and happy – with him.

Still, the thought of returning to Berlin terrified her. She sighed. "I wish we didn't have to go back."

Q was thoughtful for several minutes before suggesting, "We could stay in Italy."

Hilde stared at him, trying to process the implications of his words. "You would really consider such an idea?"

"Yes. The situation in Germany will only get worse. Right now, we're safer than we might ever be again."

They continued to discuss the possibility of never going back to Germany, but the idea was only that – an idea. Neither one of them was truly serious about it.

When they'd almost reached the village, Q stopped when he spotted a lone man coming up the mountainside. "Stay here for a moment," he urged Hilde, putting a hand on her arm as he waited to get a better look at the man coming towards them.

Hilde squinted her eyes and then gasped. "Isn't that the Russian agent you were supposed to meet with?"

"It is. It would seem that Sicily is not so big after all."

～

An hour later, Q left his wife at the hotel room to get cleaned up and changed for dinner and promised to return soon. Just outside the village, Q met the agent, who introduced himself as – yet another – Pavel, and they embarked on a walk through the fields.

"I still can't believe you found me."

"That's my job," the man said with a smirk. "Thanks again for warning me about von Blomberg. Now that your wife is safely back at the hotel, will you tell me what you discussed with him?"

Q couldn't be sure, but he believed he heard suspicion in the agent's voice. "He offered me a job."

"A job?" Pavel asked, open-mouthed.

"Yes, he wants me to work for him at the Ministry of War. I declined."

"Are you crazy?"

Now it was Q's turn to drop his jaw. "Why? No! I can't possibly work for him, now can I?"

Pavel shook his head. "This is quite unusual, but it's a perfect opportunity. Think about all the intelligence you can gather from inside the Ministry of War!"

Q hadn't thought about that. What Pavel said made sense, but he didn't like the idea one bit. To work with the enemy – day in, day out. No. No. And no.

"I don't think I could do that. I'd be afraid I'd blow my cover at the first opportunity."

The agent scrutinized him. "Maybe you're right. But you should definitely think about it." He handed him a slip of paper with the name of Harro Schulze-Boysen and a telephone number.

"Who is this?"

"He's the leader of a Communist resistance group."

"Military?" Q asked. He'd heard the name but couldn't immediately place his affiliation.

"Air force. He's managed to maintain contact with the Soviet Union and the American authorities and has been warning both countries about the threats of war coming from within Germany."

Q took the paper and tucked it into his pocket. "I'll contact Schulze-Boysen, even though I believe working alone is safer."

"Not in this case. You must join with others who feel the same way you do and are working on orchestrating the demise of the Hitler regime. It will not be easy, but there is strength in numbers. Remember that."

"I will. Do you have any news from Germany?"

The agent shrugged. "Nothing special. On the surface, Germany and the Soviet Union appear to be on friendly terms. But the suspicion is high on both sides."

"This I know," Q said.

After discussing Stalin and how he was ruining the ideas of the November Revolution, Pavel gave him a last warning. "You need to be careful once you return to Germany. War is in the air, more so now than ever. It's no longer safe for you to visit the Soviet trade mission. We will contact you from now on."

"How will I know it's your people?" Q rubbed his chin.

The Russian narrowed his eyes, thinking, then broke into a broad smile. "Ask them if the hike up Mount Etna is strenuous. The answer will be, 'Not if you intend it at night.'"

Q almost choked on that hilarious sentence. "I will certainly remember that."

# CHAPTER 10

S everal weeks later, it was the end of summer, and Q and Hilde returned to Berlin. After spending four months in Italy and Switzerland, they felt like a distant relative who's the only one to notice how much a child has changed and how many new things it has learned while they were gone.

Much in contrast to the relaxed and peaceful atmosphere on their honeymoon, the atmosphere in the German capital was dire, to say the least. They felt the steady decline of everything "good and human" at every step. Swastika flags hung out of the windows, reminding the passers-by of who ruled the country. There was open harassment on the streets by violent Brownshirts who didn't even attempt to hide their abuse.

Anyone and everyone could become the victim of scorn and maltreatment by SS or SA officers roaming the streets, but the Jews had to take the biggest share of vile persecution.

During the last few months, a strict racial segregation had been implemented throughout Germany. Jews were no longer allowed in the public parks, swimming pools, libraries, or in fact any place people would spend their leisure time.

The Nazis had even gone so far as to segregate the compartments on the trains and buses, and during rush hour or in certain parts of the city,

Jews weren't allowed the use of any public transportation at all. Q wondered how they were supposed to go to work.

He decided to check up on his friend Jakob Goldmann, from whom he hadn't heard since before they left on their honeymoon. But when Q paid a visit to Jakob's apartment in the center of Berlin, he didn't live there anymore. The landlady recognized Q from when he'd sublet a room from Jakob. She seemed uneasy as she explained that she'd had to terminate Mr. Goldmann's lease because she couldn't afford to do business with *those* persons.

Q thanked her and left, fuming inside about the injustice. The landlady had repeatedly praised Jakob for being such a good tenant. Quiet, clean, and always paying on time. And now he was considered undesirable because he belonged to *those* persons. He fisted his hand and punched the air, murmuring curse words under his breath.

*I'm not going to give up. Ever.*

The next day, he contacted Harro Schulze-Boysen and arranged to meet with him two weeks later. Schulze-Boysen picked him up with his Mercedes limousine at a busy intersection near the Reichstag. He'd been briefed by Pavel and knew Q's history. He explained the ways his own organization worked and then said, "Doctor Quedlin, I'd be more than happy to integrate you into our resistance network."

Q hesitated, because working alone definitely had its merits. "I already told Pavel that I'm not entirely convinced it's safe or prudent to liaise too closely."

Schulze-Boysen furrowed his brows. "We have an extensive network of resources at our disposal. And with your connections to the science world, we could distribute our leaflets much more broadly."

*Leaflets?* Q didn't believe distributing anti-Nazi leaflets was a suitable way to end the terror regime. "I still believe it's safer for both of us not to work together, except in emergencies. But may I ask your advice in another affair?"

"Certainly." Schulze-Boysen's mouth twitched, showing his bemusement.

"Generalfeldmarschall von Blomberg has extended a job offer to me, and I need to find a way out."

The bemused smile disappeared, and Schulze-Boysen's jaw dropped nearly to the floor. "What?"

Q explained the situation, and his counterpart seemed to grow more pleased by the minute.

"That is brilliant. Brilliant," Schulze-Boysen said, turning the steering wheel. "You absolutely have to take von Blomberg up on this offer. This is a golden opportunity. Think about all the intelligence you can gather working directly for the Ministry of War."

Q's stomach churned at the thought of inventing weapons for the *Wehrmacht*, the German army, "You don't understand what that would entail. I would have to betray everything I stand for. Day after day. Everyone around me – including myself – has to believe I'm a die-hard Nazi. I'm not sure I could maintain that façade for long." He paused and zoomed in on Schulze-Boysen. "I have no idea how you can stomach it."

The other man laughed. "You get used to it. It's like wearing a coat. One I take off as soon as I reach my home."

"I don't think I could." Q shook his head.

"Well, at least consider it. It would be of great service to our cause."

"Agreed."

Schulze-Boysen stopped the Mercedes to let Q exit the car, and in the blink of an eye, the limousine disappeared around the corner of the street. Q didn't attempt to follow the automobile's path with his gaze; he was too busy making sure that nobody followed him on his way home.

Since his return to Berlin, looking over his shoulder had become a constant habit. But for the first time in weeks, he loped, and a kernel of hope entered his heart. All was not lost. There were more people willing to stand up and fight for their freedoms – he and Hilde were not alone.

Another week went by, and Q had thought long and hard about Schulze-Boysen's advice to accept the job offered by von Blomberg, but he couldn't bring himself to act upon it. Instead, he hoped the Generalfeldmarschall would forget all about the job offer he'd extended.

But unfortunately, towards the end of October 1937, that hope was crushed as two uniformed SS officers arrived at his office, demanding to talk with Q.

The sight of the despised Nazi officers sent icy chills down his spine, and the sealed letter with an official-looking seal in the hands of one of them didn't help either. Was this how they delivered arrests nowadays?

"Heil Hitler!" the officer saluted, clicking his heels.

Q let out a tiny breath and forced himself to return the salutation with the same enthusiasm. "Heil Hitler! What can I do for you officers?"

"We have an important message for you and have been asked to return your answer to the Minister of War."

Q's knees almost sagged in relief. They hadn't been sent for his head – but for his brains. He accepted the letter, and retreated to his desk, pulling out a letter opener from under a pile of paper.

With two pairs of perplexed eyes fixated on the sharp object in his hand, he carefully opened the envelope and retrieved a single sheet of paper with the official letterhead of the Ministry of War.

He leaned against his desk and began to read, the letters dancing in front of his eyes.

*Wilhelm Quedlin,*

*I trust you and your wife returned from your journey to Italy and you are ready to serve Führer and Fatherland by offering up your intellect and knowledge for the furtherance of our cause. The job I mentioned to you is still available, and I know you have most likely been waiting for confirmation that my offer was valid.*

*Consider this letter that confirmation. I will expect to see you in my office on Monday at 11 a.m. to discuss the details of your service for the greater good.*

*Please present this letter to your current employer, should you need to excuse yourself from work.*

*Welcome aboard.*

*Werner von Blomberg*


Q swallowed hard and raised his head to look into the curious eyes of the SS officers staring at him. "Officers, please let the Generalfeldmarschall know that it is my greatest pleasure to accept his invitation. I'm looking forward to meeting him at his office this coming Monday, eleven o'clock sharp."

The SS men clicked heels again and left the office, leaving Q with a dizzy feeling. He popped onto the swivel chair and dropped his forehead to his desk. Whether he wanted to or not, he'd soon be working for the devil himself.

A million thoughts stormed his brain, but it was the image of devastation he'd seen on the slopes of Mount Etna that stayed with him and churned his gut. How could he live with the certainty that thousands would be killed in the future with weapons invented by him?

~

Q arrived in front of the Ministry of War with time to spare. The impressive grey stone building overlooked the Landwehr Kanal, an artificial canal branching off from the Spree River.

At this time of year, the trees lining the riverbank were entirely bare, having shed their leaves weeks ago. They stood erect, raising their empty branches into the sky like pointed index fingers warning about coming doom.

He entered through the big wooden portal. The door creaked like a crow as it closed behind him and the blood congealed in his veins. The huge entry hall oozed terror, and it took all his strength not to turn on his heel and run.

Q announced himself at the reception desk, invitation letter in hand, and a uniformed officer ushered him into von Blomberg's office and announced, "Sir, Doctor Quedlin is here."

Von Blomberg greeted him with the obligatory "Heil Hitler" and then sat again behind an impressive dark wooden desk. *Probably oak.* Behind him on the wall hung the ubiquitous picture of Hitler and a swastika flag. Two smaller swastika flags adorned his desk, along with a picture of Luise and another woman.

Q's eyes widened as he took in von Blomberg's appearance. Before him didn't sit the jovial, good-humored man he'd met back in Italy, but a man with an ashen-grey face and bloodshot eyes that testified to a great deal of stress and little sleep.

With consideration of the uniformed officer standing next to him, Q opted for the formal salutation, "Herr Generalfeldmarschall, you requested to see me?"

"Yes. Please have a seat." Von Blomberg gestured towards one of the empty chairs.

Q did as he was bidden, unable to shake the feeling that something was very wrong.

"Doctor Quedlin, thank you for coming." A slight pause. "Unfortunately, things have changed in the last forty-eight hours, and I am not able to discuss your employment at this time."

"Sir?" Q wasn't sure whether to be elated – or terrified.

Von Blomberg sighed and then pushed himself out of his armchair to pace the length of his office. "You will understand that I cannot go into details, as these are matters of national security."

Q nodded. "I absolutely understand, sir."

Just as Q stood to bid his goodbyes, von Blomberg turned to him and said in a low voice, "I am getting married in January. Come back early February."

Relief washed over Q. "I will do that. Congratulations on your wedding."

The Generalfeldmarschall accepted the well-wishes with a grimace. "If only it was all cause for happiness."

Q took his leave, not wanting to hear an explanation for the minister's strange comment. In public speeches or on the international stage, Hitler always mentioned that he was more than willing to accommodate for peace, but the meeting with von Blomberg had given a different impression.

*The Wehrmacht knows there will soon be war, and the only question is where, not when.*

Back home, he told Hilde about the peculiar meeting with von Blomberg, and she beamed at him. "See? No reason to worry. You've just gained three months."

"Yes. But what then?" He rubbed his chin.

"*Liebling*, don't worry so much. A lot of water will flow under the bridge until February, and many things can happen."

He kissed her on the mouth. "What would I do without you, Hildelein?"

She giggled. "Worry yourself sick?"

～

The holidays came and went, and they kept watching for news of von Blomberg's marriage to Luise. It finally came the second week of January. Hilde broke the news to Q as she brought home a newspaper showing the picture of the newly married couple standing next to their marriage witnesses – commander-in-chief of the air force, Herman Göring, and the Führer himself.

But just two weeks later, more alarming news emerged. Von Blomberg had drawn the eyes of everyone towards himself and his new bride, eyes that only looked for the bad things. And Luise turned out to be one of those bad things.

Hilde and Q sat on the couch together as the news of Luise's criminal history came from the radio. "Shush," Hilde said and turned the volume up.

*"...the 25-year-old former typist and secretary has a long criminal record ranging from theft to impersonation to moral indecency, which apparently has been excused by our Führer because she promised betterment.*

*"But the police came up with another, even graver offense. The entire nation is shocked to the bone by the horrific crimes she committed against decency and racial purity by posing for pornographic photos a few years back. Those unspeakable actions were further aggravated by the fact that those photos had been taken by a Jewish photographer this woman had been living together with..."*

Hilde switched off the radio, because what followed was the usual bashing of Jews and the unspeakable "crime" of an Aryan woman mingling with a sub-human and thus impurifying the master race.

The scandal was fierce, and a few days later, Werner von Blomberg abdicated from all of his official functions, supposedly for health reasons.

"Can you believe an intelligent man in such a high-level position could trip over a woman?" Hilde asked.

"No. I thought he would have checked her background before marrying her."

Hilde grinned. "Well, on the bright side, you won't be keeping that second meeting with him, will you?"

Q nodded. "Definitely not. How was work for you today?"

Hilde shrugged. "It was fine."

She'd taken such a long leave of absence that she'd been afraid her position would no longer be available upon her return to the insurance company. But the opposite turned out to be true. "We have so many claims to process, the company is desperately seeking additional skilled staff."

"Same at the Biological Institute. We're swamped with research orders, but not enough men to do the work."

"Or women." Hilde pouted, and Q took her hand in his. "You know what I mean. It's actually ironic. A few years back, the Nazis coerced women into staying home and raising children, and now that they need the men for their war efforts, they change course and encourage the same women to come back to the factories."

Hilde leaned against Q's shoulder. "Erika has been promoted again. They've given her twice as many people to oversee, including the new accounting department staff."

"Congratulations. She must be doing good work."

Hilde rolled her eyes. "I believe it has more to do with her Party book than with the quality of her work."

"Oh, when did she join the Party?"

"About a month ago." Hilde sighed and turned to look into Q's eyes. "Erika is one of my best friends, but we have to be careful. Since she became enamored with that SS officer, she's changed."

"We will. Let's go to bed." Q stood and pulled Hilde from the couch. While doing her evening ablutions, she thought about her company. On the surface, nothing had changed. The economy was picking up, and everyone seemed to look forward to better times. But there was an ever-present underlying tension. People watched their words, careful not to accidentally make anti-Nazi or pro-Jewish comments.

It was too dangerous.

# CHAPTER 11

Things in Europe were starting to unravel at an alarming rate. The Gestapo was quickly becoming one of the most feared groups in Berlin and across Germany. Luckily, Q hadn't been the focus of any of their investigations, but he couldn't say the same for some of his colleagues.

On March 12, 1938, completely different news surprised the German population. The long-awaited war was over before it began.

Hitler had marched with his troops into Austria and declared his home country a federal state of Germany, which he now called *Großdeutsches Reich*, Great German Empire. And what happened? Nothing.

The cabinet of Nazi supporters in the Austrian government willingly agreed to the annexation, and all over Austria and Germany, spontaneous celebrations took place with people dancing in the streets.

Q couldn't help but wonder throughout the next days. Hitler's triumphal march to Vienna was accompanied by cheering and flower-throwing crowds. Did those people not know what awaited them?

It was a surreal occurrence and culminated in Hitler's enthusiastic speech in front of thousands of Austrians announcing the entrance of his native country into the German Empire.

Q wanted to puke.

But apparently, he was the only one to think that way. As spring passed, Q found himself in a constant state of worry. Even his work at the Biological Reich Institute proved increasingly challenging. His area of expertise – plant protection – wasn't deemed *war important*. Q had thought this an advantage because the authorities wouldn't interfere with his research, but he soon found that was wishful thinking and the opposite was true.

He constantly had to justify his plant protection research, and more than once had been forced to stop the work, whether due to lack of materials and funds or because he didn't get access to a vital piece of information that had been deemed a military secret.

More and more of his colleagues were forced to change the focus of their experimentation to fit the needs of the Third Reich and the war effort. It was only a matter of time until Q would have to oblige as well.

*Biological warfare.*

That was what the government wanted. New biological weapons to use against Germany's enemies. The Nazis considered this research pertinent to winning an upcoming war and began to scrutinize the scientists more closely than in the past. Everyone had to produce a Greater Aryan Certificate, proof that parents and all four grandparents were Aryan. Q groaned as he remembered the months and months of struggle to get the required Catholic baptism certificate of his Hungarian grandmother when he needed the *Ariernachweis* to receive his marriage license one and a half years ago.

The scientists had been given four weeks to produce their respective Aryan Certificates, and at the end of the month, all but one colleague had handed it in. Very few Jews were still allowed to work in critical industries, and that colleague was one of those unfortunate ones. The next day, the Gestapo stormed the building and dragged him from the facility.

According to the rumors, the poor fellow was half Jewish, enough for the Gestapo to consider him a threat to national security and treat him accordingly. Q and his colleagues pretended not to see or hear anything, going about their daily work, hoping they'd be left in peace.

But the nightmare wasn't over yet. More Gestapo officers arrived to thoroughly question all colleagues before anyone was allowed to leave for the day. Lined up in the large courtyard, they were led one by one to a small room for interrogation.

Q could barely breathe when his name was called out, and he followed the Gestapo officer with a wildly beating heart. It took his eyes a few moments to adjust from the bright sunlight in the courtyard to the dimly lit room, the office of one of the accountants. Now an important-looking Gestapo man with soulless grey eyes and all the insignia of importance on his uniform presided behind the desk. Lower-ranking officers flanked him on either side.

"Name and profession."

"Doctor Wilhelm Quedlin. Chemical engineer."

"Party book."

Q clenched his jaw to disguise a shiver. "I'm not a member of the Party."

The Gestapo man looked up, his stare boring into Q's skin like a red-hot iron rod. "Why not?"

*Because I hate everything the Nazis stand for.* Q raised his chin and returned the stare as steadfastly as he was capable of. "Sir, I don't understand much of politics. My science is my life."

Apparently, this answer didn't satisfy the interrogator because it prompted a whole new set of questions about Q's loyalties, his activities, and his general opinion about the Führer and Fatherland.

Q answered all the questions as meekly as he could, but at the umpteenth repetition, his temper broke through. "You are hindering my work. I need to return to my experiments."

No sooner had the words left his mouth than Q realized the foolish mistake he'd committed. He only had a very short amount of time – if any – to correct his error, and quickly apologized. "Gentlemen, I apologize for my outburst. I was in the middle of a time-critical experiment that is of the utmost importance to Germany and her people."

The Gestapo officer looked at his notes and then scoffed. "You work with plants. How can that be of vital importance to the Party?"

Q swallowed back his first response and calmly explained, "I'm working on orders from the highest authority on methods to increase agricultural production. Our Führer wants to assure that German people won't have to suffer through years of famine as we did during the Great War."

Judging by the pained expression on his face, the well-fed man behind the desk remembered all too well the terrible hunger he'd experienced two decades ago. The palpable tension in the room eased up and Q lowered his head and waited.

"Well, then you better get back to work. We wouldn't want to interfere with the intention of our Führer."

"Thank you, sir," Q answered and turned to leave but was called back.

"Doctor Quedlin, consider joining the Party. Questioning would have been unnecessary if you'd had the proper paperwork."

Q thanked him for the suggestion and tamped down on the hatred he carried for everything Nazi. He went back to his laboratory, hiding his fear as best as he could. He knew it had been a very thin line that had kept him from being arrested today, and he vowed to do nothing that might draw more scrutiny from the Gestapo.

He feared for his life. Like everyone these days.

Once he was sure the Gestapo had taken their leave, he packed up his briefcase and headed home. At the sound of the slamming door, Hilde came from the small kitchen with a towel in her hands and asked, "What's wrong, my love?"

"I can't take it anymore," he burst out, tossing his briefcase to the floor and sinking down into the couch.

"Can't take what?" Hilde queried, coming to sit beside him.

"The Nazis. The war preparations. Germany! We have to leave the country if we are to ever be happy again."

"Leave? But where would we go?" Alarm was written on her face.

"America. They appreciate scientists there. I have a future there. We do. What do we have here? Nothing but more fear and censorship."

"But America is so far away." Hilde seemed so small as she sank deeper into the couch beside him, and he wanted to console her.

Q put an arm around her shoulders. "I know. And this is very sudden. But we wouldn't be alone. My cousin Fanny married an American dentist a few years back and went to live with him in Forest Hills, New York. I'm sure she would be willing to help us."

Hilde said nothing, and after a day or two, the discussion naturally slipped to the sidelines as more pressing matters came forward.

# CHAPTER 12

Hilde stepped out of the bathroom. She should be excited about this evening's event, but she was having trouble mustering up any enthusiasm. Her company had made it possible for all of their employees, and a guest, to watch the movie *Olympia – Fest der Schönheit/Fest der Völker* by Leni Riefenstahl in the Ufa-Palast.

The movie was all the rage in Berlin – a beautiful homage to the Olympic Games – Games of Beauty and Games of Nations, held in Berlin two years earlier. Normally, Hilde would be excited about such an outing as Leni Riefenstahl made excellent and captivating movies. But Leni was also a very good friend of Hitler and lately all of her movies had been nothing more than blatant propaganda for the regime.

"You look lovely, Hilde," Q complimented her, folding up the newspaper he'd been reading and getting to his feet as she stepped into the room.

She gave him a smile and then smoothed a hand down the skirt of her dress. It was a very smart outfit, navy blue with large white polka dots scattered all over it. A small ruffled collar with a tie combined with the pencil skirt design and white jacket completed the outfit. She pulled on her gloves after pinning the navy blue hat to her hair and then turned to look at Q. "Are you sure we need to go?"

"If you don't go, it will certainly be noticed, and the idea is to keep a low profile. It's better to show up and make sure the right people notice you and then leave as soon as it is practical, rather than stirring up questions as to why you were absent."

"I know all of that," she sighed, "I'm just tired of being bombarded by Nazi propaganda at every turn."

Q put his hand on the small of her back. "I understand that, but this is what we need to do now. We'll watch the movie, attend the reception for a short time, and then leave."

Hilde nodded and stepped out of the apartment while he held the door for her. They took his automobile to the Ufa-Palast, and Hilde made an effort to smile and act like she was enjoying herself as colleagues greeted her and Q.

During the break, Q and Hilde left the building through a side entrance to fill their lungs with fresh air. Some of her colleagues followed suit. When Q stopped and stared off into the distance, a peculiar stiffness filled his body. Hilde whispered, "What's wrong?"

"Come with me and pretend nothing's out of the ordinary," Q breathed into her ear and led her around a corner while kissing her neck. Hilde giggled. After being married almost two years, he certainly didn't need to take her into a dark alley to kiss her.

But as soon as they were out of sight of her colleagues, a man stepped from the shadows and Q released her to greet him. "Jakob Goldmann. I was worried sick about you. Your landlady–"

Jakob pulled him in for a friendly hug. "Q, it is so good to see you. I didn't want to get you into trouble, but when I heard that Hilde's company rented the Ufa-Palast tonight, I hoped to see you," Jakob said, stepping back and giving Hilde a smile.

"You look awful!" Hilde said, and it was true. Since she'd last seen him a year ago, he'd aged at least twenty years. His shoulders slumped forward and at twenty-eight, he already sported salt-and-pepper hair. Lines sharp enough to be seen in the dimly lit alley had furrowed his face and given him the look of a broken man.

"What have you been up to?" Q wanted to know.

Jakob shook his head. "Things are not good. Each day life for us Jews gets a little harder. After my landlady terminated my lease contract, I had to move in with my parents."

Hilde felt awful for him. He'd been one of Q's best friends, and she knew that Q felt guilty for not having kept in contact with him after they returned from Italy. She put a hand on Jakob's arm and asked. "How are your parents?"

His eyes glistened. "Dead. Both of them."

She gasped, covering her mouth with her hand as tears sprang to her eyes. Jakob looked at her and tried a small smile. "Don't cry for me."

She nodded, swallowing back her tears because she could tell that he was barely keeping his own emotions together.

"My mother was forced to return from retirement. The Nazis said she was a work-shy parasite, and sent her to work in a factory producing military goods."

"That's horrible!" Hilde shouted, righteous anger building in her breast. Jakob's mother was a fragile person and anyone who'd met her knew she wasn't fit to work.

Q took her arm and said, "Shush. We don't want your colleagues to hear us."

Jakob cleared his throat. "Momma died one week later from a heart attack. With her fragile condition, the hard work and long hours were too much for her."

"Oh, Jakob! I'm so sorry," Hilde said, losing the battle to keep her tears hidden. She ducked her head and surreptitiously wiped them away.

"And your father?" Q wanted to know, placing a comforting arm around Hilde's shoulders.

"My father stopped talking the day my mother died. Not one word. When the Nazis found out, they took him away, supposedly to a mental home. I wasn't allowed to visit, and they wouldn't even tell me where he was. A few days later, a letter arrived to inform me my father was dead."

Hilde was openly crying now, and Q clasped his friend's shoulder. "I'm so sorry, my friend. You need to leave Germany before it's too late."

"But–"

"No buts. Now that your parents are both gone, there's nothing left to keep you here. You must go if you want to survive."

"Where should I go? All of the European countries have imposed quotas on receiving Jewish immigrants from Germany."

Q tilted his head, thinking. "The farther away, the better. Go to America. They are in need of young and brilliant scientists like you."

"Do you really think they'll give me a visa?"

"You'll never know if you don't try," Q urged his friend. "Do it for me. So I'll know you're safe."

Hilde wiped her cheeks and added, "And if you're successful, we might come and visit you."

Jakob chuckled. "You two are good friends. I'll think about it."

Too soon, it was time for Q and Hilde to slip back inside the cinema before anyone was the wiser. Jakob hugged them both once more and promised to find a way to let them know what was happening with him. Before entering the cinema, Q waited while Hilde visited the bathroom and splashed some cool water on her face.

When she returned, she felt only slightly better, and even more anxious for the evening to come to an end.

# CHAPTER 13

T hree months later, Hilde and Q came home to find a letter from Q's cousin Fanny in America. She told them about her life in Forest Hills, New York, and asked about the well-being of the other family members. The letter ended with an invitation to visit her and her husband for a few weeks.

"What do you think, Hilde?" Q asked. "Should we try to get travel visas for America?"

"That sounds exciting," Hilde answered. "I'll get three weeks of leave next summer."

Over dinner, they made plans for their upcoming vacation across the ocean and Q teased Hilde about her excitement.

Just as they finished eating dinner and Hilde was washing the dishes in the kitchen, the telephone rang. Q answered it. "Wilhelm Quedlin."

"It's Jakob."

"Jakob, it's good to hear from you." Q gripped the telephone receiver tighter. Since he'd last seen his friend at the Ufa-Palast, he'd only heard bad news. Jakob had been dismissed from his job, repeatedly harassed by Brownshirts when running errands, and he'd been denied visas by several European countries.

"I have good news," Jakob said, and Q released his breath. "I received my visa to emigrate to America. The final paperwork arrived this afternoon, and I'm already booked on a ship out of Hamburg three days from now, on November tenth, to travel to New York."

"That's great news! Congratulations!"

"Thanks. I'm so relieved. This ship will take me to safety. Finally." Jakob hesitated. "Q?"

"What, my friend?"

"I hate to ask…but the situation with the trains…do you think there's any way you could drive me to Hamburg?"

"Of course I'll drive you down. It's the least I can do."

"Thank you. It means a lot. I need to take care of a few more things, given that I most likely won't come back…" Jakob's voice broke.

Q could feel the pain in his friend's heart. It wasn't easy to leave everything behind and embark on an uncertain adventure. "Don't worry. You'll do just fine. And you'll find yourself a nice young woman soon enough over there."

Jakob tried a chuckle. "I'm sure I will. It's not safe for you to come to my place. Can you meet me by the train station? Seven o'clock Thursday morning."

"Sure. See you then, and take care." Q hung up the phone just as Hilde exited the kitchen, drying her hands with a towel.

"Who were you talking to?" she asked.

"Jakob. He's got a visa for America." Q took Hilde in his arms and whirled her around, then set her back on her feet. "He asked me to drive him to the harbor in Hamburg on Thursday."

"Oh. That's wonderful. We might even be able to visit him there next summer." Q loved to see the genuine smile on her face. Maybe the first in many weeks. But then, she wrinkled her nose.

"What's wrong, *Liebling*?" Q asked.

"Nothing. I just thought…if I ask for two days' leave, I could come with you. We could visit my family for the weekend."

"That's a terrific idea. We'll do that," Q agreed.

～

Thursday morning arrived, and Q and Hilde arrived at the allotted place in time, but Jakob never showed up.

"Where is he?" Hilde asked, worry in her voice.

"I don't know. This is unlike him. He's usually overly punctual."

They waited in the automobile and Q turned the radio on, searching for a musical program to help release some of the tension that was quickly building. Instead of a musical program, he could only find news report after news report. Giving up, he let the radio play, and horror seeped deep into his body at what he heard.

Last night, November 9, 1938, the Nazi regime had launched a terror campaign against the Jewish people in both Germany and Austria. *Reichskristallnacht,* the Night of Broken Glass, as the radio speaker called it.

Q's stomach churned at the vivid detail of the violence that had occurred throughout the night. The radio speaker didn't even try to hide his enthusiasm as he recounted all the atrocities committed against the Jewish citizens. Ransacked homes. Sledgehammered businesses. Demolished schools. Burnt synagogues. Profaned graveyards. Hundreds of Jews murdered. Thousands arrested and sent to concentration camps.

"How did we not know this was happening?" Hilde asked, tears in her eyes.

"We don't live in an area where there are any Jews." Q's voice was barely audible.

"You don't think that something happened to Jakob? Did he live in a Jewish part of the city?"

Q nodded and immediately started the automobile. "Jakob was living in his parents' house. So yes, he lived in a Jewish quarter." He drove towards that part of the city, and as they passed by Jewish businesses and homes, the devastation was harrowing.

Deserted streets with bodies lying where they'd fallen. Smoldering fires. Q swallowed hard. "Hilde, this is probably not a good idea."

"Don't you want to know?" Hilde wiped her tears.

Q nodded, tears clogging his throat at the senseless acts of violence in plain view. "Maybe he needs our help. We have to get to his place."

They drove the rest of the way in silence. When the debris in the street made it impossible to drive any farther, he parked and opened the door for Hilde, and they picked their way towards the small house where Jakob's parents had lived.

Q took a deep breath before he pushed the door open and entered the hallway. Then he froze. Jakob lay at the bottom of the stairs, his lifeless eyes staring up at the ceiling, his skin swollen and battered, a pool of dried blood beneath his head.

Q swallowed back the bile that rose in his throat and turned, intending to keep Hilde from seeing this, but he was too late. She took one look at Jakob's body and screamed. The windows in the staircase resonated with her voice and Q was afraid they'd burst.

He grabbed her by the waist and pulled her out of the building, burying her head against his chest in an effort to calm her down. "Shush!"

Hilde's muffled screams filled the air, and Q looked up and down the street, fearing upset neighbors – or worse – to bombard them with brickbats. But no one came running. Q noticed a curtain moving in one of the buildings, but the street remained abandoned.

Soon, Hilde's screams eased into sobbing, and he wished he could release his emotions in the same way. Despite the grief, his eyes stayed dry. The weight of guilt for his friend's death pressed on his shoulders, making it difficult to breathe. *I wasn't there to help him. If I only had urged Jakob to leave the country earlier, he'd be safe on the ship by now. I should have made more of an effort to keep in touch with him, to protect him. He was my best friend...*

"Don't do this." Hilde looked up at him with puffy tear-stained eyes, clasping his cheeks in her hands.

"Do what?" Q asked, his voice husky with unshed tears.

"I know you. You're feeling guilty for what happened. But there was nothing you could have done to prevent it."

"I could have tried–"

"Tried what? To stop the Nazis from looting?"

Q nodded. She was right, but it didn't make things any easier. He looked back towards the building. The windows were broken, furniture was smashed, belongings were strewn about...it looked like a war zone.

"I want to say a prayer for him. You don't have to join me."

"Of course I will; he was my friend, too," Hilde answered, straightening her spine and her resolve.

He stepped back inside the building, keeping Hilde close to his side and said a quick prayer for Jakob's soul. It was the only thing they could do. He wished there was some way to organize a proper burial, but under the circumstances, it was impossible. As cruel as it was, he and Hilde had to return to their automobile, leaving Jakob lying there at the bottom of the stairs.

Q drove them back to their place, glancing at Hilde frequently. Her face had turned ghostly white, and she was terribly quiet, sitting perfectly still, except for her hands. She was worrying her fingers to the point where he finally reached over and covered them, knowing she was going to injure herself if she continued.

"Hilde?"

"I want to get out. I just to get want away from all of this."

Q squeezed her hands. "We should drive to Hamburg as we planned. It will get us away from Berlin for a few days, and your sisters will distract us."

"Without Jakob? Who should have embarked on the ship to start a new life..."

"We have to move on, Hilde. As hard as it is, there is nothing we can do for Jakob. But we can help ourselves by giving our minds a small reprieve from the grief."

Hilde nodded, settled into the seat, and closed her eyes.

"Sleep, *mein Liebling*, and dream about your sisters," he said.

The trip to Hamburg wasn't the joyous event they had originally planned, but one of sorrow and worry. Hilde's family was equally agitated upon their arrival. Hamburg had experienced the same outbursts of violence as Berlin, and while the quarter of the Dremmer family had been spared, they'd heard the radio reports and worried.

But Carl and Emma had made it a rule not to make any negative comments in front of their teenage daughters because they were afraid Julia or Sophie might blurt out something inappropriate at school.

Nobody wanted to get caught criticizing the Nazi regime, as that was a sure way to become the next victim. Thus it was only in the evenings after the girls had gone to bed that Q and Hilde felt comfortable voicing their concerns to her parents.

"I just don't see how these atrocities can continue," Q stated.

Carl nodded. "I agree with you, but what are the options? The Jews are powerless to fight back, and anyone even suspected of showing them sympathy is likely to be treated as a traitor."

"But where will our nation end up if everyone just stands by and turns a blind eye?"

Carl stared for long moments at Q and Hilde before he said, "You two are young and without responsibilities. But I just turned fifty-three and have a wife and two teenagers depending on me. I may not agree with what the Nazis are doing, but I can't afford to battle them."

Q didn't want to go down that route and changed the topic of the discussion. "A few days ago, we received a letter from my cousin Fanny in America. She invited us over to visit."

Emma joined the discussion. "You should definitely go while you still can. Once you have children, travelling that far won't be so easy."

Hilde giggled. "Q's mother gave us the same advice before we embarked on our honeymoon." Then she kissed Q lightly on the cheek and whispered in his ear, "It sounds like everyone is waiting for grandchildren."

Q smiled. He was getting the same impression. "We were planning to visit Fanny next summer."

"You shouldn't wait too long," Carl said and lit a cigarette, offering one to Q. "Who knows how long it will be before we are at war, and you won't be able to leave the country for leisure trips?"

Q nodded. It had been time-consuming to secure the visa and papers for their honeymoon in Europe; how much more challenging would it be two years later to travel to America?

"We'll send a letter to Fanny right away."

# CHAPTER 14

The *Kristallnacht* was only the first of many terror campaigns against the Jewish people in both Germany and annexed Austria. Q was in a constant state of alert, a premonition of worse things to come looming in his subconscious.

His faith in the good of humanity had been severely shattered as he witnessed time after time what people could do with their hatred. Nothing was the way it was before, and Q was appalled by the actions of his compatriots.

As the New Year arrived, he was still dealing with guilt over Jakob's death, moping around without finding joy in even the things he liked most.

"Q, you have to stop this. You are not responsible for Jakob's death," Hilde said once and again, but Q refused to listen. His mood had been steadily declining, and he was slipping into a deep depression. The only thing to lighten his mood was planning their upcoming visit to his cousin Fanny in America.

"What is the weather like in Forest Hills?" Hilde asked as they sat over dinner.

"June through August are the hottest months of the year. Fanny wrote the temperatures can be well above 80° Fahrenheit, which is close to 30° Celsius."

Hilde smiled. "I'll need summer dresses. Maybe I should start to do some shopping?"

Against his will, Q had to chuckle. If life were only that easy. He doubted Hilde could buy summer dresses right then. Not in January and not in a Germany singularly focused on war.

Without warning, his good humor turned into anger, and his frustration burst out. "The whole damned nation is focused on war. Every industry has been re-purposed to keep the war machine running smoothly. There's no liberty to develop my researches. All my work is redirected to research war-relevant things they want to use as weapons."

Q pushed over an empty glass as he talked himself into a rage.

He went on, "Can you believe those narrow-minded officials in charge laughed at the inventions Otto and I presented them several years ago? And now they are feverishly trying to produce something similar, and yet inferior."

Hilde moved the glass out of his reach before she filled it with water. "I thought you were relieved that the government didn't buy your inventions?"

"I was. I am." Q sighed. "I couldn't have lived with the knowledge that my inventions would be used to kill innocent people simply because of their heritage. But it still hurts that those arrogant men refused my work and think they can do better on their own." He paused and ran a hand through his hair. "And you know what is the worst?"

Hilde looked reluctant to ask. "No. What?"

"I used to think of a weapon as being neither good nor bad; it just *is*. But humans will always abuse them. Allow any of those masculinity-driven lads free use of a weapon and he will use it against his fellow human. Hatred, fear, and the sense of power will do that to him."

Hilde put a hand on his arm. "You're exaggerating, my love. Mankind is not that bad, and things surely will get better."

"No, they won't." Q buried his head in his hands, the evil of the entire world weighing him down.

"Maybe we should look at extending our trip to America to several months, rather than just visiting for a few weeks?" Hilde suggested.

He looked up, surprised. A frisson of euphoria rushed through his veins. "You would? I mean... our trip to America is the one thing to make me happy, but whenever I think about having to leave and come back here, I fall back into my depressed state of mind."

"Then we should apply for immigrant visas for America," Hilde said.

Q looked at her with wide eyes. She was the one to resist that idea when he first mentioned it. But so many things had changed during the last year. The situation in Germany was hopeless. Hitler would never back down until he got everything he wanted. Austria. The Sudeten territories. What would be next on his list?

"Isn't that being cowardly to use the easy way out and run?" he whispered.

"No. You've done so much already." Hilde put a hand on his arm. "Maybe you'll be of better use against the Nazi regime from outside, where you can concentrate on your research work. Like this echo-sound system to locate ships and airplanes you told me about."

He'd almost forgotten about his echo-sound theories. The Royal Air Force had shown interest but had asked him to deliver a working prototype, not just theories on paper.

"Maybe you're right, and it's not cowardly to emigrate. I guess I'm not cut out to be a hero."

"You are my hero," Hilde said and circled the table to sit on his lap. For the first time since finding Jakob's body, Q was filled with hope and excitement at the possibilities that lay before them.

He held her close and said, "Let's go to the embassy first thing in the morning and turn in our applications for immigrant visas."

# CHAPTER 15

S everal weeks later, they received a letter with the denial of their requested travel visa. The reason stated was that immigrant visa applicants couldn't also hold a travel visa – probably out of fear that those persons would simply not return when their allowed time was up.

Q and Hilde were suitably disappointed, but still hopeful. The drawing for the waiting numbers under the quota for Germany would take place later in the year and they decided to travel then. Meanwhile, they tried to live as normal a life as possible.

When *Gone with the Wind* came to the motion-picture theater, Hilde convinced Q to take her to the premiere. It had occupied the headlines for weeks, and all her friends wanted to see Scarlet O'Hara and Rhett Butler. It was a welcome distraction from dull reality.

Hilde was wearing a new two-piece dress with a fitted, pencil skirt, and a fitted jacket that fanned out below her waist like a short skirt. The long sleeves and deep burgundy color gave her skin a healthy glow. The matching three-inch heels made her feel like Scarlett herself.

She giggled and daydreamed about a dashing Rhett Butler carrying her away on his horse. She couldn't understand why Q thought the movie was silly.

"You truly didn't like it?" Hilde asked as they walked home.

"No. Scarlett was a selfish brat."

"Yes, but she endured so much – didn't you feel even a modicum of sympathy for her?" Hilde pouted.

"Not really. I agree that war is awful and she lost so much, but that doesn't excuse her behavior. Not in my book."

Hilde sighed and shook her head. "We'll just have to agree to disagree."

"Very well." Q paused and looked at her shoes. "Are you sure you want to walk home in those? We can always take a tram."

"No. It's such a lovely evening, and I need some fresh air."

"You look beautiful," he said, pulling her close to his side.

"Thank you." She tucked her handbag beneath her elbow and slipped her gloved hand in the crook of her husband's arm. The small hat she wore had a piece of netting that fell over the top to just below her eyes. This kind of netting was the current fashion and seemed to be showing up on most of the new hats this year.

She looked up at her husband and grinned. "You're looking rather dashing yourself this evening."

Q grinned back at her. "I can't let you receive all of the admiring looks, now can I?"

Hilde fingered the fabric of his new linen suit in a light heather grey. The pants were cuffed at the bottoms, and a large lapel adorned the jacket that Q had buttoned only once, in the middle. He'd paired the suit with a crisp white shirt and a white cravat tied around his neck, tucked into the neckline of the shirt.

As they readied themselves for bed, she said, "You definitely could give Rhett Butler a run for his money as far as looks go. Thanks for taking me to see the movie."

"Hmm. I might ask some favors in return." He pulled her into the bed beside him.

～

Hilde was still smiling the next day as she arrived at her office. She looked at her schedule to see she had a meeting with one of her biggest clients that morning. His industrial company produced lubricants and filters for machinery.

Herr Becker arrived, worrying his fingers; he fidgeted on the seat she offered him. This was not his usual behavior.

"Herr Becker, thanks for coming. It's been a long time, and I wanted to go over those statistics with you. The number of occupational accidents in your Berlin factory has soared recently."

"Frau Quedlin." The sturdy man in his fifties looked at her like a schoolboy caught in mischief and folded his hands. "We have already implemented measures to decrease the number, if this is what worries you."

Hilde looked straight into his brown eyes, and Herr Becker evaded her glance. "I'm sure you did. But what strikes me as unusual is that our insurance company settles only a fraction of those accidents. Are you not satisfied with us anymore?"

Herr Becker lowered his head. "No, it's not that." His voice fell to a whisper. "The Berlin factory has been assigned one thousand new workers."

Hilde smiled, pleased for his growing success. "Congratulations. That's excellent news." When the man's face fell, and his eyes took on a pained expression, she lowered her voice and leaned closer. "It isn't good news?"

"Not really." He leaned over the desk and whispered, "They're Czech workers."

She still didn't understand. "And...?"

Herr Becker sighed. "Workers displaced from the occupied territories forced to work for the *Reich*."

"You don't mean...?" Hilde gasped.

He sighed again, misery flashing across his face. "No. Look. I'd rather employ people working out of free will, but I don't have much choice. The authorities have raised my production quota, and without those Czech workers, I cannot reach it. There's just no way to find one thousand workers on the market." The man leaned back, intently studying the tips of his shoes.

Hilde took a few moments to process his words. It didn't make sense. "I understand why your occupational accidents have gone up, but why did the claims go down at the same time?"

Herr Becker coughed. "Because we don't insure them. They're

considered second class workers and get none of the benefits our own employees do." He was talking himself into a rage, and Hilde was glad that the colleague she shared the office with had called in sick for the day.

"Their working conditions are horrible. They get less payment and have to work longer hours. They have to do all the dangerous and dirty work, sometimes without the necessary instructions or protective gear. They live in camps. And the *Reichsarbeitsamt* requires me to give a weekly report on their performance and behavior. Anyone found lacking faces severe sanctions."

"Sanctions?" The blood left Hilde's face, and she felt a slight dizziness.

"Yes. The work office even provided me with special supervisors for them, and more than once, I saw one of the supervisors mistreating the workers. But my hands are bound. The only thing I can do is forbid punishment at the factory because of the implications for the general work safety. But what happens at the camp, I don't know. Some don't come back the next day."

Hilde stopped breathing altogether.

"If I don't reach the production quota, someone else will," Herr Becker added in a defeated voice.

Just then, her boss entered the room. Herr Becker jumped up and greeted the newcomer, "Heil Hitler."

"Herr Becker, I was told you were coming in today. How are those new workers doing?"

The despondency and complaints of a few moments ago changed before her eyes and Herr Becker answered with a loud and cheerful voice. "Having those workers has been a great addition to the cause. I can't thank the government enough for seeing the need and taking such prudent actions to help my company perform the best it can for the Reich."

"That is good to hear." Her boss glanced over at Hilde, and she quickly ducked her head. "Is Frau Quedlin taking care of your needs?"

Herr Becker readily came to her aid. "Yes, sir, she is an excellent representative of the company. Unfortunately for your company, we aren't required to insure the new workers."

"I know. Don't worry about that. If you need anything else from us, don't be afraid to let Frau Quedlin know. We all need to do our best for the Reich. Have a good day." Hilde watched her boss leave the office and then bid her goodbyes to Herr Becker.

She probably should have been shocked, but everyone kowtowed to the Nazi ideals when pressed. *Including myself.* While she never openly praised the government, she had long ago stopped saying anything negative in regards to the Nazis, Third Reich, and Hitler.

Like everyone here, she just wanted to survive.

# CHAPTER 16

DENIED.

Q stared down at the paper in his hands…his hopes and dreams burning to ashes. A letter from the United States Embassy with the concise message that his and Hilde's number hadn't been drawn in the immigrant visa number lottery. But they were encouraged to apply again next year.

*One year?*

That seemed like an eternity given the current conditions. Hilde was staring at him, and he cleared his throat before re-reading the letter to her. He wasn't fooled by her attempt to put on a brave face. The disappointment was too obvious.

"Well, it looks like we won't be travelling to America this summer. Nor will we make a permanent move anytime soon."

Hilde's eyes welled with tears as she nodded and he took her hand in his. "Maybe we should take another trip to Italy?"

"Yes, that would be something. See the places we didn't on our honeymoon." Hilde leaned against his back, looping her arms around him, and he knew she longed for the blissful time they'd spent away from Germany.

"I'll request the travel visa tomorrow. I guess I need to write Fanny and let her know we won't be visiting this year after all." Then he stood and headed for his office to grab pen and paper.

It took him a few minutes to tamp down his disappointment before he sat down to write his cousin a letter.

*Dearest Fanny,*

*I hope this letter finds you and your family in good health and spirits. I'm writing to bring you the unpleasant news that Hilde and I won't be visiting you this summer after all.*

*Fate has prevented us from taking the easy way out, as we did not get chosen to receive immigrant visas. I have to confess that Hilde and I were looking forward to the opportunity of fleeing to the comfortable security of America, but that is not to be at this time.*

*No, the powers that be have different plans for us. May I ask that you keep us in your thoughts and prayers as we continue to live out our lives here in the midst of this turmoil?*

*Your cousin,*

*Q*


He placed the letter in an envelope and then let Hilde know he was going to walk down and place it in the post. His mind was slowly adjusting to the reality of his future, and by the time he returned to their apartment, he had a new resolve.

His will to destroy the Nazi regime had weakened as he'd given way to the hope of leaving this fight to others, but now he found a new strength and resolve burning in his chest. *If it's my fate to stay here, then I will fight back however I can.*

"Hilde?" he called to her, watching as she came from the kitchen with a questioning look on her face.

"Q?"

"I've made a decision. I'm convinced that we're meant to stay here and do all in our power to destroy this regime from the inside."

Hilde nodded and joined him on the couch. "What's your plan?"

"How do you know I have a plan?"

She grinned. "You were out walking and thinking. When this happens, you always come back with a plan."

He put his arm around her shoulders and chuckled. "You know me too well, *Liebling*. I decided to take Harro Schulze-Boysen's advice and start looking for work inside the government. The best way to gain intelligence about the regime is to be intimately connected to the regime."

Hilde frowned, and he tried to put her mind at ease. "I will be careful, but this is something I need to do. It's something I can do."

~

Several days later, Hilde received a letter from Zurich, Switzerland. She turned it in her hand to decipher the sender's name. *Adam Eppstein*. It took her a few moments to remember who that was. Her former boss and head of treasury at the insurance company. He'd been fired back in 1933 for being Jewish, and she hadn't heard from him since that day.

*Esteemed Frau Quedlin,*

*I have to apologize for not writing earlier when we received notice of your matrimony. My wife and I have cut all ties to our former home country, but when we heard about the latest developments in Germany, I wanted to reach out to thank you.*

*I will never forget the day I was fired, and you were there for me, helping me to pack my things and giving me advice I didn't want to hear. You told me to take my family someplace else. Someplace safe.*

*It took me about one year to realize you were right. As much as I loved my home country, it had changed to the point where I couldn't raise my children there anymore.*

*In 1935, I finally found the courage to apply for a job in Switzerland. And after several months, the Zurich Kantonalbank offered me a position in their treasury department. My wife and I had difficulties adapting to the peculiar dialect they speak here, but our children now speak it like natives.*

*Leaving Germany has not been without its hardships. But every day we are thankful that we're here. The Swiss have been very good to us, and we have found many good friends.*

The letter paused, the ink dripping as if Adam Eppstein had become lost in his thoughts for a moment. As the letter continued, the handwriting was shaky, and Hilde had difficulties deciphering the next sentences.

*When we heard about the Kristallnacht, my wife had a nervous breakdown, so worried about her relatives, and mine, still living in Germany.*

*It took some time, but we eventually discovered that most of our male relatives were sent to labor camps.*

*My heart is torn as I write this letter. My family and I will always have you in our hearts and prayers. You truly were our guardian angel, and I believe without your assistance my life would have been forfeit many years ago.*

*I know things in Germany are getting worse, and I urge you to take all precautions and not to draw attention to yourself.*

*I hope someday in the future, we may meet again and I can thank you in person.*

*Your grateful friend,*
*Adam Eppstein*


Hilde folded the letter carefully, tears streaming down her cheeks. Her hands were shaking violently. Her stomach rebelled as fear and emotion surged through her. She tossed the letter to the small table sitting near the couch and placed her hand over her mouth, fighting the urge to vomit. But a few moments later, she kneeled over the toilet and emptied the contents of her stomach.

She rinsed her mouth out afterwards and wiped down her pale face with a damp rag, then made her way on wobbly legs to the bedroom, where she sank down on the edge of the mattress.

# CHAPTER 17

Over the next few weeks, Hilde continued to get sick. Not wanting to worry Q, she managed to keep most of her sickness from him and was convinced that stress and anxiety were the cause of her sporadic illness.

Some mornings she would wake and throw up before she could even dress for the day. Other times, she'd feel fine, until her stomach suddenly rebelled at the smell of food.

That pattern continued until the end of June, where she vomited every single morning and then worsened. When she'd felt sick all day long, every day for five consecutive days, she made an appointment with the doctor for that afternoon.

Several hours later, she left the doctor's office, conflicting emotions raging through her body. At home she impatiently waited for Q, waiting to share the news.

"I had an appointment this afternoon," Hilde assailed him with as soon as he opened the door.

"A new client?" Q asked.

"No…the meeting wasn't at work. I actually didn't go to work today."

Q looked up at her then. "You didn't go to work? Are you sick?"

Hilde shook her head, hiding the smile that wanted to break across her face. "I haven't been feeling well lately, and it seemed to get significantly worse this morning." She held up a hand when Q started to speak. "I'm all right. I went to the doctor. That was the appointment I spoke of."

"What was his diagnosis?" Q searched her eyes, and Hilde found she couldn't continue this small word game a moment longer.

She cupped his jaw. "His diagnosis...in six months, you're going to be a father." She watched his eyes go from concern to disbelief. He looked down at her still flat stomach, placing a hand there reverently as the reality of her words took shape in his mind.

"A baby? You're pregnant?" he asked in a hushed voice.

Hilde nodded. "I know the timing is bad–"

"Never! I'm going to be a father!" Q exclaimed, pulling her to her feet and dancing her around the living room. "This is the happiest news ever!"

Hilde laughed and giggled as he swung her around and then kissed her soundly.

"Stop!" she shouted, and as soon as he set her down on her feet she dashed to the bathroom.

Q came after her and held a washcloth for her. "I'm sorry. What did the doctor say about the way you've been feeling?"

Hilde cleaned herself and answered. "Morning sickness. The doctor said it may go away, but every pregnancy is different."

Several weeks later, the all-day sickness had receded to a mild morning sickness. Hilde was still able to work, but by the time she returned home each afternoon, she was exhausted and needed a nap.

After lengthy discussions, Q had convinced her not to travel to Italy, but to stay home for the summer. She was fine with that but needed some sort of break in her normal routine.

Q must have noticed her discontent. "Hilde, what if we invited your sisters to spend some time with us here during summer vacation?"

"I guess we could," Hilde said.

"You always have so much fun when you girls get together. Why don't you invite them to the city? You can take your vacation time and relax a bit."

Hilde smiled tiredly. "That's a good idea. Maybe if I could relax for a bit, this sickness would get better." She slipped down in the covers, then added, "But I don't want them to know I'm pregnant. We haven't told any of our family yet."

"That decision is up to you." Q kissed her on the nose and then wrapped his arm around her.

Hilde nodded, and the next morning called her parents to invite her sisters. Julia, unfortunately, couldn't visit because she'd been sent to a farm in Mecklenburg with the *Reichsarbeitsdienst*, a compulsory labor service for high school graduates. But Sophie was overjoyed with the invitation, and they made arrangements for her to travel as soon as the school year ended.

At work, Hilde informed her boss that she wanted to take her vacation time as planned after all, and he wished her a relaxing time off. Q helped her ready their apartment for her sister's arrival. When the day arrived, she met Sophie at the train station.

"You're here," Hilde said, hugging her sister tight for a long moment.

"I'm so excited! Thank you for inviting me. I was bored at home. Julia is gone, and Father says I'm too young to join the *Bund Deutscher Mädel*. Julia is only four years older than me." Sophie's eyes glinted.

Hilde smiled and looped her arm with her sister's. "Is that your only piece of luggage?" she asked, referring to the small suitcase her sister carried.

"Yes. I'm ready to go have some fun. And do some shopping."

Hilde smiled. "Lunch and then shopping." The two girls had a quick lunch of soup and a sandwich at a small restaurant. After lunch, they wandered through the shops and then made plans to visit a few museums and art galleries.

Over the next days, Hilde and Sophie moved about Berlin, shared laughter, and did all the entertaining things teenagers would do. Q had to work, but he joined them in the evenings and on weekends. It was almost as carefree as before Hitler came to power.

More than once, he told Hilde that he was ever so relieved to have Sophie around to take care of her. And just like that, her morning sickness abated. One day it stopped, and Hilde hadn't even noticed.

On Hilde's twenty-seventh birthday on August 23, Q surprised his two women with tickets to visit the open air musical *Der Mond* by Carl

Orff. It was an opera-like production, based on the fairy tale *The Moon* by The Brothers Grimm.

After the last applause ebbed away, the three of them gathered their things to walk to Q's car.

Hilde looped her arm into her husband's and swooned over the beautiful music and the opulent stage designs. "Thank you, my love. This was such a wonderful birthday present."

Q couldn't answer because someone called out his name. "Wilhelm Quedlin!"

They stopped to see a man in a dark suit walking toward them. Hilde raised a brow at her husband, but he didn't seem in the least worried. Instead, he waved a greeting. "Erhard Tohmfor, I haven't seen you since we left the University."

"Yes, Q. Good to see you. How have you been?"

"I've been fine. Erhard, may I introduce you to my wife, Hilde, and her sister, Sophie."

"Ladies, it's a pleasure to make your acquaintance." Erhard Tohmfor kissed the hand of both women and explained, "Q and I go all the way back to first-semester chemistry."

"It's true," Q said, "but somehow we lost contact when we started our doctorates in different departments."

"I would love to catch up, but I don't want to take any more time from your evening out. Why don't we go to lunch one day next week?" Erhard suggested.

"Sounds fine with me. How about Monday at noon?" Q mentioned a restaurant near the department store *Kaufhaus des Westens*, and Erhard smiled and promised to meet him there at noon. He bid his goodbyes and Q escorted the two women home.

# CHAPTER 18

M onday arrived, and Q entered the restaurant to meet Erhard. The place offered a choice of three lunch specials and was crowded with people taking advantage of the offer. Q chose a goulash with boiled potatoes, Erhard ordered *Kassler* with sauerkraut. When the waitress delivered their meals, each one paid his share and Q inhaled deeply. "That smells delicious, doesn't it?"

Erhard already had his fork lifted, ready to dig in. "Yes. I'll bet it tastes even better. I'm hungry as a wolf."

"So, tell me, what are you doing for work?" Q asked Erhard after taking a hearty bite.

Erhard chewed and swallowed a piece of *Kassler*, groaning in pleasure at the taste of the smoked pork chop before answering, "I'm working for Loewe Radio."

Q raised a brow. Loewe Radio produced all kinds of advanced radio equipment for the military, but they were also the manufacturer of the *Volksempfänger*, a small and affordable radio designed for everyone's use. He grinned at the memory of how he'd bought one of the first ones several years ago and *enhanced* it to receive short waves. The good old *Volksempfänger* still served him well, including bringing in strictly forbidden foreign radio stations.

"My, my. You certainly work for an *interesting* company."

"Yes. It's wonderful. I started there in 1934 and was just recently promoted to the manager of the chemical laboratory. We have the most advanced technology at our fingertips and enough money for research." Erhard beamed and went on to talk about their research in the field of radio engineering. "We're currently working to bring motion pictures into the homes of the people with our *Einheits-Fernseh-Empfänger E1.*"

Q had heard about the E1, which was similar to the *Volksempfänger* radio, but with images. This modern device was also called television, and up until now, it had been prohibitively expensive for normal people.

"Congratulations," Q said. "Sounds like you enjoy your job." *Unlike me.* Apparently, Erhard didn't have to bother about budget cuts and diversion of research to military purposes.

"Yes, I do. There's so much going on right now. The E1 is for everyone, but apart from that, we're working on pioneering technology. Wireless transmission. Remote controls. Position tracking via sound waves. It's a scientist's paradise." Erhard gestured with his hands and Q was transported back to their university days.

They'd shared the same communist ideals and dreams for the future. While the scientist part of his brain understood Erhard's enthusiasm for the new technology, the humanist part felt betrayed. "You've changed," Q said.

Erhard lifted an eyebrow. "How so?"

"You're working for the regime. That's a betrayal of what you used to believe in. Peace. Equality. Freedom. Everything your company does is geared towards war, even the E1!" Q had raised his voice and pushed his empty plate away.

Erhard gave him a sharp look and then looked around the restaurant. "Not here. Wait a few minutes and then follow me."

Q's jaw dropped when Erhard rose from the table and wandered down the hallway leading towards the kitchen. Curious, he waited the prescribed minutes before following the man he'd shared so many things in common with years earlier.

Erhard was waiting for him and pulled him out a rear door, into the alleyway behind the restaurant. He looked around. They were alone. "Are you still a *Gesinnungsfreund?*"

Q gave his friend a searching look. "Are you asking if I still share the same opinions as I did when we were at university?"

When Erhard nodded, Q said, "Yes. My opinions haven't changed."

"Well, neither have mine." Erhard paused and then explained softly, "I thoroughly enjoyed the research work I'm able to do at Loewe. But when the company was Aryanized last year, and the owners had to emigrate to America, I wanted to quit."

"So why didn't you?" Q asked, pressing his lips together.

"Because I was offered the position to oversee the entire chemical laboratories and the production process."

Q squinted his eyes and Erhard held up a hand. "Now, before you judge me, listen carefully. I took this position because it gives me the opportunity to work against the government by sabotaging the production of military equipment."

"What?" Q's brain needed a few moments to process Erhard's words. The man standing in front of him was doing the very thing Schulze-Boysen had suggested. Corrupting the regime from within.

Both men stood in silence until Q found his voice again. "I'm sorry I misjudged you, my friend."

"No harm done," Erhard answered. He looked around again before turning back to Q, searching his eyes for a while. He exhaled deeply before going on, "I could really use someone in the laboratory. A scientist, but also someone I can trust to do the right things."

When the door opened, and several employees stepped out into the alley, Erhard and Q turned and walked towards the street. They continued walking in silence for almost a block before Q looked at his friend and asked, "Can I sleep on it?"

Erhard nodded. "But don't wait too long because–"

His sentence was halted when two Gestapo officers stopped directly in their path. "Papers!" they demanded. Despite the August heat, they were dressed in long black leather coats and jackboots.

Erhard turned and saluted them with the *Hitlergruss*, Q following likewise, clenching his jaw. The Gestapo officers scrutinized his and Erhard's papers thoroughly before handing them back.

But instead of letting them go, the taller officer seemed to enjoy the change in his routine and started to ask question after question. "Where do you work?"

"Loewe. We produce radio equipment for the Wehrmacht," Erhard said and presented his employee badge.

"And you?" The other officer nodded at Q.

"I work for the Biological Reichs Institute," Q answered, handing over his own employee card. His neck hair stood on end at the prospect that these officers were bored and looking for trouble.

"Why are you two wandering around Berlin instead of working?" the officer with the soulless grey eyes asked.

"Your behavior is very suspicious," his partner added,

Q swallowed hard and glanced at Erhard, who didn't seem in the least intimidated by the Gestapo. Erhard lowered his voice conspiratorially and said, "You are very observant. My partner and I are on a secret mission, penned by the Führer himself, to find enemy radio senders."

Q blinked at the blatant lie, but Erhard even produced a simple voltmeter from his pocket and showed it to the officers. *A voltmeter? To find a radio sender? If those men have even a modicum of grey cells, they'll know this is bullshit.*

But the men's eyes were glued to Erhard's lips as he explained the operating mode of this advanced technical device, sprinkling in just enough technical gibberish to keep them confused. Both officers tried their best to act as if they understood everything he was telling them and actually thanked Erhard for his important work.

Q silently laughed at the men's gullibility as they finally left, even saluting Erhard as if he were someone very important. He managed to hold his tongue until the officers were a fair distance away before turning to his friend with a nod and a smile. "Very well done, my friend."

"That was refreshing, wasn't it?" Erhard chuckled.

Before they said goodbye, Erhard held him back. "Be careful, my friend. There has been a huge surge in military contracts at Loewe in the last few months, and they all point to September. So far the war has been easy on us, but something much bigger is coming. Something the English and the French can't ignore."

Q nodded. "This I believe. Not because I have knowledge like you do, but it's a feeling in the air."

"One more reason to work for Loewe. You would be in a reserved profession. Protected somewhat even, as you've just seen."

"I need to speak to Hilde about this. I will be in touch, I promise."

Erhard gave him a hard look and then relaxed. "I understand. I look forward to hearing from you soon."

Q took his time returning home from work later that day. The conversation with Erhard weighed heavily on his mind, and he'd thought through things a thousand times. Now he needed to speak with Hilde.

As he entered the apartment, bursting with the urge to communicate, Hilde and Sophie were in the process of preparing dinner in the kitchen. He gritted his teeth and said hello. What followed was an endless chitchat about their day as they ate, interrupted with a question here and there about his meeting with Erhard.

Q bit his tongue. This wasn't for young ears. After eating, he excused himself and retreated to his study. Pretending to work, he listened to the noises in the apartment until – finally – he heard the door of the guestroom close and steps approach his study.

Hilde peeked inside. "Sophie is asleep."

"Good." He all but jumped out of his chair.

"What's wrong with you?" Hilde asked, but Q shook his head and grabbed her hand. "Come for a walk with me."

Hilde grabbed an auburn cardigan from the hook by the door and pulled it over her short-sleeved summer blouse before following him outside. It was well after ten o'clock, and the moon was casting a dim light onto the deserted street. Q increased his pace, pulling her behind him until they came to a vacant bench.

"Sit," he told her but made no attempt to join her.

"Q, you're starting to worry me," she said and stood again. "You've been anxious since you came home."

"I want you to send Sophie home. Tomorrow."

She took a step backwards, her hand going to her throat. "What? Why? We're having so much fun together."

He pressed his lips together. "I need for you to trust me on this and send her home. First thing in the morning."

Hilde looked at her husband, crossed her arms over her chest, and shook her head. "Not unless you tell me why."

Q looked at her. "I don't want to have to explain myself…"

"Well, if you expect me to send my sister home tomorrow, you had better do so. I'm sick of your secretive behavior. You think I didn't notice your sneaking out at night, the hushed phone calls, the hidden papers in your study, and your growing agitation? I'm not stupid, you know."

He sighed. "No, you're not." He wrapped her in his arms, kissing her hair. "I wanted to protect you. With you carrying our child and your sister here, I just wanted to give you a carefree summer."

Hilde leaned into his chest. "That's sweet of you, my love, but how can I be carefree if I sense your anxiety? Tell me what's wrong."

Q looked at her for several long moments before he forced his breath out and said, "War is about to start."

"War?" She shook her head, looking confused. "We've been in one war or another since the annexation of Austria one and a half years ago."

"Yes. But something big is coming. A real war. Bad and ugly. My old friend Erhard Tohmfor confirmed my own suspicions today."

"When?" Hilde whispered.

"Very soon. Sophie needs to go home. Immediately. Please?"

Hilde nodded. "I'll take her to the train station first thing in the morning. There's a morning train to Hamburg…" Tears glistened, then spilled down her cheeks. "Oh, Q, it's really going to happen?" It broke his heart to see the fear in her eyes.

"I'm afraid so. Sophie will be much safer with her parents than she would be with us in the capital."

The next morning, they explained to a very disappointed Sophie that she had to cut her stay in Berlin short and return to Hamburg immediately. Hilde helped Sophie pack and Q drove them to the train station.

As Hilde waved goodbye to her sister, Q saw the tears stream down her cheeks. "We'll see her again," he assured his wife.

A few days later, on September 3, 1939, France and England declared war against Germany after Hitler's invasion of Poland on the first.

# CHAPTER 19

By November, normal life had become a distant memory. In hindsight, Q could easily identify the cornerstones of the carefully planned attack on Poland. Just three days prior to that date, the German government had instituted ration cards.

From then on, everything a person needed to survive – including food, textiles, and commodities – was being rationed. Each household, depending upon the number of people living there, was given a *Lebens-mitelkarte*.

Q had to give the government credit for that. It was a clever move to handle the panic they knew would ensue as Germany entered into *total war*, and at the same time, it prevented hoarding of food.

As soon as Sophie left for Hamburg, Q told Hilde about the job offer from Erhard – and the subversive tasks coming with it. As always, she supported him in his fight against Hitler's regime, but he could tell that she still wished they'd gotten their immigrant visas for America.

Armed with the employment contract from Loewe, Q entered the labor bureau and sat on one of the wooden benches in the long, empty hallway. A cleaning lady came along, mopping the floor until it sparkled.

In stark contrast to five years ago, the hallways were empty. The Nazis had achieved full employment of the German workforce. *But at what cost?* Q fisted his hands. This charade was ridiculous!

The door next to him opened, and a man with horn-rimmed glasses called him inside, gesturing for Q to take a seat after exchanging the obligatory Hitlergruss. The room was furnished with wooden desks, chairs, and cabinets that had seen better days. On the wall behind the desk hung a portrait of Hitler, flanked by two swastika flags. A shiver ran down Q's spine, and he grabbed his briefcase tighter.

"You're looking for a job?" the official asked with a friendly smile.

"No, sir. I came here to ask permission to quit my job at the Biological Reich Institute and–"

The smile disappeared. "Papers!"

Q retrieved the papers from his briefcase and handed them to the official, who studied them for a long time.

"Doctor Quedlin, your request is highly unusual. Why do you want to quit your current position at the Institute?"

"Sir, as you've seen from my papers, Loewe offered me a position to oversee research and development of radio technology–"

"Yes, I can see that," the middle-aged man snapped. "But if everyone in critical industries changed their positions whenever they wanted, we could never win the war."

*Of course. Hard-boiled Nazi.* "Sir, I understand your concern. The labor bureau has a much better knowledge of the needs of our Fatherland than the single worker. And I would never dream of quitting the job I have so wisely been assigned to. I came to you to gain clarity, whether the position at Loewe will allow me to make a better contribution to the war effort."

The smile returned to the official's face. "It's a rare occurrence for scientists like you to accept the superiority of knowledge of the labor bureau."

Q's eye twitched, but he forced a pleasant smile on his lips. "Thank you."

"Now explain how your new position is of use for the Führer and Fatherland." The official leaned back in his chair and folded his hands, watching Q attentively.

"The position I have been offered from Loewe would enable me to work directly on projects to benefit the Wehrmacht and ultimately the safety of our soldiers. Now that we are at war, this should be my first concern and the work in plant protection – albeit important – must take second priority."

The official leaned forward, enthusiasm in his voice. "The war will soon be over. Poland was conquered in four weeks. Next will be the French. They will be just as easy to defeat. And our Führer has plans for more."

Q didn't happen to agree but nodded nonetheless. "Aren't you worried about Stalin?"

"No, of course not. Our governments signed the non-aggression treaty and the Soviet Union has served us well dividing Poland."

Bile rose in Q's throat. The Soviet Union had been touted as an enemy of Germany for many years, and now suddenly they were best friends.

While Q was dealing with his emotions, the official put the required stamps on his employment contract and handed it back with a smile. "Do well for the regime, Doctor Quedlin."

"Thank you, sir." Q stuffed the papers into his briefcase and left the room, a sick feeling in his stomach.

Back at the Biological Reich Institute, he handed his approved written notice to the director, and a huge weight fell from his shoulders. At Loewe, he would be able to do something more meaningful.

Ever since Hilde had told him she was expecting their first child, an unexpected anxiety had taken hold of him. Money.

If something happened to him, he wanted to have the assurance that Hilde and the baby could live comfortably without his income. She'd grown used to a modest amount of luxury, and he didn't want her to have to skimp.

With that in mind, he had intensified his effort to sell the commercial rights to another one of his patents. Surprisingly, it wasn't all that hard because with the war in full mode, the companies were lining up for the lucrative military contracts and some of his patents in the area of gas detection had become very sought after.

As he returned home, Hilde awaited him with a letter in hand. She looked even more beautiful now with her rounded belly, rosy cheeks, and shiny hair. Q kissed her mouth and her stomach, saying hello to mother and child, then took the letter from her.

Despite her protests, he retreated to his study to open it. He hesitated a few moments with a pounding heart before he meticulously slid open the envelope with the letter opener his mother had given him as a wedding gift.

Moments later, he stormed into the living room and stopped short in front of Hilde, carefully lifting her up and twirling her in one circle.

Hilde giggled. "Good news?"

"Yes, *Liebling*. Drägerwerke agreed to buy another one of my patents for the modest sum of...drum rolls... twenty-five thousand Reichsmark."

"Twenty-five?" Hilde furrowed her brows and mentally calculated, "That's...oh, my! That's more than a five-year salary for you."

Q puffed out his chest. "I know. It's incredible, isn't it? I'll call your father to ask how to best invest the money. I want it to be there for you and the baby in case something happens to me."

Hilde's eyes clouded over. "Nothing will happen to you, my love. Don't jinx it."

"You're right," he said. "But I want this money to be our assets of last resort. With this war raging on, you never know."

After dinner, Hilde sat down to rest and knit a coat for the baby. Q retreated to his study and placed a phone call to his father-in-law.

They exchanged a few pleasantries and then Q cut to the chase. "Carl, may I ask you a question about taxes?"

"Certainly. Although I'm more experienced in tax laws for companies and not for individuals."

"It seems I'll receive a modest sum of money for one of my patents."

Carl chuckled into the phone. "How modest exactly? Small amounts are tax exempt."

"Twenty-five thousand," Q said, and picked up the letter opener, rubbing the amethyst stone with his thumb. According to his mother, amethyst was his lucky stone.

"Congratulations–" Carl said, but Q cut him short.

"No, don't. Not before I actually hold the money in my hands."

Carl laughed. "Fine. With that amount, you have to pay the complete additional war tax of five percent. Apart from that, I don't think there are further tax implications."

Q shook his head. "I wonder what's coming next? On top of extra taxes and food ration cards, you must ask for permission to change your job, and getting a travel permit is next to impossible."

"Everyone says it'll soon be over," Carl said.

"That's what they want us to believe." Q rubbed the amethyst again.

"So, how do you plan to use that money?" his father-in-law asked.

"Well, Hilde and I have discussed this. I think we should spend a small part of it buying high-quality things that will keep their value, even if we get another hyperinflation."

"Good idea. Like what?" Carl inquired.

"Jewelry and antique furniture were the two things that have come to our minds." Q grinned at the memory of the sparkle in Hilde's eyes at the mention of jewelry.

Carl exhaled loudly, and Q imagined him puffing out smoke. Carl probably had lit a cigarette as he settled in his chair to take the phone call. "Those are sound choices. You should also invest in gold coins. Now, mind you, you'll need to purchase them as secretly as possible and keep them hidden in a very safe place. I would suggest burying them somewhere."

"We don't have a garden, and I wouldn't want to bury them anyplace where someone else might find them. Or we could bury them in your garden... In case something happens to Hilde and me."

Carl raised his voice. "Enough of that depressing talk. Nothing will happen to you. Neither of you is a Wehrmacht soldier."

Q pressed his lips together. Even though the country was at war, almost everyone pretended nothing had changed. *Maybe people needed this form of denial to cope with the danger?* "But people are worried. Some of my colleagues in Berlin spent their summer vacations and weekends helping out for free at the farms outside the city."

"Yes, the same thing here in Hamburg. They want to secure connections if food becomes scarce," Carl said, sounding pensive. "I can still feel the hunger years after the Great War in my bones. That was an experience I don't want to repeat, and I certainly don't want my girls to have to live through it."

"One more reason to invest our money safely. Thank you for your advice. Hilde and I will certainly treat this blessing carefully, should it come to fruition."

"Is there a chance it might not?" Carl asked.

"In these days and times, anything can happen."

"Well, I'll keep my fingers crossed. Are you still planning to come up for Christmas?"

"Yes. I need to buy train tickets because of the fuel rationing." Q grimaced and scribbled a note on a piece of paper.

"Let us know what day and time you will be arriving, and we'll meet you at the train station."

"We will. Thank you again. See you soon."

# CHAPTER 20

Hilde shifted in her seat, trying to find a comfortable position. The train rattled through the countryside towards Hamburg. The fields were dusted with white frost and wafts of mist gave the landscape a mysterious appearance.

"I hope we'll get snow for Christmas like we did last year," she said and leaned against Q's shoulder.

"Statistically, Northern Germany has had a white Christmas every ten years over the past fifty years," Q answered, and she boxed him in the chest. He chuckled at her and glanced at her immense belly. "See the positive side. In your current state, you wouldn't want to shovel snow."

"No. But I would want to sit behind the window with a hot cup of tea, watching my husband do it." She giggled and then pressed a hand to the side of her stomach.

"What's wrong, *Liebling*?" Q asked with a worried tone.

"Nothing. Just the baby kicking me again." Hilde breathed and took the hand off her belly to reveal a protruding bump the size of a baby foot dancing across it. "Look, it's moving."

Q chased the bump with his hand and chuckled.

"I hope it'll decide to be born sooner rather than later," Hilde said with a tired voice. In her last month of pregnancy, she felt like a walrus and every movement had become cumbersome.

Q's eyes took on a look of panic. "The baby isn't due for two more weeks. I told you it wasn't prudent to travel to Hamburg. What if you go into labor early? Here on the train?"

Hilde laughed away his concern. "We've discussed this at length already. The journey takes only a couple of hours. And the midwives in Hamburg are as good as the ones in Berlin should our pumpkin decide to arrive early."

At the train station in Hamburg, they exited the train, and her father met them on the platform. He gave Hilde a big hug and an appreciative glance. "My little daughter has grown up. And soon you'll be a mother yourself."

Her stepmother, Emma, had already prepared dinner for them. The next morning, everyone helped to decorate the tree for Christmas Eve – mouth-blown glass bowls from the Ore Mountains, hand-made straw stars in several forms and colors. As a finishing touch, Carl decorated the fir tree with real candles – used ones from last Christmas, but candles nonetheless.

Even though Hilde's half-sisters, Julia and Sophie, were much too old to believe the *Christkind* angel brought the presents the family still pretended it existed. It was one of the coveted traditions nobody wanted to give up.

But this year it was difficult to get into the spirit of the season. The war hovered over the country like a black shadow, ready to swoop down and wreak havoc. Emma collected everyone's ration cards, including the extra cards Hilde received because she was pregnant, and managed to put together a veritable Christmas feast.

"Full-fat milk! This is a gift from heaven," Emma exclaimed as she scrutinized Hilde's extra rations.

"That skim milk we mere mortals are allowed to buy is absolutely awful," Q said in agreement. "I'm convinced they've watered it down in addition to removing the fat and cream."

Emma smiled. "Q, would you go to the pantry and fetch me a bar of chocolate that I've hidden on the top shelf?"

When he came back with the chocolate in hand, Hilde's mouth watered. It was so hard to get these little indulgences nowadays. But

Emma took it from his hands and melted it in a double boiler. Soon the smell of melted chocolate filled the house and one by one, every family member showed up in the kitchen.

Emma poured the full-fat milk into the melted chocolate and whipped up a delicious chocolate pudding for their dessert. Then she put it in the pantry to cool down, locked the door, and hid the key in the pocket of her apron. "This is for tonight. Now, everyone get ready for Mass."

After church, Sophie jumped up and down. "Can we open gifts now?"

Everyone laughed and Carl chimed a tiny bell. The family gathered around the tree and opened their presents. Most of the gifts Hilde received were things for the unborn baby. Home-knitted rompers, diapers, a woolen blanket, and small boots to insulate tiny feet against the winter cold.

She thanked everyone before turning her attention to the large box Q had carried with them on the train. He'd been very secretive and had teased her about her curiosity.

"Open it, sister," Sophie urged enthusiastically.

Hilde smiled and pulled back the wrapping around the box. When she opened it, she gasped in delight. Inside lay an expensive fur coat with a matching scarf and leather gloves.

"Let me help you try it on," Q said, setting the box on the floor and pulling her to her feet. He retrieved the coat from the box and helped her slide her arms in, but with her bulging belly, it wouldn't even come close to covering her.

Everyone laughed. "Your baby needs to come soon so you can enjoy your gift," Julia said with a grin.

Hilde kissed Q. "Thank you. It's so beautiful. And warm. I'll wear it as soon as our child is born."

The days wore on, and Hilde enjoyed the time with her sisters and – surprisingly – with Emma. The more time she spent with her stepmother, the more she came to like her.

～

Q enjoyed the time off before he started work at Loewe in January 1940. He and Carl retreated frequently into the older man's study to smoke a cigar or cigarette and discuss politics.

Q said, "I don't buy into the official propaganda that the war will be over in no time at all."

"But the conquest of Poland went so smoothly. Maybe Hitler will stop at that," Carl argued.

"I doubt it. Not every country is going to fold like Poland did. And Hitler will only be satisfied when he's conquered all of Europe." *And more.*

Carl clenched his fist and raised it in the air. "I hate these damn Nazis! I feel so powerless. I wish there was something I could do."

For a short moment, Q was tempted, but he bit his tongue. It was too dangerous to tell his father-in-law the truth about his new job. The small measure of satisfaction Carl would get from knowing wasn't worth the risk of Q's secret getting out. He changed the subject, "How does Sophie like school this year?"

"She hates it. Since the war started, the quality of instruction has declined rapidly. Most of the young teachers were drafted, leaving only the ones nearing retirement."

"And Julia?" Q inquired.

Carl looked angry and then resigned. "She started *Reichsarbeitsdienst* this summer. She says she wasn't meant to become a farmer, but what can she or I do? She'll be there for a year…maybe the hard work will be good for her."

Q highly doubted that, but he held his tongue.

The discussion turned to their planned travel to America. "How did your cousin take the notice that you couldn't come to visit?" Carl asked.

"She was disappointed, as we were. But in hindsight, I can see that if we had journeyed to America to visit Fanny, we wouldn't have come back because of the war's breaking out."

He and Hilde had discussed this fact many times. They would have lost all ability to communicate with their families – and to return home. "It seems the gods had different plans for us."

Carl picked up on the unexplained statement and asked, "Plans?"

Q glanced at his father-in-law but laughed it off. "Just a figure of speech, Carl."

# CHAPTER 21

Hilde looked down at the baby in her arms with wonder in her eyes. She'd given birth to a bouncing baby boy several hours earlier, and like all mothers, she was filled with joy.

"What shall we name him?" she asked Q, who sat beside her on the bed.

"We discussed several names, but I still like Volker."

Hilde smiled and nodded. "I like that name as well." She looked down at the tiny infant and ran a finger down his cheek. "Do you like that name, little one? Volker? It is yours."

The bell rang, and Q got up to open the door for the visitors. Hilde heard muffled voices and footsteps growing louder. Then a happy voice called from the doorway. "Knock, knock."

Hilde looked up to see her friends, Gertrud and Erika. "Come in and meet Volker."

Gertrud leaned over with her huge belly and hugged Hilde. "He's perfect," she said and added, "I'm so envious. I have another eight weeks to go."

"Time passes quickly. You'll see," Hilde assured her friend.

Then it was Erika's turn to hug the young mum and her baby. "Congratulations. You're not going back to work anytime soon, are you?" she asked.

Hilde shook her head. "No, I don't want to go back to work for at least a year. I don't trust anyone to care for my pumpkin."

"Good. You need to have another child soon for the Führer. My husband and I are already planning on a third one."

Hilde shivered. *God help me if I produce children for the Führer.*

Erika had been completely taken in by the Nazis since she married a dashing young SS-Officer, Reiner Huber, son of the well-known SS-Obersturmbannführer Wolfgang Huber. Their wedding one year ago had made the gossip columns, and Hitler himself had sent his congratulations.

"You should have named him Adolf. That would have been an honorable name," Erika continued, and Hilde exchanged an eye roll with Gertrud. Erika's love for everything Nazi bordered on the ridiculous. She'd even named her three-month-old twins Adolfine and Germania.

Hilde hid her face and turned her attention back to Volker while Erika continued to praise the regime. "Have you heard about the Führer's new plans to rid Germany of the inferior Jews and Eastern European races?"

Both Gertrud and Hilde groaned but didn't dare interrupt Erika's flow of words. Finally, Gertrud spoke up and reminded Erika that mother and son needed to rest.

When Q came back into the room after the women left, he saw the concern in Hilde's eyes. "What's wrong, *Liebling*?"

"Nothing. It's just…Erika. She used to be my best friend and now all she talks about is Nazi rubbish. It saddens me."

Q sat down on the bed and fondled her cheek. "Don't feel guilty. You can't do anything to change her mind."

"I know." Hilde sighed. "But she drains my energy. I'd rather not see her again."

"Then don't," Q said.

*If it were only that easy.*

A few days later, her mother and stepfather visited. Annie showered her grandson with compliments. "See how cute he is with his bright blue eyes and the light blond curls. He looks just like his father." Then she leaned over to take Volker in her arms, but stopped midway, holding the baby in the air with both hands, as if offering him to someone.

Annie's eyes took on a puzzled look in her struggle to figure out how to hold her newborn grandson.

"Mother, just hold him close. Support his head and don't squeeze him too tightly," Hilde suggested.

Annie attempted to follow Hilde's instructions but was confronted with another problem: baby drool. She desperately tried to hold him close while at the same time keeping his mouth turned away from her immaculate white blouse.

She gave up after a few tries and handed him back to Hilde. "You hold the baby. I can appreciate him better from over here."

Hilde bit her tongue as the almost forgotten pain of being abandoned by her mother came rushing back and compressed her chest. Now that she was a mother herself, the mere thought of giving her child to someone else stabbed her heart.

"Well, you should both get some rest," Annie said only a few minutes after her arrival. "We'll see you both later."

Later that day, when she told Q about her visitors, Q chuckled. "That's just like Annie. I guess she'll never change."

They were sitting together on the couch, Q's arm resting around her shoulders while Volker slept like an angel in his crib. Hilde sighed. "I wish Father and Emma could be here."

"I know. But Hamburg is too far to travel for a quick visit. Especially with all the travel restrictions in place. But we can send them pictures."

"Yes." Hilde snuggled up against him. "You know, now I can see how good a person Emma is. She's done her best to be a mother to me; I just didn't want to accept it back then."

"Yes, Emma is a good person, and she's done a good job raising you," Q said, but Hilde had already dozed off in his arms. He carefully spread her out on the couch and covered her with a blanket.

She moved and murmured in her sleep, "I just wish my own mother was more like Emma."

266

# CHAPTER 22

As winter gave way to spring, and the time approached for them to apply for immigrant visas again, Q and Hilde decided to forego it. Their place was in Germany.

Q had begun working at Loewe as head of production. From the first day on, he and Erhard had weekly meetings every Monday to discuss "quality control" of production. Usually, they conducted this meeting in Erhard's office behind closed doors, but at times they had to inspect the production lines and the laboratories. At those times they talked in code.

Erhard would raise his eyebrows and mention that the defective goods rate was too high, and Q knew it was time to think of a way to raise it even further. If Erhard insisted he make sure certain spare parts arrived in time for a particular project, Q knew he was to delay the order and explain it away as a change in the technical requirements.

Soon enough, they ate lunch together and discussed everybody and his brother, but mostly politics. Q enjoyed those lunch breaks because Erhard was the only person – apart from his wife – with whom he could be candid. A refreshing change in an environment where he'd had to watch his every word for so many years and never voice his true opinions.

One day during their lunch break, Erhard said, "Q, we need more help."

"Why? It would be an added risk."

Erhard sighed. "The director called me into his office last night. He wants to promote me to his personal assistant starting next month."

"Congratulations," Q said with thinned lips, looking anything but pleased.

"I know, it's less than ideal because I will be tied up with administrative tasks and can't help much with our cause. But if I decline the offer, I will draw suspicion and might be of even less use."

"Then I'll do it alone," Q said.

Erhard shook his head. "No. You can't oversee everything on your own. And in many cases, you need a second signature for certain activities."

"I can still get your signature," Q stubbornly insisted. "Besides, we don't know whom we can trust. It would put our entire cause at risk."

"Shithead," Erhard murmured.

"I heard that!" Q growled, and Erhard sent him a crooked smile.

"Let's give it a few more weeks and then discuss this again," Erhard suggested.

"Very well. I'll get these things taken care of." Q packed up his empty lunch box and left the room.

Later that week, Q and Hilde took baby Volker to Q's mother. At seventy-four years old, Ingrid had trouble walking and rarely left her apartment these days. But she loved Volker and the baby adored his grandmama.

That night, she'd agreed to watch over the infant so Q and Hilde could go out with Q's friends to the moving pictures. Hilde fussed over Volker, distressed over the idea of leaving him for even a couple of hours.

Q and his mother exchanged looks behind her back and Ingrid said, "Hilde, sweetheart, it may have been a while, but I raised four children."

"And she helped to raise my brother's four children as well," Q added.

Hilde reluctantly put Volker in Ingrid's arms. "I know, but it's the first time I've left him."

Ingrid skillfully hugged Volker to her chest and smiled at Hilde. "You two go out and have fun. Volker and I will do the same."

Q had already opened the door when Hilde turned again and gave Volker one last kiss on his head. "If he cries, he's hungry. I have put a bottle of milk in the kitchen, and it needs to be heated. But not too hot. You have to measure the temperature against the skin on your wrist–"

Ingrid laughed. "Sweetie, you go and have fun. Volker will be just fine with me." She cuddled his little hands. "Won't you, little pumpkin?"

"Can we go now?" Q asked his wife and escorted her out of the tiny apartment and down the stairs. "We have to hurry or the picture will already have started."

Leopold and his wife had already purchased all their tickets and waited for them in the foyer.

"Here you are." Leopold waved them over. "You're late."

Q looked at Hilde and grinned. "She couldn't separate from Volker."

Dörthe laughed. "Ours are two and four already, but I remember those times." She put a hand on Hilde's arm. "In a few months, you'll be thrilled if you can leave him with his grandmother for a few hours."

Hilde tried to put on a brave face, but everyone could see she was still worried about her son.

"Let's go inside," Leopold suggested.

As always, the theatre was packed. Nowadays, there wasn't much else to do for leisure. The popular picture *Wunschkonzert*, a love story with complications, had been Hilde's choice, but Q didn't mind.

Before the feature was shown, they had to sit through several horrible propaganda films about the inferior race of the Jews.

"I'm sick and tired of being made to watch garbage like that," Leopold complained as he bought a soft drink for Hilde and wine for the others during the break.

"Those short films would be hilarious if it weren't so sad," Q added.

Hilde nodded and softly stated, "When I was taking Volker for a promenade in his pram today, I saw two women wearing yellow stars. They looked so...despairing. Beyond hope."

"All Jews must wear them now. It's to single them out," Leopold said with a firm nod of his head. "Has anyone heard from Jakob?"

Q and Hilde exchanged a sad glance and then Q explained, "Jakob was killed during *Kristallnacht*."

"What? How did you find this out?" Leopold wanted to know, and Dörthe put a hand over her mouth.

"We were about to drive him to Hamburg Harbor. Instead, we found him dead at the bottom of the staircase of his parents' house..." Q swallowed hard, blinking back the tears. "If you had seen the destruction...it made me ashamed to call myself a German."

A few people passed behind them, and Leopold snapped at Q, "Watch your mouth!"

Q squinted his eyes at his friend. He'd thought Leopold was anti-Nazi. The bell rang, and they returned to their seats to watch the feature. As they prepared to bid each other goodnight after the film, Leopold took him aside and said in a lowered voice, "Compulsory service is coming up very soon. They need more soldiers for the Wehrmacht."

Q nodded. Something was in the air; the military contracts at Loewe had risen to a new level. "Thanks for the warning. I'm working with Loewe in a reserved position for important military projects."

"And you enjoy your important work there?" Leopold asked, his eyes glaring daggers at Q.

"I do. It's very rewarding." Q opened his mouth to tell Leopold about his resistance work, or the fact that sabotaging military production was how he was able to enjoy his job so much. But then he closed it again. He and Leopold went back to high school, and he had trusted him completely – until about an hour ago.

Even if Leopold approved of his actions – which Q still believed his friend did – the knowledge might compromise Leopold's safety. Or the safety of the employees at the paint factory he owned.

# CHAPTER 23

As spring gave way to summer, baby Volker continued to grow, and each time Hilde looked at him, a surge of love rushed through her. But each time she looked at the baby, she also saw her two-year-old self.

The memory of how her own mother had left her at her grandmother's house stabbed her heart. Hilde caressed Volker's sleeping face – and saw herself screaming after her mother. "Don't leave me alone. Come back."

Nightmares had haunted her for years until she'd found tranquility in Q's love, but now everything came rushing back with full force. She breathed through the pain and blinked away some tears as the doorbell rang.

"Mother, what are you doing here?" Hilde asked, the words coming out raw. It was as if her very thoughts had summoned her mind's tormentor to her door.

Annie smiled and stepped inside. "I've come to see my grandson."

"He's taking a nap but should be waking up soon. Would you like a cup of ersatz coffee?"

Her mother grimaced. "*Muckefuck?* God, I have no idea how you can drink that trash."

"Nobody likes it, but it's all you can get with the ration cards."

Annie nodded sagely. "I'll have tea then. Next time I will bring some real coffee for us."

Hilde could only wonder how on earth her mother obtained real coffee. Probably some high-ranking admirers of her famous husband who showed their gratitude with small perks.

She led her mother to the sitting room and went to the kitchen to make tea for them both. She carefully carried the tray back to her mother.

"Thank you for the tea," Annie said, taking a sip before leaning back and playing with her long pearl necklace.

"You're welcome. How are your husband and Klaus?"

"Fine. Although your brother might get drafted soon. He's almost twenty."

Both women paused and Hilde racked her brain for something she might tell her mother. The baby cried, but before Hilde was up, he stopped. "Why did you abandon me?" she blurted out before she could stop herself.

Annie was shocked speechless for a few moments. "What? You ask this now? That was a long time ago and should be forgotten by now."

Hilde shook her head. "I will never forget. It still haunts me."

Her mother blushed, her hand returning to the string of pearls hanging around her neck. "You don't understand. I was very young when you were born. I could barely take care of myself, and having the burden of an infant–"

"I was a burden?" Hilde asked, barely keeping herself together.

"Well, burden might not be the right word. Times were difficult because of the Great War, and I was all alone. I needed time for myself. I'm sure you can sympathize."

Hilde scowled at her mother. "No. I can't sympathize. You always put yourself first, even before your own daughter. You could have left me at Grandmama's for a weekend or even a few weeks or months, but forever?"

Annie grabbed her necklace tighter and rubbed the pearls between her fingers. "It was as much your father's fault as it was mine. Why didn't he take care of you?"

"Because he was a soldier at the front!" Hilde jumped up and paced around the couch table. "How on earth was he supposed to take care of me? Take me with him into the trenches?"

"Now you're exaggerating," her mother scolded. When Hilde didn't stop pacing, tears spilled from Annie's eyes. "If I could do it all over again, I would have found a way to keep you with me. Not a day goes by that I don't wish I could have done things differently."

Hilde stopped, stupefied at the sudden change in her mother's tactics and stared at her. Even though she was sure Annie's remorse was fake, she couldn't help but sense a glimmer of hope. "You do?"

Annie nodded, wiping a few tears from her eyes. "I promise I will make it up to you."

"Mother, you don't have to make it up to me. Maybe we should just leave the past...in the past." Times were bad enough. Hilde didn't need to add to it by holding a grudge against her mother.

Annie got up and gave her daughter a small hug. It wasn't a grand gesture, but Hilde was choked up by the presence of something resembling an honest emotion in her mother's eyes.

Another cry from the baby drew both women toward the bedroom. Annie seemed intent on making things right and actually held Volker a few minutes, despite baby drool wetting her silky cardigan.

In the summer of 1940, Q and Hilde moved to a bigger apartment in Berlin Nikolassee. The two-story apartment building offered a big front lawn fringed by hedges and a smaller garden in the back accessible to all tenants that included a sandbox and a swing for the children.

Hilde loved the new apartment and the surroundings. The quarter of Nikolassee was far enough from the city center to be as quiet and peaceful as Berlin could be. Within walking distance from their new home was a large green area with several lakes, including the huge Wannsee.

During summer, Hilde and Volker spent many afternoons at the beach of the lake, playing in the sand, splashing in the shallow water near the shore, and enjoying life. On some days, Hilde completely forgot about the war, but on other days, she was harshly reminded of the reality.

Today was such a day. Hilde and Gertrud had taken a stroll with the prams along the shore of Wannsee. Just before they reached the bridge to the island of Schwanenwerder, an affluent residential area, a bunch of SS-officers appeared out of nowhere, stopping the entire traffic – pedestrians, bicycles, and the sporadic automobile.

A black Mercedes limousine rolled across the bridge to one of the big mansions on the island. "Goebbels," Hilde said to her friend; "he's living on the island."

Gertrud pursed her lips. "I wish this war would soon be over. I'm worrying day by day about my husband."

Hilde nodded. The poor man hadn't even seen his three-month-old daughter yet. She put a hand on Gertrud's arm. "He'll come home. You'll see."

Her friend dabbed a few tears with her handkerchief, and as soon as the SS officers who'd blocked their way had disappeared, they continued their walk. Hilde kept her own worries to herself. Q hadn't been drafted because he worked in a reserved profession at Loewe. Nonetheless, she feared for his safety every single day.

"At least your husband is at home." Gertrud's voice broke into Hilde's thoughts.

"That's a small relief. I'm afraid he would refuse to join up because of his pacifist ideals." *And his hatred for Hitler.* "And you know the punishment for conscientious objection…"

"Everything was so much better before the war." Gertrud nodded.

Volker and Luisa, Gertrud's daughter, started crying jointly.

"Time to feed the lions," Hilde said, and they walked to the next bench to nurse their babies. As both of them suckled happily, Hilde continued, "My mother urges me to wean Volker, but it's next to impossible to buy full-fat milk, and how will an active toddler survive on skim milk?"

"I know. There's never enough quality food to be had with those darned ration cards. And I had to cut up one of my old aprons to sew a dress and a jacket for Luisa because I'd used all our textile rations for a new blanket."

"I know. Thankfully, Q is not very picky, and neither is his new boss, so I didn't have to buy a new suit for him and was able to use all the textile rations for Volker. I was also lucky that our neighbor handed me down a few things from her son."

Gertrud smiled. "How does Q like his new job?"

"He loves it." *Because he's one of the key players in a sabotage group and also gathering intelligence for the resistance.* "Erhard Tohmfor, his boss, is a friend from university, and they seem to get along very well."

"Have you met him?" Gertrud asked as she put Luisa back into her pram.

"Yes. He and his wife have visited us on a few occasions. Erhard is a wonderful person, a natural born leader. He brings out the best in every single one of his employees." Hilde sighed. She longed to voice her fears about Q's resistance work to someone, but even though Gertrud definitely wasn't a Nazi – unlike Hilde's former best friend Erika – that topic was off limits.

After she'd bid goodbye to Gertrud and Luisa, she pushed Volker's pram home and told him about all her worries and fears. He responded to her concerns with a happy smile and some sort of gibberish.

"You're a downright slaphappy little fellow," she cooed to her son. "Don't worry. There's nothing we can do about it."

Since the birth of Volker, she and Q had steered clear of that topic. She didn't ask, and he didn't tell. But she had eyes in her head, and she noticed when he came home all agitated, or went out late at night, hiding papers under his jacket. He thought she was asleep, but she lay there awake, praying he would come back.

It was during those times when she would get up and go to the nursery to stand by Volker's crib and watch him sleep – her heart full of love but heavy with fear.

∽

The first half of 1940 was full of whirlwind military successes – the Führer's short succession of *Blitzkriege*. Hitler's Wehrmacht conquered Denmark, Norway, Belgium, Luxembourg, and the Netherlands.

Then, Hitler sent his troops into France, through the dense forest the Allies once thought impenetrable. Much to everyone's surprise, the Wehrmacht marched into Paris in a campaign that lasted just six weeks.

Eight days later, Q came home in a foul mood. "I can't believe it."

He took a closely guarded bottle of schnapps from the cupboard and poured himself a shot. "France surrendered. Do you have any idea what that means?"

Hilde didn't.

"That maniac is now dominating all of Europe together with his old crony Mussolini in Italy. With Franco's Spain and Stalin's Soviet Union friendly countries, there's not much left to occupy and subdue." He downed another shot. "Did you hear Hitler's speech on the radio?"

"No. I was out walking with Volker."

"Hitler called himself *Größter Feldherr aller Zeiten,*" Q said. "Biggest general of all times!"

"He honestly compared himself to Napoleon?" Hilde asked, rolling her eyes.

Q nodded, his scowl growing deeper. "He did."

Hilde snuggled up against Q on the couch. "On the positive side, let's hope he ends the same way his megalomaniac idol did."

Q stared at Hilde. "What?"

"His empire collapsed, and he died exiled in Saint Helena."

"I know what happened to Napoleon," Q said. "But what makes you think that Hitler can be stopped? Who's left to stop him? The English?"

Hilde searched his eyes but found only defeat in them. "You can't give up faith. There are many brave persons like you and Erhard. Men and women who actively work to overthrow the Nazi regime. It may seem impossible now, but the night is darkest just before sunrise."

Q wrapped her in his arms and murmured, "That's why I love you so much. You never let me give up."

But the night had yet to become darker.

Hitler started a strategic bombing of England – the Blitz. In return, English bombers attacked German targets. Each time she saw or heard the planes flying overhead, she held her breath and prayed they would deliver their deadly load someplace else.

One day, they received notice from the government that every personal automobile had to be turned in for the war effort. Only doctors and food suppliers were exempt.

Hilde crumpled the piece of paper and threw it against the wall, but

Q only laughed at her silent protest when he came home. "We never could get enough fuel to use it anyway."

She moped around for days at the loss of their means of transportation, until Q surprised her with two bicycles.

"Q, they are wonderful!" She smiled, incredibly pleased.

"Aren't they?" He beamed. "Now we can spend our summer making excursions around the green parts of Berlin. Just imagine, we could take a biking tour around the Wannsee with the entire family. Maybe even sleep on one of the farms. It would be like a vacation."

Hilde's mood brightened at her husband's enthusiasm. "I would like that, but how do we transport Volker on our bikes?"

"Oh." His face fell, and he furrowed his brows in thought. "Wait…" He left her standing and rushed off into his study room.

She shrugged. Some things would never change. Still smiling, she took Volker for a walk in his pram.

Q didn't mention the bicycles again, but a few days later, he brought home an old metal basket. The sturdy basket was made of unbroken wire net around all its sides, except for one. There it showed two holes in the net, each the size of a big fist.

"What's this?" Hilde asked, eyeing the thing suspiciously.

"This is…" he paused, his grin growing bigger, "Volker's new bicycle seat." He pulled mother and son behind himself into the shed and attached the metal basket with pieces of scrap metal and wire to the front of the bicycle's handles. A few movements later, Volker leaned haphazardly against the edge of the basket, his feet placed through the holes in the net.

Hilde jumped to support her son. "Q. This is great, but don't you think he's still too small to sit in such a contraption?"

Volker snickered and explored the basket curiously.

"See. He likes it." Q beamed proudly. "Should we embark on our first tour?"

"No way. He can't even sit yet, much less keep his balance while we're riding the bike." She picked up Volker and sat him down on safe ground. "Thanks, Q. That is such a great idea, but our first tour will have to wait a few more weeks."

# CHAPTER 24

Summer gave way to fall. Leaves started to change, and the temperatures began to drop. Q was having one of his weekly quality control meetings with Erhard. The ongoing war had brought the company a surge of contracts, and Q had his hands full with overseeing and sabotaging the production lines. There was no time left for intelligence work.

"Erhard, we need to talk about enlisting some more help," Q said after he'd closed the door to the office.

Erhard raised his head. "Didn't you reject this very idea several months ago?"

"Yes. And I'm still convinced it's a risk, but with all the new contracts, I don't have any time to gather intelligence and keep in contact with our Russian friends. And…" Q scratched his head.

"And what?" his friend asked.

"If something should happen to me or you, we need another person to continue our work."

"Hmm." The seconds on the clock kept ticking away. Erhard rubbed his chin. "I actually have someone in mind."

"Who?"

"One of the head chemical engineers. Martin Stuhrmann."

Q raised a brow. "Stuhrmann? He's in the Party. How do you know he's on our side?"

Erhard took a moment to explain. "You've heard of Arvid and Mildred Harnack?" When Q nodded, Erhard continued, "They are old acquaintances of mine and part of a resistance group."

That was new to Q.

"Stuhrmann is a friend of a friend of Mildred Harnack. More than once, he's voiced his discontent with the Nazi ideology."

"Just because someone doesn't like the Nazis doesn't mean he's willing to work against them." Q shook his head. "We should test him before we tell him anything."

"Test him?" Erhard asked.

"Yes. We'll feel him out, then set a trap to see whether he's trustworthy or not. We'll take it from there." Q's head was already spinning gears, trying to come up with a plan.

"Fine."

In the following weeks, they started having their lunch with Martin Stuhrmann. He was in his early thirties, a solid and dutiful engineer who always triple-checked the requirements. His brown hair showed an accurate side parting and his hazel eyes carefully observed his environment.

Q and Erhard made it a point to frequently discuss technical developments and politics, paying special attention to those technical innovations that benefited the military and the ethical implications.

After several weeks of doing this, they decided to set up a trap. Erhard called him to his office and closed the door. Martin seemed surprised that Q was also present, but didn't say a word.

Erhard started his attack. "Martin, I noticed the quality of production with your team has gone down again. Several times in the last few weeks, we had to throw away entire batches. And yesterday, the paste for the cathodes was contaminated and made unusable."

Q joined in. "When I ordered changes to the conveyor belt, the needed tool broke and stopped production for several hours."

When both men finished speaking, Martin was pale and trembling. He looked at Erhard with terror in his eyes and asked hoarsely, "Are you implying that I sabotaged the production line?"

Q and Erhard shared a look, then shook their heads in unison. "We're not pointing any fingers, but we do believe that someone might be intentionally causing these types of problems, thinking they might be helping to shorten the war and end Hitler's reign."

Martin's shoulders shivered. "No one would do that. Sabotage is a severe crime, and if caught, that person would be shot on the spot...or worse."

"Right." Nothing else was said, and they left it to poor Martin to figure out what had just been said.

Erhard then changed the subject. "So, when we have won the Total War, do you think life in Germany is still going to be worth living?"

Martin seemed confused. "Of course. I mean, isn't this what the government is telling us?"

Q added, "Or do you think it would be better for everyone if the war were to end now even if Germany wouldn't win?"

Both men watched Martin closely – this was the make or break test. What they had just asked him was very dangerous. If Martin were a Nazi, he would immediately tell the *Betriebsobmann*, the shop steward, or talk directly to the Gestapo.

Martin watched them with big eyes and responded with a question of his own, "Are you implying that our Führer doesn't know what's best?"

Q and Erhard cocked their heads but remained silent for a minute. Finally, Erhard said, "Thank you, Martin. That's all for today."

Martin left the room scuffing his feet, and Q had to suppress a chuckle. "Poor fellow. He's absolutely confused now."

Erhard agreed. "Yes. But his reaction will tell us where we stand. If he sings, it would be disappointing, but not life-threatening–"

"For us." Q completed the sentence. "Because you'll simply present evidence of Martin's sabotage acts to the Gestapo and they won't believe a word of what he said."

"Yes, and you will be my witness if that is needed. I already made a note in my journal that we suspect someone is sabotaging our production and that we've started interrogating people."

"But if he keeps quiet, we'll know he's on our side. Just how long should we wait?" Q asked.

"I think three weeks is a prudent time."

Martin told no one. The *Betriebsobmann* did show up in Erhard's office several times during the next two weeks, but it was always about routine work. One time, he reported on working accidents, another time to ask for time off for the employees to attend a Party rally, and so on.

It was a tense three weeks.

Erhard and Q had just finished another one of their "quality control" meetings when Q said, "I guess it's time to enlist our new helper."

"It is. But we won't tell him anything about our underground work – not yet."

Q nodded. He and Erhard understood each other. "Caution is the mother of wisdom."

"You're right, we can't be careful enough."

When Martin arrived, he looked slightly uneasy but took a chair at the round table in Erhard's office.

"Martin, you've done well since our last meeting. I need you to carry out an important task with the utmost discretion." Erhard said.

Martin's hazel eyes went wide. "Certainly."

Q leaned back in his seat and observed the two men at the table with him. Erhard, his long-time friend and partner in crime, sat on his left. Nearly forty years old, his blond hair was cut almost military-short and his piercing blue eyes seemed to be able to look right inside the head of those talking to him. His demeanor showed the signs of authority, while Martin, on the other hand, seemed to be sitting on hot coals.

For a moment, Q felt guilty about dragging Martin into their resistance activities.

"I need you to gather drawings, technical data, and fabrication orders...everything one might need in order to start a serial fabrication outside of Loewe. Can you have this ready by the end of the day?"

It was an unusual request, but Erhard was the boss, so Martin didn't dare to oppose him. He nodded.

After Martin left, Q raised his voice. "We should tell him the truth. He needs to have the chance to say no."

Erhard nodded. "And we will. Tonight."

The next day, the three met again for lunch. "How did it go yesterday?" Q asked them.

Martin grinned like a light bulb. "Great. I wanted to give the papers to Erhard in his office, but he asked me to keep them until the evening. He told me he'd be waiting for me at the corner of Siemensstraße. I actually found this a bit strange and was somehow worried – but more curious."

Erhard chuckled. "Martin passed our test with flying colors, and I asked him if he wants to work for our cause."

Martin blushed at the praise. "You know, I was initially worried you'd accuse me of sabotaging the production, but when you mentioned the time after a total victory...I remembered our earlier discussions and noted there was a common denominator. I suspected you two were doing some kind of subversive work–"

"No such thing." Q stopped him. "We don't ever mention those words. You understand?"

"Yes."

Erhard added, "The less you know, the safer it is. For everyone. Don't ask. Just do."

Martin paused for a moment. Fear, anxiety, and pride fought for dominance in his eyes until he took a deep breath. "You're right. I know what happens to people who oppose our Führer."

"If the time is right, you'll get to know more. I have known you long enough to know you are on our side. Now it's time to work until we've succeeded. One day we will harvest the fruits of our work."

"Well said, Erhard," Q commented on his friend's little speech.

The three men got up, and Q and Martin left the small canteen together. On the way to the laboratories, Martin barely contained his thrill. "When will we start? And how?"

"Slow down. I'll teach you our production lines and all the problems that could happen."

Two days later, during their lunch break, Erhard said, "Martin has solved his first task very well; now I have another one for you two."

Q saw the eagerness in Martin's face and chuckled. *Was I that enthusiastic ten years ago?* It seemed that, for Martin, their resistance activities were an exciting game, a challenging competition to outsmart the government.

Erhard's voice cut through his thoughts: "...I need you to make two short-wave transmitters."

Great. That would give them the opportunity to communicate with Moscow and possibly other countries. Q's mind leaped forward, trying to figure out where they could hide those transmitters. "We could disguise them as prototypes."

Both Martin and Erhard stared at him as if he'd lost his mind. "Disguise our employees as prototypes?"

"No. The transmitters. If we use one of the radio control boards the Wehrmacht has ordered and–"

"Q, stop." Erhard cut him off. "I just told Martin that we need to screen all employees for reliability in case of an eventual upheaval. See why we need help? You'll take care of the transmitters while Martin oversees our employees."

Q scowled at his friend, but then he grinned. "Certainly. I'll go and tinker with the equipment. Martin can talk to the others all he wants."

"Now let's go over the production goals for this week," Erhard said and fixated on Martin closely. "Always remember, our main goal is to increase production waste, but this must be handled carefully. It must always be due to a material defect, and never negligence of our personnel."

"If we raise the slightest suspicion that someone could be causing these problems, we'll all be in hot water," Q added.

Martin nodded.

In recent months, it had become more and more difficult to contact the Soviet agent. Thus, Q's focus had shifted from giving technical information to the Russians to doing anything that opposed the German government – sabotage, gathering important war information, and preparing for a life after this terror was over.

He still hoped that the German people would see Hitler for who he truly was and stop the charade. After an upheaval of the entire nation against their rulers, they'd need new, trustworthy people in place, and with Martin's help screening the personnel, Loewe would be prepared.

# CHAPTER 25

A s December arrived, Hilde and Q once again took the train to Hamburg to spend Christmas with her parents. It had been surprisingly easy to get the required travel permits. Not even the Nazi regime dared to interfere with German Christmas traditions, and visiting family was one of them.

Hilde leaned against the window and watched the landscapes pass by. Wherever she looked was destruction – the result of the continuous air raids. She sighed deeply and Q took her hand.

"I hope this war will end soon," she said. "It's getting worse every day."

"It will end," Q answered, "one way or another. Either we win the war and Hitler subdues all of Europe, or our country will be destroyed completely. The Allies will be even harsher than after the Great War if they win." Q shuddered.

"I was too young to remember the Great War," Hilde said and retreated into her thoughts while Volker was peacefully sleeping on Q's lap. She'd thought about returning to work next year, but Q had convinced her to stay at home with their son.

He'd handed her all the administrative tasks associated with his private research. Not that he invented much anymore. He was always afraid his inventions would be abused in the name of war.

But he still worked with a patent lawyer to sell the commercial rights connected to earlier inventions to other countries. Most of the technical things she didn't understand, but her typewriting skills came in handy with all the needed correspondence.

Sometimes he'd let her type up technical instructions regarding the radio production at Loewe. *He thinks I don't understand, but I do.* Her transcriptions would be given to the Russians either by Erhard or himself. She never asked, and he didn't tell, but she knew. She could see it in his eyes, in his posture, when the tasks he gave her belonged to his intelligence work.

She sighed again and looked at her sleeping son. Volker was a darling little boy with white-blond hair, bringing happiness to their lives without even trying. He'd inherited his father's curls and bright blue eyes, but her mouth and nose. *I'd give anything to see him grow up in a world of peace.*

"It's his first Christmas," she said, twirling one of his curls around her finger.

Q nodded. "And he'll celebrate his first birthday in less than three weeks."

"Do you think he understands what's going on in this world?" Her voice betrayed her fear.

"I doubt it. He's too young. But we'll make it as normal and harmonious as possible – for everyone."

"I feel a bit guilty that my parents haven't been able to see him sooner."

"It just wasn't possible to make the trip, neither for you nor for them."

"I know, but..." Volker stirred in his sleep but didn't open his eyes. They smiled at each other and stopped talking, not wanting to wake the tired child.

Some time later, the train stopped in Hamburg, and Emma met them at the train station. "Oh, look. How cute you are, darling! You look even sweeter than on the pictures your Mommy sent me. Say hello to your *Oma.*"

Volker looked at her with bright eyes, apparently understanding every word, because he raised his little hand to touch Emma's face and babbled some incoherent sounds.

Hilde laughed. "He's intelligent."

"That's because he's my son," Q said with pride.

On their way to the Dremmer home, they witnessed the remains of the horrible air raid over Hamburg a month ago. Hilde involuntarily shivered. "Emma, we're so relieved nothing happened to you."

Emma stopped for a moment, and her lips tightened. "We were lucky, but many others weren't."

Changing the subject, Emma filled them in on the news of the family. "Julia won't come home for Christmas. She'll stay at the farm with the *Reichsarbeitsdienst.*" Her face softened, and her eyes glowed. "She's been offered a job in the administration of the farm."

"Aren't you worried about her being so far away?" Hilde asked.

"Worried? No. At least in the countryside, I know she's getting enough food. And it's safer. The bombers tend to concentrate on the big cities."

Hilde wanted to ask her stepmother why she wouldn't leave Hamburg and stay with Sophie in the countryside, but she already knew the answer. Just like herself, Emma wouldn't leave her husband alone.

For a moment, her heart filled with sadness because Ingrid couldn't be with them. Q adored his mother, but she was too old and fragile to make the journey to Hamburg. Instead, she spent the holidays with her other son, Gunther.

Hilde grimaced. She and Gunther had never gotten along and had developed a pattern of avoiding each other, even after he'd moved back to Berlin with his family a few years ago.

"What are you thinking?" Q interrupted her thoughts.

"Nothing."

"Then why are you looking so worried?"

"It's just…I was thinking about your mother, and then Gunther. All of his sons, except for the youngest, have been sent to war. It must be so awful for Katrin and him."

"Since when are you fond of my brother?" he teased.

Hilde gave him a small smile. "Not of him, particularly, but I can understand the anxiety he must go through to have three of his sons at the front lines, waiting, hoping, and praying every day that they will come home."

Q squeezed her hand. "I know. Let's hope this war will end sooner rather than later, and his youngest will be spared the experience."

Emma interrupted them. "How old are your nephews?"

"Twenty-four, twenty, eighteen, and fourteen."

"Fourteen. One year younger than Sophie," Carl said.

"It's a crime against our youth! How can they be children in a world like this? How can they be happy and carefree when disaster is looming above their heads?" Q had raised his voice, and Hilde gave him a hug.

Everyone knew he was right. If the war continued, it was only a matter of time before teenagers like his nephew would be sent off to fight.

"Well, we won't let anyone ruin our Christmas holidays. No more talk of the war. Dinner is ready," Emma declared.

During dinner, they caught up on each other's lives. The company where Hilde's father did the taxes and handled the accounting department had changed and now exclusively produced war goods. Uniforms for the Wehrmacht, to be precise.

And just like that, they'd reverted to the topic of war. Emma shot her husband a sharp look and Hilde hurried to ask her sister, "Sophie, how is school going this year?"

Sophie made a face. "Awful. If there is school at all."

"I'll bet you do like the days without school," Q said, and Hilde thought she saw a mischievous light in his eyes. Despite his passion for science, he must have been a terrible student at school. She made a mental note to ask Ingrid about Q's school years.

"No. Those are even worse." Sophie pouted. "They make us work."

Q chuckled. "Well, I believe work isn't bad for you."

"This kind of work is," Sophie insisted. "For an entire week, we have to do our share in supporting the Reich. Like harvesting produce at the farms and orchards, or collecting old metal to produce more weapons."

Hilde swallowed hard. The Nazis used school children for war production?

Sophie had talked herself into a rage, and not even the stern glances of her mother could stop her flow of words. "I hate it! At school, they make us listen to the daily report of the Armed Forces, telling us about the great victories of our soldiers and then make us discuss the strategic masterstrokes of our Führer."

"Enough," Carl intervened. "I believe your mother wanted to hear nothing more about the war."

A long silence ensued until Volker rescued them with his cheerful nature and his need to play. He insisted on being put down on the floor, and everyone welcomed the distraction.

Volker had been pulling himself up on furniture for the last few weeks but had yet to trust his balance enough to let go and take his first steps. Now with a big audience, he clapped his tiny hands and then took two steps before plummeting to the floor.

Hilde jumped up with tears of pride in her eyes and hugged her son, praising him for his grand achievement.

# CHAPTER 26

The next day was Christmas Eve.

Traditionally, they would decorate the tree together, but as Hilde looked around her parents' small home, no Christmas tree stood in front of the window. Trees were hard to come by and expensive. Instead, her father had gathered a few branches, tied them together, and affixed them to a wooden stand. It wasn't much, but it would have to do.

It took them all of five minutes to decorate the branches in a traditional fashion with a few of the precious glass bowls and some straw stars. Hilde was looking at the small manufactured version of a Christmas tree and could only shake her head. The Nazis had tried very hard to turn the Christian celebration into a profane festivity they called *Julfeier*.

Without much success, though if there was one thing the German people would argue about with their government, it was their beloved Christmas traditions. Not even the most die-hard Nazi supporters liked the idea of a *Julfeier*.

Hilde recalled a propaganda flier she and Q had found on the train to Hamburg. She'd forgotten about its existence and now pulled it out of her pocket.

"This is what is circulating out there," she said to Emma.

Emma gazed at the flier, then dropped it as if it were poison. "Over my dead body! We've used glass bowls and straw stars since I was a child, and it will stay this way until I die."

Hilde picked the flier up and put it in the trash. The images of an SS officer hanging swastika ornaments on a Christmas tree made her stomach churn. *Nothing is holy anymore! Not even the birth of the Holy Child.*

When she returned to the living room, Emma was muttering under her breath and still livid. It would be funny if it weren't so sad. Like most Germans, Emma would never openly criticize the Nazis, but that was before they had attempted to interfere with Christmas and the traditions she held dear to her heart.

Now she was acting like a lioness whose children were being threatened. Carl joined them, and upon hearing what had his wife so upset, he excused himself and returned with a leaflet of his own.

"These were being distributed at the company a few days ago."

Q took it and read it aloud while everyone laughed.


*Reference: Discontinuation of this year's Christmas Holidays*

*Due to the circumstances caused by the war, this year Christmas will be discontinued.*

*Reason: The Holy Joseph has been drafted to the Wehrmacht.*

*The Blessed Virgin Mary has been mobilized as a munitions worker.*

*The Infant Jesus has been evacuated due to constant air raids.*

*The Magi didn't receive an entry permit.*

*The Star of Bethlehem had to be blacked out.*

*The Shepherds went into the trenches.*

*The Stable has been converted into a gun emplacement.*

*The Straw has been seized by the troops.*

*The Diapers of the Infant Jesus had to be delivered to the textile collection.*

*The Crib has been given to the National Socialist People's Welfare.*

*And because there is only the donkey alone, it doesn't make sense to celebrate Christmas.*

. . .

As Q ended his recital, he glanced at the flyer and then at Carl. "They were handing these out at your company?"

Carl paled. "The company officials were already away for the holiday. When we came back from lunch, they were lying on our desks."

"Whoever made and distributed these leaflets risked their lives for it. We need to burn it immediately," Q said.

"Q, aren't you over-reacting just a bit?" Emma questioned.

"No. Being in possession of this could land us all in jail."

Carl added, "Emma, he's right. I should have never taken the leaflet. By bringing it to our home, I've endangered us all."

Q stepped towards the sink and lit the leaflet on fire. When he could no longer hold it without singeing his fingers, he dropped it into the sink and then washed the ashes down the drain. Then he turned and looked at Hilde and the rest of her family.

*How many more Christmases will be like this?* Hilde wondered.

In the evening, after dinner, they opened the presents, which were rather modest and useful this year. Warm winter gloves for Emma. Hand-knitted stockings for Sophie. Cigars for Carl. A sweater for Q, and a shawl for Hilde. The only person showered with gifts was little Volker.

Carl had gone all out and had overhauled the old wooden sled his daughters had used many years ago. At first, Volker was rather skeptical, but when his grandfather had taken him on his first trip around the house, he never wanted to be separated from his sled again. After much yelling, his parents relented and put the sled beside his bed, where he could see and touch it.

Emma had collected all of their ration cards as soon as they'd arrived and gone shopping. The extra food rations given to all "true" Germans for Christmas had been a blessing, and on the 25th of December, Emma made a mouth-watering festive roast with baked potatoes and lard.

The entire home smelled of food and for once everyone forgot about the hardships of the war. Hilde helped her stepmother in the kitchen and watched with surprise as Emma took the finished roast and cut it in half. She carefully wrapped one portion together with baked potatoes and placed it into a brown paper package. In the end, she placed some cookies into a storage container and placed it on top of the meal.

"Hilde, would you like to take a walk with me?"

Curious as to what Emma was up to, she nodded and dressed Volker in his hat and coat before settling him into the pram. Emma placed the food package under the blanket at Volker's feet, and they took off for a walk.

They walked for quite a while before Emma veered them off the road to a small house. The shutters hung from their hinges, the windows broken and scantily replaced with wooden planks, the formerly nice gardens a picture of devastation. No smoke curled out of the chimney. The house had definitely seen better times, and considering the shameful state it was in, Hilde seriously doubted that anyone still lived there.

Images of the past stormed her head, and Hilde suddenly remembered. A Jewish family with three girls around the ages of Julia and Sophie had lived here for years. She swallowed back the picture of the neat and tidy girls playing in the garden while their mother lovingly attended to the vegetables and flowers.

"Are they still living here?" she whispered.

Emma gave her a meaningful look and a nod. "Yes." Then she took a quick glance around and disappeared with the package to the back door. Hilde heard a quick rapping on the door and felt a new level of admiration for her stepmother. Her own mother would never do anything selflessly without expecting something in exchange.

Several moments later, Emma hurried back to join Hilde and the baby. They returned home and had almost reached their street when Hilde asked, "Does Father know?"

Emma nodded. "There's not much we can do, just tiny bits here and there." She paused and turned to look at Hilde. "I've come to the realization that this war is not good for our country."

"You are a good woman. I wish I had realized this twenty years ago –Mother."

Emma's eyes watered as she hugged Hilde tight. "This is the first time you called me 'Mother.'"

"I know," was all Hilde could whisper before she broke out in tears as well, and the two women clung to each other until Volker made it known that he was tired of their walk.

Back at home, they found Sophie playing the flute while Carl and Q were absorbed in a political discussion about the consequences of this war.

When they entered Carl's study, his dark eyes flickered as he said, "To hell with all the home front talk. Goebbels can keep hammering the same idea into the minds of everyone. I don't buy any of it."

Q imitated Goebbels's voice and recited, "Everyone has to do their share to support the soldiers at the front."

Hilde laughed softly, "You could do the voice-over for the propaganda movies."

Q shook his head and made a face at her. "Funny."

During the next days, Hilde learned just how much Emma cared for her family. Like most housewives who had the means, she'd been growing vegetables in a small garden behind their house.

She must have worked hard during the summer because the cellar was fully stocked with homegrown carrots, potatoes, onions, and a variety of other vegetables she had preserved in simple ways.

There were still winter vegetables out on the patches, including several heads of cabbage. From that, she had made her famous sauerkraut by chopping up the vegetable and letting it stand in vinegar for a good fourteen days.

One day, Emma produced a special treat for the family from her secret storage. She made pancakes and topped them with homemade strawberry jam Julia had sent from the farm. With a shortage of sugar and sweets, the simple pancakes with jam were like heaven.

Every other day Emma would take a walk, hiding a brown bag with food beneath her coat.

# CHAPTER 27

Q, Hilde, and Volker returned to Berlin in the first days of 1941 on a train ride fraught with adventure. Getting tickets had been difficult. With the absence of private vehicles and the increased rationing of petrol, the trains were overcrowded.

After the holidays, everyone needed to get back to work and even though private "leisure travel" was frowned upon, nobody had let Nazi ideology or war keep him or her from visiting far away relatives.

Q stored the pram together with their suitcases in the baggage coach and then followed Hilde and Volker to their wagon. They found a place crowded with several other people in a compartment. Q wasn't entirely happy. The continuous air raids over the capital and Hamburg were a constant threat, and he feared the train would be forced to stop.

To be safe, he'd taken a bag with enough food and drink for a day inside the train and crammed it onto his lap. He looked at Hilde, who looked beautiful and relaxed with sleepy white-blond Volker on her lap and her new flaming red shawl around her shoulders. A hidden worry nagged at him.

"How are we going to carry Volker if we have to rush from the train?" he asked her.

Hilde smiled. "Why should we have to rush?"

"If the air sirens go off and–"

"Q, there haven't been air raids in days. Why should the Allies start today?"

"Maybe because nobody expects it? Or because they're back from Christmas holidays just like we are?"

"You're overthinking this," she said, kissing the top of her son's head.

"Maybe I am." Reluctantly, he kept silent for a while, but then he looked at her again. "I'd really feel better if we were prepared. Just in case."

She sighed dramatically. "Since when are you such a pessimist?"

"Please."

"Fine. What do you want me to do? Tie him onto my back?"

It wasn't such a bad idea, but looking at her bright red shawl, he thought of a better one. "We'll use your shawl."

"Seriously?"

"Yes, stand up." He apologized to the other passengers and moved Hilde around, strapping little Volker to her chest. He wrapped her shawl around her body twice in a crisscross fashion before tying it in the back. Volker seemed to enjoy it, and Q grinned. "That will do. Now you won't have to hold him in your arms if we have to run."

Under the amused glances of the other passengers Hilde sat back down, trying to find a comfortable position. Not more than half an hour later, the abhorred sound of the air raid sirens screamed their warning. The train stopped, and the passengers were ordered to rush into a nearby forest to take refuge.

After three such interruptions, Q and his family finally arrived safely in Berlin, much later than they expected.

Several weeks after their return to Berlin, Q, Erhard, and Martin had another of their weekly meetings. Martin had become a very enthusiastic member of their small sabotage group and wanted to include even more people in their resistance effort.

"That's not a wise idea," Erhard replied with a shake of his head.

"But we could do so much more–"

Q jumped in. "Involving more people can only result in damage to our cause. And not just the cause, but to us and everyone involved. If we do too much, we'll attract suspicion."

Martin opened his mouth to argue his case, but Erhard cut him off, "Look, between the three of us, we have the entire production process under control. We don't need more people on the inside."

Martin finally nodded, and they moved on to other topics, including if and how they would keep in contact with other resistance groups. After a heated discussion, they decided that only Erhard would connect with other groups while Q kept in touch directly with Moscow via the Russian agent.

"And what's my task?" Martin asked, disappointed like an eager schoolboy.

"You have our back in case something happens," Erhard said, but Martin didn't seem convinced. "Look, you're in the Party–"

Martin blushed. "I know, but I only joined because everyone did and it helped me to get promoted."

Erhard looked at him. "I'm not judging you, Martin, not at all."

"I will resign from the Party. I'll do it today," Martin said, agitated.

Q's jaw dropped. "That's a bad idea. Very bad."

Erhard nodded in agreement. "I concur with Q. People would start getting suspicious if you resigned from the Party right now. It would draw too much speculation upon you, your family, and this company."

Martin's shoulders slumped, and he was a picture of misery.

Q sympathized with him. "Wait – being in the Party is a good disguise. You have access to Party meetings and can hear about things we never will. In fact, your task is to stay on friendly terms with the shop steward and keep an eye out for any signs that someone might suspect we're not working in the best interest of our Führer."

Martin beamed like a light bulb with the assignment of this important task.

After he left, Q took Erhard aside and asked, "Aren't you afraid Martin might be too enthusiastic and give us away?"

"No, on the contrary. I believe he understands our point and his new task will serve us well, you'll see."

Apart from sabotaging the war production and copying all of the classified technical documents to distribute them to their contacts, they'd started to prepare for the time after Hitler.

"We just have to open their eyes to how ridiculous and megalomaniac the war and Hitler actually are, then the German people will rise up in a revolution," Q said.

"Yes, but how can we make the leading managers of the company doubt the government without exposing ourselves?"

"I don't know yet, but we'll find a way. Have I told you about that satirical Christmas leaflet my father-in-law found at his workplace?"

Erhard chuckled. "Yes, it actually was quite funny."

"So there are like-minded people who won't keep quiet anymore. Not that I think leaflets are enough to overthrow Hitler, but they are a start to make people think – and doubt."

A week later, Q was sitting at his desk, deep in concentration. He was copying top-secret material to make a blueprint for a serial production of radio equipment somewhere else when Martin walked into the laboratory.

Q looked up and frowned at him. Martin of all persons should know he didn't appreciate interruptions when he was deep in thought. But instead of retreating, the intolerable fool stepped forward, not paying attention to where his feet landed. He tripped, spilling a full mug of ersatz coffee all over the papers in front of Q.

Q jumped up, opening his mouth to angrily reprimand the young man when he became aware of the two Luftwaffe officials, two men in Gestapo uniforms, and the shop steward right behind Martin.

He swallowed hard and busied himself with removing the sodden papers and wiping up his workspace while the shop steward shot Martin a sharp glance. "Can't you take better care, Stuhrmann?"

Martin made his best effort to look contrite. "I'm so sorry."

But the shop steward had already gestured for him to shut up and addressed the officials, "*Meine Herren,* please rest assured that no liquid is allowed in the production hall. Our workers have to go to the break room for any refreshments. Unfortunately, scientists insist they get special treatment."

The Luftwaffe major seemed to be in a good mood because he merely nodded. "Yes. Yes. Now let's continue with our inspection."

The shop steward clicked heels and said, "Major Schmid, please follow me to where we produce the state-of-the-art radio equipment for our armed forces. Our head of production, Martin Stuhrmann, will answer all your questions."

Q glanced at Martin and nodded a silent *thank you* before the group crossed the laboratory and walked through the door to the production hall. Q returned to his work with trembling hands.

That evening, when Q headed home, he was still shaking from the encounter.

Dinner was cold – again.

# CHAPTER 28

I'm sorry, my love. I couldn't get enough coal to heat the oven in the kitchen. The little I got I used to heat the living room," Hilde said.

"I don't care."

She looked at him and frowned. "What's wrong with you, my love? Did you have a bad day?"

Q merely nodded. "I'll tell you when the baby is asleep."

Two hours later, they sat together on the couch and she snuggled up to him while he told her everything that had happened.

"It sounds like Martin proved himself today, if you still had any doubts about him."

He kept quiet for a while, stroking her arm. "I don't know how much longer I can do this."

"You need to stay strong and continue. I'm afraid all the time, and there will always be times when we want to give in to our fear, but I know you – you need to stand up for what you believe in."

"But at what cost?" Q asked her.

"What if everyone just gave in? There would never be an end to this. Our country needs people like you."

His voice was tired when he answered, "I'm not sure our country is worth the effort anymore."

Hilde ran her hand through his curls. "Then do it for our son. For his future, so he can grow up in a country worth living in. Be a good example for him."

Q turned his head and kissed her. "I admire you. You are so strong, and you make me want to be a better man. You're the best life's companion I could ever have wished for." They kissed again, and he promised, "One day, when this war is over, we'll enjoy our lives again. Just like during our honeymoon. Only better."

Hilde snuggled close in his arms. "I hope that day comes sooner rather than later."

She heard the air raid sirens in the distance, just as on almost every night. Both of them held their breath, ready to get Volker from his crib and rush into the cellar of the building, which served as a bomb shelter, but the sirens faded away.

Hilde sighed. "I'm so thankful we moved out here. If we still lived in the center, we'd have to spend almost every night in the shelter."

"Yes, it was a good decision, for several reasons. There's not much out here worth bombing, only lakes and greenery."

"Yes." Hilde shivered in his arms, and he asked, "Are you cold, *Liebling*?"

"No, I believe I haven't told you. Last week when Volker and I visited your mother, we passed in front of our old apartment building." Her voice broke. "It was bombed out and completely uninhabitable. Oh my God! Will this nightmare ever end?"

The next day, Q went back to work with a fresh sense of purpose and renewed courage. They'd just received a huge order to deliver a new and enhanced portable transmitter to the Wehrmacht by June.

The urgency in the date of delivery made Q wonder which country Hitler wanted to attack next. He and Erhard discussed the possibilities, and as the list of countries not already under Nazi control wasn't very long, they came to the conclusion it must be England.

Just how to warn them? They didn't have contacts within the English government.

Q sighed in desperation, and instead, they worked on a plan to delay production of the portable transmitters. Q got right to work and accidentally destroyed an important tool needed to make the prototype. It was the only one Loewe had – unfortunately for the company – and he walked into the director's office, head bowed and shoulders dropped.

Shifting from one foot to another, he started his apology. "Sir, I'm so sorry, but when I tested the radio frequencies of the prototype for the Wehrmacht, our measuring device blew up."

The director scolded him for his imprudence and raised his voice loud enough to attract Erhard Tohmfor into his office. "Sir, is there a problem?"

When Erhard became aware of Q staring guiltily at the floor, he could hardly hide a smile and looked in the other direction.

"Yes. Doctor Quedlin has ruined some measuring device that is needed for the new prototype!" the director shouted.

As always, Erhard had the situation under control and answered calmly, "Director, I agree this is rather unfortunate. I have mentioned time and again that we need backup tools in case such a thing happens. Unfortunately – as you know – it is almost impossible to procure anything non-essential. The government seems to believe that our tools don't have a shelf life, but they do. Most of our tools are far too old to work reliably."

Now it was Q's turn to stare at his toes to hide a grin. While Erhard was right on the general condition of their equipment, this particular tool could have served for another thirty years, if he hadn't crossed two wires before using it, thus effectively ruining the measuring device. It had been a nice little explosion.

In his early days as a scientist, he'd always been afraid to ruin something and had been overly careful, but now he felt an immense surge of adrenaline whenever something went wrong.

The director spoke again. "Fine. Order a new one. Make it urgent."

Erhard nodded, and Q left the office, putting on his most contrite face. Back at the lab, he gave Martin a silent thumbs-up when he told him about the ruined device.

Martin nodded and explained, "We also have a problem with the fabrication machines for the casing. They started failing, and it took me an entire day to find the cause."

"I hope you were able to fix it." Q smirked.

"Unfortunately not. The motors have seized up due to poor-quality transmission oil. It had too much particulate material in it, and I had to throw everything away. We need to wait for the next batch to arrive."

*Particulate material as in sand and metals shards you poured into the oil?* "It's so hard to buy high-quality raw materials. I wonder what is next?"

For Q and Martin, it was like a game, trying to outdo each other in wreaking the most havoc on production progress. Sometimes Erhard had to slow them down and caution them to be more subtle in their sabotage work.

~

Summer arrived, and Q finally received the answer as to where Hitler had his sights set next.

The Soviet Union.

Erhard and his wife were visiting Hilde and Q the night the news broke that Hitler's troops had mounted an attack against the Soviet Union because Stalin had been plotting against Germany.

Hilde raised her hand to her mouth. "Weren't our two countries supposed to be allies?"

"Well, apparently not anymore," Q responded.

"I can't believe Hitler attacked his friend Stalin and mounted the largest offensive so far in this war," Erhard said.

His wife shook her head, the shock still lingering in her eyes. "Obviously, the accusation about plotting against our country must be fabricated."

Q's hands curled into tight fists. "We must increase our efforts. If Hitler wins this war against Russia, his next goal is the entire world."

The next day, the Russian agent contacted Q. He'd relayed intelligence to Pavel for several years now and almost considered him a friend.

Pavel didn't have good news for him. "I'm leaving for Moscow today, and we won't be able to meet again. I can't tell you if and how you'll be contacted from now on. As I speak, all agents are being recalled home."

"I wish you well, and have a safe trip home." Q swallowed. "Tell your leaders that we are at your disposal for anything needed to shorten this war. Neither my helpers nor I have changed opinions."

The agent produced a map, which he tore into two halves; he gave one part to Q, "If another agent contacts you, ask him for the other half of that map. If he can't produce it, he's not on your side."

"What about asking if the hike up Mount Etna is strenuous?"

"Who told you that?" Pavel asked, confused.

"The other agent, the one I met in Sicily."

"Oh." Pavel's eyes clouded. "I didn't know about that. Well then, to be on the safe side, ask for both."

# CHAPTER 29

On a hot summer day in August 1941, Hilde met with Gertrud and Erika and a number of youngsters at the Wannsee beach. It was the favorite gathering for mothers with small children, a getaway within the city limits to forget the sorrows of war, even if only for a few hours.

Despite Hilde's intentions not to see her former friend and converted Nazi anymore, Q had encouraged her to reconnect with Erika. Her father-in-law was SS Obersturmbannführer Wolfgang Huber, and Hilde might be able to gather some valuable information she could pass along to Q.

As always, Erika was singing the praises of Hitler, and Hilde did her best to swallow down the bile forming in her throat. She wanted to punch some common sense into that woman. Did she even understand what garbage she was regurgitating?

Thankfully, Gertrud steered the conversation to safer topics. Children. Erika had just given birth to her first boy three months earlier. She raved about the baby's Aryan looks, his blond hair, and his tall frame.

Hilde bit back a sharp remark. The boy looked like any baby, with little to no hair, and not especially tall or strong. On the contrary, he was cute and chubby.

After a while, Gertrud said, "Hilde, I envy you."

"Me? Why?" Hilde wanted to know.

"You still have your husband around. Mine has been transferred to the Eastern Front. We just saw him for a few days of leave of absence. "

Gratitude spread across Hilde's body even as she felt sorry for her friend. Q's resistance work was dangerous, but maybe not as dangerous as the front. "Yes, I'm so grateful he's working in a reserved profession."

Erika chimed in, "Q is doing valuable work, but my husband is following in the footsteps of his father and has recently been promoted. He's in Paris." Her eyes became dreamy. "He wrote me that I should be able to visit soon, when little Adolf is a bit older and can stay with my mother."

Hilde shivered; she still couldn't wrap her mind around the fact that Erika had named her children Adolfine, Germania, and Adolf. *Disgusting.*

She tucked that thought away and turned her attention to the children. Volker was now a year and a half old and was walking around like a pro. He was an active little boy but lately had been having problems with his digestion.

"Volker has been sick again this week. He's thrown up two nights in a row, and I'm seriously worried. If I could only get some healthy food for him, and not the crap we can buy with the ration cards."

"Hilde, everyone has to make sacrifices for the war. You shouldn't be complaining." Erika sent her a scolding glance.

Hilde hid her hurt at this reaction and soon found an excuse to leave. Q might find it valuable to stay in touch with Erika, but she couldn't stomach her former friend's Nazi talk one minute longer.

Several days later, Q came home, tired as usual. The constant anxiety and the secrecy were taking a toll on him, and Hilde thought about something to cheer him up. She'd been keeping a sweet secret from him, waiting for the right moment.

Now as he complained once again about the futility of his sabotage efforts, she decided this would be as good a moment as any other. "Q, you must carry on. You need to be a good example for your children."

Q started to respond but then her last word gave him pause. "Children? As in more than one?" He looked at her, and she saw the happy smile on his face.

"Yes, I'm pregnant again."

Q grabbed her and spun her around the room. "I'm so happy, and I love you so much."

But as slaphappy as they both were, Hilde was also worried. They were in the middle of the worst war of all time, and they were going to bring another child into the world?

He sensed her unease and assured her, *"Kommt Zeit, Kommt Rat!"* Time will tell.

# CHAPTER 30

Q needed Hilde out of the house. And not because she was pregnant. He needed to think what else he could do – about dangerous things.

He'd never been able to hide something from Hilde, and she would only worry if she found out.

When yet another broadcast praised the virtues of the *Kinderlandver-schickung* – the evacuation of children from the big cities into the countryside – he raised the topic with Hilde.

"Absolutely not! I will not leave Volker in the hands of some Nazi nurses," she growled.

That was a point for her. Volker would soon turn two years old and was too young to understand, but Q wouldn't want him indoctrinated with the Nazis' ideology. "So why don't you go with him?" he suggested, trying to sound casual.

"And suffer their indoctrination day in day out? It's bad enough to hear Erika singing Hitler's praises; I don't need to listen to a bunch of overenthusiastic nursery teachers."

"Maybe you could go and stay at your parents' place for a while?"

She scoffed. "Hamburg is as much a target of the bombings as Berlin. In fact, it's worse for them. We've only had the occasional air raids."

Q sighed. This wasn't going the way he wanted it to. "What about Julia? She's on a farm near Magdeburg, and that's only a few hours' train ride from Berlin. You could take Volker there. It might even help with his digestion problems."

"I don't want to leave you here alone. Who knows if I'll ever see you again?"

"*Liebling*, nothing will happen to me. But you're six months pregnant, and you need to rest. Face it, Berlin isn't safe anymore. You aren't getting enough sleep because of the air raids. Things need to change."

Hilde nodded. He was right. Even though their quarter hadn't taken a hit, not a day or night went by where they weren't forced to leave their beds and seek shelter. It was wearing her down both physically and mentally.

"Q, I don't want to leave you–"

"It won't be forever, but you need a break. Please take Volker and stay with Julia for a while. I'll join you for Christmas. That's only a few weeks away."

Hilde finally agreed. Normally, it was almost impossible to obtain a travel permit for personal or leisure travel. But because Hilde was pregnant and had a small child with her, she made a convincing case that she had to leave Berlin for a while and she received her travel papers without any problems.

Two days before she travelled, she came home livid and recounted what had happened as she stood in line waiting for her turn to get the travel permit stamped.

"You won't believe this, Q! That official saw that I was pregnant and congratulated me."

"Well, that isn't a reason to be angry, or is it?"

"Yes, it is. His exact words were, 'Congratulations on giving our Führer yet another Aryan child.'"

Q put his hands on her shoulders to calm her down, but couldn't stop himself from laughing out loud. "I hope you didn't punch him in the face."

She scowled at him but then joined his laughter. "I wanted to, but the urge to vomit on his shoes was bigger."

"You didn't…?"

"No, I didn't. I managed to get hold of a waste paper basket. You can't imagine how fast my papers were stamped and finished."

On the morning of December 6$^{th}$, he took her and Volker to the train and sent them off to Magdeburg.

# CHAPTER 31

The next day, Q met with his old friends Leopold and Otto. It always gave him a stab to the heart because they'd always been a quartet – until Jakob was murdered in the *Kristallnacht*.

So many things had happened since then, most of them bad. The friends had a silent understanding not to talk about politics, but today was different. As they sat in the bar, the usual music broadcast was interrupted by an urgent message and someone raised the volume on the radio.

*"We interrupt this program to bring you a special message. Our esteemed ally, Japan, has successfully beaten the United States of America. In a surprise attack, Japanese bombers attacked the Naval Station located in Oahu, Hawaii, crippling and destroying both their mediocre Navy and Air Force. Even now, Pearl Harbor burns and Germany celebrates our ally's victory.*

*"The Führer is very optimistic that the war will soon be won, and Germany will prevail over her enemies. The spiteful United States of America has paid for its interference, and other nations will soon reap their just rewards at the hands of German soldiers."*

Turmoil ensued in the bar, everyone talking at once. Most of the guests – all of them in uniform except for the three friends – echoed the opinions of the radio speaker, but Q thought differently. *Thank God. Now*

*America will have to officially enter the war.* "It's over. Germany is going to lose this war."

"I wouldn't be so sure. Hitler won't be stopped," Otto responded.

Q had yet to figure out on which side Otto stood. He'd not joined up but pulled a few strings to have his research work at the University be classified as *reserved profession.*

The same was true for Leopold. He owned a paint factory and seemed to be unbothered by the Nazis. While Q trusted Leopold completely on a personal level, he didn't necessarily trust his political convictions. It would be wiser to keep quiet.

"You're probably right," he said and changed the topic. "Have you been able to crack down the hydrogen cyanide molecules, Otto?"

Otto nodded. "We're working on it. It's highly poisonous and extremely flammable." Q exhaled in relief as the subject was safely navigated into a direction they all were comfortable with.

When they bid their goodbyes, Q was convinced that he needed to do more. Much more. Sabotage and intelligence gathering wasn't enough. He wanted to do something bold, something that would forever change the course of history. But what?

As he walked to the tram station with Leopold, they could see the red lights of the Tempelhof Airport in the distance. Suddenly, Q had an idea. He sent Leopold off on the tram and opted to walk home. It would take him three or four hours, plenty of time alone to think through his new idea.

The next day, he stormed into Erhard's office. "I have a brilliant idea!"

"Care to share it with me?" His friend chuckled.

"That's why I'm here. Let's take a walk, and I'll explain it to you."

"A walk? It's nine o'clock. I have work to do." But as he looked into Q's excited face, he took his hat and coat and left his office. On the way out he advised the secretary, "Fräulein Golz, Doctor Quedlin and I have an urgent appointment to visit with one of our suppliers. We'll be back in about an hour."

As soon as they'd left the company grounds and were out of earshot of anyone, Q started to explain. "I thought we could produce remote controlled blinkers."

"Blinkers – what for?" Erhard asked.

"That's the good part. With the remote control, we can make them start blinking when hostile aircraft are incoming and–"

"But how would we know when hostile aircraft were coming?"

Q thought for a moment. "Just like anyone else. Via the air raid sirens."

"Fine. And where do we position those blinkers and why?"

"We'll install them on the roofs of military buildings. When they start blinking, the English pilots can easily spot the strategic buildings to bomb and avoid civilian targets."

"Hmm." Erhard stopped walking. "It is a brilliant idea. And it could save thousands of civilian lives."

Q grinned. "Yes, it's fantastic, and we have all the means to do it. We can use one of the production lines on the weekends to make the blinkers, and we can easily build two or three remote controls as well."

"But we would need to be near the buildings because the range of the remote controls isn't very far," Erhard objected. "We could only light two or three buildings at the same time, and how fast can we get there once we hear the sirens? From where you live, it'll take much too long to get to any strategic military building."

"I haven't thought about that." Q shook his head and took up walking again. "What if we use the short-wave radio transmitters we're building for the Wehrmacht? I'm sure I can come up with a way to alter the blinkers so they could receive the radio signal. This way we can light all the buildings from wherever we are."

Erhard nodded. "Yes, we just have to keep the transmitter with us at all times."

"We should let Martin in on the plan," Q said. With new hope and a sense of accomplishment, they returned to the factory, but right before they reached the grounds, Erhard asked, "Just how do we get those blinkers onto the buildings? It's not as if we can simply go up there and assemble them."

# CHAPTER 32

Hilde shared the train compartment with a young woman who looked exceptionally dirty and unkempt – like someone who'd just crawled out of a heap of rubble. She couldn't hold back her curiosity and started a conversation with the girl, who introduced herself as Annegret.

Annegret confirmed her fears, telling her that she had been bombed out that day.

"Oh, I'm so sorry. That must have been an awful shock," Hilde said with genuine empathy, but before she could ask more details, the ticket officer entered and Hilde presented her papers.

Just as the man was about to return her papers, a Gestapo officer entered their compartment. Even though Hilde's papers were in order, she still felt shivers running down her spine. The picture of SS men beating a handbag thief to death was too deeply ingrained in her brain. As was the ever-present fear that they'd uncovered Q's resistance work and came to arrest her.

She waited with bated breath and tried not to show her relief when he finally returned her papers and turned his attention to Annegret. "Papers?"

The young woman suddenly looked like a frightened rabbit. *Well, doesn't every normal citizen hold her breath in the presence of the Gestapo or SS?*

The stern expression of the Gestapo officer softened as he read out loud Annegret's name and repeated it before he came to attention. "Fräulein Huber, may I say how sorry I am for your loss."

"*Danke.* I'm still in shock," said the girl and Hilde eyed her suspiciously.

Her suspicions only grew when the officer sang the praises of the late Obersturmbannführer Wolfgang Huber – Erika's father-in-law. Oh my God, that young lady couldn't be his daughter. It had been a while since she'd seen her at Erika's wedding, but she clearly remembered Annegret's high-pitched voice, which was in total contrast to the soft, subdued tone of this girl.

As soon as the officer left their compartment, Hilde accused the girl, "You're not Annegret Huber. Who are you?"

The girl's hand flew to her chest. "Of course I am."

Hilde shook her head at the girl's audacity. "You're lying."

"Why do you say that?" The Annegret impostor stared at her with pure terror in her eyes.

"I know Annegret, and you are not her."

The girl sagged and finally opened her mouth, "Look, the bombing today hit directly over the building in Nikolassee where I lived."

Hilde paled and grabbed her sleeping son tighter. She closed her eyes for a moment and prayed Q was okay. Even if her building had been hit, he could have been at work. He liked to work late. *Please. Please. Let him be fine.*

She gathered all her strength and forced out the words, "We live there. Where exactly was the hit?"

The young woman reached over to take her hand. "How horrible. Just about the whole block at the Rehwiese Park was flattened to the ground. Only the smaller buildings across the railway track weren't damaged."

Hilde sagged in relief and murmured, "Thank God."

"The alarms came too late, and most of the inhabitants didn't make it into the shelter. I was lucky because I got trapped under a broken staircase. Herr and Frau Huber, and Annegret, they're all dead."

"What is your real name?"

A long pause ensued before the girl finally answered. "Margarete Rosenbaum."

*She's a Jew. That's why she's lying.*

"All I want is to live." Tears pooled in Margarete's eyes, and she was barely able to form the words. "I was their maid for two years, but Herr Huber wanted to send me away by the end of the week."

Hilde had a good idea where a Jewish girl would have been sent. "Continue."

"I took Annegret's papers and then pinned the yellow star on her blouse. I just want to survive. Please."

Hilde didn't answer. Instead, she turned her head and looked out the window at the darkness beyond. *How far down can this country go?* A twenty-year-old girl had to assume someone else's identity in order to stay alive. This wasn't her country anymore.

She pondered whether she could help the girl but finally decided that the best she could do was to ignore everything that had happened during the last thirty minutes.

"I won't tell anyone," Hilde said and looked away again.

Volker awakened a little while later, and Hilde was thankful for the distraction. It was after dark when the train arrived in Magdeburg. As they stepped carefully down onto the platform, the girl helped her to unload her baggage and her son. Hilde met her eyes for a moment and said, "Good luck, Annegret."

Then she turned and stepped into the embrace of her sister Julia.

Initially, Hilde enjoyed her time on the farm with Julia. It was much more peaceful and relaxed than in the capital, but after a few days, she missed Q and her friends.

Julia had to work, like everyone else, and Hilde got increasingly lonely as the days turned into weeks. Hilde offered to help, but at seven months pregnant, she wasn't of much use with the hard work.

Volker wasn't much company either because he was now old enough to enjoy playing with the other children and the animals. The active little boy loved the animals, but he liked the handcarts even more. He would spend hours placing things into a handcart and then pulling it around, like a toy wagon.

Hilde was happy that he was enjoying himself, but she longed for Q to arrive for Christmas.

"I'm so glad you're here," she said with tears in her eyes when she finally met him at the train station.

"I've missed you and Volker so much," he said, hugging and kissing her.

They celebrated Christmas with Julia, but nobody was in the mood to enjoy it, except for Volker of course. Q was unusually distracted, and Hilde worried about him. Something had happened, but he wouldn't tell what it was.

When it was time for him to return to Berlin, she said, "I'm ready to come back with you."

"Hilde, I really think you should stay here until the baby is born."

"No! I won't have my baby so far away from you and my friends. Besides, I don't want to be alone any longer."

"It's safer here than in Berlin. You know that a big part of Nikolassee was reduced to rubble right after you left."

"I know, but I would rather die by your side than live without you."

He took her into his arms and whispered in her ear, "It's not yet time to die, Hildelein."

Q finally gave in, and right after New Year's they returned home. Despite knowing about the bomb damage to their quarter, she was still shocked to the core to see the sad remains of what used to be a thriving place.

One day, Hilde put Volker into his pram and walked to the building where Wolfgang Huber once lived. There wasn't much left of it. The entire building had collapsed in shambles, and only the back wall stood half intact.

An eerie cold seized her, and she sent a prayer to the sky, asking to keep Margarete safe, before she hurried away.

Apart from that, things had returned to normal, if one could call this life normal. But something was off, and the more time passed, the more certain Hilde became that Q was hiding something from her. She'd never seen him in such a state of anxious excitement, but whenever she asked him about it, he brushed it off. "I'm just worn out by the constant worry, and the raging war."

She could tell he was lying to her, but she didn't have the strength to confront him. With less than one month until the baby was due, she needed all her energy to keep her small family fed and keep Volker under control. The cute little man had developed into a little daredevil, and he missed the freedom of the countryside where he could play and run for hours on end.

She sighed. She wasn't entirely sure she wanted to know what Q was up to. In any case, a discussion with him would have to wait until the baby was born. Emma had agreed to stay with them for a month to help with Volker and the household chores, so Hilde could dedicate herself to the newborn.

# CHAPTER 33

Q jumped up, and his chair fell back. "It's not possible!"

Martin, Erhard, and he had come up with and discarded idea after idea. Infiltrating a construction company and pretending to have to do maintenance work on the roof. Climbing up like a cat burglar. Landing with a makeshift parachute. Overwhelming the security guards. Getting security clearance for some of the buildings. They just couldn't get access to the roofs of those darned buildings.

Martin and Erhard looked at each other before they nodded. "It was a good idea, but we just can't get those blinking lights up on the roofs. All buildings of strategic importance are too closely guarded."

Q sighed with disappointment. "We had everything worked out. The production of the blinkers, the remote control, the radio transmitters, everything...but we can't get them up there."

Erhard put a hand on his shoulder. "Don't take it personally. We'll come up with another idea to torpedo the war effort."

Martin nodded. "Yes, we can make a change, we just need another idea."

The three men tossed around a few ideas over the next days, but nothing to be taken seriously. During their next quality control meeting, they discussed the radio transmitters for the Wehrmacht when Q suddenly said, "We'll make a remote-controlled bomb."

318

The others looked at him with their jaws nearly on the floor. "A bomb? Certainly we could do that, but why?"

Q suddenly knew exactly what he had to do. "To assassinate Hitler."

"To…what?" Martin drawled, the words barely making a sound.

"Yes. I will assassinate the Führer," Q reinforced.

"That would certainly solve some problems," Erhard said.

All three of them started tossing ideas around with ardent zeal. In moments, the disappointment over their failure to find a way to install the blinkers on the roofs was forgotten, and they outplayed each other with ideas for their newest project.

"We need to find a weakness…a time when he is less protected and thus vulnerable," Martin suggested.

They made a plan of action and distributed tasks. Erhard would feel out other resistance groups, and Martin would keep his eyes and ears open at the weekly Party meetings for any information they might use. Q was tasked to find out Hitler's daily routine.

Several weeks later, they had to abandon the idea of assassinating Hitler – he was too well protected. Many before had tried, and nobody had ever succeeded. People outside his inner circle couldn't get close to the Führer anymore.

"What about Goebbels?" Erhard suggested. Goebbels was Minister of Propaganda and one of Hitler's most devoted followers. His excellent public speaking skills combined with a virulent anti-Semitism made him a dangerous weapon and an important pillar of Hitler's power.

"Goebbels?" Q asked. "If a more moderate person came into his position, that might lead to better conditions for the Jews and less support for the war amongst the civilians."

"Let's take the next week to think about it," Erhard suggested.

Q returned to the laboratory and started his daily work. For weeks, he'd been thinking about a way to shorten the war and speed up the tumbling of the Thousand-Year Reich. Could they have found the solution?

But could killing someone in cold blood be justified, even if done to save hundreds, maybe even thousands, of lives?

In March 1942, Hilde gave birth to her second baby, another son, and Q was proud as a peacock. He instantly fell in love with the cute little baby with a down of straight brown hair, much different from Volker's white-blond curly locks. But he shared the same blue eyes as his brother and Q himself.

"Hilde, he looks exactly like you," Q said.

She took a look at the baby's crumpled face and laughed. "I hope not." Then she stroked his tiny head with her palm and held him against her chest. "What shall we name him?"

"He looks like a Peter, doesn't he?"

"Peter? Well, I like it."

Q knew that Hilde had secretly hoped for a girl and had already chosen a girl's name, but for a boy they'd still been undecided between three or four options.

Emma, who had already arrived a few days ago, came into the bedroom with Volker holding her hand.

"I wanna see the baby!" Volker shouted and rushed toward the bed.

"Slow down!" Q scolded him. "Your brother, Peter, is very tiny and you will crush him with your weight."

Volker instantly looked guilty and slowed down his steps. Then he glanced at his mother with a questioning look in his eyes, and Q saw how a warm smile spread across her face as she nodded. Volker crawled onto the bed and carefully caressed his baby brother's hand.

Q's heart constricted, seeing the three of them like that, happy and united in love. He couldn't – no, he wouldn't – be responsible for tearing them apart. Something had to give.

Emma put a hand on his arm and said, "We should take a picture of them."

He nodded and went to his study to retrieve the photo camera to capture this moment of love.

~

The weeks went by, and the more Q thought about the planned assassination attempt, the more worried he became. Not for himself, but for Hilde and the boys. The possibility of destroying their happiness lay hard on his conscience, so hard that one day he decided to visit his mother.

"Wilhelm, what a surprise," Ingrid said as she opened the door for him.

Q fidgeted with his hands. "Hello, Mother. Can I come in?"

"Certainly, my darling. But what brings you here, in plain daylight on a workday? Is everything fine with Hilde and the boys?"

"Yes." He didn't know what else to say. *They're fine for now, but soon their lives might be torn to pieces – because of me.*

His mother smiled. "I'm getting old. The last time all of you visited, I had to sit in my armchair the rest of the day and relax. Volker surely is a handful, but Peter is such a sweet and content baby. They're so different from each other."

"Mother..." He looked at the woman he'd loved his entire life and longed to tell her the truth.

"Son, I'll make us an infusion." She led him to the tiny kitchen and made an herb tea. "I'm sorry, I don't have coffee."

"Nobody has real coffee anymore..." Q sat down and stared at his mother's back, while she boiled water. He wasn't sure why he'd come here. She wouldn't be able to help. Nobody could.

Ingrid carried two steaming cups and sat down at the kitchen table with Q. "What do you have on your heart?"

The burden of his conscience weighed him down, and he couldn't look into his mother's eyes as he handed her an envelope stuffed with money. "Will you keep this for me? If anything happens..." He couldn't bring himself to finish the sentence.

His mother put her hand under his chin and raised his head to look into his eyes. She would be able to see right into his soul, like she always had. Now she would scold him for being such a foolish and egotistic man. But she didn't.

After a long time, she said, "Wilhelm, I'm worried about you. You've always been a freethinker, but these are not the times to play hero. What-ever you are up to, I don't want to know about it. But promise me one thing...be careful."

He nodded. "I will."

321

She kissed his forehead and took the envelope. "I'll guard this until you come and take it back."

"Thank you, Mother. I love you." He rushed out to hide his glistening eyes. *Damn! Damn! Damn!*

A few weeks later, Q came up with the perfect solution to protect Hilde and the boys in case he was found out.

One night when the children were asleep, he took Hilde's hand and led her to the couch. "Hilde, I want you to hear me out. Things are getting more dangerous, and I worry about you and the boys. I need to keep you safe."

She made a face.

He continued, "If we are no longer together, nobody will hold you responsible for my actions."

"What?" she demanded, her eyes wide open with shock.

"We'll feign a fight, and you will leave. Take the boys someplace safe where my actions won't reflect on you."

"Absolutely not! There's no way I'd do that. Without you, I might as well die right now." She jumped from the couch and stared at him, her hands resting on her hips.

"Hilde, please be reasonable. If you can't think about yourself, think about the children."

"My answer is no. This discussion is over." Turning on her heel, Hilde took herself off to bed.

The next morning before he had to leave for work, he brought the subject up again. "Hilde, just say you'll think about it," he pleaded with her.

But she was adamant. "I will not! Nothing will make me change my mind about this. We are a family, and we will stay together until they force us apart. That's the end of the discussion."

This went on for a few days, until he finally relented. "Fine. We'll stay together."

For the first time since he'd brought up the topic, she smiled at him. "Finally, you're coming to your senses."

# CHAPTER 34

Hilde put two mugs of ersatz coffee on the breakfast table and watched her sleepy husband as he took a big gulp. "God, how I hate this *Muckefuck*! Isn't there real coffee to be had anywhere?"

She hid her smile at his outburst and took a sip of her own, then grimaced. "I don't know why I still drink that stuff. Maybe we should instead try one of the suggestions from the propaganda ministry."

"What?" Q looked at her and raised a brow.

"They now want us to use common weeds as food."

"Weeds? You can't be serious." He put down his mug. "Although I'm not sure anything can be worse than this. If we at least had sugar…"

"See here." She showed him a leaflet that had been distributed to all households and summarized the contents. "The solution to our malnutrition apparently is growing along the roadsides and in the wooded areas. Here's a recipe to make a salad of stinging nettle, common dandelions, and cabbage thistle. Ugh." Hilde put the leaflet down and grimaced.

Q grinned at her. "Hmm – I can see the children running to the table for their share of stinging nettle. Any more pearls of wisdom in there?"

She scanned the leaflet and shook her head. "Not much. They advise the good German housewife to collect those 'nutritious herbs' along the sides of the road to prepare a healthy meal for our families. Apparently, those adjustments to our diet will help us live even better and healthier than before the war."

"Well, then let's take a walk along the Autobahn and see if we can find ourselves a good lunch."

Hilde tossed the leaflet onto the table in disgust. "What a load of bullshit!"

Her outburst caused a laugh to spring from Q's lips. Normally she was much better at controlling her response. But the war and the constant threat of being discovered had frayed her nerves.

Q sighed, running a hand through his hair. "This is the price we have to pay for Hitler's delusions of grandeur. I'd dispose of him if I could."

His remark was casual, but Hilde was shocked nonetheless. *Would Q actually kill the man, given the chance?*

Her heart constricted. Suddenly his strange behavior, the need to get rid of her and the children, everything fell into place like a jigsaw. She took a deep breath to calm her racing heart, but she didn't dare ask. She wasn't even sure she wanted to know.

Germany was in the middle of the worst war in the history of mankind, but the Nazi regime failed to acknowledge the hardships for the civilians and touted their war successes. According to the media and leaflets, everyone not willing to suffer for their leader was a traitor to the nation and should be treated as such.

Hilde often stood for hours in line to buy food or clothing. Keeping an entire family well fed wasn't an easy task, and she was grateful that she had enough milk to nurse Peter. It was one less problem that weighed down on her shoulders.

Peter was such a contented baby, and Hilde barely noticed his presence. He would be happy to play with an old piece of cloth and lie in his crib babbling at himself. He'd even sleep through the frequent trips to the bomb shelter, and she'd often joke with Q that you could literally drop a bomb beside his head without waking him.

Volker, on the other hand, had become a handful and hard to manage. He was very intelligent for his age and more curious than was good for him. He kept Hilde on her toes around the clock. During the day, he ventured out, and at night, he was plagued by nightmares.

The trips to the shelter were something he abhorred and feared. Almost every night, she had to drag a crying toddler down into the cellar. But what else could she do? He was too young to understand and too old not to understand.

Q helped her as much as he could, but as the war wore on, everyone was required to work overtime and put in weekends. Vacation was a word of the past. And to be honest, what would they do during vacation?

Hilde sighed and put down her needlework. She'd resorted to mending and re-mending Volker's clothes, attaching pieces of textile to make the pants and shirts cover his growing legs and arms. Right then, she was cutting up an old skirt of hers and making it into matching shirts for the boys.

When would this end? Desperation took hold of her, and she shed a few tears.

On Sunday, Leopold Stieber and his wife came over to visit, with their children. Hilde offered them some bread and herb tea.

When Dörthe saw the green liquid, she raised her brow. "You're not picking weeds at the side of the street, are you?"

Hilde laughed. "I wouldn't. They could just as well ask us to sweep up the dust on the streets and stretch the flour with it."

Dörthe grimaced. "Ugh."

"No, I grew lemon balm and peppermint on the windowsill."

Leopold and Q joined their discussion, and soon they were telling jokes about the bad conditions.

Leopold said, "This one is good: Someone tried to commit suicide by hanging himself, only the rope had been made with such poor quality material, it couldn't withstand his weight and broke.

"He then tried to drown himself in the river, but the suit he was wearing contained too much wood, and he ended up floating and couldn't make himself sink.

"Despondent, he returned home and went back to living and eating only the official rations the government gave him. He was dead two months later."

Everyone shared a laugh; it was better than crying in despair. Only

Dörthe sent her husband a scathing glance. "You should know better than to tell such a joke. We could all be sent to prison."

"Come on, Dörthe, we do need to have some fun."

The Stiebers soon left and the daily routine returned. Hilde made it a habit to take turns visiting her mother-in-law and her own mother. She also took many pictures of the boys and regularly sent letters to Emma and Carl.

Her relationship with her mother had steadily improved over the last year. Hilde had finally accepted Annie's selfish nature and tried to not let it bother her.

Her mother seemed to make an effort to change, and she was always excited to see the boys – for a short while. Volker's explorative spirit and Annie's immaculate apartment didn't mesh well.

"I can hold the baby for you. You keep Volker away from my glassware."

Hilde sighed and handed Peter to his grandmother. Some things would never change. Peter seemed to be quite taken with his grandmother and soaked her blouse in baby drool, which earned him a sour face but no complaint.

Meanwhile, Volker tried to discover how fast he could run from one end of the living room to the other, cheering himself on and clapping his hands after each turn.

"He's much too wild," Annie complained, and Hilde tried to distract him with a picture book she'd brought along.

When Peter began to fuss, Hilde said, "I'll take him back, he must be hungry."

As she began to nurse him, her mother gave her a disgusted glance. "You shouldn't be doing that. It's not ladylike. It would be better to give him a bottle."

"I disagree. Besides, the milk is bad, even when it's available. How can you feed an infant only skim milk?"

Annie retreated into the kitchen, and it soon started smelling heavenly. She returned a few minutes later with two cups of coffee. Real coffee.

Hilde finished nursing Peter and then laid him against her shoulder. "Oh my God, Mother, where did you get real coffee?"

But her mother chose not to answer, and instead, sipped at the cup. "It's good, isn't it?"

It was. The full aroma of sweet and fruity coffee with just a hint of pleasant bitterness exploded on Hilde's taste buds. "Hmm. Wonderful."

A few minutes later, Hilde said, "In the tram, I overheard a conversation. Their neighbor got caught trying to stockpile food from a farmer and has been sent to one of the labor camps."

Annie nodded. "Well done. *Im Krieg ist sparen Deine Pflicht.*"

Hilde raised a brow at her mother's attitude. "Do you really believe it is your duty to skimp because we are at war?"

"Yes. It's also a crime against the Fatherland to keep more rations than someone is assigned."

"Says the woman who has real coffee in her home," Hilde responded, unable to keep the bitterness from her tone.

Annie shrugged, not looking the least bit embarrassed. "My husband is a famous opera singer. I can't well decline if people want to show their appreciation for his talents."

"Did you know that people are actually killed in those so-called labor camps? Especially those in Poland?"

"Those are just silly rumors." Annie set down her empty cup and waved her hand, as if she could wave away the truth so easily.

"Are they?"

"Does it matter if they're true? The Jews deserve it for ruining Germany. The least they can do is work to help bring her back to her former glory."

"Mother, they're being killed." Hilde scowled.

"I don't believe that for a minute." Her mother stood up and looked at the clock on the bureau. "I'm afraid I have to leave now. Robert is singing tonight at the State Opera."

"Well, give him my best wishes. I'll come by next week again."

On her way home, Hilde pondered over the fate of those deported to one of the labor camps. She hadn't believed the news when Q first brought it to her attention. But he'd sworn it was true; it had reached him through some secret channels from someone working for the Polish resistance.

Yes, all the signs pointed to its being the truth. No one had ever come back to tell. She remembered the young woman she'd met on the train to Magdeburg. SS-Obersturmbannführer Huber's maid. Why was she so afraid, if she didn't have inside knowledge? Something only a few of the initiated knew about.

# CHAPTER 35

Q spent many sleepless nights and anguished days arguing with his conscience. He was a pacifist and had always prided himself on believing in the good of mankind.

But in light of the atrocities the regime had committed and continued to commit, he felt the urge to change the course of history.

He wrote in his diary…

*Is one human life worth more than another one? Is one life worth less than a thousand?*

*Who am I to take the decision out of God's hand of who should live and who shouldn't?*

*Is it my mission to go against the basic rules of mankind and murder one person to try and save thousands?*

*Am I any better than the worst of the Nazi followers if I raise my hand against a fellow human?*

*No, the die is cast, and I should not waver in my faith to do the right thing. I believe the gods have put me onto this world for a reason.*

*If I do not survive, I'm consoled by the fact that I always acted in good faith. I hope my children and history will one day forgive my deeds and see them for what they are: a desperate attempt to turn the wheel around for a world worth living in.*

. . .

Q closed the diary and hid it on the top shelf in his study. Then he went to work. Summer was in full bloom, the blossoming chestnut trees a stark contrast to the burnt buildings lining the streets of Berlin. No major street had gone unscathed by the continuous bombings.

Martin and Erhard were already waiting for him. During the last weeks and months, they had meticulously worked on their assassination plan, adding detail after detail – coming up with an idea, only to discard it when they gathered the next piece of information about Goebbels.

They had investigated everything about him. His daily routine. His office. His home. His family. His travels. The people he spent time with. Finally, everything began to fall into place, and their plan was slowly taking shape.

"His office is too closely guarded," Erhard said.

"But we don't want to harm his family, so his house is out of the question," Martin said and then added, "Have you seen where he lives?"

"No." The other two shook their heads in unison. Martin had been tasked with that part of the operation, and as a devoted Party member, he'd even managed to get an invitation to one of the pompous parties Goebbels liked to host.

"He has bought the estates of two exiled Jewish bank directors and joined the properties. The mansion he's built to replace the two former ones is simply outstanding."

"We wouldn't get inside anyways," Q cautioned and rubbed his chin. "He lives on that upper-class island Schwanenwerder in the Wannsee, right?"

Martin nodded, and Q continued, "I live not too far away from there. We used to take bicycle tours along the Wannsee. As far as I know, there's only one bridge connecting the island with the mainland. The Schwanenwerder Bridge."

"I know that bridge. There's not much traffic; only inhabitants are allowed on the island nowadays," Erhard said.

Martin agreed. "He has to cross that bridge every morning and every evening. It's the perfect place to plant our bomb."

"We have to think about it," Q said, and everyone agreed. They decided that Q should have a look at the bridge on the weekend since he lived the closest to it. They would meet the following week to discuss further steps.

Back at home, Q wanted to tell Hilde what he was up to. He opened his mouth several times to explain, but no words came out. Whenever he looked into her trusting blue eyes, his throat went dry.

No, he just couldn't bring himself to destroy the little peace of mind she still had.

Always in tune with her husband, Hilde picked up on his worries. "What's wrong, my love? You've been incredibly tense these last weeks."

He sighed. "I am. All of this anxiety is taking a toll on me. But I don't want to bother you with it; you have your hands full with the boys."

Hilde studied his face intensely, and he forced himself not to flinch. "We should go for a walk to the Wannsee beach on the weekend – it will help to get your mind off whatever troubles you."

*Hell no!* "That's a good idea. We have to hold onto what little happiness we have left in these dark days," Q answered and felt like a traitor. How could he concentrate on his family when the potential crime scene lay in plain sight? On the other hand, it would be the perfect excuse to take a closer look at the Schwanenwerder Bridge.

The next Monday, Q returned to Loewe and his partners in crime with a plan. The small wooden bridge was the perfect target.

"We can plant our bomb beneath the bridge, and I'll detonate when Goebbels's Mercedes passes over," Q explained.

"We have to find out the times he passes over the bridge and set a timer," Erhard said.

"No, that's too hit-or-miss. I'll wait nearby and trigger the remote control right when the car rolls over the bomb. Because the bridge is so old, cars have to go slow. It will be easy to identify the exact moment."

Martin shook his head. "I don't like it. It's too dangerous. If someone sees you–"

"This is the crux. I initially wanted to hide behind the trees, but that's too suspicious. I need a legitimate reason to linger near the bridge, maybe for hours…"

Erhard jumped up and shouted, "Fishing!"

"What?" Q asked, quite puzzled by the sudden outburst of his friend.

"Fishing. You disguise yourself as a fisherman and wait on a boat in the water with the fishing rod in hand a short distance away from the bridge."

"That's a fantastic idea. That will work," Martin chimed in, and even Q had to agree that this definitely could work. "Now we only need to secure the boat and the fishing equipment."

"It's a deal then," Erhard stated. "Let's start building our bomb."

Building the bomb was the easy part because they could tap into the resources at Loewe. Martin was tasked with building the bomb itself while Q and his wireless equipment department handled the remote control unit. His employees, of course, thought they were working on a new prototype for the Wehrmacht.

It took Q plenty of time and a considerable amount of effort and money before he was able to obtain the boat and fishing equipment.

Once the equipment was in place, they just had to determine at which times Goebbels would most likely cross the bridge. Martin and Q worked out a schedule so that they could take turns observing their target.

# CHAPTER 36

Q was waiting for his tram to arrive when a teenage boy joined him at the tram stop.

"Are you Herr Quedlin?" the boy asked.

"Yes." Q nodded, wondering what he could want.

"I have a message for you. Open to page seven." With these words, the boy handed him a newspaper and quickly disappeared around the corner.

Q's curiosity was piqued, but he didn't dare open the paper in plain sight. Instead, he meticulously folded it twice and stored it in his briefcase. Only when he was home, in the safe confinement of his study, did his shaky fingers find page seven.

He gasped. A note lay inside: *Meet tomorrow at six p.m. at Westkreuz train station. Bring your half of the torn map.*

His heart raced. Q hadn't heard anything from Moscow since Pavel had left Berlin more than a year ago. Communication was difficult these days, and from Erhard, he knew that the other resistance groups also had trouble staying in touch.

What if this was a trap? He retrieved his half from his desk and scrutinized it carefully. Could anyone have known about the map?

Hilde called out to him. "Q, dinner is ready." He stored the map and the note in his briefcase and exited his study to have dinner with his family.

Later that evening, he told Hilde about the note he'd received.

"If this was a trap, how would they know about you and the map the Russian agent gave you?" she asked.

"The Gestapo has means to get everyone to talk." He shuddered, remembering the horror stories he'd heard.

She put a hand on his arm. "This may be so. But I believe the Gestapo wouldn't go to so much trouble if they wanted to arrest you. They'd burst in here and haul you away."

A shiver of fear ran down his spine. "You're right. I will go to the meeting place."

The next day he was sitting on pins and needles, unable to concentrate on his work. More than once, he opened his briefcase to feel the map tucked away inside a newspaper. The hands on the clock in the laboratory moved excruciatingly slowly until it was finally time to leave.

Q arrived at Westkreuz Station, which was crowded with workers on their way home. As if by magic, a man appeared and asked if he had a map of Berlin. *This must be my contact.* Cold sweat broke out on Q's forehead. Unlike the other agents he'd met, this one clearly was German and not Russian. Q barely remembered the question he was supposed to ask.

"Is the hike up Mount Etna strenuous, *mein Herr*?"

The man looked confused and then laughed. "Not at all. Only if you intend it at night. Didn't you trust the map, comrade?"

Relief flooded his entire body, and Q shook the agent's extended hand. "Never can be too careful, comrade. Can I see the map, please?"

They sat on one of the waiting benches, and the agent handed him a newspaper with the map inside. Q laid it beside his own. They fit perfectly.

"Satisfied?" When Q nodded, the agent introduced himself. "Gerald Meier, Wehrmacht deserter and proud member of the Red Army."

"You probably already know who I am," Q said and leaned back to watch a few pigeons fighting for crumbs. Before the war, old men and women had come here to feed the birds, but nowadays nobody had food to spare.

"I thought all agents had been recalled," Q asked. "How did you get back into Germany?"

"That's quite a story. Care to take a ride?"

Q nodded, and they jumped on the next suburban train. Gerald gestured to keep silent until they reached their destination. After a fifteen-minute ride, they got off at one of the deserted suburban stations that only saw crowds twice a day.

They found another waiting bench and sat down. "I parachuted into Sweden about a month ago and made my way down here," Gerald said. "Because I'm German, I've had no problem getting along, and I've been living in Berlin with some old friends."

Gerald Meier probably wasn't his real name, if he really was a Wehrmacht deserter.

"How do you make contact with Moscow?" Q asked.

"I have a transmitter."

"Why me?"

"My superiors gave me a list of contacts I should try and re-activate. Pavel was sure you'd still be on our side. Is that so?"

Q nodded. "My opinions haven't changed. In fact…"

"In fact, what?"

"Nothing. What kind of information do you need?"

Gerald squinted his eyes and looked sharply at Q before nodding. "Basically everything you can give us. Headquarters will decide whether it's important for their strategy or not. A summary of production at Loewe would be a good start. Together with blueprints for any and all new advances you've made in the last year. Especially wireless transmission, echo-sound, and this new radar thing everyone raves about."

"I can do this, but it will take some time. A week at least."

"Fine, meet me a week from now. Same place, same time." With a nod, Gerald stood and walked away.

Q was left alone in a deserted train station with plenty of information to think about. He would have a lot of work to do.

# CHAPTER 37

H ilde had just put the boys to bed when she heard the door.

"You're late, Q. I was worried."

He took her into his arms. "I'm sorry. I wish someone would invent a telephone that we can always carry with us. Then I could have advised you."

Hilde laughed. "How would that work? Should we always drag along a cable reel? Maybe loop it around our necks."

"No, it would need to work without a cable." He furrowed his brows and crossed his arms over his chest. "In fact, a few years back, the Canadian David Hings invented a portable two-way radio and called it a Walkie-Talkie. The problem with those Walkie-Talkies is that their range is very limited, and they work even less reliably in a city with many buildings, but I might be able to–"

"Q, you digress. Tell me about the meeting with that...man."

Q relayed what happened, closing with, "I have to replicate as many technical instructions as possible until next week."

"I could help," she offered.

"You? Absolutely not. I'm not dragging you into this." He plopped down on the couch. "Is there dinner left for me?"

Hilde smiled. "Yes, I kept it warm for you. And nice change of topic."

"You know me too well." Q smirked. "But I am hungry."

"Fine. I'll set the table for you."

Hilde thought this was the end of the discussion. Since the birth of Peter, Q had been overly protective and had tried to keep her away from his resistance work. It was a wonder he'd told her about the Russian agent.

She frowned at the memory of his hilarious suggestion of making her leave after a feigned fight. *Over my dead body.* An icy shiver ran down her spine, and she pushed the foreboding away. There wouldn't be any dead bodies. Not hers. Not Q's. Not anyone's.

But three days later, Q came home from work with a pile of papers and asked her to type them up later in the evening.

Hilde eyed them suspiciously. "What's this?"

"Just some technical material," he said without going into further detail.

But Hilde knew.

She retrieved the children and seated them at the table for dinner. Q's face shone with pride as he looked at his sons. While Volker was the spitting image of his father, Peter took after his mother. Barely six months old, he was already sitting at the table with them and eating the same, albeit mashed-up, food.

After dinner, Q read a book to Volker while Hilde rocked Peter to sleep on her lap. When both children were sound asleep, Q and Hilde retreated to his study.

She'd often done the writing and copying for him, and sat down at the typewriter, ready to have him dictate the technical texts to her.

"No, wait," he said. "I want you to layer several papers on top of each other."

Hilde observed him layering white paper, blueprint paper, and brown paper before he handed her the pile. "Here, put this into the machine."

"Why do I need to do this? We haven't done it this way before."

"Hilde, I just want to try it this way. Besides, it's better that you don't know everything. You need to be able to say you had no knowledge about the technical things you were typing."

She exhaled a long breath. "Fine. Let's start." *I'll bet this has to do with meeting that Russian agent.*

When she had filled the paper, she took it out, removed the white paper from the pile, and replaced it with a new one. The letters on the white paper were slightly smeared, but still legible. *Why did he want the letters to be smeared?*

Q now met with Gerald on a weekly basis. He handed him all the intelligence he, Erhard, and Martin could possibly gather, not only from Loewe but also from every source they had access to. Erhard and Q were still active members of several scientific circles, and Martin often got hold of classified material via his Party connections.

Gerald always praised the good quality of the information, and more than once brought back a message from Moscow on how much they appreciated the detailed intelligence about position finder beacons, a bomb that automatically steered by means of light, and even a technical paper on the use of hydrogen peroxide to propel torpedoes of V-weapons – weapons of retaliation.

"Do you think this will help to shorten the war?" Q asked.

Gerald tried to say something uplifting but then shook his head. "I'm afraid not. Despite the messages of endurance from the official channels, there's nothing that gives me new hope. The Wehrmacht is overrunning our Red Army, and I'm afraid Russia is in danger of losing the battle of Stalingrad."

On the next meeting, Gerald was strangely withdrawn. He avoided eye contact with Q and even stopped joking about the pep talks from his superiors.

"Something wrong?" Q asked him.

"No. Everything is all right; I guess all the tension is taking a toll on me." Gerald squirmed.

"Me too. You have no idea how often I wanted to jump ship."

"No. Now's not the time. We might be getting closer to victory," Gerald said.

Q doubted that, but he had an ace up his sleeve: the assassination attempt on Goebbels. It had to happen soon because winter was coming and the Wannsee might freeze up. Preparations had been ongoing throughout summer, and despite various setbacks and postponements, they had finally settled on a date. December 1st 1942.

He knew he was playing a dangerous game and wanted to get it over with before he met Gerald again. Then he'd be able to bring some good news. *I hope.*

"I think we should wait and not meet again until December. I'm swamped with work and can't give you much useful information at the moment," Q said.

Gerald flinched. "No, we have to meet before that. Moscow depends on your intelligence reports. We're so close to making progress in the battle of Stalingrad."

"Fine." Q sighed. "Give me at least two weeks and let's meet at the end of the month." It would be two days before the assassination and might even give him a small reprieve to have something else to think about.

That night, Q returned home and dropped a bomb on his wife. "We're going to assassinate Goebbels."

Hilde swayed and held on to the table before plopping down on her chair. She gulped several times. "You're serious, aren't you?"

"Dead serious."

A nervous giggle escaped her mouth. "Why you?"

Q stroked her head. "It has to be done, and I'm in the best position to do it."

They sat on the couch into the wee hours of the night, holding onto one another. Hilde whispered, "Two weeks. I'm afraid."

"I'm afraid too. But I have Martin and Erhard covering for me. Nobody will ever know I was near that bridge."

Martin would help him attach the bomb the day before the planned attack, and he would cover for him at Loewe while Q was sitting on the water in his boat waiting for Goebbels's limousine to cross the bridge.

Hilde trembled in his arms. "Please calm down," he urged her when she started to cry. "Tell me what you've done this week."

Hilde dried her tears. "I started weaning Peter. He's such a big boy now and eats so well with us. It's a bit sad but will give me more independence."

Q hugged her. "Yes, our baby is growing rapidly. And Volker, he's such an intelligent boy. When this war is over, we might add a little girl to our family, what do you think?"

She leaned against him and laughed. "With our luck, it will be a third boy."

"Doesn't matter. Let's go to bed and practice."

As they passed the nursery, Hilde disappeared inside to give the boys a kiss and then returned with a winter coat in her hands.

"I finished this today. I made it for Volker from one of your old jackets. Now he will at least have a memory of you if you should die."

Q took her into his arms and promised to take every precaution. "Even if I get caught, there's nothing they can hold against you. Remember that. I will love you for eternity."

He took her to their bedroom and made sweet love to her, holding her afterwards until the sun rose over the horizon.

# CHAPTER 39

The days crawled by at a snail's pace as Q prepared for the assassination. Everything was finished, and all they had to do was wait.

Meeting Gerald after work was a welcome distraction from Q's anxiety. He didn't have much to report because his thoughts had been focused solely on the attack. But still, he'd managed to copy a few construction drawings.

Q arrived at Potsdamer Platz by underground and surfaced onto the square. The November wind chilled his bones and fog wafted across the vast square.

As he approached the meeting spot on the stairs leading up to the train station, he was suddenly surrounded by Gestapo officers. "Halt! You're arrested."

Q's heart sank. Did they mean him? He looked around, seeing no sign of Gerald, only the six Gestapo officers. His pulse raced, and despite the cold, sweat formed on his forehead. "Is there a problem, officers?"

"Put your hands up! You are arrested for crimes against Germany and the Party."

Q did as he was asked, putting up no resistance as two officers grabbed him rather roughly and dragged him to a waiting car. They pushed him inside, and the car took off with him and the three Gestapo men inside.

"What have I done?" Q asked, trying to keep the fear and nerves out of his voice.

The senior officer looked at him and sneered, "You will be informed of the charges against you, but not here. You are coming with us."

Q sent up a silent prayer to the gods above to keep his family safe. The image of Hilde holding Peter in her arms, with Volker standing by her side as he left this morning, filled his mind.

*I love you, my darlings!*

After ten years of spying and trying to bring down the regime, he'd finally been caught.

*It is over.*

# PART III: UNWAVERING

# CHAPTER 1

*November 30, 1942*

Hilde Quedlin repeatedly glanced at the clock on the sideboard while she sat on the floor playing with her children. Three-year-old Volker played with wooden blocks handed down from his aunts while nine-month-old Peter relentlessly tried to balance on his hands and knees. He was so close to crawling, and Hilde's heart filled with pride and joy as she watched both of her little rays of sunshine.

Worry seeped into her. Today, Q had met the Russian agent after work and should be coming back any minute. Time crawled as she prayed for her husband's safe return home.

She sniffed the distinctive smell of a full diaper and huddled Peter in her arms to carry him to the nursery. The little man was less than enthusiastic to be disturbed in his crawling exercises and kicked his little feet against his mother.

Hilde laughed. "Easy, little man. I'll let you down again when you're clean and fresh."

When she returned to the living room, she glanced at the clock again. *Why hasn't Q returned?* It usually didn't take that long.

A sharp knock on the door interrupted her worries. He'd probably forgotten his keys. She settled Peter on her hip and patted Volker's head as she passed him to open the door.

It wasn't Q.

Fear gripped her at the sight of two officers in long black leather coats. Gestapo.

"Frau Quedlin?" one of them asked

Her voice failed, and she could only nod.

"You are under arrest."

Despite the baby warming her, the blood chilled in her veins. "What? Why? I don't understand…" Hilde said, terror in her voice.

"All will be explained to you, but you must come with us now." The younger officer said, his dead steel-blue eyes seeming to look through her.

"No, please…my children. There is no one else here to watch them," Hilde pleaded and pressed Peter tighter against her. He didn't like the treatment and kicked to be set down.

The senior Gestapo officer looked at the little boy. With straight, light-brown hair and blue eyes, he was the spitting image of his mother, and Hilde thought she saw a glimpse of compassion in the officer's eyes, but she could have been wrong.

At that moment, Volker came rushing from the living room and froze in his tracks at the sight of the black-coated men. He clung onto Hilde's skirts and peeked around her knees. Volker was the epitome of an Aryan child. Hilde had let his hair grow, and his white-blond curls framed his pale skin and bright blue eyes in the cutest way possible. When he grew into a man, he would look exactly like his father.

"They'll be taken to the children's ward," the younger officer said, dissolving her illusion of leniency.

"No, please…let me call my mother…" Hilde's heart stopped at the notion of Q's and her little rays of sunshine fending for themselves in some orphanage.

"Call her," the older officer said, silencing the protest of the other one. "We can search the place while we wait." He stepped into the foyer, causing Hilde to stumble back, and she watched in growing horror as three more officers rushed inside and began opening the drawers and cupboards, rummaging without care through the contents.

"Please, what is this about? My husband is–"

The younger officer turned on her. "Your husband has already been arrested. Make your call."

Hilde swallowed hard and ushered Volker into the kitchen. With shaking hands, she placed Peter in his high chair.

"Mama?" Volker shrieked, watching with wide eyes as the Gestapo officers ransacked the house.

"Shush. It will be okay, Volker. Mama's calling grandma to come stay with you for a bit. Won't that be fun?" Hilde picked up the phone and dialed her mother's number with trembling fingers. A stone fell from her heart when Annie answered on the third ring.

"Annie Klein."

"Mother, it's Hilde. I need you to come stay with the children. Please...the Gestapo is here and say I must go with them." Hilde's voice was wobbly, and she had to lean against the wall to steady herself.

"The Gestapo? What have you done this time?" Annie wanted to know, her voice accusatory, causing Hilde to flinch.

"Nothing, there must be some mistake. Please, could you come right away?" She hated to ask her mother for this favor. Annie was probably the least suitable person to take care of the two active boys, but who else would rush to her house with the Gestapo present?

"I do have to get ready to go to the opera tonight, but I guess I could cancel it and come over."

"You have no idea how much this means to me..." Hilde sighed. At least her children would be safe.

"I'm not doing this for you, but for my grandchildren." Annie gave an annoyed sound. "I thought your days of troublemaking had stopped when you got married."

Hilde chose not to argue with her mother. "I will tell them you are on your way. Thank you."

But Annie was gone. She'd hung up the phone without responding or offering her daughter a word of reassurance. When Hilde looked up, the senior Gestapo officer was standing in the kitchen, watching her with narrowed eyes.

"My mother is on her way. She doesn't live far away, and it will take fifteen or twenty minutes…" Her voice strangled as emotion closed her throat like a vice.

"Fine. We will wait for her arrival."

Hilde nodded and rushed to Peter, who had started wailing from his chair. She picked the frightened child up, and his little arms wrapped around her neck. "Shush, Mama's here."

The senior officer continued to observe her with cold eyes, giving Hilde the chills. Her heart was beating an erratic rhythm until she'd gathered enough courage to address him.

"Please, can you tell me what's happening? Why am I being arrested? Why was my husband arrested?" Her eyes searched the face of the officer for an emotion, anything. But it was as animated as a marble statue.

"You will be informed of the charges against you once we arrive at Prinz-Albrecht-Strasse 8."

The breath stuck in her lungs even as cold sweat broke out on her palms. Hilde hugged her baby tight. *Gestapo Headquarters.* The words reverberated through her body, sending tremors into every limb. The ornate building looked nice enough on the outside, but everyone had heard the rumors about what went on inside the three-story stone building. Horrible visions filled her mind, and an icy hand grabbed at her heart. It was all she could do not to break down in tears.

"Mama, I'm hungry," Volker whined, coming to lean against her knees where she sat.

Hilde brushed a hand over his head and hugged him close. "Grandma Annie will be here soon, and I will have her get you something to eat, all right?"

Volker was such a good little boy, and he nodded, turning to look at the Gestapo officer in silence. Hilde wanted to hide her children away from the horror that she feared was to come into their lives, but she was powerless to do so.

Fifteen minutes later, her mother swept into the kitchen, a look of incredulity on her face. "Hilde, what is the meaning of this?"

"Mother, I–"

Annie turned away from her daughter and addressed the Gestapo officer with her brightest smile. "*Kommissar,* I'm Annie Klein. My

350

husband, the opera singer Robert Klein, and I are devoted followers of our great Führer. Hitler has more than once graced the performances of my husband with his presence. I'm awfully sorry for the inconvenience my daughter has caused. She was always a troublemaker. It's her father's fault. He left us when she was still a baby. I was so young…" Annie dabbed a tear from her eye and put a hand over her heart before she continued, "…it will always lie on my conscience that my own daughter wouldn't follow the path of virtue like any good German woman should. But rest assured, I will make sure the same won't happen with my grandsons. They're in good hands with me."

Hilde stared at Annie, anger exploding through her at the blatant lies her mother was telling. It wasn't her father who had left. He'd been a soldier in the trenches of the Great War. Her mother had eloped with her soon-to-be second husband, the glamorous opera singer Robert Klein, and dumped two-year-old Hilde on the doorstep of Annie's mother-in-law.

The Gestapo officer waved his hand. "Let's go."

Hilde's breath caught in her throat, and she found that she was unable to move even if she'd wanted to.

"Go with him," Annie urged and shoved her out of the kitchen, taking a screaming Peter from her arms. "We'll be fine, won't we?"

"Thank you, Mother," Hilde croaked, glancing back at her children while she forced her feet to take one step after another away from them.

# CHAPTER 2

Q's entire body was itching with anxiety. The Gestapo had taken all his personal belongings, including his watch, and then shoved him into an interrogation room before they disappeared. The room was empty except for a rickety metal table and two worn-out wooden chairs. Q sat down and stared at the grey stone wall.

For a while, he counted the seconds to keep track of time and take his mind off what was to come. But that hadn't helped him find some semblance of calm. Neither had pondering on a tricky scientific problem. Nor holding onto the thought that even the Gestapo couldn't prove Hilde was involved. Despite his efforts to block out the reality, angst seeped into his bones. Agonizing, strangling terror.

Q had lost count of the minutes and hours when the door finally opened with a bone-chilling creak, and a senior Gestapo officer stepped inside. By now, he didn't care anymore. Anything was better than sitting in the empty room, waiting for the worst, and letting his imagination run wild.

"I am *Kriminalkommissar* Becker. You are in very severe trouble."

"What are the charges against me?" Q hoped the *Kriminalkommissar* didn't hear the cracks in his voice.

*Kriminalkommissar* Becker shook his head. "I ask the questions, not you. You are an intelligent man, so you know it's in your best interest to answer them quickly and honestly." Becker slammed his hands on the table and leaned forward. "Let's begin. State your full name."

Q took a breath. "Wilhelm Quedlin."

"Your age?"

"Thirty-nine."

"Are you married?"

Q lifted a questioning eyebrow. "Yes, but you know that already."

"Answer my questions," Becker snapped, his voice hardened as his steel-grey eyes clearly showed his annoyance.

"Your wife's name?"

"Hildegard Quedlin. Born Dremmer." Q fought the impulse to jump up and ask Becker how long these stupid questions would continue. If they didn't already know this information, everyone gave too much credit to the Gestapo. Why did Becker waste time asking non-relevant things?

"Where do you work?"

Q's jaw clenched at yet another stupid question. "I work at Loewe Radio Technologies."

"And what do you do at Loewe?" Becker's grey eyes pinned Q in place, which told Q that they were finally getting somewhere.

"I work with the radio transmitters and research." Q tried to answer as truthfully as possible without giving away anything the *Kriminalkommissar* didn't already know.

Becker pulled out a packet of papers from a briefcase and threw them on the table. "You gave these papers to an agent."

"I don't know what you mean. What agent?" Q's heart thumped in his throat as he recognized the blueprints he'd given to Gerald a while ago. *Oh God, they must have caught him, too.*

"You don't recognize these papers?" The *Kriminalkommissar* smirked and pushed the papers across the table.

Q thumbed through them, the chill seeping deeper into his bones as each page revealed itself. What lay before him was the entire collection of intelligence he'd given to Gerald over the last two months. Some of them had been typewritten, but many drawn by hand – Q's hand – and some included handwritten comments. There was no sense in denying they were his work.

"On a second glance, I do recognize some of them," Q said, feverishly thinking about his next move. How much did Becker know?

For a moment, a cruel smile flickered on Becker's lips. "Good. And how did they get into the hands of the agent?"

"How should I know?" Q challenged Becker.

Becker gave Q a nonchalant smile. "Look. I've been friendly with you so far, but I can easily change that. Do you want me to call in my men?" The question was as indifferent as his facial expression. He might have been asking about the weather instead of threatening torture.

Q shook his head, swallowing down the rising fear. "No."

"Who is the man you gave the papers to?" Becker demanded, seemingly uninterested as he inspected his fingernails.

Q decided to give Becker what he wanted. His own life was probably not worth a single *Pfennig* anymore, but he could at least try to protect Gerald. "He was a Russian agent and called himself Pavel."

"Pavel, is it? Any last name by chance?" Becker leaned across the table, his cold eyes fixated on Q's.

Q felt like a rabbit staring at a snake, but shrugged casually. "No. Sorry. He never mentioned his last name."

Without warning, Becker jumped up and knocked the table over until the hard edge pressed into Q's lap. Becker leaned on his edge of the metal plate, and Q winced but refused to give the *Kriminalkommissar* the satisfaction of crying out in pain.

"You're lying," Becker snapped, his lip curled in disgust, adding more of his weight onto the table.

"No...ahh...he said to call him Pavel," Q forced out the words, and the pressure on his thighs subsided slightly. "He was very careful not to tell me anything compromising."

"Didn't it strike you as strange that your *Russian* Pavel wasn't a Russian at all?" Becker asked, his voice once again conversational.

Q's fingers dug into his legs. The Gestapo knew everything about Gerald. He wasn't to be saved anymore, but Q decided to stick with the Pavel version.

"Not Russian?" Q shook his head, his face a mask of confusion. "Now that you mention it, I remember thinking his German was flawless. He must be one of the Volga Germans."

354

Becker put the table back on its four legs and changed the topic. "Do you confess to the crime of spying on the Party?"

"No." Q pointed at the papers that had fallen to the floor. "I merely gave technical information to a country that used to be our ally."

A warning light flickered in Becker's eyes, and Q understood the message. He needed to play by Becker's rules if he wanted to get out of this interrogation alive.

"That's called high treason," Becker said with a smug smile on his face that widened as he noticed the fear spreading across Q's. "For how long have you been committing this hideous crime?"

It probably wouldn't make any difference to his sentence, but if he told Becker he'd been in contact with the Soviet trade mission since before Hitler's *Machtergreifung* ten years ago, the Gestapo would investigate every single person he'd had contact with during the last decade. Johanna and Reinhard from the communist literature club. His friends Leopold, Otto, and Jakob. No, not him. Jakob was dead. Killed by the Brownshirts. Every single engineer and scientist he'd shared information with. His colleagues at the Botanical Reichs Institute. His patent lawyer. Harro Schulze-Boysen. Erhard Tohmfor. Martin Stuhrmann. Hilde. He needed to protect them at all costs.

"A year, give or take a few months," Q hedged.

Becker's nostrils flared. "Give me the names of everyone else involved."

Q shook his head, giving him his most earnest look. "I worked alone."

"That is a lie. Your wife helped you."

Q gasped. The seeping chill in his bones intensified. *Not Hilde.* "No! She would never. She's innocent. My wife has no idea of my actions. She would never approve. It was all my own doing."

*Kriminalkommissar* Becker didn't respond. Instead, he stood and retrieved one of the scattered papers from the floor. He scrutinized it, as if intently interested in its contents. Q had a sense of foreboding. A very bad foreboding.

"There are no corrections on this sheet. Do you know how to type this well?" *Kriminalkommissar* Becker tapped the documents in front of him.

Q shook his head. He was a dismal typist. "It is true that my wife often typed the information I needed, both for my patents and for my intelligence work. But, as you can see, those are complex technical documents, and she had no idea of their meaning. I always let her believe it was a technical description I needed for my research."

A rap on the door interrupted their conversation. Q wasn't sure if he should be relieved or more frightened.

"*Herein*," Backer called out, and another Gestapo officer peeked inside, making a gesture Q couldn't decipher. Becker nodded in response, then scooped up the papers and walked to the door. Just before stepping into the hallways, he turned. "Doctor Quedlin, I said this at the beginning of our little chat, and I will say it again. You are in severe trouble. The way I see it, you'll be accused of high treason and receive the death sentence."

Q's mouth went dry. He knew the punishment for treason, and he'd been expecting it for such a long time, he thought he'd come to terms with the prospect of such a sentence. But hearing it from Becker's mouth was totally different than imagining it in his own mind.

*I want to live!*

Becker stood in the doorway, closely observing Q's struggle with that prospect before he spoke again. "But I'm no monster. You are an intelligent man, and I'm sure you'll see the benefits of my offer. If you agree to work with us and give us the names of everyone involved in your subversive work, I will see that you receive a mild punishment. Or none at all."

The door closed with a creak, and Q's mind raced with a million thoughts. Here was his chance to save his life. This interrogation had been short and easy. The next one wouldn't be.

A short time later, two officers stepped into the little room and escorted Q to a holding cell. They shoved him inside and slammed the door shut. Q gazed at the empty five-by-eight-foot space that was now his. The ceiling hung barely above his head. It reminded him of an oversized closet, and he wondered how long he would be kept here before they moved him or...killed him.

The cell was completely made of stone and brick, the walls a dull grey. Previous prisoners had scratched or drawn on the walls, no doubt in the quest to leave some bit of evidence of their existence and suffering.

A shiver ran down Q's spine. Reluctantly, he sat on the corner of a bloodstained mattress lying on the floor. A rough woolen blanket was the only dressing on the mattress – no sheets or pillow. He looked away from the stinking bucket standing in one corner. Q forced down the bile rising in this throat and closed his eyes.

When he was certain he wouldn't throw up, he opened them again and inspected his cell more closely, peering into the dimness surrounding him. There was a small window with iron bars over the glass, but the glass was opaque and would only let in a small amount of light when the sun shone. A single bulb hung from the ceiling, but it was switched off. This time of year, it got dark around four-thirty in the evening, and he had no means of estimating the time that had passed since his arrest.

Judging by the rumbling of his stomach, it was past midnight by now. The guards had thoughtfully left a bowl with an unidentifiable, stinking liquid in the corner opposite the bucket, but he wasn't hungry enough to force it down – yet. He had no doubt, though, that in a few days from now he'd be gratefully devouring whatever food arrived.

# CHAPTER 3

Hilde sat in the car, squeezed between two Gestapo officers. Despite the chilly November day, she was sweating. The air was too thick to breathe and pure panic tied up her throat.

The car passed the familiar streets and places of Berlin, but she had no eye for them; neither for the natural beauties of Nikolassee where she lived, nor for the once majestic art nouveau buildings that had been reduced to rubble – skeletons rising into the sky as a reminder of the harrowing war raging across the world.

Hilde's limbs were numb with fear when the car arrived at Gestapo Headquarters, and she was shoved into the building. Inside the dreary interrogation room, she was left alone. Paralyzed with fear, she plopped down on one of the two chairs and lifted a hand to her chest. She clasped the red jasper pendant on the gold necklace Q's mother had given her for their wedding. *This is the lucky stone for your zodiac sign*, Ingrid had said. Hilde could use some luck now, although luck alone wouldn't be enough. She would need a lot of strength and endurance to bear what was to come.

The door opened, and a Gestapo officer walked in and shut the door with a long creak. "Frau Quedlin, I am *Kriminalkommissar* Becker."

Hilde inclined her head, trying to hide her fear. *Kriminalkommissar* Becker took a seat opposite her at the metal table and leaned back in his chair. He could be called handsome, with his broad shoulders, short blond hair, and classic features, if it weren't for his soulless grey eyes.

Becker observed her for a few minutes and suddenly smiled what seemed to be a genuine smile. Hilde felt the fear easing out of her system. Maybe the rumors were highly exaggerated, and this wouldn't be as bad as she'd imagined. If she could convince him that she was innocent, he might even let her return to her children.

"I have a few questions to begin with. Could you please state your name, including your maiden name?" Becker's voice was pleasant, friendly even.

Hilde nodded. "Hildegard Quedlin. Born Dremmer."

"Age and place of birth."

"Thirty. I was born in Hamburg on August 23, 1912." Hilde focused on answering his questions, suppressing the tremble in her voice.

"You are married to Wilhelm Quedlin?"

"Yes, *Herr Kriminalkommissar*."

"Do you have children?"

Hilde cast her eyes down, the thought of her two precious babies bringing tears to her eyes. "I have two sons. Nine months and three years old."

"Could you find someone to care for them right now?" Becker asked, showing an empathetic smile.

Hilde met his grey eyes and believed she saw a spark of compassion, but it disappeared as quickly as it had appeared. She willed her tears away and said softly, "I was allowed to call my mother. She's with them now."

"That must be a relief for you," Becker said and leaned forward. Hilde shivered. Despite the polite, even friendly, manner this man emitted a bad aura.

She nodded. "Yes."

"Your husband was arrested earlier today and will most likely be accused of treason. What do you have to say to that?" Becker launched his question without warning.

Hilde caught her breath. *Treason?* She knew what that meant. Q had warned her about the consequences, but she'd always believed such a thing would only happen to other people, not to them. They'd been careful. They wouldn't be caught.

"I...don't understand. My husband is a good man, a good citizen."

Becker sat up tall and pierced her with his steel-gray eyes. *He doesn't believe me.*

"Frau Quedlin, you don't strike me as being stupid. In fact, I would venture to say you are more intelligent than most women. It would be in your best interest to tell me everything you know about your husband's subversive activities. Who he met with. How long this has been going on. How he makes contact with them. Everything."

"*Kriminalkommissar*, I'm as shocked as you are. This must be a misunderstanding. My husband is a gentle man–"

Becker slammed his hand down on the table, making her jump. "Who has been working with the resistance! And if you thought for one minute about your two sons you'd tell me everything you know."

"I don't know anything." Hilde shook her head. "If he really worked against our government, which I doubt, he never told me. He was devoted to his work, making radio transmitters for the Wehrmacht. He's not a spy." The lies came easily enough.

Becker scowled at her, then withdrew some of the papers she'd typed for Q and slid them across the table to her. "Do you deny typing these?"

Hilde looked at the papers and inwardly cringed. Despair took hold of her. She steeled her spine and stuck to her story. "I've never seen those papers before."

"You are denying that you deliberately tried to disguise the typewriter these directions were written on? You are denying that you were the person operating the typewriter?"

"Yes." She nodded fervently.

"Do you have a typewriter at your home, Frau Quedlin?"

"Yes." Hilde's mind whirled, and she had difficulties following the staccato of Becker's questions.

"Do you know how to type?"

"Yes."

"And is it not true that you often helped your husband by typing up his research and documentation for his patents?"

"Yes, but I don't understand where this is going."

"And is it not true that you assisted him in copying secret and confidential documents, using blueprint and brown paper to distort the letters, making identifying the typewriter much more difficult?"

"I have typed things for him on blueprint paper, but not…I haven't done anything wrong. My husband likes to make copies of his research, and he would dictate, and I would type. I never understood the technical contents of what I was typing. And surely, he would never copy secret and confidential material–"

Becker slammed his fist on the metal table again. The screeching sound curled Hilde's toes. "Stop babbling."

Hilde nodded, her eyes wide open. She expected him to hit her and was grateful when he leaned back and apologized.

"Please forgive my manners, Frau Quedlin. But I hate being lied to. And you are lying."

"I haven't done anything wrong," she protested.

"You need to come up with a better story than that. Preferably the truth. This could be smooth and easy. You could be back with your children in no time at all. Or…"

Her blood froze in her veins.

Becker slid the papers back to his side of the table and stood up. "Well, maybe you just need some time to think about things." He opened the door and called two junior officers into the room. "Take Frau Quedlin to her cell. She requires more time to think about the truth. Frau Quedlin, I will see you tomorrow."

# CHAPTER 4

Q was alone in his cell, which was a surprise. He'd heard of ten to twenty prisoners being crowded into spaces as small as this one. While companionship might have been nice, he was actually thankful for the opportunity to think.

For ten years, he'd been waiting for this moment, fearing how his life might end if his resistance efforts were ever found out. The fear had always been present in the back of his mind. Every time he'd sabotaged the war production at Loewe, stolen another piece of intelligence, or met with the Russian agent, his life had been a catastrophe waiting to happen.

At least this constant worry was gone now. A tiny trace of relief took hold of him before the far-reaching consequences of his capture shattered all sense of relief, and a different kind of fear took hold of him. The certainty of torture and agony gripped him like the cold hand of death.

But death wasn't cruel like the Gestapo bloodhounds were, and Q was sure that at some point in the near future, he'd welcome death as salvation from his torment. Despite Becker's friendly façade, Q had seen the determined gleam in his grey eyes. The determination to get what he wanted, at all cost, by all means necessary. If only men like Becker would put their unwavering determination to a worthwhile cause and not destroy their fellow humans.

Q shuddered. *Kriminalkommissar* Becker had offered him a deal.

Promised a mild punishment, a release, if Q worked with the Gestapo. The only thing he had to do was confess to his activities and rat out everyone else. It was the easy way out, and Q was more than tempted to take it.

But he couldn't do that to his friends. Have them pay for his deeds? No. How would he be able to live his life as a traitor? A true traitor who betrayed his own ideals, not some despicable government. And what if this was just a ploy to get him to talk?

No, Q wouldn't fall for their tactics. In the solitude of his cell, his will was strong. Whether that would hold true during his next interrogation, he didn't know. *I'm not a hero. Not a soldier trained to endure pain. I'm just a scientist. An ordinary man.*

How could he ensure he didn't betray his friends when the Gestapo came back for him? Q relaxed on the stinking mattress and did what he knew best: think. He devised a plan.

He would tell the Gestapo everything they wanted to know. Every little detail about his sabotage work at Loewe. How he'd copied the blueprints and given them to "Pavel." He'd talk so much, *Kriminalkommissar* Becker wouldn't have the time to ask about names. Because names he wouldn't tell. Those he'd take to his grave.

*Hilde.*

Q's heart grew weary. Images appeared in his mind. Their wedding day. Climbing Mount Etna. Holding Volker for the first time. Sadness choked his throat. Would he ever see her and his sons again?

He hoped she was safe. She was just a woman, a mother. Not even the Gestapo could believe she had something to do with his resistance activities.

Q listened to the silence. All he could hear was a distant shuffling. Other prisoners? Gestapo coming for him? The shuffling stopped. Judging by the small, opaque window near the ceiling of his cell, he was in the cellar of the building. The infamous Gestapo cellar? Q willed his mind to go down another road, but the threat of what was to come kept him circling back.

*What happened to Gerald?*

*Kriminalkommissar* Becker had been in possession of some of the paperwork Q had given the agent the last time they'd met. Gerald was a

Wehrmacht deserter, and everyone knew what happened to them if they got caught.

Fear and cold crept into his bones. Sleep was impossible, and Q stood up to pace the tiny cell. Walk and think. Had he made the right choices in his life? Should he have stopped his subversive work? Not planned the attack on Goebbels? Never married Hilde? A thousand questions assaulted him. But no answers.

Much later that night, when he sank onto the mattress again and wrapped his freezing body with the rough blanket, his last thought was that he'd do everything again.

~

Hilde sat in a cell very similar to Q's, thinking about the horrific events that she now thought of as *Fateful Monday*. After the interrogation, they'd taken her down a narrow stairwell, into one of those clammy and moldy basements that always reminded her of a medieval dungeon.

Goosebumps rose on her skin. After the uniformed man shoved her inside and closed the door, the silence became deafening. The window was barred and opened into a grey light well. Nobody would hear her cries. But she didn't cry. Not yet.

Hilde paced the confines of the small room, her arms wrapped around herself. She was grateful for the cardigan she'd grabbed when the Gestapo had arrived for her. It was cold in here. But she'd have frozen even in plain sunlight because of the fear and sorrow filling her heart.

*Kriminalkommissar* Becker told her that Q had been arrested, too. She'd assumed that all along, but having the certainty had knocked the breath out of her lungs. Q would probably be held in the same building, and she willed herself to *sense* his presence. If he was nearby, she could tap into his strength and envision him holding her the way he'd done so many times in their eight years together.

It worked, and she calmed down – until images of her babies crept into her mind and tears started streaming down her cheeks. She'd weaned Peter just the week before, and for that she was thankful because it would have been so much harder for both of them if she were still nursing him. But she missed snuggling him next to her as he went down for a nap. She missed talking with Volker and watching his mind work as he played with his toys.

She consoled herself with the fact that her mother was with them. Despite Hilde's differences with Annie, she'd take good care of her grandsons.

*It's only for a few days at most.*

Hilde plopped onto the mattress on the ground and wrapped a stained, stinking blanket around her to find some warmth. But sleep was elusive, and she lay there, remembering the good times she'd shared with her husband and children.

Two weeks earlier, the weather had been unseasonably warm, and she and Q had taken both boys to the park. Peter had giggled and babbled in his pram. Volker and Q had walked hand-in-hand, both shuffling their feet through the autumn leaves. The little boy had fired a million why-questions at his father. *Why are the leaves falling from the trees? Why is it autumn? Where did the summer go?*

Hilde cried some more. Would they ever experience such a peaceful and happy outing again? She rolled over, allowing her tears to flow unchecked, and prayed to God.

*Please. Allow me the chance to leave this place and return to my children. Please let me live to raise them, so they don't have to grow up without a mother like I did.*

She and Q had discussed this exact situation, and she knew what he expected her to do. She'd always waved it away, but now that the situation had arrived, she struggled with the prospect of betraying her own husband. Put all the blame on him. To save herself.

Sleep finally claimed her in the wee hours of the morning, but her dreams were plagued with visions of her next interrogation. *Kriminalkommissar* Becker had been nice enough, but she knew that was simply a façade designed to break her down.

365

# CHAPTER 5

I t was still dark outside when two Gestapo officers hauled Q from the mattress, waking him from a fitful sleep. He didn't even have the time to put his shoes on, and of course, there was no breakfast either. He followed them without complaining. It wouldn't help.

This time, they took him to a different interrogation room: one without a table and only a single chair placed in the center of the room with a bare light bulb hanging overhead. The men shoved him into the room and ordered him to sit in the chair. Q did as they requested, trying not to think about whatever was to come. His stomach growled, reminding him that he hadn't eaten in eighteen hours.

*Kriminalkommissar* Becker entered a few moments later, finishing a bun that smelled of ham. Q's stomach growled. Becker wiped his mouth with his hand and smiled at him. "Good morning, Doctor Quedlin. I trust you had a good night's sleep?"

Q remained quiet at the bait the *Kriminalkommissar* was throwing at him. Becker acknowledged his silence with a smirk and walked towards Q, circling around the chair. He came to stand behind him, and chills of anticipated agony rushed down Q's spine.

"Have you had a chance to reconsider your answers to yesterday's questions? Are you ready to tell me who you were working with?" the voice came from behind.

Q shook his head. "I worked alone. Nobody else knew what I was doing."

The next moment, Q was hurled through the air and braced his arms to cover his head before it smacked against the cold stone floor. He blinked as his eyes watered and the metallic taste of blood filled his mouth.

"Get up," Becker said.

Q pushed himself back to his feet and sat in the chair once again, wiping the corner of his mouth with his hand. A streak of blood appeared.

Becker stroked his knuckles and approached Q until he towered over him, staring down at him with dead grey eyes. "Who are your partners?"

Q swallowed and answered again, "I worked alone. Nobody else knew what I was doing—"

"That's a lie! It would be in your best interest to cooperate with me."

"I'm willing to tell you anything about my subversive work," Q hedged, and when Becker agreed, he felt a slight reprieve in his terror and started to talk. About the blueprints, how he gave all his research to the Russians. Everything. He talked for such a long time, he almost fooled himself into believing Becker would be satisfied.

"Now, tell me who helped you."

"I worked alone," Q insisted and received another blow to his jaw. The pain dizzied him, and for a minute he saw red stars.

"Gerald Meier said differently," Becker said.

So, they'd caught the Russian agent. Q clung to the hope that Gerald hadn't mentioned Erhard's name. Thankfully, Gerald hadn't known about Hilde and Martin. At least those two were safe.

"You arrested him, too?"

"Yes, and your friend Erhard Tohmfor."

*No. Not Erhard, too.* Q yearned to know if Erhard was still alive, but he was too afraid to ask. His own survival looked dimmer by the minute. It was too late to cover for him. Erhard was not to be saved either way.

"Erhard Tohmfor was my friend," Q explained, meeting Becker's eyes. "I believe he might have known about my stealing intelligence and my sabotage acts but turned a blind eye to it. He was never actively involved."

367

This time, the end of a wooden bat connected with Q's back and doubled him over, forcing all the air from his lungs. Again and again. The agonizing pain exploded into black stars, and his breathing rattled as he panted for air. He must have passed out; when he came to, his arms and legs were shackled to the chair and Becker towered over him with a cup of deliciously fragrant coffee in his hand.

"Oh good, you're awake," Becker said with a smug grin. "Let me tell you something. My department arrested the agent you knew as Gerald six weeks ago."

Six weeks? Even with his damaged brain, Q knew this wasn't possible. *Kriminalkommissar* Becker was lying. Because if it was true...

"But how? I met him just last week..." Q whispered, making an attempt to clear the fog from his mind.

"Well, unlike you, this man made a wise choice." Becker stared down at him. "He agreed to act as a double agent for us in exchange for his life."

This was surreal. Unbelievable. But probably the truth. Suddenly, the pieces of the puzzle fell into place. That was why Gerald had started to ask all those questions. And why he'd insisted on another meeting before the assassination attempt.

Q's entire worldview shattered with this revelation. A double agent. The feeling of betrayal hurt as much as the physical pain from Becker's beatings. The person he'd trusted as a comrade for the same cause had betrayed everyone to save his own life. He swallowed hard, trying to hide his shock.

"You thought you could trust this Russian agent, but really..." Becker chuckled, his grin growing wider, "a man as smart as you...you should have known how treacherous the Russians are."

Rage mixed with hurt and pain, and before Q could stop himself, he blurted out, "Well, this agent was, in fact, a German, so you see that only goes to show how treacherous the Germans are."

Becker's fist shot out and caught Q on the right side of his face, just a few inches below his eye. Thanks to his cuffs, he didn't fall off the chair this time, but his vision grew blurry as his eye immediately swelled and his mouth filled with the metallic taste of blood.

"Remember, we are not stupid. Gerald has told us everything about you. Scum." Becker spat in Q's face. "He's given us all the information you shared with him on your long walks together. We know everything. We also know about Erhard's role in your little sabotage effort."

Q was still sorting out the information when Becker struck again.

"We arrested your wife yesterday. Let's hope she's more cooperative than you are." Becker bared his teeth in what was probably supposed to be a smile, and Q's heart squeezed.

*Not Hilde.*

Q looked up. "*Herr Kriminalkommissar,* my wife is innocent. I never told her about my resistance work. She knows absolutely nothing. You must believe me. She is innocent in all of this."

Becker looked at him with a calculating eye. "Who else besides Erhard and your wife was working with you?"

"No one, I swear. It was just Erhard and myself. Hilde had no idea what she was typing. She's not a scientist. She couldn't know."

"I'm fed up with your lies," Becker said and waved at another man. "Take him away."

This time, they shoved him into a cell slightly bigger than the one he'd spent the first night in. This one, though, was crowded with at least ten other prisoners. None of them looked any better than Q probably did, but they moved around, groaning, to make space for the newcomer on the hard stone floor.

Q was terrified. *The preferential treatment has ended.*

# CHAPTER 6

Hilde woke after a fitful sleep and stretched her cold and aching limbs. Muffled noises from the hallway outside her cell reached her ears, the first sign of other persons being held down here.

When the door opened half an hour later, she backed up against the protection of the wall and watched warily to see who'd come inside. A uniformed Gestapo officer waved his baton, pushed a tray inside with his foot, and then left without a word.

Hilde waited until she heard the bolt on the door engage before inspecting what she assumed was breakfast. She gulped down the foul-smelling water, then suspiciously eyed the piece of bread and the bowl with an indefinable whitish mash. Even though her mind rebelled, her stomach reminded her that they'd conveniently forgotten to give her food last night.

She held her nose and forced down half of the disgusting mush. Then she chewed the hard-as-stone piece of bread, not knowing when she might be given a chance to eat again.

Before long, another officer arrived to deliver her to *Kriminalkommissar* Becker. He was sitting at the table in what looked like the same room she had been interrogated in the day before. The officer who'd escorted her leaned against the wall behind her.

"Good morning, Frau Quedlin, I hope you were not too uncomfortable last night?" He smiled and gestured for her to take a seat.

Hilde shrugged. "When can I go home?"

Becker steepled his hands atop the table, his eyes never leaving her. "That depends entirely on you and your willingness to cooperate. I have two wonderful children myself; you must be missing your sons. Is it the first time they've spent the night without you?"

She barely could press out, "Yes," before her eyes watered at the thought of her two babies.

"It would be such a shame if they became orphans," Becker mused, seemingly more to himself than to her.

That remark hit her harder than a punch to her stomach. She must have made a groaning sound because Becker now smiled at her benevolently.

"Well, well, Frau Quedlin. I have a soft spot in my heart for children, and therefore will make you an offer. Give me the names of everyone involved with your husband and the resistance effort he was part of. Everyone. Even the people you only suspect to be against the government."

Here was her chance to go home to her children. All she had to do was betray everyone she knew and name ten, twenty, or thirty people Becker could go after.

"Does that mean I can go home again?" she asked, her voice cracking.

"Possibly," Becker agreed and smiled again. But his smile never reached his soulless eyes. Hilde was sure he was lying. Even if he wasn't, could she live with her conscience if she did what he demanded?

"I would love to tell you, but I don't know anything or anyone. I didn't even know that my husband was engaged in this abhorrent behavior until yesterday." She tried to sound as honest as possible.

"Now, Frau Quedlin, that is not quite the truth. Let's talk about those papers you typed out for your husband." *Kriminalkommissar* Becker slid some additional papers across the table to her.

Hilde looked at the papers, several of them simple patent requests and mundane notes she'd typed up for Q's research. She saw no harm in identifying them and nodded. "I remember typing these, so yes, I typed these for my husband."

"For once, you're telling me the truth," Becker said and produced the papers he'd shown her the day before and placed them side by side. "These papers were typed on the same typewriter."

Hilde's heart fell.

"Now explain to me why you lied yesterday?"

"*Kriminalkommissar* Becker, I'm sorry. I didn't recognize the papers. I typed many things for my husband. He's horrible at working the machine and oftentimes brought his research notes home and asked me to type them up." She wanted to jump up and run away, which was a rather stupid notion, given that she was inside the best-guarded building in Berlin. "I'm just a simple mother of two children, and frankly, I never gave much thought to what I was typing. It was usually at the end of the day when I was tired from caring for the children and our home."

"Haven't you ever wondered why your husband brought such sensitive material home with him?" Becker demanded to know.

Hilde's neck hair stood on end. "I didn't think it was sensitive."

"Don't you know that it's a crime to steal classified material?" Becker thumped the table with his fist.

The table jumped, as did Hilde.

"No, he wasn't stealing. It was all his own work," she defended Q.

"How do you know?" Becker asked.

"I…he is an honest person."

"An honest person? So why did he betray Führer and Fatherland then?"

Hilde shrugged. Whatever she said, it would be wrong.

Becker stood and walked around the table to put a hand on her shoulder. Her entire body stiffened. Then she felt his breath at her ear, and she closed her eyes.

"Do you love your husband, Frau Quedlin?"

"Yes."

The hand grabbed her chin and turned her face until she was forced to stare into his eyes. "Does he love you?"

Hilde nodded.

"And still, you want to make me believe you had no idea about his political opinions. That he hated the admirable ideas of our Führer and collaborated with our enemy? That he was a communist in his heart?"

Hilde moaned as the grip tightened. "Yes. I mean, no. I didn't know any of that."

"So why didn't you admit to typing those papers yesterday?" Becker asked again, squeezing her chin harder.

"I already told you, I didn't recognize them." Becker moved away and her face burned. Her skin probably showed the marks of his hand.

"Now, let's keep to the truth, shall we?" Becker breathed into her ear, both his hands moving across her shoulders to rest around her neck.

Hilde gagged in panic. "I…I don't know. I panicked. I thought maybe those papers had something to do with my arrest."

"So, you knew there was something wrong about those papers?" he asked again and tightened the grip around her neck. Hilde thought he'd strangle her. Her pulse throbbed erratically as her vision began to dim. She kicked with her legs, clawed with her hands. She was desperate for air. Then she was free again.

As she gulped in precious oxygen, Becker strolled to the other side of the table and sat down. He steepled his hands again. "Talk."

Terror held Hilde's mind in her grip, and she couldn't think of anything intelligent to say. "No…I never thought there was something wrong with the papers. But yesterday, when you told me that my husband was accused of treason, I panicked. I thought maybe those papers had something to do with it."

"And you deemed it wise to lie to the Gestapo? Don't you know we have the means to find out the truth?" The threat in his voice made her shudder.

"I'm sorry."

"So, what exactly was in those papers?"

"I don't know."

Becker waved his hand, and Hilde's arm was jerked behind her back, probably by the officer who'd leaned against the wall. She screamed in pain. The pressure increased and she screamed until Becker waved again, and she was free.

"The truth, Frau Quedlin."

She was sobbing and holding her sore shoulder, her words coming out in ragged exhalations. "The truth is I never knew anything."

"I don't believe you. See this." Becker held out the piece of paper with blurred letters.

Hilde tried to hide her gasp, but it was too late. Becker had already noticed her reaction.

"You recognize that one, right?"

"Yes." She did. Very well. It was the piece of paper where Q had given her explicit instructions to use several layers of paper on top of each other. Q's words rang in her ears. *It's better that you don't know. You need to be able to say you had no knowledge about the technical things you were typing.*

"Why are you suddenly so nervous, when you had no idea what this was all about?" Becker smirked at her.

She was as good as dead. There was no sense in denying anymore. Her visceral reaction had given her away. Her brain was worn out, and the pain still lingered in her arm, making her unable to form a clear thought.

"At the time I was typing it, I didn't think much of it because my husband was very peculiar with his inventions, but now after my arrest, it seemed suspicious to me."

"You admit that you were helping your husband in his traitorous activities against the Reich?" Becker's voice was friendly, but his next words stung. "You scummy whore."

Tears shot into her eyes. The lack of sleep and food, the constant interrogations, had taken a toll on her ability to focus. "I don't. I...knew nothing. And I didn't do anything wrong."

"And still you paled when I showed you the papers, you piece of scum."

There had to be something to turn this situation around. Hilde racked her frightened mind for an excuse. Anything. "I thought, that maybe... my husband...some shady business...trying to sell his research to a competing company. A little cheating...but not treason...never...he was loyal."

*Loyal to his convictions. Just not to the monster who's our Führer.*

"Bullshit. You knew exactly what you were doing. Treason." Becker stared at her until she squirmed and then stated, "We have arrested Erhard Tohmfor."

Hilde caught her gasp, but tears pooled in her eyes, and she had to blink them away.

Becker was a well-trained interrogator and caught her tiny lapse. He pressed her for more answers: "Was Tohmfor involved in your husband's traitorous activities?"

"He was his boss. An honest person."

"Was he a traitor as well?" Becker shouted.

"My husband isn't a traitor, and neither was Erhard!" she spat out and earned herself a slap to her face. She tasted blood on her lip as the heat exploded across her cheek.

"Your pig of a husband is the worst kind of traitor. And so are you. And Erhard Tohmfor. And who else? Give me names!"

Hilde started crying. She didn't care anymore if Becker hit her or not. Maybe it would be better if he believed she was about to have a breakdown.

"Who else do you associate with?"

She swallowed and panicked deep inside. *The Gestapo would already know this information, right? Or should I lie?* Going with her first thought, she opted for a middle way. "My best friend is Erika Huber, the daughter-in-law of the late *SS-Obersturmbannführer* Wolfgang Huber. We often come together so our children can play."

If *Kriminalkommissar* Becker was impressed by her connection to Wolfgang Huber, he didn't show it. Instead, he continued to ask the same questions over and over. Hilde stuck to her line of defense, that she hadn't known what she was typing, and never once mentioned the name of Martin Stuhrmann – the person who'd helped her husband to prepare the assassination plan on Goebbels.

The questions had become friendly again, but Hilde wasn't fooled. Inside the man sitting across from her was a cruel and sadistic monster enjoying the horror he inflicted.

# CHAPTER 7

Q slumped against the wall in a ball of misery. His right eye was partially swollen shut, and the bruise on his left cheekbone was throbbing with every breath. But after having looked at the other prisoners in his cell, he felt privileged.

As bad as he felt for himself, he worried about his wife and friends more. Hilde arrested. Erhard arrested. Q wondered if Martin was safe. So far, his name hadn't been mentioned. *This means they don't know about him.* Gerald hadn't known about his existence, and now Martin's destiny lay in the hands of his friends. Q would rather die than betray him, but he wasn't sure how long he'd be able to hold on to that plan…and whether Hilde and Erhard could do the same.

*Hilde. My love. It's my fault she's here. I have fed her to the wolves, and because of me, she's suffering now.* His heart was in a tight knot. If only he could save her.

Several hours later, the Gestapo came back for him. This time, they took him down a different hallway. Downstairs. While walking, he heard the cries of fellow prisoners, muffled by the thick stone walls. Some were merely the pitiful whimpering of men pushed to the breaking point.

These sounds shook him to the core, and by the time he was pushed into a windowless room with a chair and a large tub of water, all he could do was keep his knees from knocking together. *Kriminalkommissar* Becker stood in the room with an evil grin on his face.

"Traitorous pig!" Becker attacked him right away, followed by a long torrent of abuse. As he protected himself the best he could, he learned that Gerald had told the Gestapo about the assassination attempt on Goebbels. The Gestapo had then searched his home and found several drawings, including one for a remote-controlled bomb.

"A remote-controlled bomb? *Herr Kriminalkommissar*, such a thing does not exist." Q had decided to play dumb.

"We found the drawings for such a device in your apartment," Becker shouted.

"Merely an idea. My mind is always filled with ideas, but exactly how would a remote-control device work? What method of transmitting the signal would be used? One day such a device may exist, but for now, it is simply a figment of my imagination." Q's teeth were shattering with anxiety and pain, but he managed to keep his voice steady.

"Liar! So far, I've treated you with kid gloves,[the metaphor refers to gloves made of soft kidskin] but this will change if you don't cooperate." Becker turned and stormed from the room, the other officers joining him.

Q was alone with only the sounds of the tortured souls in the other interrogation rooms for company.

After a few minutes, Becker returned with the drawings. "These are yours?"

"Yes, those are mine. I am an inventor, *Herr Kriminalkommissar*. I am always dreaming up new and innovative gadgets. It is why my services were so valuable to the Loewe." Of course, he'd never shared this specific device with his employer.

"Do you deny planning to assassinate our propaganda minister, Goebbels?" Becker demanded, picking up a wicked-looking stick with leather thongs attached to the end.

Q's eyes were fixated on the stick in Becker's hand while he tried to focus on answering the question. "I admit I thought about it. It was a mind game, though. Gerald and I tossed around some ideas. We pondered whether it would diminish the Reich's power and shorten the war, or not." The more Q talked, the more confident he became. "But without having access to a powerful bomb, or the mythical remote control device to detonate it with, it was simply a dream. There was no way to make it a reality."

Becker didn't look convinced, so Q continued speaking, "I'm a scientist. I'm always inventing things, in theory, but other people have to actually build them. My ideas stop when I put them down on paper."

"It is unfortunate that you insist on sticking to this story," Becker said and nodded toward the two officers who'd followed him into the room. They grabbed Q, dragged him to the tub of water, and tossed him in.

The impact with icy water took his breath away, and when he was finally able to inhale, Q was plunged beneath the water and held there until he felt his lungs would explode if he didn't take a breath. This torture continued for most of the day. The only relief he got was when *Kriminalkommissar* Becker would return and ask him the same questions, over and over again.

Q stuck to his story, convinced they would continue with the same procedure whether he told them what they wanted to hear or not. And for once, he was speaking the truth. As far as he knew, there was no such bomb in existence yet, except for his own prototype, which Martin hopefully had destroyed by now. He'd heard rumors about this kind of powerful bomb's being in the experimental stage, but nothing official.

Late in the afternoon, when Q had long ago lost feeling in his frozen limbs, and even his thoughts had become viscous, Becker pulled him one last time from the tub of water and repeatedly beat him with the leather thongs.

The strikes slashed his ice-cold skin and brought sensation back into Q's body – excruciating pain. Hot fire burned his skin even as he shivered and shook from the cold and pain that racked his body.

"Tell me what I want to know, and you can go," Becker said many hours later.

Q barely lifted his head and answered with a battered voice, "I've told you everything. I'm a scientist. That drawing was mine and mine alone. A dream that will never come to fruition."

Becker looked at Q's battered and bruised body and evidently decided that Q must be telling the truth. He shook his head, instructing the other officers to help him back to the chair. "We will assume you are telling the truth about the drawing."

The *Kriminalkommissar* paced the room and then turned with an evil smile. "It's a shame, really. A man as bright as you. You could have worked for the Reich and become rich and powerful. But you chose to squander your brilliance by working for the enemy."

"I never wanted money. I always wanted progress. Progress *for* the people, not against them."

The remark earned him another slash with the whip, and Q chose to keep his next words for himself: that he wanted later generations to think honorably of him, which was why he stood up against Hitler, the person he thought would bring doom to his beloved Fatherland Germany. *National Socialism isn't good for anyone except for Hitler himself.*

"By the way, your friend Tohmfor confessed. Everything." With these words, Becker left the room. Q was alone with the two brutes who'd taken pleasure in almost drowning him for hours on end. He feared the worst.

But nothing happened. They dragged him back to his cell, where he fell on top of several fellow prisoners. *I'm still alive*, was his last thought before he fell into fits and bursts of an exhausted sleep.

# CHAPTER 8

Q's trial took place on December 18, 1942, less than three weeks after his arrest by the Gestapo. It wasn't held in the normal courtrooms, but as a *Geheime Kommandosache,* a secret trial. Q wasn't even allowed a lawyer to defend him.

It wasn't illegal because the Gestapo law of 1936 gave the organization carte blanche to operate outside of, around, and without any concern for the law. In fact, the SS officer and former head of legal affairs in the Gestapo, Werner Best, had once said, "As long as the police carry out the will of the leadership, it is acting legally."

Q was handcuffed to the seat of the accused while a judge presided from a high bench. *Kriminalkommissar* Becker and the double agent, Gerald Maier, sat to Q's left. Behind his back, more than two dozen Gestapo officers and supporters filled the room.

His heart leapt when he saw Hilde entering the room, handcuffed and accompanied by a Gestapo officer. Q sought her eyes, and when she looked his way, his heart broke at the devastation visible on her face. A bruise on her sunken cheek testified to the abuse she'd endured, and he wanted to scream. Or at least to walk over, take her into his arms, and kiss the pain away. Her dress bagged on her, and that sparkling twinkle in her blue eyes he'd loved so much had disappeared.

From his place, he could glance at her out of the corner of his eye without turning his head. Throughout the trial, he exchanged glances with her, conveying his unconditional love. He hoped that by some miracle, she'd forgive him for the mess he'd gotten them into.

Various Gestapo officers testified and Q listened as the evidence against him was stacked up. Documents were presented, including the drawing for the remote-control bomb device, and testimony was given in regards to his planned assassination of Goebbels.

The judge finally called an end to the testimony and leveled an ice-cold stare at him. Q inwardly quaked beneath the man's gaze.

*"Aufstehen Angeklagter!"*

Q pushed himself to his feet, holding back the groan of pain from his beatings in the previous days. He braced a hand on the table in front of him for a moment, and then forced himself to stand tall. *I will not give them the pleasure of seeing me broken.*

"Doctor Quedlin, you are accused of treason against the Party. The evidence has been presented. What do you have to say for yourself?"

Q glanced at Hilde, who sent him a barely visible nod, and then back to the judge, "I am guilty of committing the acts of subterfuge that have been discussed here today, but I did it to fight a regime of injustice. I would do so again. I acted in line with my conscience, a conscience that abhors what the Reich has done to my Fatherland. I would go to any lengths if it meant ridding Germany of this evil."

The small courtroom erupted in shouts for his death and curses aimed at his person. The officer seated next to him stood and grabbed his arm tightly, promising retribution for those bold statements.

Hilde had listened in growing horror as the evidence against him was presented. Until this moment, she hadn't grasped the extent of the Gestapo's knowledge about Q's intelligence and sabotage activities. They had been watching him and many others for months before arresting them.

She didn't understand everything that was said, but apparently, the Gestapo believed that Q had been the head of a sabotage group at his company, while at the same time belonging to a much bigger resistance network they called the *Red Orchestra*. Dozens of members, including the well-known Luftwaffe *Oberleutnant* Harro Schulze-Boysen, had been arrested and were now tried by the same court.

A sense of pride filled Hilde as she observed Q standing unbroken in the courtroom. In his eyes, she'd seen a sea of pain. She sought out his glance every so often, trying to make him understand that she didn't blame him. That she'd forgiven him, if there ever was something to forgive. *If only I could have a few moments to speak with him.* But rows of benches, bars, and handcuffs separated them.

Her pride about his unwavering steadfastness transformed into plain horror when he was asked to defend himself. Hilde pressed a hand over her mouth. Wasn't it outright stupidity to deliberately enrage the judge and the spectators? Wouldn't it have been better to admit guilt but restrain from adding fuel to the fire? The ensuing uproar was deafening, and for a moment, she feared someone would kill Q right on the spot.

The judge slammed his gavel on the bench several times, yelling at the spectators to calm down. A deadly silence ensued. At the end of it, the judge pronounced his sentence.

"The defendant, Doctor Wilhelm Quedlin, is found guilty of treason against Führer and Fatherland. He is sentenced to death." The judge paused for a moment and then added, "Get this piece of trash out of my courtroom."

Q's sagging shoulders were the last thing Hilde saw before she sank down, hiding her face in her hands. Silent tears streamed down her cheeks. Both of them had known what the punishment for treason was, and that no one in the resistance could hope for mercy from the government. But knowing it as a theoretical fact and hearing with her own ears that the man she loved was sentenced to death were two different things.

Her heart broke into a million pieces, leaving a hollow place behind.

Q was shoved towards the door, passing by her place. He was too far away to touch him, even if she stretched out her hand. He frantically turned his head, and she caught one last glimpse into his loving blue eyes. A powerful energy passed between them. She would stay strong. She still had her sons to care for.

# CHAPTER 9

H ilde spent the next two days in a state of trance in her cell. Since Q's trial, she'd not been interrogated, and while she loathed *Kriminalkommissar* Becker and his constant abuse, the uncertainty of what was to come was almost harder to endure.

At first, the other women in her cell had tried to console her, but soon enough had given up. Each woman had her own problems. Prisoners would come and go, and many of them were incapable of walking, eating, or even talking after yet another interrogation. It seemed as if no one was any worse off than anyone else.

Hilde slumped against the cold cement, huddled into a ball, crying until she'd used up all her tears. Three weeks in the hands of the Gestapo and no end in sight. She hadn't been allowed a lawyer or a visitor; hadn't even been allowed to write a letter. She had no idea whether her mother had been able to bury the hatchet and telephone the man she despised so much, Hilde's father, Carl Dremmer, and his second wife, Emma.

Had Annie at least informed Q's mother, Ingrid? The poor woman had turned seventy-six this year and had buried two of her sons and her husband already.

Worry about her children gnawed at Hilde's soul, eating at her spirit bit by bit. Just when she wished she would die in this hellhole, a Gestapo officer came for her. Her neck hair stood on end as he pushed her upstairs into a room furnished with a single chair and a table. Several minutes later, the door opened, and Hilde almost gasped at the sight of a neat and tidy woman.

"Here," the woman said and put a mug of water and an envelope on the table. Then she left without another word.

Hilde gulped down the cool, clear water before she reverently touched the envelope with her fingers, tracing the lines of Ingrid's old-fashioned handwriting. It took her several attempts to tear open the envelope with her trembling hands.

*Dearest Hilde,*

*I have been filled with the greatest sorrow since Frau Klein informed us about your and my son's arrest.*

*Every day I hope to hear that this was an unfortunate mistake and you and my Wilhelm have been released. Every day I have prayed that both of you will be able to spend Christmas at home with your children and me, the way we had planned.*

*If you are allowed to write, let me know how I can help, and if you need anything.*

*Frau Klein moved into your apartment in Nikolassee with the two boys, and she tried her best to care for them, but she also has to care for her sick husband. This is why she agreed to send Volker to your father in Hamburg. Unfortunately, my own health is declining rapidly, and I could not offer to care for my grandsons, even though you know how much I love them.*

The letters blurred before Hilde's eyes, and she had to blink rapidly to clear them. Her two little boys. She missed them so much. She'd been very worried about Peter, with his being so little, but even more so about Volker. He was such a sensitive boy, and she could only imagine how this new situation was affecting him. And now, to be separated from his brother!

He was usually excited to be with Grandma and Grandpa. Perhaps they could make him believe this was just a Christmas vacation? She wiped a tear away and continued to read.


*Please rest assured that both of your children are fine for the time being. My prayers and thoughts will always be with you.*
  *Ingrid*


Hilde sighed. She read the letter several times, and then folded it up and put it inside her bra, right over her heart. At least she had one connection to the outside world. Some time later, *Kriminalkommissar* Becker entered the room.

"Frau Quedlin, how are things at home? I understand you had a letter today?" Becker asked with a fake smile.

"Fine," she bit out, too raw to play his games. The letter had jumbled her emotions.

"That is excellent." Becker leered and took another step toward her. "It is unfortunate that such a beautiful woman like you married such a despicable bastard."

"Q is..." Hilde stopped. Why did she even care what Becker said? It was all part of his game.

He lifted an eyebrow. "Did you want to say anything?"

"No, sorry, *Kriminalkommissar*, I didn't want to interrupt you." Hilde steepled her hands, trying to steel herself for what was to come.

"Well, well. You are coming to your senses." His hand brushed her shoulders, and her entire body stiffened. "Your scumbucket of a husband has reaped what he sowed. The Reich will not let her enemies go unpunished, and he will pay the price for his treasonous acts. Execution. Doesn't that word melt on your tongue?"

She glared daggers; if looks could kill, Becker would be dead by now.

"Execution. Say it. Say 'my scumbag traitor of a husband will be executed.'"

Bile rose in her throat as she repeated his words.

Becker showed a pleased smirk. "Well done, Frau Quedlin. I have the feeling you're beginning to cooperate. There is still a chance for you to save yourself, if you'd rather not follow in the footsteps of this *Drecksau*."

Hilde fought the urge to spit at him. *How dare he!*

"Tell me names. Every single person you suspect of having collaborated with the enemy. And you're free to leave."

Becker said it with an enticing smile, as if it were true, but Hilde only saw the hate, the cruelty, and the sadism in his eyes. The very things she'd suffered from in those past three weeks. Something snapped in her.

"I will tell you nothing! You have destroyed my life, taken me away from my children, beaten and abused me when I knew nothing about my husband's intelligence work. What makes you think I will believe you now? You...you...evil..." ...*bastard.*

As she thought the swear word, she instinctively ducked from the expected beating. But nothing happened. When Hilde looked up again, Becker was grinning from ear to ear, applauding her outburst.

"Are you done?" he asked, which only served to fuel the fire burning within her soul.

"No." She slammed her fist on the table, raising her voice, "I want to go home. I'm innocent. My children need me."

*Kriminalkommissar* Becker crossed his arms over his chest. "There is a way you can go home. Tell me what you know."

"I...know...nothing!" In her rage, she shoved the chair, knocking it over on its side. She paused as silence filled the room, sure this would have consequences.

Becker, though, seemed to be satisfied by witnessing her state of complete breakdown and ordered someone to take her back to her cell. There, she sank down onto the cold floor, pulled out the letter, and cried for a long time.

# CHAPTER 10

For two long days, Q had been trying to come to terms with his death sentence. He'd assumed his life was forfeit the minute he'd been arrested. That assumption had now been confirmed in a secretive trial before a Nazi judge. And despite having expected the outcome, it still had hit him in the bowels. The look of agony on Hilde's face when he'd glanced into her eyes one last time.

*Will I ever see her again? Or my sons?*

Fear gripped him harder with every passing minute. It wasn't so much the fear of death, because his rational brain understood it would be quick and rather painless. What had him in tight knots was what might come before that last breath.

*Kriminalkommissar* Becker had more than once stated how enraged Hitler himself was at Q's audacity to collaborate with the enemy *and* plan an assassination attempt on Goebbels. He'd never been shy with hints on *what else* his brutes had in store for uncooperative prisoners.

In the solitude of his death cell, Q's mind went down a dangerous path, envisioning and recalling the most appalling rumors he'd heard over the last years. Now that his trial was over, he'd never be shown in public again. What reason did the Gestapo have to keep him in one piece?

Terror took up every last cell in his body until he made a momentous decision. If he were going to die anyway, it would be on his own terms, by his own hand. Once he made the decision, he felt a peace and calm settle in his spirit. It would be his last act of defiance against this evil regime. With the prospect of agonizing torture, it was an easy, almost joyful task to plan his own demise.

The sun set and the guards distributed what they called *food*. Q all but grinned at them, in the certainty that he'd never see their abhorred faces again. He waited until everything grew quiet beyond the doors of his cell. It was the perfect time. Nobody would make the rounds until morning.

He removed his glasses and broke them into pieces. Then he slipped beneath the wool blanket, the shards of glass clutched in his fingers. Q closed his eyes and thought of Hilde and his two little boys, and he almost lost his courage to go through with his plan.

*Please forgive me.*

He pressed the shard of glass against his left wrist. The pain was slight, the rush of blood over his fingers warm and calming. After he slashed his right wrist, he waited for the inevitable to happen as he sensed his very life seeping into the mattress beneath him.

"Wilhelm Quedlin! *Aufstehen! Augen auf!*"

Q was floating on a cloud, looking down at the tiny city of Berlin, when a voice repeatedly insisted he open his eyes and stand up. He ignored the pesky voice, but it wouldn't shut up. Then hands grabbed his shoulders and shook him.

"*Er lebt.*" He's alive.

*How disappointing,* Q thought and finally opened his eyes. Same cell. Same guards. Only this time, they were actually trying to save his life. *Stupid bastards. Let me die.* They wrapped his wrists with pieces of cloth, and fuzzy snippets of conversation reached his brain.

They pulled him from the mattress and attempted to get him to stand, but he'd lost too much blood, or not enough. He sank down to his knees, wavering like a tree in the storm.

"Take him to the hospital," someone said.

Q let everything happen to him like a puppet on a string, unable to move or talk. He was thrown onto a flat board and deposited in the back of an ambulance. A wave of nausea assailed him as the ambulance rushed off with the sirens wailing.

The drive to the prison hospital, Alt Moabit, didn't take long, and he was carried into the hospital ward. A stern-faced nurse and a physician examined his wounds and stitched the torn flesh of his wrists back together.

"Stupid man," the nurse said with a scowl. "You're lucky you didn't die."

Q's voice wouldn't work, or he would've told her how unlucky he was.

He was wheeled into a tiny cell with a large window in the center of the wall, but he couldn't get up to look outside. As punishment for his attempt to take his own life, he was held in solitary confinement, wearing leather mittens, and tied to his bed so he wouldn't do something stupid again. The nurses fed him the minuscule half-rations, and for the rest of the day, he was alone with his thoughts. Nothing to occupy his mind. Nobody to talk to. No books to read. Nothing.

Q almost chuckled at the irony of fate. The same people who had sentenced him to death wouldn't let him commit suicide. No, even his death had to be on their terms.

For most of the time, Q floated in a cloud of haze, trying to escape reality by solving mathematical puzzles, but not even his brain worked the way it was supposed to. The itching and burning wounds reminded him of his desolate situation, and the leather mittens over his hands made things worse.

The slashes didn't heal properly, and in the following days, the physician had to re-open the wounds twice to drain the infection from them. By the second day, copious amounts of suppuration soaked through his bandages. The young nurse gave him a wary smile before she exchanged his bandages. What she saw must have been awful because a look of horror crossed her face, and she hurried away to call the doctor.

After some consultation, they agreed to give Q penicillin.

"You shouldn't waste your precious penicillin on a man condemned to death," Q argued, but nobody took notice of him.

He slipped into a state of despondency; the infection, the constant hunger, and the boredom were taking a toll on his body and soul. As he lay in his bed, hour upon hour, without books or any form of human interaction aside from the nurses twice a day, his mind began to unravel. It circled in a downward spiral.

Hilde.

His sons.

Gerald's betrayal.

His imminent death.

*When will they come for me? How will I die? By firing squad? By guillotine?*

# CHAPTER 11

Hilde had finally been allowed to write a letter and was given a few sheets of paper and pen and ink. She stared at the blank pages for the longest time, thinking of her beloved family and wondering how Volker was adjusting to his new life with his grandparents in Hamburg.

Her father, Carl, had just turned fifty-seven years old, and she constantly worried about his health. Mother Emma… she smiled at the name. She had never called her stepmother "Mother" until Volker was born and Hilde became a mother herself. It was only then that she started to understand, and their relationship had improved.

She envisioned her half-sisters, twenty-one-year-old Julia and seventeen-year-old Sophie. Hilde wondered how much they had changed since she last saw them. There was so much she wanted to know. So much she wanted to say. But she was afraid of who else might read every word. Hilde sighed, and a tear fell as she began to write…

*My dear Mother and Father,*

*Finally, I'm allowed to write. You were probably very scared when you received the news. I am fine, as far as one can be fine in my situation. Except for the horrific thoughts that follow me day and night.*

*Pappa, please take my best wishes for your birthday, even though they come late. I wish you, from my deepest heart, love and all the best for the new year of your life; above all, health. You know you are supposed to relax and not work so much.*

*Was Volker already with you for your birthday? You are now allowed to write me whenever you want. I believe you will be given the address you must write to. As you know, all letters will be read by the appropriate officials first.*

*I don't know anything about you and the children. Please write me about your lives. I miss you all so much. I only know that Volker is in Hamburg with you. I hope he is fine, at least I have wished so.*

*I hope he is not too much of a burden for you, dear Mother Emma, now that both of your daughters are also back to living with you. As long as Julia is not working, I hope she can help you, and the little boy gives you some pleasure and not only work.*

*We had been so looking forward to our first Christmas at home. The first time with our own Christmas tree, and also the first time with two children. How many Christmas holidays have we spent with you? Little Volker will think this celebration exists only at your place.*

*It consoles me that he will believe it is a good custom and not some rupture in his life, and that he doesn't have to be somewhere with strange people and strange children.*

*Thankfully, Mother Annie agreed to take care of my sons when I was arrested, but I haven't seen or heard from her and have no idea how Peter is. There is so much I'd like to know. I was supposed to be allowed a visit from her a while ago, but nothing happened.*

*Was Julia in Berlin, and was it she who took Volker with her to Hamburg? I'm longing to know the details of his trip.*

*It was a true stroke of fortune, in my misfortune, that I finished sewing Volker's winter coat. I finished it on Friday, and Monday, November 30, was my unlucky day.*

Hilde jumped when a guard yelled her name. She set down the pen and stood, her legs shaky beneath her. But he was only there to tell her she'd be transferred to a regular prison the next day.

"Pack your things and be ready," he yelled at her.

*Which things?* Hilde wanted to ask. She possessed nothing except the clothes she was wearing and the letter from Ingrid. She'd been wearing those same clothes continuously since the day she'd been arrested more than three weeks ago, except for the two times she'd been stripped bare by her interrogators. Hilde stiffened at the memory.

It took several minutes until she was able to pick up her pen again. With a heavy heart, she continued to write…

*When I finished the coat, I even told Q that if I were to die now, at least he had a memory of me, and that he would have to remind Volker that his mother loved him enough to spend many day and night hours making it especially for him.*

*I really said it as a joke. I had no idea what a horrible fate was already hovering over us.*

*But now, when he wears his winter coat, you can remind him of his mother. I hope he doesn't forget me and doesn't endure the same fate I did when I was his age. I still remember, as if it was yesterday, living with always-changing relatives.*

*Not that they treated me badly, but I always knew that my mother didn't want me, and I longed to be back in my parental home. Knowing that the name of my mother was never mentioned, would be fearfully avoided, didn't make things better. Volker should know that I'm still here, and that I always think about him, and I hope deep in my soul that I will soon be together with him again.*

*If you have some, please show him pictures of me. Believe me, it will be solace for him even when he doesn't seem to be unhappy. Seeing pictures of his mother will help him remember me and keep our close relationship.*

*And he should not forget his little brother either. He shall know that he and Peter belong together always. Volker, despite his almost three years, is not a mindless child anymore, and I want him to stay so thoughtful.*

*We have always talked with him as if he was an adult, and his daddy has often said that he is a complete person. And now this complete person's life has changed a great deal. He had to give up those painting lessons with Auntie Stein, those he liked so much. Maybe you can write her a letter and have Volker paint something for her; she will be so happy.*

*He had to leave the kindergarten where they just started with the advent celebrations and the Christmas carols and the other children of his age with whom he played so nicely. I'm sure he will also miss the nice little garden where he spent many hours a day outside.*

*I hope so much that all this he can have back very soon. Please do not misunderstand me; I know he is treated well by you, better than anywhere else except with me. And this is the reason why I want Volker to stay with you. Peter is, thank God, too small to comprehend all this. But it is even harder for me to leave him at this cute age.*

*All the joy he brought to my heart, every moment I spent with him. Oh God, it is so hard, but still not the hardest thing to do.*


Hilde could not go on. Her shoulders shook too hard for her to continue writing. And even if she had been steady, she wouldn't have been able to see the paper through the blur of tears. She missed her children so badly. She was so afraid for them. For Q. For herself.

Christmas was in two days, but saving a miracle, she'd spend it in prison. Alone.

Amidst total darkness and desolation, she spotted the smallest silver lining. Tomorrow, she would leave the awful Gestapo headquarters behind and be transferred to a normal prison. A place without constant interrogations. A place where prisoners were treated like human beings. A place where she might be allowed clean clothes and a shower.

A shower! After three weeks in this hellhole, her clothes were covered in dried blood, dirt, and sweat. Mold and stench oozed from every thread.

Hilde curled up on the hard cot and fell into a nightmarish sleep. In that horrid place, it wouldn't take her mind long to slip into madness. It wasn't until morning that she felt steady enough to finish her letter.

. . .

*You cannot imagine with how many tears I'm writing this letter. My first letter in this dreadful time of my life.*

*I can only write about my children because I have focused all my thoughts on them to help me in the darkest hours. Thinking of them warms my heart, but sometimes makes all of this so much more painful.*

*But I also know, and this has given me consolation, that with you and Pappa, I will always have support. And that you will not be the only ones.*

*Now I must talk about the reason for my letter, the instructions on how to handle Volker. It is natural that he has to be integrated into your way of life, but I must warn that he wakes up very early, around seven. If with you, he wakes up earlier, then he will have his naptime earlier as well and go to bed earlier in the evening.*

*My biggest wish in that regard is that he continues his naptime. He still needs it. At our house, he sleeps at least two hours and is still able to fall asleep immediately in the evening.*

*But he needs quiet and darkness when he is supposed to sleep, especially during the day. If he doesn't sleep, it's because he hasn't had enough exercise, especially outdoors.*

*My second wish is that he plays a lot outside, even if it rains. We have always played many hours outside, and I used to also let him play alone. It is my explicit wish, and he is used to doing so. Volker knows he's not supposed to step on the street. I have actually had to beat him two times because he did so. The second time, I hit him with a stick, the only time ever. He was seriously scolded and then spent half a day locked in a room.*

*But he had only followed other children; alone, he wouldn't have run onto the street. If he does the same thing at your place, I ask you to be as strict as I was because this is vitally important.*

*I grant my permission for you to give him a good smacking so he knows this is not just an empty threat when he doesn't do what you tell him. I'm sure it will work, but you have to be rigid and not grandmotherly. Because now you must replace his strict mother.*

*I will ask Mother Annie to send you his handcart to play outside, as well as the sleigh he received last Christmas to keep him occupied. When it gets colder, he will need winter shoes because those from last year will not fit anymore. Mother Annie will have to apply for them.*

*I already applied for a pair of slippers for him. You should have received the ration coupon by now. All of this you will need to coordinate with Mother Annie. Give Volker gloves, scarf, etc. for playing outside.*

*I would love it if you could let him paint as often as he wants. Maybe you can help him with this. He loves painting.*

*Next, I must talk to you about nutrition. You know how badly sick Volker was and how long it took to recover from his stomach sickness. Therefore, please excuse me if I am very thorough about his nutrition because I do not want you to have the same problems with him again.*

Hilde found great comfort in writing her son's daily requirements down, knowing this was the only motherly thing she could do for him right then. She guided Mother Emma on the foods he could eat and how often, letting her know what settled well on his stomach and what proved to upset it. When Volker turned three, he would get additional coupons for the extra nourishment the child needed. She hoped Emma and her father wouldn't be financially burdened by any of this.

Hilde wracked her brain trying to think of anything she had forgotten. She hated burdening Mother Emma with so many instructions, but what else could she do? She couldn't be a mother to her son right now, so all that was left was to mother as best as she could from afar.

When she was certain that she had covered everything, she rushed to finish the letter so it could be on its way to her beloved family…

*I have a bad conscience about making you so many rules; I hope you don't think it's too much. May I ask you or Julia to please write me soon, letting me know in great detail how you all are? I'd like to know how Volker behaves, if he's healthy, if he is nice, what he does every day and how you spent Christmas, everything. I want to know everything.*

*Julia is such a good writer, please tell her to do this favor for her older sister.*

*Wishing you and my little sweetie a wonderful Christmas and a happy New Year. I'm sending greetings to everyone.*

*Your always thankful Hilde*

She squeezed in some extra words on the last sheet of paper she had been given.

*My beloved little Volker,*

*Your mother had to write a letter because she couldn't come herself and this is why she's very sad.*

*But you spent Christmas with Grandma and Grandpa – this is fun, isn't it?*

*I hope you'll always be a good boy and do what Grandmama tells you. Maybe then there will be something nice under the Christmas tree, that lovely tree with so many lights.*

Hilde stopped and drew a Christmas tree with candles and ornaments onto the paper.

*I have painted a Christmas tree for you, can you do the same? Try it and then send it to your mother with a letter. Please don't forget your little brother, Peter, who is with your other grandmama for Christmas.*

*But soon we will be all together again in our apartment in Niko-lassee. Do you remember it? And then you can play again with your kindergarten friends.*

*Now, be always a good boy and please think once in a while about your mother who loves you more than anything in the world.*

Hilde stared at the letter as tears rolled down her face once more. She folded the sheets of paper over, addressed the envelope, but didn't seal it. The censors would do that for her.

When the guard came for the letter, she was out of tears,; despair had crawled into every crevice of her being. Desperation was becoming her constant companion, and her ability to stay strong was slipping away with each passing hour.

Later in the morning, they came to transfer her to the women's prison. As soon as she left the Gestapo cellars behind, her spirits rose.

The new cell was about six by ten feet. It featured a bunk bed, a table, and a chair. Most importantly, there was a window where sunlight streamed inside.

Pure luxury.

# CHAPTER 12

C hristmas had passed, and the year 1943 had arrived when Q's wounds finally started to heal, and the constant mind-fog cleared. Two weeks tied to his bed in solitary confinement had made him hungry for any kind of human interaction.

As this wouldn't happen, he talked to himself aloud to break the monotony of his existence. He held vivid discussions with himself and was surprised when, one day, a different voice filled the room.

He hadn't seen the young nurse before, or perhaps he just hadn't paid attention to her. She was little more than twenty years old, with a round face, straight blonde hair, and vivid blue eyes.

"Are you feeling better, Herr Quedlin?" she asked him.

No, he definitely hadn't seen her before because nobody had ever addressed him by his name in this hospital. Usually, the nurses and doctors only barked orders at him. "*Hinsetzen. Essen. Aufstehen.*" Sit up. Eat. Stand.

"Well, yes," he managed to answer.

When she untied him and took off his mittens, he wasn't surprised. This had been the usual routine after the first few days. The nurses would untie him, give him his food, then sit in the corner, watching him while they read or wrote something.

Not this one. She helped him sit up, handed him the tray, and moved the chair to sit beside him.

"I'm Schwester Anna," she said.

Seen up close, she was much too thin. Like everyone in this country. While there wasn't a famine like during the Great War, the rations didn't allow anyone to put on fat.

"Thank you, I'm Wilhelm Quedlin," he said, out of training as to how to hold a conversation with another person besides himself.

She giggled. "I know that."

When he'd finished eating the piece of bread and two potatoes, she smiled at him and apologized. "I'm sorry, but I have to tie you up again."

Then she was gone. Q longed to see her again, but with her blonde hair and fair skin, she looked like an angel, and he came to the conclusion that she had been a trick of his isolated mind. A friendly *Kranken-schwester* who actually talked to him? No way.

The next day she came back and started a conversation.

"You do know I've been sentenced to death, Schwester Anna?" he asked her.

"Yes. We were told."

"Doesn't it strike you as ironic that you're nursing me back to health then?" Q rotated his wrists in all directions.

"It does, but that's my job." She paused for a while and lowered her voice. "You're luckier than your friends. Harro Schulze-Boysen, his wife, and another dozen members of the Red Orchestra were executed on December twenty-second."

"I knew he was arrested, but not that they'd already executed him," Q said. Apparently, Schwester Anna believed him to be part of Schulze-Boysen's network.

Another irony of fate. He and Schulze-Boysen had agreed not to work together, and yet he had been found out because they used the same contacts in Russia. According to what Q had heard in his trial and then put two and two together, the entire resistance network had been discovered when the Gestapo captured a female Russian parachutist last summer. She possessed a list of more than two hundred contacts, which the Gestapo had been able to decipher.

"The poor man, he'd been in Gestapo custody since last September. But he never wavered in his convictions," the nurse said.

Q's eyes widened in shock. Since September? Why hadn't he known until his trial about Schulze-Boysen's arrest? Would he have been more careful? Stopped meeting Gerald? Would he still be free, together with his wife and sons?

Q barely noticed when Schwester Anna tied him to his bed again and left; too many emotions flooded his system. Guilt. Regret. Fear. He'd insisted on doing things on his own when he should have kept up with the news better.

After many hours of second-guessing himself, analyzing all the possibilities, weighing the pros and cons, he finally found some calm. *There was nothing I could have done, and no way I could have known. I wouldn't have done a thing differently.*

When *Schwester* Anna returned in the morning, he'd been waiting for her, anxious to pepper her with questions. "Where did they shoot him?"

"He wasn't shot. He was hanged," she said while untying Q.

"Hanged?" Q raised an eyebrow. Military people like Schulze-Boysen were normally executed in front of a firing squad. Civilians were usually beheaded with the guillotine. *But hanging? When did the Nazis begin killing people by hanging them?*

Hanging was considered a discreditable and cruel method of execution. In a few rare situations, the drop broke the victim's neck, but more often than not, the rope merely compressed the throat, making breathing impossible and giving the victim a painful few minutes of suffering as they were suffocated to death. Their faces swelled and turned purple as the blood stopped its circulation, then blessedly, they would convulse and pass from this life.

"Yes. He made a statement before they dropped him." She turned her head away and whispered…

*"Wenn wir auch sterben sollen,*
*So wissen wir: Die Saat*
*Geht auf. Wenn Köpfe rollen,*
*Dann Zwingt doch der Geist den Staat.*
*Glaubt mit mir an die gerechte Zeit, die alles reifen lässt!"*

. . .

Even if we should die,

> We know this: The seed
> Bears fruit. If heads roll, then
> The spirit nevertheless forces the state.
> Believe with me in the just time that lets everything ripen.


Q didn't know what to say. Just reciting Schulze-Boysen's last words could get the nurse arrested if someone overheard her.

She turned to look at him with watery eyes. "So many brave men and women have been executed. Schulze-Boysen was so strong. He was brutally tortured, and yet he never said a word or betrayed anyone working with the Resistance. He didn't even beg for his life."

"You shouldn't voice these things here. People have been arrested for less," Q warned her.

A smile appeared on her face. "Would you turn me in?"

"Of course not. But the walls have ears. You never know who's listening, or whom to trust," he said, tasting the bitterness of Gerald's betrayal.

In this moment, the door opened, and the head nurse peeked inside. She scowled at Anna. "Hurry up, you are needed. And have I heard chatter in here?"

"Yes, *Oberschwester,* I just told the prisoner to finish his meal so I can leave. I'll be with you in a minute," Schwester Anna answered.

The next day, another nurse attended him.

When she left, it finally dawned on him, what his sentence actually meant. Death.

Of course, he had known the meaning on an intellectual level, but now, he felt the weight of it in every cell. His body took on a life of its own and started shaking violently, and for once, he was thankful to be tied to his bed. After hours of howling, screaming, and fighting, he finally fell asleep.

When he woke up the next morning, he consoled himself with the fact that at least Martin would continue their sabotage work at Loewe, even without Erhard and Q. In case of an upheaval within Germany, Martin would also be able to lead the company into a new era.

# CHAPTER 13

The deafening sound of air raid alarms penetrated Hilde's dreams on January sixteenth. The next moment she was wide awake. It was her first alarm in prison. She heard the guards rushing along the hallway and waited for someone to open her cell door. But nothing happened.

Her cellmate, a resolute Polish woman in her fifties with little mastery of the German language, said, "Prisoners stay in cells."

Hilde looked at her in shock. That couldn't be true. Their cell was on the third floor, and they were sitting ducks for the British bombers.

"No, no," Hilde protested. "We need to go to the shelter. Or at least to the basement of the building."

"Yes. Stay," the woman said and stretched out on her cot, sliding a rosary through her fingers and murmuring a verse in Polish that Hilde assumed to be *Hail Mary*.

Not sure whether the protection of the Virgin Mary would extend to a Protestant, Hilde wrapped a blanket around her slight form and cowered in the corner of the cell. The building shook as bomb after bomb detonated nearby. Dust and pieces of the plaster walls fell to the floor, and she coughed in the dusty air.

The air raid continued for most of the night and finally stopped sometime after the sun came up. Covered with dust, Hilde climbed the ladder to her bunk bed, eyeing the peacefully sleeping Polish woman with envy before she fell into a fitful sleep.

A few days after the bombing, the guard announced a visitor for Hilde. It would be the first person from outside she'd seen since her arrest almost two months ago.

Hilde entered the visiting room to find a man she hadn't seen before.

"Frau Quedlin, my name is Müller, and I'm your lawyer." He extended his hand to her.

Hilde took it, baffled. "My lawyer? But–"

"Frau Klein has retained me to defend you and your husband."

"My mother?" Hilde asked, confused by his words.

"Yes, your mother, Annie Klein, has hired me to mount a defense against the Gestapo's accusations."

Hilde couldn't believe it. It wasn't at all like her mother. The same person who hadn't even written a letter had gone to all the trouble to hire a costly lawyer to defend her?

"Please tell her that I'm very grateful, but I can't..."

The lawyer waved her objection away and pulled a sheaf of papers from his briefcase. "Let's sit down and get over the paperwork first. Shall we?"

Hilde took a seat and eyed the papers.

Herr Müller explained about his duties and his fees, then slid the first document across to her and handed her a fountain pen. "This is a full power over your and your husband's estate for your mother. According to the contract, she has to use it in good faith to cover all expenses related to your children and to pay my fees."

Hilde shook her head, her earlier surprise replaced by the bitter knowledge of her mother's ulterior motives. Annie never did anything if there wasn't an advantage to her.

"I know this may seem like picking over bones, but it actually is the best solution. Your mother, Frau Klein, has the best intentions."

*Yes, the best intentions for herself.*

After a long pause, Herr Müller tapped the paper. "Your trial is scheduled in less than a week."

"I will sign it, fine, but you need to get my husband's signature as well," Hilde said and reluctantly took the pen.

"Of course I will, Frau Quedlin. As soon as I'm allowed to visit him."

The lawyer asked her about her side of the story, and she repeated everything she'd already told the Gestapo. He might be her lawyer, but she was sure someone was watching or listening, so she made sure that she didn't confess to having done anything illegal. Nor would she ever mention Martin's name. As far as she knew, he was still at liberty.

"Very good. That should help." Herr Müller finished scribbling notes and looked at her with a sad expression in his eyes. "You have been accused of high treason."

"High treason?" Hilde's voice quivered.

"Unfortunately, yes."

"This is ridiculous. I've done nothing to justify..." Her voice broke, and she took a deep breath.

"That is what we need to prove at trial."

"But...how can they...?" Hilde closed her eyes and willed her voice to work. "What are my chances?"

"This I don't know. I promise I'll do my best, but I will be honest with you. Your trial is considered *Geheime Kommandosache*."

"What does that mean?" Hilde wanted to know.

"It means the normal sharing of information is suppressed. I asked for copies of the evidence against you but have received nothing. We won't see the evidence they intend to use until the day of the trial."

"But that's unlawful!" Hilde was livid. She stood up and paced the small room. "How can they do this? There are laws in place for a reason."

"Laws they do not have to follow."

Desperation gripped her. "Is there nothing that can be done?"

"I am going to do my best for you. Furthermore, I've started the paperwork to appeal Doctor Quedlin's sentence. I won't be able to over-turn his conviction, but I'm hoping to get his sentence changed to life-long imprisonment instead of execution." With a glance at his watch, Herr Müller stuffed his papers back in his briefcase and stood up. "My time is up, but I will be back. Have a good day, Frau Quedlin."

*A good day?*

# CHAPTER 14

Q was lying on his bed, trying to exercise his weakened and sore body within the little free-moving space he had when the door to his cell opened. Judging by the sun streaming in through the window, it was around noon. A very unusual time for anyone to enter his room.

At the sight of the head nurse, his heart sank, but she greeted him with something similar to a smile.

"Herr Quedlin, you have a visitor." She released his hands and feet and helped him sit on the edge of the bed before ushering in a thin, well-dressed man a few moments later.

"Doctor Quedlin, allow me to introduce myself. I am *Rechtsanwalt* Müller, and I am here to represent you," the lawyer said and extended his hand.

"Who sent you?" asked Q, suspicious of being allowed a visitor after all these weeks.

"Your mother-in-law, Annie Klein, has retained me to represent you and your wife against the charge presented and your conviction."

Q nodded, trying to grab hold of what the man was saying. "Have you seen my wife?"

"Yes, I have. She sent me to tell you she's fine and looking forward to her trial with hope, as she's innocent."

Q smiled at the evidence that Hilde had stuck to their plan to lay all guilt on him and pretend to be an unknowing helper.

"Do you know when her trial will be?" he asked.

"As a matter of fact, in three days from now. But I'm here to talk about your case, not hers, if you understand." Herr Müller glanced at his watch. "We have only twenty-five minutes left."

Q raised a bandaged hand. "Excuse me, but first, why now? Why is the Gestapo allowing this?"

"Well, it is my understanding that Frau Klein is well connected. She personally asked *Kriminalkommissar* Becker for this favor, and it was granted to her."

*A favor? Since when is being allowed a lawyer to defend yourself a favor?* Q wanted to scream but refrained from doing so. It wouldn't help. He'd be grateful for this *favor* that actually was a basic right – or had been before Hitler came to power.

Herr Müller pulled some papers from his briefcase and handed them to Q with a pen. "These papers transfer all legal power over your estate to your mother-in-law so that she may continue to care for your children and pay my fees. I need you to sign on the line next to where your wife signed."

Q's thankfulness disappeared. He wasn't at all surprised that Annie had figured out a way to benefit from his and her daughter's arrests. His first impulse was to refuse, but his children needed food and clothing and a place to live. All of this cost money. Yes, he had given his mother an envelope with money to stash away, but this money wouldn't last for long if it was the only source of income for his children.

"I knew there was a catch," he sighed in disgust as he signed his name. It rankled that he was forced to transfer all of his property and wealth to his mother-in-law – even if it was for his own defense and the good of his children.

Herr Müller proceeded to talk about his plans to appeal Q's sentence and turn it into lifelong prison instead of a death sentence.

As long as *lifelong* meant the duration of Hitler's Third Reich and not Q's life, Q didn't mind. He was convinced that the "Thousand Year Empire" wouldn't last but another year or two at most.

At the end of their half-hour discussion, the lawyer tucked the papers away. "I've also contacted Ingrid Quedlin and Gunther Quedlin."

"You've talked with my mother and brother?" Q asked, perplexed.

"Yes. Your brother has kindly offered to help as much as is needed," Herr Müller said while getting ready to leave.

"Please give my best wishes and my thanks to him," Q said hesitantly. Gunther was a lawyer himself, but Q wasn't sure how he felt about dragging his brother into this mess. He'd had enough grief in his own life, having been forced to retire from his job at the Ministry of Education shortly after the Nazis came into power due to being a member of the Social Democratic Party.

"There appears to be some tension between Frau Klein and your side of the family."

Q gave a chuckle, the first one in a long time. "More than you imagine. My mother hates Frau Klein. Gunther hates Hilde and Frau Klein. Frau Klein hates her ex-husband, who is Hilde's father. She also hates his second wife. Hilde hates her mother. And believe it or not, even my mother and brother have been hot and cold for as long as I can remember. In this family, nobody talks with anybody and grudges are held onto for life."

The attorney chuckled and shook his head. "It's really a shame when families cannot get along with one another. Really a shame. Good day." Herr Müller shook Q's hand, then knocked on the door to be let outside.

As they waited for the door to open, the lawyer turned to look at Q and said, "Propaganda minister Goebbels has called for total war. He's supposed to hold a speech in the Sportpalast."

Q paled. Goebbels's *total war* was one that had been rumored as a last resort. The Reich would be monitoring all civilian activities. Anything that didn't directly help the war effort would be shut down, and the people put to work elsewhere. No one, not even the rich, would be able to escape the demands of the Party.

He also knew that if it had come to this, the war would continue mercilessly until one of the parties surrendered unconditionally. And it wouldn't be the Allies. The hardships the German people had suffered were only just beginning.

# CHAPTER 15

*January 27, 1943*

Hilde looked into the heavily spotted mirror and braided her hair as best she could. The day of her trial had arrived, and she wanted to look like a good, and innocent, German housewife.

Everyone, including her lawyer and the prison guards, had told her that, in the worst case, she'd be sentenced to five to ten years in jail. The most probable outcome was one to two years, and with some luck, she'd be allowed to go home today.

Normally, prisoners were allowed to take a shower once a week, in groups of ten. Ten women. Three showers. Twenty minutes. Still, it was a luxury compared to the Gestapo cellars.

But today, she'd been given twenty minutes alone in the showers in order to look nice for her trial. It was a special concession given by Frau Herrmann. She was in her early twenties, and her wavy blonde hair fell down on her shoulders, giving her an angelic look. But that wasn't the reason the women called her *Blonde Angel*.

They had given her the nickname because she was always helping the prisoners in one way or another. She smuggled secret messages in and out, never withheld news from the outside, sneaked them extra rations or other small favors when possible, and always had a nice word and smile on her lips – for everyone. She truly was an angel.

Hilde smiled. She'd learned to find joy in the smallest things, like taking an extra shower.

Her fingers trembled as she finished braiding her long brown hair. She'd spent the time since her lawyer announced the date of her trial vacillating between hope and despair. He hadn't visited again, nor had anyone else. Not even *Kriminalkommissar* Becker and his henchmen.

Not that she missed them, but it had left her with far too much time on her hands to think. About the past. About Q. About her two little boys. About her mother and the future…it was an emotional ride.

"You look nice," Frau Hermann said. "Your automobile is waiting for you."

*My automobile is waiting for me?* Hilde suppressed a giggle but nonetheless felt a tiny bit like royalty.

Frau Herrmann escorted her down and handed her over to two male police officers. "Good luck."

The police weren't unfriendly and helped her get into the back of the truck. Apparently, normal police still had some manners.

The truck stopped, the door opened, and another prisoner climbed inside. His nose had been broken, and green and black bruises disfigured his face. It took Hilde a few moments to recognize the newcomer.

"Hello, Erhard," she said.

He blinked and looked at her with a dull expression on his face. His eyes probably had to adapt to the darkness in the truck first.

A police officer jumped inside and shackled Erhard to the wall opposite her.

"Hello, Hilde," Erhard greeted her, his voice thick.

"No talking," the policeman ordered and jumped out. Hilde heard him bolt the door, and a few seconds later, the vehicle started moving again.

With barely audible whispers, she talked to Erhard. His wife had also been arrested, but they'd released her after a few days.

Hilde decided to take it as a good omen.

The truck stopped in front of the courthouse, and she and Erhard were escorted up the steps and seated together on the defendant's bench.

Despite their not being allowed to speak to one another, his mere presence gave her strength.

Hilde scanned the room for her lawyer. She thought he would be seated beside her, but she finally found him sitting next to *Kriminalkommissar* Becker on the prosecution's side. Her stomach sank.

To her right was the judge's bench, and to her left, the audience. Most people in the audience wore a uniform, except for one man with curly blond hair.

Her heart leaped as she sought his eyes. Q looked miserable. He was thin and weak; the fire in his curious blue eyes had dimmed. She sent him a smile and hoped he could see in her eyes how much she loved him.

The trial began. Erhard's case was first. He'd confessed to being a tacit accomplice, hoping to receive a jail sentence.

After a pause of several minutes, where she leaned her shoulder against Erhard's to give him some comfort, the trial continued with her case.

Herr Müller argued for her innocence. "Your honor, Frau Quedlin is a housewife and mother. She has given the Führer two beautiful sons. She didn't understand what she was typing for her husband. Furthermore, she had no active role in the sabotage at the Loewe radio factory."

*Kriminalkommissar* Becker argued the charges against her and stepped forward. "How does a woman, living in such harmony with her husband for seven years, not know he's a traitor to the Reich? I tell you, she knew what she was typing and even encouraged his criminal sabotage activities."

"I do not see any evidence to convince me she was not complicit with the espionage and sabotage taking place," the judge agreed with Becker.

"This woman deserves to pay the ultimate price for her part in defying the Party, the Führer, and the Reich," *Kriminalkommissar* Becker demanded.

Herr Müller argued the exact opposite fiercely: "Your honor, this woman doesn't deserve to die for her unknowing actions. Even if you deem her guilty – and I believe she isn't – of complicity, according to paragraph…"

Hilde didn't understand most of the legal gibberish, except that her actions were of such minor importance to the operation that she should be punished with a prison sentence of no more than two years.

Hope settled in her heart. She gathered all of her strength and energy around her, showing a mask of airiness to the cold and contemptuous Nazi supporters in the courtroom. On the inside, however, she was worried not only for her own life but also for the well-being of her two little boys.

When some official-looking person announced a recess and Hilde was taken outside, dread boiled in her belly as something became clear…

These Nazi devils were barrelling ahead to kill anyone who opposed them. Was it Erhard's and her turn now?

# CHAPTER 16

Q sat in the courtroom, well aware of the importance of this day for the fates of his family. Even the most die-hard Nazi supporters in the audience seemed to agree that while Erhard deserved the death sentence, Hilde should get away with a few years in prison.

The shy smile on her thinned face and the carefully braided hair in pretzel style surely had helped to win the sympathy of the judge, too.

When Q was told to get up and leave the courtroom to await the judge's decision, his weak legs barely held his body weight, and he had to lean on the bench to stand. He moved slowly towards the exit, his stomach growling in protest.

In the prison hospital, he'd received only half rations. Half of the smaller prisoner rations, not the ones for civilians. After just two months in custody, his clothes bagged on him, and it was only thanks to the suspenders that he didn't lose his pants.

He was afraid of what the judge would decide but chose to stick with hope. Erhard had been incredibly brave and steadfast during the trial – an example of courage in the face of terrible odds. Not once had his friend cried, whined, or begged. But simple courage and honesty weren't traits honored by this regime.

And Hilde…if she weren't already the woman of his dreams, he would have fallen in love with her today. Even when *Kriminalkommissar* Becker had demanded capital punishment, she hadn't even flinched.

The guard cuffed Q's left hand to the bench in the waiting area and left. A few moments later, another guard showed up with Hilde in tow. He cuffed her to the same bench.

Q's heart lurched. Suddenly, the room seemed to beam with sunlight.

"The judge will have lunch and render his verdict in one hour," the guard said and disappeared.

Q looked at his beautiful wife and reached for her arm with his free hand. Her skin was so soft, but her eyes widened in horror. Q followed her glance down to the bulging scar on his wrist.

"What happened?" she whispered.

Q felt his face flush, but he met her eyes. "After my sentencing, I decided I would rather take my own life than allow these devils to take it from me. But I failed."

"Oh, *Liebling*! What did they do to you?" Hilde asked, lifting his wrist, and kissing the scar softly.

"They moved me to the prison hospital, and I've been there ever since." He didn't tell her about being kept in solitary confinement or the fact that he'd been tied to his bed most of the time.

"I've missed you so much," Hilde said with tears in her eyes.

"My love. I've thought endlessly about you and our boys."

Hilde nodded, and her tears spilled over. "Will we ever see them again?"

Q lifted his hand and cupped her jaw, searching her eyes, wishing there was some way he could make this all go away for her. "They are being cared for, and that is what counts right now."

Hilde nodded and laid her head on his shoulder, their hands intertwined. Q kissed her forehead, then sat with her, closing his eyes and soaking up this moment. This one hour might be all the time in this life he'd be allowed to spend with her, and he vowed to keep these memories deep inside his soul. For eternity.

"Remember when we first met?" he asked her, not really expecting an answer. "You were so beautiful and full of life. Your laughter at the moving pictures had me intrigued even before I'd seen you. I knew then that you were the woman for me."

Hilde turned her head and looked up at him. "We've had a good life together, haven't we?"

"Yes. And no matter what happens, know that I love you with all of my heart and soul."

"I love you, too." She stopped speaking and leaned as close to him as her handcuff allowed. The warmth of Hilde leaning against him seeped into his soul, mind, and body.

They stayed like that, remembering the good times. They laughed, giggled, and cried. They packed their entire life together into this time.

She was his soulmate and would always be. In this life or the next.

Far too soon, the guards returned and took them back into the courtroom for the proclamation of the sentences.

The judge entered the courtroom and instructed Erhard to stand. The tension was palpable, and Q's neck hair stood on end.

"Doctor Erhard Tohmfor, it is the ruling of this court that you are found guilty on all counts and are hereby sentenced to death by execution."

The audience applauded. Erhard's face showed the shock for a short moment before he gathered his composure and stared defiantly at the judge.

Q sent his friend a short nod in acknowledgment of his courage.

"Hildegard Quedlin, stand."

Hilde squared her shoulders and stood erect and tall, despite the fact that she must be scared to death.

Q wished with everything in him that he could be there to hold her hand in this moment. He closed his eyes, listening for the words that would spare her life.

"Frau Quedlin, I have looked at the evidence that has been presented to this court. I find it incredible that a woman so in love with her husband would not be aware of his subversive activities. I, therefore, find you guilty of cognizance of high treason and sentence you to death by execution."

Q's eyes popped open. *Sentenced to death? Not prison? God, no! That cannot be true.*

But it was. Hilde's gasp of dismay could be heard among the murmurs in the audience. Apart from the gasp, she stood upright and unwavering, defying everything the judge stood for.

Judging by the puzzled then smug look crossing *Kriminalkommissar* Becker's face, not even the Gestapo had expected such a harsh verdict.

The judge slammed his gavel down on the bench and left the courtroom.

Q's mind remained in a fog as he tried to take in what had just happened. He barely noticed the guard leading him to the waiting vehicle outside, murmuring something that sounded like *Sorry*.

When Q's eyes had become accustomed to the darkness inside, he couldn't believe what he saw. Hilde.

Q looked at the prison guards and silently thanked them for their compassion. There seemed to be good hearts buried beneath their harsh appearances. The door was bolted from the outside. He and Hilde were alone.

He swept her into his arms. He touched her beautiful face, scrutinized it, trying to memorize every single line, the sweetness, her bright blue eyes, her red and soft lips.

He kissed those lips. Careful at first, but soon, red-hot fire passed between them. They both knew this would be their last kiss. They wrapped their arms around each other and hungrily devoured the other's mouth.

When they had to come up for air, they whispered words of love, but also cautioned each other to be strong.

He locked eyes with Hilde and felt the fire in his body ignite – the fire that had been burning between them from the first moment he saw her and that had never ceased to burn during all those years. Not even now, when they both were sentenced to death.

"I love you," she whispered.

"I'm so sorry, darling." Q kissed her neck, intent on memorizing the feel of his wife in his arms.

"It wasn't your fault. Don't you ever blame yourself for this awfulness." She looked at him, sad, but steadfast in her conviction.

A rock fell from his shoulders. Not even after her harsh sentence did she blame him. Much too soon the door of the truck was opened, and one of the guards peeked inside. "We have to leave."

Q nodded and said to Hilde one last time, "I love you." Then he was hurried away and could only wave to the disappearing car.

# CHAPTER 17

For days after the trial, Hilde refused to talk to anyone. Her cellmate, the Polish woman, had been transferred to some other place, and she was alone in her cell.

The other women on her level soon decided to let Hilde grieve and didn't insist on making conversation. Everyone understood that a death sentence was hard to swallow.

On the third day, the Blonde Angel appeared with a pretty young woman and introduced her as Hilde's new cellmate Margit Staufer.

Hilde did her best to ignore the woman – although girl would be more appropriate. She couldn't be much older than eighteen. But seeing the newcomer so lost and sad tugged at her motherly feelings, and she couldn't keep to herself any longer.

"I apologize for my earlier rudeness. I'm Hilde. Welcome to this humble place." She made a gesture taking in the entire cell.

For a short moment, the girl's face lit up. "Thank you. I'm Margit."

"You look so young," Hilde said, wondering what she could have done to end up here.

"I turned nineteen three months ago." Margit bit her fingernails and looked hesitantly at Hilde. "How long have you been here?"

"I was arrested two months ago."

Margit's eyes widened. "That long?"

Hilde nodded, not mentioning her death sentence. The two women talked about their lives, and soon became friends.

Two days later, Margit received a huge package.

Hilde watched as Margit opened the large box and unpacked more food than Hilde had seen in a long time. Her stomach rumbled at the smell of smoked ham. The minuscule prison rations were enough not to starve, but they never left her sated.

Margit generously shared the food with Hilde and waved away her weak protest.

"If I want more, my family will send me more. Please eat."

"Thank you." Hilde took tiny pieces of ham, fresh bread, apples, and even a morsel of cake. It was the first time in months that she didn't feel the constant nagging of hunger.

After a while, Margit asked, "So, what did you do?"

Hilde looked at Margit, trying to gauge if she really was who she pretended to be. It wasn't unusual to plant spies in prisons to get information the regime wouldn't otherwise find out. But Hilde was already convicted, so what difference did it make?

"My husband relayed intelligence to our enemies, and I was accused of helping him."

Margit scowled. "These Nazis...they are an insult to true Germans everywhere."

"Shush! Aren't you afraid someone will hear you?" Hilde urged her.

"I will not be silenced." Margit threw her head back.

Hilde smiled. Margit was the spitting image of herself – a decade ago when she'd been young and hot-blooded. Determined to right the injustices around her. Before she'd grown up and stopped voicing her concerns openly, afraid of the consequences.

*And what has that brought you? Nothing! Absolutely nothing!*

Looking back on her life now, she wished she'd done more. Taken a more active role in the resistance efforts instead of just supporting Q's work. But she'd had children to take care of...still, a pang of jealousy hit her as she witnessed Margit's carefree manner. The girl simply refused to succumb to the necessities of life or let the Nazis threaten her.

Over the next days, Hilde and Margit became friends. Hilde enjoyed their conversations and the point of view of a teenager. In Margit's life, everything was still easy – black and white.

Having someone to talk to relieved the boredom and helped keep her mind busy. It was only when she lay down to sleep, and the cell grew quiet, that her mind rolled back to Q, her little boys, and the death sentence that loomed over her head.

# CHAPTER 18

After Hilde's trial, Q was told he'd be transferred to the Plötzensee prison. His initial thrill at leaving the solitary confinement of the Moabit prison hospital was crushed when *Kriminalkommissar* Becker walked into his hospital cell with a satisfied grin.

"Prisoner. You couldn't wait to be dead, could you? But let me tell you that I'm the one to decide when and how it happens, not you. And I might just let you rot in prison for a while; wouldn't that be fun?"

Q chose not to take the bait. *"Herr Kriminalkommissar*, what a surprise to see you here."

"I happened to be in the area and thought I would let you know that your mother has requested permission to visit you."

"My mother?" Hope flared in Q. Usually, prisoners had the right to receive visitors once per month, and his old mother had gone to the trouble to visit Becker in the Gestapo Headquarters across the city from her place to receive a visiting permit.

"I denied it," Becker stated.

Q felt his spirit deflate. So much for seeing his mother one last time. He swallowed down his angry retort and asked, "May I ask why?"

"You have shown so little cooperation, I decided you didn't deserve the privilege of visitors," Becker said with a cruel smile.

Since when had yet another lawful right become a *privilege*? Hatred

421

for the Gestapo officer choked Q, and it was all he could do to hold his tongue and keep from verbally attacking the horrid man. He slumped down on his bed and stared at the floor.

"I hope you enjoy your new cell as much as you enjoyed our hospitality at Prinz-Albrecht-Strasse," Becker said and left.

This one sentence brought memories to the surface that Q had carefully buried deep down for the past month. Angst seeped into every single bone, and his entire body trembled violently.

When the nurse entered the room a few minutes later, she knew with one glance on his face what had happened and muttered under her breath, "I really don't know why we coddle the patients, and then give them back to the Gestapo."

She helped him get up and turned him over to the prison guards who'd just arrived.

At Plötzensee, the guards shoved him into a cell that actually looked like a place where someone could live. The nine-by-twelve-foot space held a chair, a table, a closet, and a bunk bed. The bed was completely equipped with a mattress and a rough woolen blanket. Compared to the Gestapo cellar, this was luxury.

Q sat on the lower bed and jumped when a voice from above said, "Hello, my name is Werner Krauss." A head with slightly too long, dark hair popped over the side and looked down at him from the upper bed.

"I'm Wilhelm Quedlin, but friends call me Q."

"Q it is then. I believe we'll have to keep each other company, whether we like it or not." Werner climbed down from the upper bed and extended his hand.

Q immediately liked the dry humor of his cellmate. Judging by the way he talked, the man must be educated.

"Well, I would say it's nice to meet you, but I think we both agree it would have been better to never meet than to meet here," Q said as he shook the extended hand.

Werner answered with a dry laugh. "I was going crazy, talking only to myself."

Over the next days, Q learned that Werner Krauss was indeed educated. He'd been a professor of literary sciences in Marburg before he was conscripted into the Wehrmacht and then transferred to Berlin. Q already looked forward to many fruitful arguments with his new cell-mate. At least something was positive in his otherwise bleak life.

At one point, Q asked Werner about the bright red pieces of cloth tied to the bars of some of the prison cells, including theirs.

"TU. *Todesurteil,*" Werner said with a crooked smile. "So everyone knows the inmates have been sentenced to death."

"Ah. You too." Q swallowed and finally dared to ask the question he'd been avoiding all these days. "How does a professor end up on death row?"

"A very good question," Werner agreed. "Via one of my friends, I made the acquaintance of Harro Schulze-Boysen. One thing led to another, and I ended up helping his group put up posters against the exposition *The Soviet Paradise.*"

"You mean the propaganda exposition they did last year in June? The one full of lies about the Soviet Union? Showing how people live in earth holes?"

"That one," Werner answered.

"And you received a death sentence for pasting up posters?" Q shook his head. He'd known that, according to the *Volkss-chädlingsverordnung,* the decree about damages to the nation, every criminal act could be avenged with the death penalty. But gluing up posters?

"That, and listening to foreign radio transmissions."

Q chuckled.

"What's so funny?" Werner asked him.

"It's just that I bought a *Volksempfänger* back in 1935 and adapted it to receive foreign radio stations. But that is the one thing the Gestapo never found out."

Werner grinned. "I won't tell them."

Werner had influential friends in the intellectual community and had secret channels to receive real news, not the Goebbels propaganda. One day in early February, he received a visitor and came back to their cell with exciting news.

"Q. We have a reason to celebrate."

"Your appeal was granted," Q asked warily. It wasn't that he begrudged his friend, but he would miss his company.

"No. That will come." Werner waved it away. "Have you heard what is going on outside these walls?"

Q shook his head.

"My visitor just told me that a few days ago, the Wehrmacht had to surrender at Stalingrad."

"*Ach*. You're sure this is true? It would be the first blow to Hitler's confidence in this war."

"It is true. Hitler refused to speak on the tenth anniversary of his coming to power and Goebbels had to give the speech for him. And, hold your breath, Goebbels has ordered to close down all theaters, moving pictures, varietées, and other entertainment establishments until February 6 to commemorate the devastating defeat of the Wehrmacht."

Q and Werner discussed for endless hours the possible implications to the Eastern front, the Western front, the public mood in Germany and in the occupied countries. They also discussed Goebbels's *total war* declaration and what that might mean for the citizens of Germany. They discussed the resistance effort and how they hoped the Russians would continue to push back the Nazi army.

Despite the distraction Werner provided, Q was riddled with guilt. Hilde had forgiven him, but he couldn't do the same. It was his fault that she'd been sentenced to death, and there was nothing in the world that could take this burden from his shoulders.

# CHAPTER 19

T hree long weeks had passed since Hilde's trial when the Blonde Angel opened her cell.

"You have a visitor," Frau Herrmann said.

"A visitor?" Hilde beamed with joy. A visitor was something all prisoners longed for, and for her, it was the first one other than her attorney.

Frau Herrmann took her to the visiting room and said, "I'll be back in one hour. Enjoy yourself."

Hilde gave her a grateful smile and entered the room where Annie was waiting for her.

"Mother?" Hilde walked the short distance to her mother, and then stopped dead in her tracks, incapable of believing her own eyes.

"What's wrong, dear?" Annie asked. "You look like you've seen a ghost?"

"I am. You are wearing my coat." Hilde wanted to slap her mother in the face for appropriating the fur coat that Q had given her for Christmas when she was pregnant with Volker.

Annie tossed her head and rolled her eyes. "Well, it's not as if you were using it, and it's such a nice coat. Besides, it's been freezing for weeks, and you wouldn't want me to catch a chill."

"You could have at least asked. I'm not dead yet, you know." Hilde longed to rip the coat off her mother.

"Of course you're not dead, my dear, or I wouldn't be visiting, would I? Hilde, let me have a look at you." Annie had the annoying habit of not replying to anything she didn't like.

Hilde sighed. Maybe her mother should have the fur coat; she wouldn't be allowed to keep it in prison anyway.

"You look good. But you should really eat more, you're too thin."

"Mother…" Hilde groaned inwardly. Had her mother no idea about reduced rations and that sort of formalities? "How did you get permission to visit me?"

"Oh, darling, it wasn't hard. Sit with me." Annie patted the chair beside her. "All I had to do was ask *Kriminalkommissar* Becker for permission. We had a wonderful chat, and he encouraged me to personally ask him whenever I want to visit. Within reason of course. He's such a lovely man and so handsome in his Gestapo uniform."

Hilde rolled her eyes. Her mother would be the only person in the world to use the words *Gestapo* and *lovely* in the same sentence.

"Trust me, there is nothing *lovely* about him," Hilde protested.

"That's because you don't want to see things as they are. I'm sure if you had decided to stay within the law, you two would get along so well. He's the dream of every mother-in-law. Polite, upright, firm in his opinions. Loyal to our Führer."

"He's a monster," Hilde hissed, and her entire body tensed with the memory of the interrogations in the Gestapo headquarters. If her mother knew Becker's true colors, she'd stop gushing about him. But Hilde wouldn't enlighten her; those dark hours were something she wanted to keep locked deep inside, never to surface again.

"Your husband is the monster." Annie shook her head. "You know none of this would have happened if you'd married a man like *Kriminalkommissar* Becker and not that dishonorable husband of yours. I will never forgive myself for not seeing through him earlier, and even allowing you to marry him."

"I don't remember asking for your permission," Hilde said tartly.

"Well, that is your problem. You don't ask your mother. You always were a difficult girl, out causing trouble and disobeying the authorities. I'm not surprised you ended up here. I should have drowned you in the first bath water I drew."

Hilde took a deep breath. She'd heard that insult so many times, she shouldn't care anymore. "Mother, it's not his fault. He has loved me like no other man ever could. I don't blame him and will continue to love him until I take my dying breath."

"See how his love has ruined your life! You don't have to die for him." Annie dabbed at her eyes.

"Mother, please." Hilde didn't want to fight with her mother. "Tell me about the boys."

Annie leaned back with a theatrical sigh. "Berlin wasn't a good place for them. I had to send both of them to your father in Hamburg. His new wife has more time on her hands than I do."

"I'm sure Emma will take good care of them." Hilde tried to keep a straight face as she nodded. It hadn't taken Annie long to figure out that raising children was a lot of work and interfered with her busy social schedule. Deep in her heart, Hilde was relieved to know her sons were in the capable hands of her stepmother.

"Thank you for helping out, Mother. And for contacting the lawyer."

Annie beamed with pride. "It was no big deal. By the way, I almost forgot. I brought food and money." She handed Hilde a package wrapped in plain brown paper.

Hilde unpacked black bread, cheese, ham, and precious sugar along with several banknotes.

"*Kriminalkommissar* Becker told me you can use the money to send extra letters if you wish. Because officially, he can allow you only one letter per month, and I assume that one will go to your sl… husband."

Hilde chose to ignore her mother's comment. After all, Annie was her only connection to the outside world and the grandmother of her sons. They would need her love and support, however meager it might be, if the worst-case scenario happened.

"Mother, I know you don't like Q, but could you please send him letters and write news about the boys? He was so thin the last time I saw him, maybe you could also send him some of the food you plan to bring me?"

Annie shook her head. "You want me to help the man who is responsible for my daughter's being sentenced to death?"

427

"Yes. Please, Mother. Do it for me. I will be happy if I know Q is fine."

Annie's nostrils flared. "Why do you still love that man? He's brought nothing but misery to you and your sons."

"I understand that you are angry with him. I really do." Hilde ran a hand through her hair, desperate to make her mother understand. "But yes, I still love him as much as I did throughout our entire life together. If it is even possible, I love him now even more, because only now do I know what I had in him and what I will lose with him."

Annie scoffed, but Hilde barreled on…

"Even if I stay alive, there will never again be a man who means this much to me. If I didn't have the children, I wouldn't want anything but to leave this world behind together with him."

"Well, it looks as if your wish will be granted," Annie hissed.

Hilde ignored her and went on. "Right now, in this very moment, I'm glad that I'm not better off than he is, that we are both in prison, both sentenced to death. He said that those nine years with me were the world for him. The memory of those experiences with me now make it easier for him to die."

Annie lifted her chin. "Is it as easy for you?"

"I agree with him. We have enjoyed the pleasures of life, as much as possible, and we always knew that we were privileged. We had a good life, and we had each other. Never once did we fight or argue, we didn't have unfulfilled desires, were always content and happy, and we have enjoyed this consciously. Few people will be able in their old age to say that they have experienced nine years of pure bliss."

Annie was quiet now, looking down at her shoes, and Hilde thought she saw some hint of emotion on her face.

"Mother, for me, it won't be hard to say goodbye to a world that no longer has Q in it. This may be some solace for you, Mother, to know that I will have an easy goodbye and death." Hilde slumped back in her chair. It was true. A world without Q wasn't the same; it didn't appeal to her anymore.

Annie sighed. "Fine. I will write him a letter and send him some food."

"Thank you." Hilde hugged her mother.

Annie moved a step away and smoothed her skirt. "Don't despair, Hilde. Herr Müller is still working on your case. He's currently weighing his options – whether it's better to appeal your sentence or ask for clemency."

Hilde nodded. "Yes, I know."

A knock on the door indicated that their hour was over. Annie stood and walked to the visitor's exit. In the door, she turned one last time. "Your half-brother will be conscripted as soon as he turns sixteen in a few weeks."

Hilde waited until she was back in her cell to digest the news about her half-brother and his future. Hitler must be desperate if he'd started conscription of underage boys.

Usually, they weren't sent to the front lines but used as *Luftwaffenhelfer*. Their main job was to operate flak and help shoot down enemy bombers. It was a dangerous job that took many lives.

Hilde was afraid for her baby brother, but in the current political climate, she knew that even if she were free, there'd be nothing she could do. All Germans had to help the war effort, whether they wanted to or not.

Those who didn't comply faced severe punishment.

# CHAPTER 20

I n Plötzensee, Q felt surrounded by goodwill. Compared to his time at the Gestapo headquarters and prison hospital, it was actually pleasant. Even the guards treated the prisoners like humans, much different than the Gestapo brutes had done.

Q had his suspicions that the prison director was not a great enthusiast of the Nazis. Of course, no such words were ever uttered, but the evidence spoke for itself.

The director could have chosen any kind of man as Q's cellmate, ranging from common criminals or forced laborers from the occupied countries to military prisoners of war. But he chose Werner Krauss. Werner and Q had been convicted in the same series of trials, and supposedly belonged to the same resistance organization the Gestapo had given the name *Rote Kapelle*, Red Orchestra. As such, it was entirely against the rules to put them in the same cell together.

When Q was told he was allowed one letter every month, he didn't have to think for one second to whom this letter would go. He sat down immediately and poured his soul onto the single sheet of paper he'd been given.

An hour later, he put it in the envelope – unsealed – and wrote Hilde's name on it. He had no idea where she was being held captive and put the word *Gefängnis*, prison, beneath her name. The censors would know where to send it.

His mother-in-law, Annie, had kept her promise to Hilde and sent him a package with food and money – no doubt his own money. The accompanying letter was curt and distant. Q unerringly read between the lines that she blamed him for Hilde's death sentence.

*And she is right. It's my fault that Hilde was arrested. I should have...would have...*

Whenever he thought about Hilde's fate, his thoughts went down a vicious spiral. It didn't matter that she'd forgiven him; he would never do the same.

Q broke the train of thought and came back to the present, stashing the money in his underwear. It wasn't that he distrusted Werner, but you never knew who might search the cell. A bundle of banknotes would be prone to disappear.

He carefully rationed the money to purchase things he found necessary for his continued sanity. In prison, he'd started smoking. It was a good way to occupy his hands and keep the constant hunger at bay.

But most of the money he spent on *Kassiber*, secret messages, to his family. Today was one of those days, and he stirred from his meanderings when the door to his cell opened.

"You wanted to speak with me," the young officer said quietly, motioning for Q to come closer.

"I have need of paper, pen, and ink," Q answered with an equally low voice.

The officer squinted his eyes and told him the price. Q stuck his hand in his pocket to retrieve a banknote and handed it to the officer, grateful that Annie had relinquished her hatred of him long enough to help him from the outside.

"I'll be back within the hour." The officer took the money and disappeared.

Later that afternoon, with his purchased pen, ink, and paper, he wrote a letter to Annie, thanking her for her benevolence.

The following day, he purchased more paper, and with too much idle time on his hands, he began to jot down his thoughts. His scientific brain needed exercise, and he took up his previous work in the area of plant protection and pest management. Without a laboratory or any kind of material, all he did was think and try to solve the problems in theory. Then he would send his conclusions to befriended scientists and wait for their answer as to whether the theory held up to a practical test.

Werner proved to be a valuable friend and discussion partner. With nothing else to do, they argued about everything under the sun. Despite not being a scientist, Werner always listened intently when Q bounced off his ideas about plant protection. Several times, he made remarks that helped Q to continue with his research.

But Werner also had a project of his own in the works. His mind was as sharp as Q's, just in a different field. As a literary professor, he had full power over words and scathing wit. In the boredom of prison life, he soon started to write a satirical novel that he called *Die Passionen der halkyonischen Seele* – The Passions of a Halcyon Soul.

Q was thoroughly impressed with the ingenuity of the novel's hidden side blows to the Nazi regime. Its protagonist was an air force officer, and it took Q only the first chapter to find out who'd been the model for the protagonist: Harro Schulze-Boysen.

While Q always teased Werner about his fine arts, he actually loved the idea and enjoyed reading or listening to the chapters as they took form. The hidden messages in the novel were powerful and mundane at the same time.

"When the Nazis are gone, your book will become a standard work, I'm sure," Q said.

"Oh, this is only the first draft. It must be polished before it will be good," Werner hedged, full of the insecurities of any writer in the world.

"I give Hitler another year or two at most," Q said, choosing to ignore Werner's remark.

"The war is plain crazy," Werner agreed. "And every time they plug a hole in one place, two new ones appear somewhere else. I can't see how Germany can hold up much longer."

Q still wasn't allowed visitors thanks to *Kriminalkommissar* Becker's intervention. But Werner was, and each time he came back from those meetings with a renewed sense of hope.

A hope that the Nazi reign of terror was coming to an end. But would it come soon enough to save them?

# CHAPTER 21

H ilde held in her hands a letter. From Q.
      She reverently opened the envelope and pulled out the sheet
of paper. Compact writing filled both sides. Reading his words, her heart
filled with love and gratitude while her eyes filled with tears.

*My dearest Hilde,*

  *While I'm writing this, my heart is full of eternal love for you. You
were the best thing that happened to me, and I couldn't have wished for a
better companion. Despite the war and everything else that happened,
those were the most wonderful nine years in my life, and I wouldn't want
to miss one minute of them.*

  *When my time to leave this earth arrives, I will go grateful and happy
to have enjoyed everything a man can ask for. With you.*

  *But at the same time, my soul is riddled with remorse. Words cannot
express the depth of my guilt over your fate. It is entirely my fault that
you're in this awful situation. It was never my intent to hurt you or cause
you any pain and, believe me, I would gladly give my life to spare yours.
If I had known the terrible consequences, I would never have asked you
to type those fateful papers.*

  *You are with me every waking second of every day. I miss you. Your smile, your sweet voice, your quick wit. Everything. My mind is consumed with thoughts of you.*

Hilde stopped reading, and a smile tugged at her lips. She didn't doubt that Q *often* thought about her, but the moment the next technical problem caught his curiosity, he forgot all about the world around him, including her.

It had happened countless times during their time together, and she'd learned to accept it as a part of him. Hilde was convinced that not even his incarceration could change the way his brain worked.

She wiped her eyes and continued to read…

*Fate has been a cruel trickster. It has given me what I most desired, then taken it away. By my own hand.*

*Unfortunately, there was no easy way out for us. The powers that be didn't allow us to leave everything behind and start a new comfortable life in America. How I wish that had occurred. Many times, I wondered exactly which powers had an influence. Earthly powers? Celestial powers? Or pure coincidence? Bad luck? We will never know.*

Hilde stopped again, wondering what their lives might have been like in America. After a while, she shook her head. Dwelling on what-ifs was counterproductive and would only bring about sadness and depression.

She picked up the letter and finished reading Q's words…

*In hindsight, it's easy to see that if we had visited my cousin Fanny in summer 1939 as we had planned, we'd never have returned to Germany because of the outbreak of the war.*

*Now I tend to believe it was more than inconsequential luck. We were meant to stay here. We were meant for greater things. It is just unfortunate that you, my dearest Hilde, got caught up in my destiny and are now paying for my convictions with your life.*

*My friends and I were fighting for a good cause. For a better world.*

434

*The world of peace and equal opportunities. A world without war. But destiny had different things in mind.*

*It seems that the world has still to learn a lesson. A lesson that must include the horrors of war to give way to a better future, of mankind rising like a phoenix from the ashes, when everything that is bad and evil has been burnt down to the ground, and the fire has fertilized the soil for good things to grow.*

*On the subject of our children, I have every confidence they will be fine with your father and Emma. Volker and Peter love their grandparents, and they will have a happy life with them.*

*Annie has kindly sent me a package with food and some necessities. If you have the chance to express my thanks to her, please do so.*

*While I am resigned to my sentence, I still have hope that yours will not be enforced. So many convicted have received clemency. Please stay strong and never lose your inner sunshine.*

*I'm counting the seconds until I receive your letter. In four weeks from now, you will hear from me again.*

*My love, until next time. Think of me and know that my love surrounds you and will never die, even if my body does.*

*Forever,*

*Q*

Hilde wiped her eyes and tucked the letter into her pocket. She touched it whenever she felt lonely and the reality of her circumstances became overwhelming.

One of those days, she and Margit were talking when the male prisoners from the adjacent building had their one free hour in the courtyard. Snippets of conversation floated inside through the tiny open window.

"I'll hang myself if this continues much longer," a male voice said.

"And what with exactly?" another voice answered.

"…can't take it anymore…the uncertainty…"

Hilde stood and closed the window. "Pour souls. You wouldn't think so, but the imprisonment is so much harder on the men."

"Just last night, I heard a newcomer scream and clamor in his dreams," Margit added.

435

When the night was clear and there were no enemy bombers in the sky, the prison walls echoed and amplified even the slightest noise.

"It's not the danger or death lurking around the corner. These are not the bad things. The real bad thing is the uncertainty, not knowing what will happen to you. It's what starts eating you up from the inside. The isolation in the cell. The hunger. Every one of those men over there would rather go to a concentration camp or a real prison than stay one day longer here on death row." Hilde stopped talking when she noticed Margit's pale face. She put an arm around her shoulders. "Don't worry, you'll get out of here."

Margit nodded. "I will. I must."

Later in the afternoon, they heard the sound of breaking glass. It came from across the courtyard and was followed by an eerie wolf-like howl.

"It's from the men's building," Margit stated.

"Yes." Hilde didn't want to think about what exactly had happened; she retrieved Q's letter from her pocket. She lifted it to her nose and inhaled deeply, savoring the lingering smell of her husband.

"You adore the letter more than the man," Margit teased her.

Hilde breathed in the scent again and smiled. "I would much prefer the man, but what can I do? This letter is all I have, and so adore it I will."

# CHAPTER 22

Today was Q's fortieth birthday. He held a letter from his wife in his hands and thought he couldn't have asked for anything nicer this day. He turned the envelope over in his hands for several long moments before he slit it open and withdrew the sheet of paper.

Despite knowing better, he hesitated to read the words. What if she had changed her mind and was angry with him, or condemned him for getting her into this situation? What if she never wanted to write to him again?

His fingers trembled as he smoothed the letter open on his lap. When he could no longer stand the uncertainty, he looked down and began to read…

*My dearest Q,*

*Oh, how my heart rejoiced to receive your letter. I keep it with me at all times and let my fingers caress the paper as if it was your cheek. At night, the letter comforts me in my loneliness, and it is as if you were with me.*

*I love you with every fiber of my body, and I will always be faithful to the love we share.*

*Please do not feel guilty about causing my harsh fate. I absolve you from all of it. Yes, I have felt desperate in recent days, but I would never have wanted to forgo the wonderful times with you by my side.*

*That said, I want you to know that I do not condone your activities against the Reich. If I had known about your intentions, I would have found a way to make you change your mind.*

Q stared at the paper in disbelief, the letters dancing in front of his eyes until it dawned on him, and he grinned. Werner wasn't the only person who could write with hidden messages. *Hope you had fun reading this, dear censors.*

He traced his fingers across the paper, bringing Hilde's sweet face back to his memory. He could actually *see* her standing in front of him, one hand on her hip, her blue eyes twinkling with mischief. His heart filled with emotion.

*But I want to stay by your side always, like I promised on our wedding day. In good times and bad times. In life and until death do us part. None of us are promised only happiness, and I never worried about bad times, because I had you, my love. Although I didn't expect death to come so soon.*

*It's funny really. You used to joke about us growing old and doddery. And I imagined us reaching our eightieth year with a multitude of experiences to tell our grandchildren, but it looks like that is not to be.*

*I hope your health is much improved and that you are finding an outlet for your brilliant mind. Mother Annie is allowed to visit me one hour every month, and I pleaded with her to give you as much help as she wished to give me. As you can imagine, she's not very fond of you at the moment, but I am relieved she did send you some much-needed things.*

*Even though I know from her that Volker and Peter are fine and healthy with Emma and my father, I worry about them every day. How could a mother not worry when she's separated from her children?*

*My rational mind tells me that Emma and my father are showering them with love and affection and will do everything to make their harsh fate as bearable as possible, but my heart tells me that only I can give them the motherly love they need.*


A smear blurred some letters, and Q sighed. He knew exactly what strained her conscience so much. Hilde had vowed to never let her children suffer the same fate she had – growing up without a loving mother.

All he could do was repeat over and over that Emma and Carl would do their best until Hilde – by some miracle – was released from prison and was free to return to her children.


*I am looking forward to your next letter. Please tell me everything you do, even the tiniest details. It is my only way to be with you and to imagine being by your side.*

*All my love forever,*

*Hilde*


Q dropped the letter to his lap and closed his eyes. With his inner eye, he reread her sentences many times and savored the warmth and love in her words. *Hilde is still alive, and she still loves me.* That was all that mattered.

Nobody knew what the future held, or how long it would last, but right now, Q was happy. Hilde's letter was the best birthday present he could have asked for.

# CHAPTER 23

A few weeks later, Hilde had another visitor. Her lawyer, Herr Müller, had come to speak with her. She'd not seen or heard from him since the day of her sentencing and wondered what news he would bring.

Hilde did her best to suppress the rising hope, out of fear she might be disappointed. Once again, she found herself in the small visiting room.

"Good day, Frau Quedlin," he greeted her with a handshake.

"Good day, Herr Müller. What news do you bring?"

"I'm afraid not much," he apologized, but after taking a look at her disappointed face, he hurried to add, "and that is good news. Actually, no news is good news. I was waiting for the dust to settle before making my next move."

"The plea for mercy, right?" Hilde fidgeted in her seat.

"Well, that's what I wanted to discuss with you. I have weighed the alternatives and have come to the conclusion that we should reconsider our original plan to ask for a plea of mercy."

"What? Why?" Hilde asked, not quite following his lengthy sentence.

"In the current political climate, we might have a better chance of success asking for a revision of your sentence. It was unusually harsh, and a more benign judge might reduce it to one or two years of prison."

"You think so?" Hilde's voice was full of hope. Several months ago, two years of prison would have terrified her, but now it sounded like a merciful option.

"I can't promise anything, but it has been done before. It would help, though, if you had influential friends who would support your claim and speak on your behalf. The kind of friends with a Party book and rank."

The only person who came to her mind was Erika, who had married the son of an *SS-Obersturmbannführer*. But Erika's father-in-law was dead and her husband somewhere in occupied France.

"I'm afraid I don't have that kind of friends." Hilde shook her head.

"Unfortunate, but we will proceed on our own then. I believe you have a good case for a revision. There's no real evidence of your involvement in any kind of resistance or sabotage activities."

"I hope so." Her shoulders sagged as she tried to kindle the spark of hope inside her.

"On a happier note, your mother has asked *Kriminalkommissar* Becker for permission to bring your son Volker with her the next time she visits."

Hilde jumped up, excitement burning like fire on her skin. "She did that? When will I see him?"

"He's not yet given a definitive answer, but he seems inclined to grant his permission."

Hilde wanted to throw herself into Herr Müller's arms and kiss him. He seemed to suspect some kind of exuberant reaction from her because he clutched his briefcase against his chest warily.

She suppressed the need to cry out in joy, and instead said, "Please give my mother my sincerest thanks for that undertaking."

A relieved expression crossed his face as he retrieved an envelope from his briefcase and handed it to her.

"This is from your mother. You might find it useful." He nodded and bid his goodbyes, the door clicking softly behind him.

Hilde all but danced back to her cell, and in her hurry to tell Margit the good news, she forgot to hide the envelope full of *Reichsmark*. But today was a truly good day, because the guard to return her to the cell was the Blonde Angel.

Frau Hermann discreetly pointed at the envelope and whispered, "I have to surrender all money to the prison director should I find any."

Hilde quickly rolled up the banknotes and stashed them in her brassiere before handing the envelope over for inspection. She couldn't help but share her elation with the friendly guard.

"Imagine, I might be allowed a visit from my son. Isn't that wonderful?"

"That truly is good news," Frau Hermann said with a smile.

Hilde never understood why this warmhearted, empathic young woman had chosen such a gruesome profession, but this was not a question she dared ask. Despite her friendliness, Frau Hermann still was a guard. No fraternizing with guards was allowed.

Back in her cell, Hilde hummed a melody. Life was good. She would see her son. And thanks to her mother, she had *Reichsmark* to buy things. Money made life in prison much more tolerable. It didn't matter that she knew the money was from the estate she and Q had worked so hard to build, nor did it matter that her mother was more than likely taking a large portion for her own needs as well.

All that mattered was that she would soon see her son.

After pestering Margit with endless details and anecdotes about her sons, Hilde sat down to write a letter to Emma. Officially, she was allowed only one letter per month and that one was reserved for Q. But with the stash of money the lawyer had given her, she could afford to pay the guards to smuggle a secret letter outside.


*Dear Mother Emma,*

*Please do not mention this letter in your reply; it wasn't sent through the official channels.*

*I want to tell you how elated I am that Mother Annie has asked for permission to bring Volker with her during her next visit. I know that you and she never got along very well, and I understand your reasons. Annie can sometimes be difficult to deal with.*

. . .

442

A smile twisted Hilde's lips upwards. That would be the understatement of the century. But her intent wasn't to cause more bad blood between her relatives. If the worst-case scenario should happen, they all had to work together for the best of the children.

*I beg you to please try to get along with her, for my sake, and for the sake of your grandchildren.*

*You will never know the amount of gratitude I feel towards you for taking both of my children under your care. Now that both of your girls are grown enough to not cause you so much trouble, you must now start over again with two little boys who aren't even your flesh and blood. I know they are in the very best hands with you.*

*But I wish that you will also see to your own health and your own well-being and ask Annie for help if everything becomes too much for you. She has full power over Q's and my estate and should be able to send money for much-needed things like new shoes or clothes.*

*Peter can wear the handed down things from his brother, but my Volker must have grown since I last saw him, and when spring arrives, he won't fit into last year's clothing.*

*Please take my sincerest thanks for everything you do. Give my beloved children a big kiss from their mother, and my greetings to Father, Sophie, and Julia.*

*Your daughter, Hilde*

Hilde folded the letter and sealed the envelope, then waited until one of the guards known to deliver secret messages came by and paid the woman for the delivery.

That night, she fell into a deep sleep filled with happy dreams until the bloodcurdling sound of the air raid sirens made her sit straight up in her bed. Margit already stood, face pale as a ghost, pounding against the cell door.

"Sweetie, there's no use in doing that. You know we have to stay in our cells." Hilde hugged the sobbing Margit. Despite her fierce spirit, she was just a nineteen-year-old girl.

The guards rushed to seek shelter in the basement of the building, while Hilde and Margit crawled under the table and cuddled against each other. This air raid must be the most terrifying in a long time.

Normally, the thick old prison walls kept most of the noise outside, but today, they creaked and shook as each bomber delivered its deadly cargo onto the city of Berlin.

The minutes crawled, and every time Hilde thought it was over, the night sky filled again with the buzzing of approaching enemy aircraft. She'd learned to distinguish the sounds of German flak, a downed British aircraft, and the dreadful bombs.

The impacts approached. After an ear-piercing detonation, fragments rippled from the ceiling, and glaring light entered through the small window. *Several of the buildings nearby must have caught fire.*

Despite the closed window, Hilde could hear the sizzling and cracking as the fire ate away at whatever was in its path. She just hoped it wouldn't reach the prison. The fire brigade would have other priorities.

The air raid lasted the entire night, and at some time, Margit and she must have fallen asleep curled together under the table because when Hilde woke from the sudden silence, it was light outside.

While there had been several bombings last year, none of them had done serious damage to Berlin. That had changed at the beginning of 1943. Since the start of the year, the constant attacks had become an integral part of life in the capital.

During the next days, the overwhelming power of the attack was the number one topic of conversation amongst prisoners and guards alike. They received word that more than seven hundred people were killed during the bombing and thirty-five thousand rendered homeless due to the destruction of close to a thousand buildings.

The guards told of the utter devastation the bombing had left behind. Rubble wherever one looked. Skeletons of structures stretching out toward the heavens. Entire quarters razed to the ground.

444

# CHAPTER 24

Q and Werner had grown accustomed to life in prison. Each of them dedicated many hours of the day to their projects. The guards joked about the feverish activities in the cell of those two intellectuals, who actually seemed to enjoy having that much idle time on their hands. But they didn't disturb them, except for the one hour of "leisure" the prisoners had to spend in the backyard.

In the afternoon, they usually argued about every topic under the sun, and once a week, the Catholic priest *Pfarrer* Bernau visited their cell to give them moral support.

The priest's main task was to accompany the condemned prisoners during their last hours and give them the last sacrament if they so wished. But apart from that, he made it a habit to visit each prisoner at least once a week and lend an open ear to everyone's sorrows.

Everyone in the prison appreciated him because he never insisted on dwelling on the Catholic doctrine, but took a more humane approach. Regardless of the prisoner's religion, he comforted with words of empathy and friendliness.

Q soon discovered that *Pfarrer* Bernau did a lot more than console. He was an educated man, well versed in theology, sociology, and politics – and a dedicated enemy of the Nazis.

It was an open secret that *Pfarrer* Bernau would help those inmates who couldn't afford to bribe the guards to smuggle secret messages in and out of prison. And, according to rumors, he'd hidden more than one Undesirable from the authorities. God only knew where he got the money, help, and fake papers to carry out his work.

The days passed, and with the infamous Judge Roland Freisler presiding over the *Volksgerichtshof,* more and more petty crimes were punished with the death sentence and Plötzensee was bursting at the seams.

One day, a young Frenchman called Pascal was put into Q's cell. The lad spoke barely a word of German, but Q did his best to practice his rusty French. Thankfully Werner's French was a lot better, and Q let him do the talking.

Curious about the background of their new cellmate, Werner questioned the young man about the circumstances surrounding his arrest.

"I was hungry. It was cold and dark. That's when I saw a woman with a handbag and stole it from her." Pascal broke out in sobs.

"Why on earth did you do such a stupid thing?" Werner wanted to know.

Pascal explained between sobs, "I don't know. But as soon as I had it, I felt so guilty and threw it away in remorse."

Q couldn't condone his deed. However, stealing a handbag certainly wasn't worthy of capital punishment. There were no words to comfort the young man who was now nearing the end of his life for doing one little stupid thing.

In the next days, more details about Pascal's arrest and trial came to light. Apparently, the court had produced witnesses, in his defense, stating the young Frenchman had rescued two children from a burning building during a recent air raid.

But the judge, one of Roland Freisler's closest followers, hadn't cared, and given Pascal the same punishment a cold-blooded murderer would have received. It was inhumane and unjust.

Even the prison director and most of the employees silently agreed with that appraisal and worked diligently to find reason after reason, no matter how ridiculous, to delay the planned execution.

Pascal was understandably distraught; the language barrier only served to increase his anxiety and desperation. After his first initial breakdown, he calmed down enough to write his memoirs.

"Now my mother and my girl will at least have a memory of me," he told Q.

Q nodded. What else could he do? He wouldn't start a philosophical discussion in French about how only a sentence of death could bring out the essence of one's life. How being confronted with your imminent death sorted the wheat from the chaff and left you with only the truest, sincerest thoughts about life.

When Pascal was finished writing his memoirs, he begged Q and Werner to promise him they would see that his letters were delivered to his family in Paris after the war.

Werner readily agreed, always optimistic that his death sentence would be revoked, thanks to the generous help from some of his influential friends.

A week later, the executioner came for Pascal.

Q wasn't particularly religious, but today he was yearning for *Pfarrer* Bernau's weekly visit. The execution of Pascal had shaken his unstable peace of mind. Once again, the unjust law hadn't known mercy. Not even in this case.

But today, the priest wasn't in the mood for a political argument. Or any kind of discussion.

"What's wrong?" Q asked, running a hand through his curly hair.

"Today was an especially ugly day. One of the men who died today wasn't at all prepared for it. I did my best to spiritually assist him, but he was so young and didn't want to accept what was about to happen."

"Pascal?" Werner asked, his voice oozing grief.

"It was awful. Yes. He was screaming and kicking and fighting when they placed him on the guillotine. The executioner couldn't do his work, and the Frenchman had to be tied in place. After the deed was done, the hangmen were visibly shaken and told me this was one of the most horrible and unjust executions they'd been commanded to undertake." The priest paused, his emotions clearly visible on his face.

Werner's hands were clenched into fists. "It will be up to the coming generations to judge, but this young Frenchman has led a correct life and one simple mistake during times of turmoil shouldn't have ended it."

The priest made the sign of the cross. "May God bless his soul. And may He help the hangmen riddled with guilt."

"They do have a hard job," Q admitted, shivers of ice running down his spine.

They remained quiet for several minutes before *Pfarrer* Bernau cleared his throat. "I do have more disturbing news from the outside."

"Tell us this news," Werner encouraged him.

"Hitler has commanded the deportation of all Jews from his *Reich*. There have been reports of mass murders during the evacuation of the Jewish ghettos in Poland. Tens of thousands are sent to so-called extermination camps."

"How do you know these things to be true?" Q asked. He didn't doubt for one instant the Nazi were capable of these atrocities, but even to him, it seemed a bit farfetched to deport and kill an entire race. The logistics of transporting and then killing that many people were unheard of.

"I may not disclose my sources, but they have seen it with their own eyes. This is genocide on a large scale. Hundreds of thousands, maybe even a million. Mainly Jews, but also gypsies, homosexuals, God forgive them, mentally ill persons..." the priest made the sign of the cross "... they use gas to kill many people in a short time. Even in my worst nightmares, I'd never feared our government would stoop so low. May God help us, for we are sinners."

"You need to be careful with whom you talk about these things," Q cautioned him. "Not all the prisoners are trustworthy."

"Yes, we have every reason to suspect there are prisoners, even TU, that would turn on you in the hope of saving themselves," Werner agreed.

*Pfarrer* Bernau gave a small smile and knocked on the door to be let outside.

448

Neither Q nor Werner mentioned the disturbing information anymore, but deep inside, Q's worry about the state of Germany grew.

*How much worse do things have to get before they become any better?*

# CHAPTER 25

H ilde had been on pins and needles since she received the official
confirmation that her eldest son would be allowed to visit for an
entire hour.

When the day finally arrived, Margit helped her comb her hair. They
both stared in horror at the bundle of long strands in the brush.

"I'm losing my hair!" Hilde exclaimed. They both knew it was due to
a lack of proper nutrition and sunshine.

"No. It's absolutely normal to lose a few hairs every day," Margit lied
and added, "You look nice. And your son won't notice."

A few minutes later, one of the guards arrived to take Hilde to the
visiting room. Her heart thundered in her throat, and with every step, she
became more anxious. *What if he doesn't recognize me? Or doesn't want
to see me?* Several times on her path through the long prison hallways,
she was tempted to turn on her heels and run away.

Volker had turned three in January and was a bright little boy. Emma
told him that his mother was in the hospital and that's why she wasn't
allowed to be with him.

Hilde wasn't sure whether she liked that lie or not, but in the end, it
wasn't her decision, and Emma insisted it would be better for the boy if
he didn't know his parents were in prison. For treason.

The guard opened the door to the visiting room, and Hilde leaned against the doorframe for a moment, gathering her strength. Volker was sitting on Emma's lap, an expectant grin on his face. He looked so grown up Hilde barely contained the tears pooling in her eyes.

She forced a happy smile on her face and called his name, "Volker?"

He turned, and once he saw her, gave a shout of glee, and rushed to throw himself in her arms. Hilde went to her knees and wrapped her arms around his little body, holding him tight until he started wiggling to gain his freedom.

"Mama, are you very sick?" Volker asked.

"I'm much better now. I've missed you so much. See how much you've grown." Hilde stood up and followed him to the table where Emma sat.

"I'm a big boy, Grandmama says so every day." He beamed with pride and started telling so many things, she barely understood a word.

Just hearing his voice made her happy. Hilde reached Emma and embraced her. "Thank you so much for making the trip to bring him here."

"Don't mention it," Emma answered and smiled, gesturing for Hilde to concentrate on Volker.

"Sweetie, can you tell me what you've been doing? How is your baby brother?" Hilde asked and lowered herself to sit on the floor.

"Peter follows me around. Like that." Volker laughed and crawled on all fours across the floor.

"You two are such a good team. Do you play together?" she asked, thinking about how Peter had always imitated his bigger brother and tried to do everything Volker did.

"Sometimes. But he always throws over my building blocks. Can you tell him to stop doing this?" Volker's big blue eyes pleaded with her.

Hilde nodded, her throat closing with unshed tears at the mention of Volker's blocks. Q had made them for him, and they'd been his favorite. It warmed her heart to know that he still played with them.

"I will, sweetie, as soon as I'm with you again. In the meanwhile, you do what Grandmama says, yes? And you take care of your little brother for me."

Volker nodded with a serious face and came to sit on her lap. "When are you coming back to us?"

She swallowed hard. "I don't know, sweetie. I hope soon."

"Will you die?" His little voice trembled.

"Oh, my little darling, don't you worry. Remember that your mother loves you more than anything in the world, and she will always think of you."

"I forgot..." Volker rushed away and came back with a sheet of paper. "I did this for you, so you will get better soon."

She took the drawing and inspected it. Four people standing on green grass. A yellow sun in the sky. And a boat. "That is beautiful, sweetie."

"This is me...and you...Papa and Peter..." Volker beamed with pride as he explained everything he'd drawn for his mother.

Hilde forgot everything around her, and much too soon the guard returned to announce it was time for the boy to leave. She hugged him tightly, whispering words of love in his ear while barely managing to hold back her tears.

"You have fifteen more minutes, I'll watch him meanwhile," the guard said and took Volker with her as Annie entered the visiting room.

It was the first time Hilde had been in the same room with both of her mothers at the same time. An awkward silence captured the place until Hilde finally gained control of her tears. "I'm sorry."

"Don't apologize. I cannot imagine what you're going through," Emma said.

"You have no idea how much his visit means to me. I will cherish this one hour forever in my heart. Thanks to both of you for making it possible," Hilde said, doing her best to swallow down the tears.

"I did have to pull a few strings, but it wasn't that hard," Annie mentioned and took the second chair at the table.

"Here. I brought you some of the things you mentioned." Emma handed her a package.

Hilde took the package. She'd have a look at it later. Now, she had more pressing issues to discuss with the two women.

"Do you have what you need for the children? Are they safe?"

"The air raids have increased, but they are safe for now. As for what they need...they are growing so quickly. I will soon need a few coupons for shoes and clothing," Emma admitted.

"Annie, unfortunately, this is upon you. With the birth certificate of the children, you can go to the authorities here in Berlin and ask for extra coupons. Then you send them via mail to Emma. And please send her money every month to buy whatever the boys may need."

Annie just stared at her. "Hilde, you think life is easy, but there is no cash left. Your husband hasn't been paid a salary since the day he was arrested, and according to his patent lawyer, royalties are paid once a year only." She sighed and waved a hand. "I checked all your bank accounts; there never was much money. One would think you had been able to save more."

Hilde started to grow angry with her mother. *I'm the one rotting in prison, not you!*

"Then sell a few things, Mother." Hilde scowled. "I'm sure my fur coat would receive a good price."

"Don't be silly, dear. Who would want to buy a fur coat in April?" Annie answered with a roll of her eyes.

Emma had watched the silent fighting with wide eyes and now entered the discussion with a calm voice. "Maybe there's something else from Hilde and Q's estate that you could sell, Frau Klein? Silverware, china, or antiques?"

"I will see what is possible and send you money by the end of the week. If you give me a list of things needed, I will also run the errands to receive the extra ration cards. While I may not dedicate too much time to that cause because I have important social obligations to attend to, I will certainly do everything needed for my grandsons," Annie said graciously.

"Thank you, Mother. And couldn't you sublet the apartment in Niko-lassee to someone? This way the boys would have a regular income."

"It may be done, but it is a lot of work and hardship," Annie protested, but quickly nodded when she noticed the stern glances of both Hilde and Emma.

"Time to go," the guard called from the doorway.

Emma pulled a small packet from her purse. "I have some pictures for you of Volker, Peter, and the rest of the family."

"Thank you two so much for taking care of my children." Hilde took the pictures and bid her goodbyes to Emma and Annie before she hurried to the waiting guard, who'd been generous enough to allow Hilde an

453

extra fifteen minutes to speak about organizational details with the two women while she cared for Volker.

Back in her cell, Hilde found Margit waiting to hear every last detail about her visit.

Hilde showed her the pictures Emma had given her. "Look, these are my two cuties. And these are my sisters…" She ran her fingers lovingly over her children's faces and swallowed back a lump in her throat. Seeing her son had been bittersweet.

"What if I never see them again?" she asked Margit through her forming tears.

"You'll be with them again soon," Margit said and hugged her.

Hilde nodded. She wanted so badly to believe it would be true. She smiled at the pictures in her hand and knew she would think back on this one hour with her son every single day while she was here. It would keep her spirits up and help her to stay sane.

Then she opened the package Emma had given her. It contained her favorite pair of black shoes, shampoo, soap, food, a woolen cardigan, two books, and several torn stockings.

"Look, Margit! Finally, I have some comfortable shoes…and shampoo." Hilde opened the bottle and sniffed. "It smells so good."

Margit laughed. "Nothing beats real shampoo. I'm sick and tired of the curd soap they give us."

They scrutinized the food and sat on the lower bunk bed to eat the fresh buns with butter.

"Hmm, real butter," Margit licked her lips. "Today is a day to celebrate."

"You know, we're actually quite fine. We have enough to eat, something to read, and Emma even sent me work to do. Mending those stockings will keep me busy for days."

"You actually think it's nice of your stepmother to send those torn stockings?" Margit pouted.

"Mother Emma has such a hard life outside, and she works day and night. Caring for my father, her own teenage daughters, and now my sons. I feel bad that I can't help more. And I can't find any joy in living such an idle life. At least mending stockings will make me feel useful…

and keep my hands and mind occupied." Hilde leaned back and took a hearty bite of the fresh bun.

After eating in silence for a while, Hilde spoke again, "You can't imagine how thankful I am that Mother Annie made the visit with Volker possible. For all her shortcomings, this one deed when it really counted has shown that she does love me."

"Yes, that was nice of her to do." Margit yawned and then asked, "While you're busy mending stockings, can I borrow one of those books you received?"

"Yes, help yourself," Hilde answered with a warm smile. It had been a very good day indeed.

# CHAPTER 26

Q took his daily walk around the courtyard outside, grateful for the one hour of exercise in the sunshine. It was his only reminder of a world outside the prison walls – a faint memory of days spent walking and playing at the lake with his wife and his sons.

Spring had sneaked upon them, and with it, more executions. Just this morning, they had come for two more inmates. They always came in the morning, every day, save for the weekends. Even the executioners worked regular hours.

This awful procedure had become a normal part of daily prison life, and nobody seemed to waste another thought on the morbidity of the situation. Even the hangmen were part of the community and did their best to make a horrific situation more endurable.

It had taken Q a while to come to terms with their habit of walking over to the prisoners for a short chat. But after a while, he came to appreciate the break in routine and trained his brain to separate the "execution business" from his own fate.

"Good afternoon, Doctor Quedlin," one of the hangmen greeted him. "Do you have a moment?"

"Certainly." Q nodded. It wasn't as if he had to go anywhere.

"About that Frenchman. It was such a shame we had to behead him. He was a good lad. We actually thought the court would give him mercy, but no such luck. We have to follow the orders of the court, but if someone had asked me..."

"Yes, such a waste of a young life," Q answered. At first, he'd been surprised that hangmen did have a conscience. He'd always envisioned them as cold-blooded monsters, but they weren't. They were just human beings with a horrible job. But they weren't cruel sadists like *Kriminalkommissar* Becker and his men.

The executioners at Plötzensee didn't enjoy their jobs.

"I remember this young man we took a few weeks back," another executioner raised his voice. "He just stood there, sobbing in the death chamber while we finished our discussion on...I don't even recall now. I felt horrible for having made him wait and apologized to him for this very rude behavior."

*Just before you killed him,* Q added in his mind.

The other executioner joined in the walk down memory lane. "Remember that con man?"

"The one who worked as a hairdresser? He was always smiling and in a wonderful mood."

Q took the bait and asked, "Why was he always in a good mood? He was on death row."

"Yes, but he was actually looking forward to his execution." The executioner chuckled and raised an eyebrow. "Don't you want to know why?"

"Yes. Sounds like a good punch line. Why was he looking forward to his execution?" Q asked.

"Because every prisoner is given six cigarettes to smoke on his last day. He was actually yearning for that day." The hangman burst into boisterous laughter.

"Everyone does what he can to deal with the situation," Q answered and ran a hand through his curls. He wondered how he would behave in his last hours. Would he remain steadfast and unwavering? Or would he crumble and beg for his life?

"Yes. But the civilians have more trouble coming to terms with their death than the military personnel. I remember this Czech colonel who begged us to properly disinfect the guillotine before it was his turn. He didn't want to catch a nasty infection."

There was laughter all around, and even Q broke a smile at that one.

"Sorry, but work calls. See you around," the other one said and waved at Q.

Q bid his goodbyes, hoping he'd be around for a while longer. After the leisure hour, he and Werner were summoned to the prison director's office. During his time in prison, Q had discovered that the director was a well-educated man who enjoyed a good discussion about science and literature. Not many inmates could provide this.

Q had the suspicion that whenever the cruelties of his jobs became too much, the prison director sent for him and Werner to occupy his mind with lighter material. They would discuss the classic German literature books found in the prison library, like Goethe's *Faust* or Schiller's *The Robbers*, carefully steering clear of any comment about current politics.

But today, the director wasn't engaged in the discussion. After a while, he interrupted them with a sigh. "You might be interested to hear that even the most loyal citizens are turning their back on our Führer. Last week, two assassination attempts on Hitler failed."

Q's head snapped around, staring at the director in disbelief.

Werner found his voice first, "Have they arrested those involved?"

The director shrugged. "Maybe. The Gestapo arrested Hans von Dohnanyi and Dietrich Bonhoeffer."

"From the *Abwehr*?" Q asked in disbelief. Since when did the Gestapo arrest *Abwehr* agents?

"Yes. Apparently, they have plotted against our Führer, and at least Dohnanyi has forged papers to help several Jews flee to Switzerland. An unimaginable deed," the director said, but somehow Q had the suspicion he actually condoned their doings.

He would never say so openly, but with every day that passed, Q's conviction grew that the director hadn't believed in the Nazi ideology for the longest time. There still was hope for an upheaval from within. If only the majority complicit so far in their silence took a stand and fought against their leader.

# CHAPTER 27

Hilde had adapted to prison life, and in Margit, she'd found a wonderful companion. Letters were the highlight of her otherwise boring life in prison, and any day she received one was a happy day.

Mother Annie rarely wrote, but Mother Emma, her mother-in-law, Ingrid, and her sisters, Julia and Sophie, took turns writing, and she usually received two letters per week.

"I spoke with the Blonde Angel this morning," Margit said with a teasing tone.

Hilde looked up from her needlework into Margit's expectant face. She took the bait. "And what did she tell you?"

"Good news. Very good news," Margit teased.

Hilde knew she had to play her game if she wanted to know what the Blonde Angel had said. "Come on, Margit, please tell me."

"I might or I might not…"

Hilde laughed and threw one of the stockings she had just mended at her. "You're as eager to tell me as I am to hear it."

Margit pouted but then broke out in laughter. "You have me there. So, the big news is…drum roll…women are not executed any longer."

"They aren't executing women?" Hilde stared in disbelief at her cell-mate, as hope spread throughout her chest once again.

"It's not official, but apparently, the executioners are swamped with work, and it was decided to stop executing women for the time being."

"That indeed is good news." Hilde took Margit by her shoulders and danced with her around the tiny cell.

The days trickled by, and every day, more concerning news from the outside reached the prison. The Eastern front had all but crumbled, and the Soviets seemed to gain footing, while the British and Americans had started a Combined Bomber Offensive, a strategic bombing campaign to disrupt the German war economy, reduce the morale, and destroy the housing of the civilian population. Rommel's Afrika Korps had to surrender in Tunisia. One hundred and fifty thousand German soldiers and one hundred and twenty-five thousand Italian soldiers became prisoners of war, and the absence of their manpower had a crippling effect on every other front.

One month had passed since Volker's visit when Annie visited again.

"You look very good, Hilde," Annie said.

Hilde sighed and shook her head. "What do I care about looks?"

"It is important, even in your situation, and I'm glad you're taking care of yourself. Do you need more shampoo?" Annie touched her carefully back-combed hair.

For the first time, Hilde noticed the grey strands in her mother's hair and the profound wrinkles around her eyes.

"No, thanks, but I could use some food. They have reduced our rations again. The only reason I'm not losing much weight is because I barely move."

"Well…what do you do in here all day?" Annie asked, raising an eyebrow.

"Not much. I think what I miss most about being in here is having work to do. Maybe you could bring me some clothes for the children that need to be mended, or some yarn so I could knit them sweaters… anything to keep my hands busy."

"I think I could send you some yarn," Annie said noncommittally. Hilde could feel something was bothering her.

"Don't worry about me, Mother. I don't deny that sometimes I am about to break down, but generally, I'm fine. There's a little window in my cell through which the sun has been shining for weeks. It's been

460

getting warmer each day, and I can see the trees beneath my window. They are blooming green with leaves."

"Yes, the spring is the only good thing we have right now," Annie complained.

"Mother, we should be grateful for what we have," Hilde scolded her. "The weather is so wonderful. Some days, all I can think about are the children and how much they must enjoy being able to get outside and soak up the sun after this long and harsh winter. Even though I can't be with them, I am happy to know they are happy."

"You can say that because you are safe in here, but outside…the constant air raids are demoralizing," Annie said, her face frowning in consternation. "Not one night goes by when we don't have to rush to the shelter. I always worry whether I will survive the night, the lack of sleep has taken its toll on my health and youthfulness, and even my best contacts can't get me real coffee anymore."

Hilde was torn between rage and amusement about her mother's grievances. Here she was, sentenced to death, and Annie complained about *her* hardships? Some things never changed.

"I really don't understand why the British have to make our lives so difficult! Why don't they go back to their island and leave us in peace? I haven't done anything, so why do I have to bear their wrath?"

Hilde chose not to answer and instead directed their discussion back to happier topics. "How is your husband? What opera is he currently singing in?"

"Oh my God, Hilde, sometimes I ask myself, how you can care so little about other people? How do you not know that my poor Robert has suffered from a severe inflammation of his vocal cords and hasn't been able to perform most of the winter? It's all the fault of those bloody British. They destroy everything!"

Hilde sighed and was actually glad when the guard announced their visiting time was over.

461

# CHAPTER 28

As he paced the tiny cell Q's eyes shot daggers at Werner. Three long strides. Turn. Four small strides. Turn.

"I can't believe you gave away all your inventions to the Soviets. A government you never understood," Werner said.

"That's not true," Q protested. "Communism is the only form of government to look out for its people. The reign of the people, no more elites, no more rich persons taking everything for themselves."

"And where did you get your information? You don't seem to know the first thing about this so-called Socialism." Werner stepped into Q's way.

Q scowled. "I can't think when I have to stand still. Get out of my way."

"Oh, oh, the mighty Doctor Quedlin is thinking. But you should stick to natural science, where you are a true creative force, and leave political sciences to others. Your philosophy of life is heavily skewed." Werner smirked and stepped aside.

"Oswald Spengler," Q said and ran a hand through his hair. "His book *Decline of the West* explains everything there is to know about the clash of civilizations."

"Phaw...Spengler was wrong," Werner declared.

"How so?" Q queried. "All humans are created equal and if everyone is working for the best of the community–"

"That isn't Socialism, my friend." Werner shook his head.

Q looked towards the window, having heard this before. "So, you would argue against his idea that all civilizations go through a natural life process of birth, growth, maturity, and then death? That all civilizations have a limited lifespan; one that can be predicted?"

"The end of civilizations is not a foregone conclusion. And Socialism is not the capitalism of the lower classes. In my opinion, Socialism is about improving the community by everyone's working equally, and ensuring that everyone is reliant on the government to the same degree and the government determines how that community will thrive."

"That's nit-picking," Q said with a smile and continued to present Spengler's important assumptions about the history of civilizations and the interaction between man and his surroundings.

Werner in turn picked every single argument apart, trying to contradict Spengler with theories of other important philosophers. Their argument continued well into the evening until they both had sore throats from too much talking.

Q was never sure if Werner really believed everything he said about Socialism and Spengler, or if he was simply arguing for argument's sake, as a way to shorten their long prison days. Be it as it may, Q cherished their day-filling arguments and carefully avoided agreeing with Werner even on the most insignificant point.

Sometimes *Pfarrer* Bernau joined their discussions, and some of their favorite topics were pedagogic and educational questions. The re-education and de-Nazification of all Germans, and especially the younger generation, would have to become first priority after the complete destruction of the German state.

Those questions would determine and influence the entire economic concept of the new Germany. At that point in time, Q had bid farewell to his previous belief that Germany would be able to escape the evil clutches of Hitlerism with its own force, while Werner – of course – clung to the illusion of a revolution from within to overthrow the current government.

"It doesn't matter which way Hitler is thrown from power," *Pfarrer*

Bernau said with a stern face, "either way the whole country will be in ashes."

With that statement, unfortunately, everyone had to agree. What they didn't agree on was how an ideal German state could be formed after the defeat.

Q partook in this discussion with mixed feelings because he was fully aware that he wouldn't be part of that new country. But maybe Werner and *Pfarrer* Bernau would.

# CHAPTER 29

Hilde should have been grateful, but she wasn't. Today was April 20, 1943, and to celebrate Hitler's birthday, he had generously allowed every prisoner to write an additional letter to a family member. Unfortunately, Q wasn't one of the *approved* recipients because he was a prisoner himself.

She scowled at the blank sheet of paper in front of her and made a face. So now she should be grateful to the man she despised most in this world. The man who was ultimately the cause of her death sentence and unspeakable suffering for millions of people.

"Aren't you going to write that letter?" Margit asked as she stuffed her hastily written words into the envelope.

"Ha. Why can't I write to Q? And why does *this man* give me a present at all? It's his damned birthday, not mine!" Hilde scribbled a skull on the paper.

"Come on, Hilde. You are the person who spends all of her money on smuggling out secret letters, rather than buying things for herself. It would be rather stupid not to seize the opportunity to write an official letter."

"I guess you're right," Hilde sighed and crossed out the skull. Then she started to write a letter to Emma.

. . .

My dear mother,

I'm wishing every one of you a very happy and peaceful Easter. The children will be joyful and happy, and you will take joy in them and with them.

I will think a lot about you, and I will imagine how the boys are searching for Easter eggs. Your place is perfect for that kind of game, and I remember how well Pappa can hide the eggs. We used to seek them for hours.

Last year, Q and I hid Easter eggs at our place, and little Peter was just one month old. Meanwhile, my sweetie will be able to walk alone, after what you wrote me in your last letter.

How much I would love to see him! I will never be able to make up for missing his first steps. His first words – it is both cute and unique how a baby starts talking. And everything else he has learned.

And he already learned a song! How much I yearn to see him clapping his little hands while humming the melody to Backe, backe Kuchen. If I ever see him again, then all of this will have passed.

It's terrible that he got the measles as well and you had to care for another sick child. I always am afraid that it is too much for you. I know how much work the two boys make, and how cranky they are when they get all the childhood diseases. Of course, it's always both of them. I hope your health will cope with this burden.

But I am so grateful that the children can be with you and don't have to go to an orphanage. And give my thanks to Sophie for making clothes for them.

Can I help somehow? If you send me material and patterns, then I can sew by hand. Or when Sophie has made little pants, maybe I can embroider them? I still have so much yarn at home it would give me the biggest joy to do some work for the children and help you out. Please ask Mother Annie to send me some, and don't forget to send me the measurements of the children. I have no idea how much they have grown. It's been such a long time...

You can have all the shoes I still have in our apartment. You wear the same size as I do and this is the least I can do for you to show how grateful I am for all your work. In these days, good shoes are a fortune, and you deserve them.

*Can I give you something else from my things? Or to your daugh-*
*ters? Just tell me what you need, and Mother Annie will send it to you.*
*You have to endure enough hardship by taking care of my children, I*
*want to help in whatever small ways I can.*

*Mother Annie sent me a huge chunk of sausage. Were those the*
*coupons from you? Many thanks for it, it is wonderful! But I didn't want*
*to have those special foods because I wanted Mother Annie to send them*
*to Q. He needs it so much more than I do.*

*Soon, it will be Julia's and your birthday. I'm sending you my best*
*wishes right now because I never know when I'll be able to send another*
*message.*

*I have told Mother Annie, if she travels to the Baltic Sea in the*
*summer, she should take the children with her. Would you allow that? It*
*would be a lot of fun for them.*

*For now, I'm sending you my best wishes for the new year in your*
*life. All my greetings to you, Pappa, Sophie, and Julia.*

*And one thousand kisses to my little sweethearts!*

*Love, Hilde*


Hilde drew a birthday cake with candles below her signature and carefully folded the letter and stuffed it into an envelope. Then she dabbed at
her eyes. Thinking about her children was joy and torture at the same
time.

"I wish I could send my sons something for Easter," Hilde
murmured.

"You and your children..." Margit teased her.

"You'll understand when you're older and have children yourself."
Hilde got up and knocked on the door to indicate she was finished writing. A guard showed up and received both of their letters.

Margit shook her head. "I doubt I will ever have children. Not in a
world like this one."

"Don't you want a family? What about your parents? I'm sure they
want that for you."

"You don't know my family." Margit knitted her brows together.

Hilde gave her a stern look. "That's right. I don't because you never

467

talk about them. You know everything about my family, and I know nothing about yours." Hilde had tried several times to get Margit talking, but this was the one topic she was very tight-lipped about.

"You really want to know?"

Hilde smiled and nodded.

"My father is an important man in the Gestapo, and my mother is a good German housewife and mother." Margit made a face. "My two brothers are officers in the Wehrmacht and my sister is the leader of her *Bund Deutscher Mädel* group. I'm the black sheep of the family."

"What did you do? You've never told me."

Margit scowled and spit on the floor. "I hate the Nazis and their stupid racial ideology…"

Hilde kept quiet as Margit paused, deep in thought. The turmoil on the younger woman's face was apparent. It would be good for her to get whatever was hurting her out in the open.

"…I fell in love with the son of our neighbors. My father was livid. Not because I kissed that boy, but because he was a *Mischling*!"

Hilde put her hand over her mouth. The daughter of a Gestapo officer and a half-Jew. Of course her father was angry.

The expression on Margit's face turned from angry to pained, and she continued with a low voice, "…The next day, he and his mother had disappeared, and nobody would tell me what happened. I wasn't allowed out for two weeks, and then my father decided to send me away to a training camp with the *Bund Deutscher Mädel*…" Margit's face brightened, and a mischievous gleam entered her eyes. "But once there I wouldn't budge. I explicitly told our leader what I thought about that whole charade."

Hilde couldn't hold back a giggle. She could vividly imagine exactly what Margit had said to the BDM leader. Hilde might have done the same thing ten years ago.

"My father was summoned, and it created quite a scandal for him. So, he decided to teach me a lesson and had me arrested."

"You can't be serious," Hilde exclaimed. Although, on second thought it might be true. Margit's family visited her often, and after every visit, her mood was abysmal.

"I am deadly serious. Father says I'll be released the day I publicly repent and swear to be a good German girl like my sister."

Hilde stared at her with wide eyes.

In the following weeks, Hilde and the other prisoners relentlessly worked to convince Margit that she should fake remorse to get out of prison.

"It won't do any good if you rot away in here," Hilde said. "Think about how much more good you can do when you are outside and work in the underground. I'm sure some of the women in here can arrange contacts for you."

Several days later, Hilde received notice from her lawyer that her petition for a revision of the sentence had been denied. She sighed as her hopes to receive lifelong imprisonment in lieu of capital punishment were shattered. Herr Müller assured her he would not give up and would now issue a plea for mercy. It was a faint hope, but it was all she had.

And if this weren't enough to dampen her mood, Margit brought worrisome news after another visit from her family.

"Occupied France is sending four hundred thousand *voluntary* workers to help the Reich make up for the German men that have been sent to the front. My father says there are over one and a half million prisoners of war earning their keep and doing valuable labor for the regime." Margit spat on the floor. "Nazi bastards."

"So many lives ruined...poor soldiers. When will this awful war be over?" Hilde said with a sigh. Some days she just couldn't take it anymore. On those days, death actually looked like a desirable option.

"My father didn't say much about the war. It seems the Allies are advancing against the Wehrmacht, but Hitler announced that Berlin is now free of Jews and that the rest of Germany – indeed, the entire Reich – will soon follow suit."

"All Jews? Everywhere? Where are they going? The camps?" Hilde's eyes widened to the point she feared they would pop out.

"Yes." Margit nodded absent-mindedly. She seemed to be absorbed by her own worry about her half-Jewish boyfriend.

"Is it true, the rumors about what happens in those camps?" Hilde whispered.

Margit glanced at Hilde and pressed her lips together. "I don't know for sure, but I spied on my father a few times, and I'm almost positive Jews are killed in those camps. I overheard him talking about how they have developed a *wonderful* way of killing many unsuspecting people in a short amount of time."

Hilde shuddered. "There are over ten million Jews in Europe. He can't kill them all. That's just not possible."

# CHAPTER 30

May had arrived, and Q sat in his cell scribbling notes when one of the guards opened the door. "You have a visitor."

Q looked up, sure the guard was talking to Werner, but Werner wasn't in the cell. "For me?"

"Yes. Let's go."

Q followed the guard, wondering who the visitor could possibly be. His lawyer wasn't due for another few weeks, and *Kriminalkommissar* Becker had made it very clear that Q didn't deserve to receive visits from friends or family.

When he saw the woman waiting for him in the visitation room, his jaw practically fell to the ground.

"Annie?" Q asked in case she was an apparition, then moved forward to shake her hand, but she waved him away.

"I'm not here to pretend to like you. You are the reason my daughter is sitting in a prison cell facing a death sentence. It's all your fault."

"It's nice to see you, too," he said when she paused in her tirade, "and I can't thank you enough for the money and food you have been sending me."

"For all I care, you could rot in hell, but Hilde begged me to send you packages," Annie clarified. "I have no idea why this woman still loves you after everything you did to her."

Q wanted to protest, but thought better of it and let her vent her feelings. There was nothing to be gained by arguing with Annie when she was like this. And what could he say in his defense? He had incurred the heavy guilt by causing pain to the person he loved most in the world.

"How did you receive permission to visit me?" he asked when Annie had finished accusing him.

"The lovely *Kriminalkommissar* Becker is a man who knows how to distinguish right from wrong – unlike my son-in-law," Annie said with a complacent smile.

Q nodded, although his opinion about Becker didn't quite match hers. "Give the *Kriminalkommissar* my best regards and tell him I'm grateful he allowed your visit. But I suppose you didn't go to all the trouble to remind me of my guilt over Hilde's fate."

"That's right, I didn't." Annie nodded. She pulled some papers from her purse and laid them in front of him. "I want you to sign these."

Q looked at them briefly. "What are they?"

"These papers will sign custody of your children over to me," Annie said and tapped on them.

Q stepped back as if struck. "No. I won't sign these. Hilde and I have already decided that Gunther is to have custody of our boys."

"Your brother? The man who despises Hilde like the devil hates holy water? You cannot be serious," Annie shrieked, clearly furious at his denial.

"I am serious. Gunther will be the custodian." Q folded his hands in an attempt to keep his calm.

"You can't honestly think your brother is a suitable custodian for two young boys? He's a socialist, for God's sake."

"Socialist or not, he's a solid citizen in good standing with the authorities, and he's a lawyer. He knows about all the administrative things to be kept in mind. Furthermore, I've written to Gunther and expressed Hilde's and my explicit wish that my boys will be sent to live with my cousin Fanny in America as soon as the war is over."

Annie paled, and it took her a few moments to gain her voice again. "You would send your innocent children into enemy territory?"

"The Americans are not our enemies. The Nazis are the enemy."

"That thinking is what has landed you in this position." Annie sneered at him. "When we have won the war, there won't be any Americans left to send your children to. They will be better off in Germany."

Q groaned inwardly. Apparently, some people still believed that Germany would win this war. It escaped his grasp how someone could be that stupid.

"I'm not giving you custody of my children. This is my last word."

"Well then, I should leave," Annie said and extended her hand as if shooing him off. A wave of nausea caught him as he noticed the diamond ring on her finger. Hilde's wedding ring.

"That ring belongs to my children, not to you," he said in a tightly controlled voice.

"It's not needed for their care at the moment, so there's no reason I can't wear it," Annie moved her hand until the diamond caught a ray of sunshine and reflected it a million times. A pattern in all the colors of the rainbow appeared on the otherwise dull grey walls.

"You could sell it and put the money aside for the boys," Q said, not taking his eyes off the ring.

"Not right now, we wouldn't get much money for it. Thanks to your friends, Germany is in such a bad shape that nobody wants to buy diamond rings, or any kind of jewelry for that matter."

"Still, that ring belongs to Volker and Peter."

"And I'll see that they get it, but after the war. Right now, it's better to keep things like this hidden, and what better place to hide it than on my finger?" Annie asked him.

Q knew he wasn't in a position to do anything about her abusing her control of his wealth. She could do whatever she pleased, and all he could do was sit and watch. It rankled deeply and strengthened his conviction to give custody of his boys to Gunther and not to her.

As Annie left, he said, "I'm not sorry about what I did, because I still believe it was the right thing to do, but I'm truly sorry that I dragged Hilde into this. Please know that I love your daughter with all my heart and soul."

473

# CHAPTER 31

Hilde sat down to write her monthly letter to Q. As always, his well-being and that of their children was uppermost in her mind.

Emma had recently sent her pictures of the boys, and she tried to decide which one to send to Q. He'd be so happy.

*My dearest Q,*

*I wonder how much longer I shall be able to write you. Things have become almost normal here, as odd as that might sound. Emma has sent me two pictures of our darling boys, and I have included one of them here for you to see.*

*It's unbelievable how fast they have grown, and even harder to imagine that they were taken from me almost half a year ago.*

*My visit with Volker was so precious, and I think of that hour with him every single day. I wish you would be allowed to see him, too, but alas, I fear you may never see them again.*

*Annie visits me every month.*

. . .

Hilde paused. It wouldn't be wise to write about Annie's constant whining about the hardships in her life, or how she used the situation to her own benefit. Then Hilde smiled and took the pen again…

*You know her; she's such a good soul. Always putting the well-being of others above her own. She never complains when Emma asks her to send much-needed funds for the boys' upkeep. Apparently, she had to sell a few of our things because there wasn't enough cash and I convinced her to sublet our apartment in Nikolassee for the time being. I hope this is in accordance with your wishes.*

*Are you receiving the packages I asked Annie to send you? I told her I will gladly do without anything as long as I know that you are well. You need the extra food so much more than I do.*

*Thankfully, my health is decent, and I haven't lost much weight because I spend all day sitting in my cell on the bed, day in and day out. Such an idle life is not something I enjoy, and I long to be useful. Annie and Emma both send me small tasks to do. But the mending, stuffing, and knitting is always finished within a few days, and I have nothing to do but sit and wait for the next package, write letters when allowed, and wish for better days.*

Hilde ran a hand through her dull, lifeless hair and looked in horror at the bundle of hair between her fingers. Q had always loved her shiny hair. If she continued to shed like a cat in spring, she'd soon be bald.

Memories of better times formed in her mind. Their honeymoon in Italy, a blissful time without worries. She gave a deep sigh and continued her letter.

*We had such a good life together, and I wanted to thank you for each and every day. I miss you and our boys more than anything, but the good memories of our time together give me solace. Please know that you are always on my mind, and no matter what the future holds, my love for you is eternal. I wouldn't have wanted to miss one single day with you, and I gladly endure everything if this is the price I have to pay for nine years of bliss.*

*How many people can say they lived life to the fullest? Those nine years with you mean more to me than a lifetime without you could. My life turned around the day I met you, and from then on I was the happiest person on earth.*

Hilde placed a kiss on the paper, and for lack of lip color, she traced the shape of her lips with the pen. When she was content with her artwork, she took the pen one last time to finish her letter.

*You are probably busy putting down all sorts of thoughts on paper, and I hope that one day they will fall into the right hands. I love your brilliant mind. I love everything about you.*

*Your Hilde*

Margit waited until Hilde had finished her letter and then pointed to the pictures lying on the mattress next to her. "Your boys are so cute."

"Yes. Aren't they? Volker is the spitting image of his father with his blond curls, but Peter takes after me." Hilde grinned. "Look, he's finally growing some hair. You can see it's dark and will be straight like mine." She handed Margit the pictures.

"They look happy," Margit commented.

Hilde fingered the pictures when Margit returned them. "My heart hurts at the thought of giving one of the pictures away, but I want Q to have one as well. So he will know what our children look like now."

"I'm sure he'll be very appreciative," Margit said.

"I'll ask Emma to replace the one I sent him, then I'll have both pictures again," Hilde murmured.

Margit laughed at her. "You and your children. I wish I could meet them one day. By the way, isn't your stepmother writing to Q as well and could send him pictures?"

"I know she is writing him, but he cannot answer her because he is only allowed one letter every four weeks and he saves that letter for me. Apparently, sending secret messages is more difficult in his prison."

"We are lucky," Margit agreed.

"I'm not so sure I can agree wholeheartedly," Hilde answered and got up from the bed. She was away from her children with only a few words and a picture here and there to keep her abreast of their growth. She wasn't tucking them into their beds at night or taking walks in the park with them. She wasn't lucky. She was on borrowed time and barely surviving.

*Is this a unique form of torture? It certainly isn't luck.*

"You know what I mean," Margit said, and after a look at Hilde's nostalgic face, she added, "Let's go for a walk."

Hilde looked at her cellmate, wondering whether the girl had completely lost her mind now, but Margit linked arms with her, and they went for a walk in their cell. Five steps, turn, another five steps, turn, while Margit pretended they were walking outside in the park and Hilde's boys were with them.

"Look how big they are! Hasn't Peter grown since our last walk? And the way he's talking. His little voice is so sweet."

Hilde giggled, and for lack of a better pastime she went along with Margit's game. "Oh yes, he walks like a big one. And he looks just like his brother did at his age. Aren't they wonderful?"

"Yes, they are."

Hilde turned and looked at her cellmate. "I remember as if it had happened yesterday how Volker walked his first steps alone between his pappa and me. A few steps from one to another. We were sitting opposite each other, and for his safety, we had put out our arms to the left and right of him. But he managed all on his own; he was so proud and beamed all over his cute little face."

Hilde became serious again. "I'll ask Emma to cut a lock from each one's hair and send it to me."

"I'm sure she will. You're lucky to have someone like your step-mother to take care of your boys. Many women who get arrested don't have that luxury and their children are sent to the orphanages or to the workhouses." Margit stopped walking, slightly out of breath.

"I really am thankful. They could nowhere have a better life than with their grandmother. My parents have a small garden attached to their house where the children can play outside."

"When I was a child, we often visited my aunt in the countryside, and I loved running around outside. We would wake up extra early, and my sister and I would rush out to explore."

"Peter is the one who wakes up early every morning..." Hilde murmured.

"Oh, yes. As soon as they are awake, small children believe everyone else has to get up with them. I have enough nieces and nephews to know."

Their happy chatter was interrupted by the guard who came to bring them dinner and reminded them of their harsh reality.

# CHAPTER 32

As May 1943 progressed, Q thought of a plan to save Hilde and asked for permission to send, in addition to his monthly letter to Hilde, a letter to Hermann Göring, the head of the Luftwaffe, who was also responsible for all military production by means of the four-year-plan.

While he was waiting for his request to be decided upon, he initiated Werner and *Pfarrer* Bernau into his plan during one of their weekly chats.

"*Pfarrer* Bernau, I wonder if I might run an idea past you?" Q started the conversation.

"Certainly. What's on your mind?" the gaunt man in his fifties answered.

"I was working on the development of a new secret weapon prior to being arrested. *Horchtorpedos*, or acoustic torpedoes, aim themselves by listening for the sound of a ship's screw. When I was still involved, we had a prototype called *Falke*, but it turned out too susceptible to faults. It often picked up other sounds and aimed for them, missing the target. Anyhow, I think I've solved the problem."

"And..." *Pfarrer* Bernau said and tilted his head.

"Well, here is my plan. I have been asked for permission to send a letter to Hermann Göring. I will offer him my solution about how to make the *Horchtorpedos* foolproof in exchange for his securing a life prison sentence for Hilde instead of the death penalty."

"That is a bold move," the priest said with a serious face.

"What makes you think he would go for this? Those torpedoes won't do much good in this war, it's too close to being finished," Werner commented.

"That's what we believe, but our government still thinks it can win this war, and they need the *Horchtorpedos* to work reliably." Q coughed a bitter laugh. "Those delusional men in power always believe a new invention or more advanced model of something that already exists will be the holy grail leading to victory."

"But you would condemn your wife to life in prison. Would she want this?"

Q shook his head. "Hitler's regime won't last forever..."

"They are calling for a thousand year Reich," *Pfarrer* Bernau reminded him.

"Yes, but we know that will never stand. At some point, the masses will either dwindle to the point the regime couldn't keep up, or they will revolt in great numbers," Q argued.

"The people are too downtrodden to even think about that kind of revolt," the priest reminded him softly, everyone having kept their voices down because of the nature of their discussion.

"I think you should do it; what is the worst that could happen?" Werner asked.

"...That my solution actually works," Q whispered, his conscience screaming to be heard.

*Pfarrer* Bernau put his hands on Q's shoulders and looked deep into his eyes. It felt disturbingly like facing the Last Judgment. "That, my son, is a dilemma only you can solve. Consider your decision carefully, and may God be with you in every step."

Q spent most of the night and the next day thinking. Was Hilde's life worth more than the lives of uncounted nameless sailors who might be killed by the *Horchtorpedos* Q had helped to improve? Was her life worth betraying his own ideals and convictions to never harm anyone? But if he didn't try to save her, how could he forgive himself for killing what he most loved in the world?

He pressed his lips into a tight line. *It's too late to use the Horchtorpedos in this war anyway. Nobody will be hurt.*

It was a lie. And he knew it.

The next day, his request for a letter to Göring was granted, and he sat down to write his offer. There was still a chance Göring wouldn't take him up on it.

# CHAPTER 33

Q was growing maudlin as he waited day in, day out for the executioners to come for him. Like the young Frenchman, he sat down to write what he considered his "legacy."

*My dear little mother,*

*Just before Whitsunday, while cleaning my cell, I received the letter you wrote on June 6. I was so delighted and moved that I, the cleaning rag still in hand, broke out in screams of joy, of consent, and of blessing.*

*Of course, I have read your letter many times since, and the need to tell you my inner thoughts became so strong that I asked for an additional letter, which was thankfully granted to me. The one letter I am normally allowed always is reserved for Hilde. For her, it means so much, maybe everything.*

*How friendly the act of the grace of the gods that I may still while alive receive an earthly manifestation of your love coming to me in the form of a simple piece of paper written by your hand. Yes, I can feel your love around me, helping and blessing me.*

*Oh, if I could describe to you what inner joy, what paradox, inexplicable and elated vibrancy, what preparedness for my fate has filled me.*

*What a peace!*

*How all those long and silent hours in prison have become a present, if I spend them meditating. Which I never had the time for before, or better, I never took the time to do.*

*But first, I want to clarify something just in case, even though I don't think this is necessary with you. All those spiritual goods that I still receive, all the maturity and rounding my soul receives, the goal of your blessing and that of the gods themselves: they are not meant in the case of my staying alive (how kitschig that sounds), of being rescued from death, and will be rendered senseless with my execution. No, I take everything with gratitude and happiness as a victory in the clear certainty that I will soon finish my life here.*

*A small joke may clarify my opinion for you...some poor fellow has written on the walls of this cell sentences like "Virgin Mary, please rescue me for the sake of my family" or "Mother of mercifulness, please lead everything to a good end" and so on.*

*Reading one, "God be with me," I could not resist scribbling under that sentence: "He is with you, but that doesn't impede him from letting you die here on the guillotine."*

*And is not my current situation, seen in the right light, a unique chance that I will not slide into death without a warning? That I not be a laggard in the sense of "tomorrow is another day," but through the certainty that within a foreseeable time my life will be over. I am eager to make each minute count and gather as much spiritual awareness as I can.*

*Everything in my cell is geared towards helping me to gain the most spiritual awareness. Look, from one moment to the next, I have been freed from all those mundane tasks like earning money, going shopping, household chores, and of work that was mediocre at best, but has used up many hours of my day. (My work at Loewe was, due to the war, far below or besides my interests.)*

*In prison, life is isolated and pre-designed. Every day is like the last, and the next one will just be like today.*

*It will contain long refreshing hours of sleep and rest, food that is very simple but not worse than the food the free people in the war-ridden country eat, punctual meals, and once a day a short walk, good discus-*

*sions with other prisoners, and even the luxury of reading good literature.*

*We have valuable books at our disposal. I just read Wilhelm Meister's* Apprenticeship, Italian Journey, *and* Götz von Berlichingen *by Johann Wolfgang Gothe. I have read Selma Lagerlöf, the Swedish literature Nobel Prize winner, and Eduard Mörike.*

*And as a special favor for me, I am allowed to work scientifically, writing down all my inventions, ideas, and experiences. Furthermore, I am debriefing my three years of work at the* Biologische Reichsanstalt *in the field of plant protection.*

*All of you spoil me and make it easy for my soul to say goodbye. Hilde sends me heroic letters, full of love, where she repeats her unwavering love for me and forgives me, despite my actions – those actions that caused so much pain not only for me but for her and our two children.*

*She absolves me from the guilt of having caused her own misfortune, pain, and threat of death. And in eternal love and connection, she wants to share my fate without quarreling over whether it is deserved or undeserved.*

*What a wonderful life's partner I have had. I see this more than ever now in bad times. Please think of her with the same love you think about me.*

*How amazingly well the children seem to be cared for. I can think only the most joyful and hopeful thoughts about them. Your letter has elated me – that you love my Volker so much that you would take him as your own. And the wonderful Dremmers.*

*My body is through the mercy of the gods completely healthy; no aches and pains hurt me.*

*Then there is my cell. I believe I'm made for prison life, for living in a small cell. Haven't you had a vision of me from a former life, where I have been writing in a cell?*

*I don't feel locked in or encaged. No, I feel safe and secure inside my cell, and the small confinements of the physical room give me the needed focus to concentrate on my spiritual development.*

*But I am still attached to my earthly life and can appreciate the small patch of sky that I can see through the window of my cell and that tree-*

*top, the sun passing by, the change of light and shadow caused by the clouds, the heat of the sun on my face, and the one thousand different things that I enjoy as an enrichment and clemency.*

*It is the life of a hermit that I enjoy after having lived a happy, conscious, and eventful life. I have enjoyed it to the fullest, traveling to many beautiful places in the world, together with the best, most loving life's partner, my wife, Hilde.*

*May I use each and every one of the remaining days to explore as much spiritual development as possible. For this reason, I thank you for sending me all your loving thoughts, which I will use to keep myself conscious.*

A noise outside distracted Q for a moment. It was the telltale sound of the guillotine blade descending.

"Still writing that legacy of yours?" Werner looked up from the novel he was working on. He must have heard the sound too.

"Yes. You know what? I'm not afraid of dying. Not anymore. It doesn't darken my day nor does it find its way into my dreams."

"That's good to know," Werner said with a smirk.

"I already experienced one death and was quite disappointed to wake up again." Q usually didn't talk about his suicide attempt; in hindsight, it had been a rash and stupid act.

"When my final day arrives, I wish to keep a dignified posture until my last breath. I won't beg and scream for my life," Werner said.

Q nodded. "We won't give our enemies and the regime the satisfaction of triumphing over our inner souls."

They remained silent for a few moments before Q spoke again: "I have researched several articles about the death penalty and different execution methods."

Werner shook his head. "So, have you decided on your preferred method yet?"

"You might find this amusing, but I found out that the physical act of dying is the most insignificant part of it. In fact, there are three main methods of execution used in Germany."

485

Werner cast a knowing smile and packed his papers aside. When Q was in discussion mood, it was best to let him talk. "I'm all ears."

"There's the firing squad, which is normally reserved for military personnel or Party members." Q stood in the middle of the cell and counted the methods on his fingers.

"Then there's the guillotine. It's borrowed from the French, and it's an expedient method of separating the head from the body. Compared to the firing squad, the guillotine is a much faster and rather painless method. It's used in our prison.

"And then there's the hanging. This is supposed to be the most painful and dishonoring one. In earlier times, it was mainly reserved for criminals, and they were often hung publicly as a deterrent example for others. It can take several minutes until the death candidate suffocates in agony. This is the method I least prefer."

Werner applauded. "I imagine you also investigated what happens to the bodies?"

"Of course," Q answered with a contented smile. "The bodies of prisoners like us aren't buried. They are taken to the University where they are dissected for medical and scientific discovery."

"Well, isn't that good news? Even after your death, you'll do great things for science!" Werner teased.

Q crumpled a sheet of paper and threw it at Werner. "I should let you continue whatever insignificant things you were doing."

Then he continued writing the letter to his mother. As much as he would have liked to share his discoveries about the different methods of execution with her, he resisted. She would probably appreciate it even less than Werner had.

*This letter will show you that I have made my peace with my fate, dear Mother. It is a fate that every human on earth shares with me, as everyone has to die one day.*

*I have dared to use my freedom of thought as an intellectual person to defy the laws of our cruel government and now have to pay the price for it. But I do it with a raised head and in the reassuring certainty of never having betrayed my conscience like so many others did.*

*If there is life after death, I can start with a clean conscience and hope to see my beloved wife there.*

*Sometimes, I believe I am making it too easy for myself, living here in my cell as an intellectual hermit, awaiting the imminent. And sometimes, I believe all of you kind souls are making it too easy for me by thinking of me with such generous and graceful thoughts, sending me letters full of love and not one single word of reproach.*

*Especially you, my dearest aged but unbowed mother, who is sending me the strength of her thoughts to make me powerful.*

*Nobody can be considered a happy person looking at death, and yet sometimes, I'm shivering in fear that my current joyful state of mind will suddenly disappear into agony. It might be harder to have to survive and foot the bill for years to come than to go quickly and full of illusions.*

*I wish that all your hopes for peace would come true. I am afraid, though, that the gods and powers that be have different plans for the world and most especially for our country. I would have accepted what the gods handed me and helped rebuild the world. A better world.*

*A world of peace, mutual respect, and equal opportunities. A world without war, hatred, and humiliation.*

*You have known me as an impatient person, always on the lookout to take fate into my own hands, to change the course of events with my own actions.*

*I believe it was my calling to stem the tide when I set the first foot on this path that has led me to where I am now. Even today, I have no possibility of knowing if I correctly understood the calling the gods gave me, or if I misunderstood my purpose of life.*

*The only thing I could do was to always keep my actions free of lowly and self-serving motives. Everything I did, I was convinced, served a greater good.*

*Now that I have been caught and my plans sabotaged, I have more than enough time on my hands to meditate in my cell. The meditation has led me to recognize one thing. One thing.*

*All these struggles in our present time were not meant to be resolved by the action of one individual. Neither were they meant to be resolved from ambush. No, the gods have planned this war to end in an open and honest fight.*

487

*This war will be fought to the bitter end with sweat, tears, and blood.*

*Not only the soldiers but also the civilians will have to show endurance and heroic sacrifice – more than anyone is now able to fathom.*

*Because I had a mission in life, I'm free of regret. The powers that be didn't wish for my intervention. I accept this wish and will leave this world without hard feelings.*

*Maybe a part of me will remain in this world, maybe I was meant to inspire creative persons to bring out their very best. Or maybe I was put into this world to procreate, and the important legacy is my two sons.*

*Maybe my work in the area of plant protection will one day serve to bring good into the world and feed many hungry people. The more the war took over our daily lives, the more my mind fled into a more peaceful and positive area which I found at the Biological Reich Institute. Even after switching to work for Loewe, I frequently visited my colleagues at the Institute, and we had many fruitful discussions.*

*The peace of the gardens, the agriculture, and the plants motivated me to work on more productive things than the destructive armaments industry.*

*Believing that there will be better times after the war where great minds are necessary to rebuild our country and to teach the simple workingman new skills and abilities, I'm sad that I won't be part of that new era, and cannot rush towards a better future with everyone else.*

*For now, I say,* "Solch ein Gewimmel möcht ich sehn ... zum Augenblicke dürft ich sagen: Verweile doch...!" *You'll know that part of* Faust II *by Johann Wolfgang Goethe. So maybe I will still experience my highest moment before those with the spade will come.*

*I'm glad that my fate has brought you closer to Gunther and his wife as well as to Hilde's wonderful parents.*

*I also want to reach out my hand to Gunther, hoping he will reach for it, forgetting his dislike for Hilde and without mentioning the past years of estrangement. I wish to reconcile with him before leaving this world.*

*Despite our differences, Gunther has generously taken over my legal affairs. May he be blessed. How comforting to know that he, too, will help to steer my sons through life, and if so much mercy would be given, helping Hilde if she might stay alive.*

*I am wishing the best to his sons, especially the youngest who is a flak soldier, with his sweet fifteen years.*

*Enough blood from our family has flowed in this war and the last one.*

Q's hand trembled, and he had to pause. His mind flashed back to a time when he was a young boy, playing with his older brothers, Gunther, Knut, and Albert. They were already in their teens when he was born.

Albert was closest to him in age and mindset. Eleven years older and a gifted mathematician, he helped Q many times with his homework. Q smiled at the memory of how they'd played in their big garden before they moved to Berlin. Q would sit on the swing and Albert would push him until he felt like he was flying into the clouds.

Years later, they discussed scientific problems, and Albert always laughed at his simplistic solutions. But Q admired his brother more than anyone else and vowed to become as brilliant a mind as Albert was when he grew up.

Sadness overwhelmed Q when he traveled through time to the day shortly after his eleventh birthday when Albert left to become a pilot in the Great War. Albert was so full of life, so confident, and looked so handsome in his uniform.

Their mother had waited until he'd walked away before the tears streamed down her face. Q hadn't understood why she cried. Not on that day.

About a year later, they'd received the dreaded telegram. *We are very sorry to inform you that your son Albert Quedlin has been shot down over France.* On that day, Q's life had changed forever. Nothing was as lighthearted as it had been before.

His second oldest brother, Knut, was the black sheep of the family. He preferred to travel instead of holding a steady job. Q had never understood Knut's wanderlust and his need to be anywhere but home.

When Q was twenty-six, his brother had embarked on one of his prolonged excursions. He wanted to travel the entire length of Norway all the way up to the polar circle. Knut was never seen again.

Their mother had clung to the hope for years that her second son would one day show up in her kitchen as he always had. But after seven years, Gunther and Q had insisted she declare him dead. His poor, strong mother.

Soon, only Gunther would be left. The oldest, most responsible of her sons. He and their mother had often butted heads because he was so stubborn in his convictions. For him, everything was black or white, no shades of grey in between. Becoming a lawyer had been inevitable.

Q pursed his lips. Gunther and Hilde had developed a dislike on first sight, and both of them had never been able to get past this first impression. He had to give Gunther great credit for helping now when he needed him most. Q hadn't had to ask; Gunther had offered his support to Herr Müller without hesitating for one second. He would be a good guardian for Q's sons.

Dusk was falling, and he continued to write…

*Now I will say goodbye to you, my beloved mother, because this will probably be the last letter I write to you, except for the day of my execution when I'm allowed to write more than one letter.*

*From now on, you'll hear about me from Hilde, my beloved wife to whom I owe everything. I dedicate my entire soul and all my rare letters to her.*

*But I would love to receive letters from you and from everyone who is able and willing to write me. They are the highlights of my reclusive life. There's no need to refer back to this letter in your answers; we do not want to bother the censors with insignificant details.*

*Your letters keep me in a good mood. News from the family and especially from my dear children keeps me connected to my former world, that's now only your world. It keeps the solitude away from my heart. It would be wonderful if the family could take turns in writing; this way not all the burden falls upon you, my beloved mother.*

*I will never forget our shared memories. Most of the past I see with a photographic memory. You at the end station of the tram line 44 where you waited for me to return from school. And your apartment. I can even smell the herb tea you used to brew when I visited. This way I never feel alone in my isolation, and every letter from the outside brings life to those pictures in my mind.*

*Please give my best greetings to everyone. With Annie Klein, you do not talk anymore? Such a pity because she is such a good soul, sacrificing, with a good heart, but little education.*

*One note to everyone: please don't put money in the letters, only stamps.*

*Today is Friday, and according to my observations, they don't come to fetch on weekends, so I'll most probably still be alive when you receive this letter on Monday, June 21.*

*Mid-summer.*

*On December 20 I almost died, and now, half a year later I'm still here. And have we not deepened our bond through this letter?*

*Goodbye. Farewell. Thank you for everything you gave me, including the healthy constitution which I hope my children have inherited.*

*We are now connected spiritually.*

*Your son, Wilhelm*


It was almost midnight, and the dusk was giving way to a few short hours of darkness. Q stared at the paper until the letters blurred. There was so much more he wanted to tell his mother, but this would be his last letter to her. Honest person that she was, she had made it clear in no uncertain words that she refused to receive secret messages from him.

# CHAPTER 34

H ilde was in a quandary. She'd been told a few minutes ago that, on July fifteenth, she would once again be allowed a visit from her sons. But she had to choose one child.

"Margit, what shall I do?" she asked her cellmate.

"That's a difficult question, indeed." Margit put a hand to her chin and wrinkled her forehead. "Which one do you want to see more urgently?"

"Of course, both of them," Hilde sighed. "The last time Volker visited was three months ago, but I haven't seen Peter since I was arrested…and I would love to see how he can walk…and talk. Hear him speak so many words with his little voice."

"Then take Peter," Margit suggested.

"I don't know. Do you think he still remembers me? He was barely nine months old when I had to leave him with Mother Annie." Hilde stood and paced the room. She looked out the small window to the trees in full blossom, and then she turned around to glance at Margit. "What if he doesn't recognize me? What if he has no idea who that strange woman is? Wouldn't that disturb his little mind?"

"Hmm, I don't think so; but then take Volker," Margit said.

"I really want to see Peter…"

"Perhaps you shouldn't think what you want, but what is best for your children," Margit suggested in an attempt to help Hilde take the emotions out of this decision.

"You're probably right...Peter doesn't even know what a mother is. If he sees me here, how strange will that be for him? It wouldn't mean anything to him." Hilde nodded. "It's more important that Volker comes to visit. I want him to recognize me as his mother if I ever get out of here."

"He does have pictures of you," Margit argued.

"Yes, but it's not the same. Maybe he won't forget me if he sees me at least once in a while. He's such an intelligent boy." Hilde smiled at the memories invading her mind. "If Emma keeps telling him about his mother, and if I hopefully get out of here one day, then I'm not just a strange aunt he's never met before."

"Won't the trip to Berlin be too strenuous for him?" Margit asked.

"No. We took him on trips when he was much smaller, and he has always liked it. He has a healthy constitution and is curious enough to enjoy new surroundings."

"Don't you think he might be disturbed? If he's as intelligent as you say, he'll find out that this is not a hospital, but a prison."

"Perhaps." Hilde wrinkled her nose as she thought for a few moments before she continued to speak. "Even if he'll be slightly deranged by the visit, if you were in my situation, wouldn't you want to see him?"

"Of course I would. So, take Volker."

"I will. And if I'm not allowed to live, then he will at least have a memory of his mother." Tears pooled in Hilde's eyes.

Three more weeks and she would wrap her arms around her beloved son again.

A few days later, a letter from Q arrived. She tore it open and devoured his words.

*My beloved Hilde,*

*Oh, how I loved receiving your last letter and that precious picture of our little boys. Thank you from the bottom of my heart. I admit, I cried when I saw how much they both have grown, but I know that they are safe and being cared for...that is all I could ask for.*

*As to your question about packages from Annie. Yes, she does send me one every month, and I'm very grateful for her continued support. It always contains much-needed food and stamps (we are not allowed to have money, but can use the stamps to buy certain things).*

*Despite my not being allowed to receive visitors, your kind mother has managed to change Kriminalkommissar Becker's mind and came to visit me.*

Hilde stared at the paper. Mother Annie had visited Q? How? Or better: Why? She continued to read with curiosity.

*I was immensely grateful and happy about her visit, but I'm afraid she didn't feel the same joy at the results of our discussion. Your self-sacrificing mother wished to attain custody over our two boys, but in line with what you and I have discussed earlier, I had to refuse her wish. Instead, I told her that my brother Gunther, who is well versed in all legal affairs, is our preferred guardian for the children.*

Hilde giggled loud enough to attract the attention of Margit, who shot her a questioning glance.

"It's just Q. He's so funny," Hilde explained and imagined how Q and her mother had been sitting in the visiting room – both of them staring at each other, and her mother growing exasperated as she grasped that she wouldn't get her way with Q. It had been like that with them for years. Q had always been polite and kind to Annie, but he'd never succumbed to her charms like everyone else did. Apparently even *Kriminalkommissar* Becker.

Hilde put the letter to her nose, Q's smell still lingering on the paper, and started to read again.

494

. . .

*I have received several letters from Emma, and even one from your sister Sophie. Please give them my heartfelt thanks if you have the opportunity to do so.*

*Not a day goes by that I don't regret the circumstances that led to your imprisonment. Please forgive me! If there were a way I could spare you what lies ahead, I would do so...even with my own life. My love, I do not want to raise your spirits in vain, but there might be hope for you.*

Hilde paused and shook her head. She bore Q no ill will and wasn't upset with him. She had supported his decisions and actions out of free will. It would have been easy to walk away and save herself had she wished to.

Q had even suggested abandoning her and the children after a feigned fight, to keep them safe. But she had objected.

She turned her attention back to her husband's letter.

*I am in good health and have been generously allowed to continue my scientific work. It is such a relief for my mind to meditate and to ponder on the solution of scientific problems. You know me well enough to understand how I tend to get absorbed in my work. It fills endless hours and time flies by. As peculiar as it sounds, I am quite happy with my current situation. The only thing I wish for is to have you by my side.*

Hilde felt a twinge of jealousy. Q was working and had something to occupy his day while she had nothing to do. She would ask Emma to send her Sophie's old school books. Then she could keep her mind occupied with practicing French or learning history.

Instinctively, she grabbed the jasper pendant around her neck that Q's mother had given her. The stone warmed quickly to the touch of her hand and never failed to give her confidence.

Her thoughts wandered to Ingrid, and a surge of empathy filled her soul. Q would be the third of her four sons to die. It was a fate no mother should have to endure. Hilde decided to ask for permission to write an extra letter next month. That letter would go to Ingrid.

Then she turned back to Q's letter, reading the many spoonerisms he wrote for her. Soon enough she was holding her stomach from laughing.

"What are you giggling about over there?" Margit asked.

"Q's letter. He wrote a number of spoonerisms," Hilde answered and started to recite, but was interrupted by a guard opening their cell door.

"Leisure time," she announced and sent them down to the courtyard for their daily walk.

"Take the letter with you and read those spoonerisms to us," Margit urged her.

Hilde nodded and folded the letter into her pocket as they joined the other prisoners in the courtyard. Hilde recited a few of the verses, and attracted by Margit's and Hilde's giggles, several other inmates and even some guards gathered around to listen.

"Let's see if you can guess what the words should have been? Drear fiend." Hilde glanced around expectantly as the women repeated the words.

One of them grinned and called out, "Dear friend."

"That's it. Now, try this one. I hissed my mystery lectures."

Margit beamed. "That one is easy. I missed my history lectures."

"Good. One more. You have a nosey little crook there." Hilde watched as the women mouthed the words to themselves.

Finally, one of the guards spoke up, "You have a cozy little nook there."

"Precisely," Hilde said.

Margit touched her arm. "Thank you for sharing those with us." She looked around at the gathered group and sighed, "We don't laugh enough around here."

# CHAPTER 35

Q had received noncommittal indications from Göring that Hilde's plea for clemency would be looked upon favorably, but nothing official. He was drip-feeding the *Kriegsmarine*, the German navy, with small albeit unimportant improvements for the acoustic torpedoes. By doing so, he wouldn't give away his discoveries before Hilde's sentence was revoked, yet nobody could accuse him of a lack of cooperation.

One day in July, Q's lawyer visited with news to share.

"I spoke with Erhard Tohmfor's wife to give my condolences for her husband's death," Herr Müller said.

A knot tied up Q's throat. His good friend was dead. Gone forever. One of the kindest, must upright men he'd known.

"How is she?" Q asked when he regained control over his voice.

"Frau Tohmfor is as fine as circumstances permit. She was arrested, but the Gestapo released her after a short time. I had hoped she could give me information that would be helpful with your appeal."

"I don't want to appeal. I've been rightly accused of treason, and I accept the power of the authorities to punish me for breaking their law. My mission in life, one I freely took upon myself, was to bring the current government down."

"There is still a chance—" Herr Müller pleaded.

"No." Q shook his head. "I would rather you spend your time and my money to bring about a milder sentence for my wife. My case is lost."

Herr Müller nodded although he clearly didn't agree. "As you wish."

"I do have a request for you, though," Q said.

"Go on." Herr Müller glanced at his watch. "We have a few more minutes left."

"Could you contact a dear friend of mine, Leopold Stieber, and ask him if he'd be willing to help care for my children once I'm not on this earth anymore."

The lawyer agreed, and Q gave him Leopold's address. When it was time to bid goodbye, Herr Müller handed him an issue of the Nazi propaganda newspaper *Völkischer Beobachter*. "You might be interested in the news."

"Thank you, I'm sure this reading material will lift my spirits," Q said with a sarcastic tone.

"It might, given that you are waiting for this war to be over. The four-year anniversary of the declaration of war by England is nearing. As far as I'm concerned, there's no person in this country who isn't waiting for the end," Herr Müller said and prepared to leave. "Someone contacted me a few days ago. The man wouldn't reveal his name, but insisted I let you know he was safe."

Q nodded thoughtfully. The lawyer didn't say another word but proceeded to hug Q, which was unusual to say the least. "I'll be back in a few weeks."

"Good day," Q answered, trying to find a reason for Herr Müller's strange behavior.

The guard searched the newspaper for hidden messages and then led him back to his cell. Absentmindedly, Q tossed the newspaper on the table and dug his hands into his pockets, where his fingers touched a piece of paper that hadn't been there before.

Q plopped onto the bunk bed and unfolded it.


*Please destroy this letter immediately.*

*After your arrest and the arrest of E, I tried to get in touch with persons I knew by name, but in vain. Everything was cut off. I didn't dare ask around, under the constant terror of being discovered myself.*

*I'm safe and continue to work as always, although the situation became more critical for me every day. But now things have calmed down, and I continue with our work.*

*It is only because of your and E's pertinacity that I am still alive. I owe my life to you for never mentioning my name. And I admire you for acting ruthlessly against yourself. Steadfast and strong. You were the brilliant mind and E was the natural born leader who knew like no other to lead us the correct way.*

*It is a way that I will continue to honor, despite the additional difficulties. I lack the connections you and E had, but that doesn't bother me. Rest assured that I will continue to work for our cause with unwavering effort, maybe even with more enthusiasm than before.*

*I learned about E's unfortunate end several days ago, and the fact that this inhuman regime has annihilated one of the best persons I've known gives me strength to carry on every day.*

*During a recent air raid, I had to hear that "we have to thank the pig Q for those attacks from our enemies."*

*You can't imagine how much I wait for the day of the planned upheaval.*

*X*


The letter was typewritten, but there was no mistaking that Martin was the sender.

Q smiled and took solace in the fact that he'd at least been able to save one of his friends. He tore the paper into tiny pieces and swallowed them. Martin had taken a big – and useless – risk writing this letter, but nevertheless, it was nice to know he continued to sabotage the military production at Loewe.

Maybe there was hope for Germany.

The next day, news about the war reached the prisoners. During their leisure time in the courtyard, nervous whispers shared the developments of the past week.

"The Red Army has launched a devastating attack on our Wehrmacht in Kursk," one of the guards said with an unusually serene face. "Both my brother and my cousin are in the 4th Panzer Army. I'm afraid they won't return home."

One of the Russian prisoners grinned and raised his hands, seemingly asking for God's help to defeat the Germans.

"It doesn't look good for Hitler," another prisoner added; "the British, Canadian, and American troops have invaded Sicily. There are rumors they have conquered all major ports in Sicily."

Q's memory returned to his honeymoon. Licata, Gela, Pachino, Avola, Noto, Pozzallo, Scoglitti, Ispica, Rosolini, and Syracuse. It seemed like centuries ago that he and Hilde had visited the ancient Sicilian ports. Back in 1937, Sicily had been peaceful, calm, and hospitable. They'd even joked about staying there forever and becoming wine farmers.

"I wonder how much longer Mussolini will resist the combined forces of the Western Allies," Q murmured.

"If the Italians can't help themselves, we'll go and do it for them," one of the guards said.

Q shook his head. "The Wehrmacht is bleeding out. Where should the replacements for the many fallen soldiers come from? Even my sixteen-year-old nephew has been drafted to handle flak."

"Pah, that's black propaganda from the enemy – our losses are minimal," the guard responded.

But Q believed otherwise. Before being arrested, he'd listened daily to foreign radio stations, and their numbers always differed widely from those presented by the propaganda ministry.

"One day, you will remember my words. In a year from now, Hitler and his Reich of a Thousand Years will be nothing but rubble. People like you will be the ones to shoulder the burden of rebuilding our country from the ashes. The suffering will be tremendous. Much worse than anything we experience now."

# CHAPTER 36

Hilde was lying on her bed, wallowing in self-pity. Volker was sick and hadn't been able to travel to Berlin.

"If I can't see Volker, I won't go to see my mother either," she whined.

"That's just stupid," Margit told her. "Any visitor is better than moping around in here. I'm sure you will enjoy seeing your mother."

"I won't. I want to see my son! My son!"

In the end, Hilde dragged herself to the visiting room, but only because Margit insisted. And maybe because she was the tiniest bit curious what news her mother would bring from the lawyer.

As she entered the visiting room, she was surprised to find two people waiting for her. It took a few moments before she recognized her half-brother, Klaus. He'd grown, and towered over her by at least a head. His shoulders had broadened, and his face had lost the chubby childlike look.

"You've grown so tall." Hilde hugged her brother.

"I'm not a boy anymore," he reminded her with the pride of a teenager who wanted to be a man, "I'm a soldier now. A *Luftwaffenhelfer*."

Hilde nodded and shook her mother's hand. "A soldier at fifteen? That's awful."

"I turned sixteen several weeks ago," he protested and did his best to stand taller.

After exchanging some pleasantries, Hilde asked the question preying on her mind. "Do you have news from Herr Müller, Mother?"

"Indeed. Herr Müller has telephoned me to announce that your clemency appeal has been filed. It will be brought to the attention of the Führer himself to decide upon. Herr Müller is confident that the Führer will give a positive answer."

Hilde shrugged her shoulders. She should be elated but wasn't.

"That doesn't seem to make you happy," Annie said.

"I'm trying not to get my hopes up too much, and I can't imagine living without my Q."

Annie shook her head. "How can you say that? He is responsible for all of this."

"Mother, I don't expect you to understand this, but only now after going through these bad times can I really appreciate how good a man Q is. He's the love of my life, never more so than now."

"How is he still alive?" Klaus asked. "I understood they have executed all traitors from that Schulze-Boysen group."

Hilde squeezed his arm at the mention of the execution rooms. "Q is working scientifically again, and the government is hoping to gain useful research from him. That is the only reason he is still alive. They'll hold him as a prisoner as long as he's useful to them and then…"

"And you still tell me he's such a good man? He's betraying his own faulty ideals and now works for the government he hated so much? To buy himself time? What about you? Why doesn't he offer his work in exchange for your release?" Annie was talking herself into a rage.

"Mother, there's nothing left for me out there, and the only reason I want to live is for the sake of my boys." It was hard to explain, but every day she felt a greater distance between herself and the outside world. She didn't belong anymore, and she didn't know if she could return to a normal life after what she'd gone through.

One moment she accepted her fate, and the next one, she was paralyzed by terror and wanted to scream, *Let me live! I want to live!*

"Your boys need their mother." Annie averted her eyes. "You will be with them, perhaps even for your birthday in five weeks."

"I'm not so sure, Mother. If Germany loses the war, they will kill all of us before the end."

"Our Führer won't allow that to happen. We will win this war," Klaus said with youthful enthusiasm. The Nazi propaganda had worked perfectly on her brother.

Annie nodded. "There, you hear it. And in the unlikely case our enemies should win, I'm positive you will have been released already. The Nazis aren't barbarians. Your plea for clemency will be approved."

Hilde put a hand over her heart, hoping her mother was right. But even if she was spared, Q didn't have the slightest reason to expect mercy. During his interrogations and his trial, and even now in his letters to her, he openly defied the Nazi ideology, calling it one of the worst evils in the world. The eighth deadly sin.

*He's made it too clear that he has been on the side of our enemies; they won't give him the satisfaction of having been right.* His unwavering opposition hadn't made things easier for her either. The judge believed she had the same convictions as her husband. While that was true, she'd been careful to never admit it.

Would she really have to die because of those two letters she wrote for him?

As for Q, if the Allies won and found out he was assisting the Reich, they would be less lenient with him and might order his death themselves. *I pity him.*

Her mother interrupted her thoughts as she stepped closer, looping her arm with Hilde's before dropping something into her daughter's pocket.

"What's that?" Hilde mouthed.

"Tranquilizers," Annie whispered into her ear. "Take them in case... you know."

# CHAPTER 37

Q had been waiting to hear back from Herr Müller with news from Leopold. In the event that both he and Hilde were executed, he wanted to secure as much support from Leopold for their two sons as possible. Leopold was a well-connected factory owner, jovial, honest and with high moral standards.

They had been friends since high school, and Q knew that Leopold had lost his parents at an early age and had later been adopted. He understood from firsthand experience how much orphaned children required moral support from different sources.

The lawyer had asked to meet with Q in the open courtyard, where it was harder for the guard to eavesdrop. The request was granted, and Q joined him, the pair walking slowly around the perimeter as they spoke.

"Did you find Leopold?" Q asked quietly, keeping his eyes straight ahead.

"Yes and no. He was captured and charged with high treason."

Q almost lost his composure, but he remained strong and asked, "What did he do?"

"You really want to make me believe you had no idea he was working in the resistance? They accused him of being a part of the Red Orchestra network." Herr Müller pierced Q with his eyes.

"I…had no idea," Q stammered. "I…he…he never told me."

"Well, your friend was discharged and found not guilty."

"They acquitted him?" Q asked, louder than intended, relief flooding his system.

Herr Müller nodded and then moved his eyes to the side to indicate the growing interest from the guards. Both he and Q started walking again.

"He must have powerful connections, but apparently not powerful enough. They didn't release him into freedom but rather transferred him to the concentration camp Sachsenhausen."

"After finding him not guilty?" Q asked incredulously.

"Yes. Unfortunately, the instrument of protective custody can be used against anyone at any time. I found out that he's doing forced labor in an industrial complex. The owner can't speak highly enough of your friend."

Q considered the news in silence, until the lawyer spoke again: "What do you know about Stieber's parents?"

"He became an orphan early on and was later adopted. His parents are nice people; I've met them several times." Q wondered why the lawyer wanted to know about Leopold's parents.

"Did you know they are Romani?"

"Romani?" Q hissed. "I had no idea." What else did he not know about his friend?

"They changed their last name shortly after they adopted Leopold and moved to Berlin to start with a clean slate. I'm not certain whether he knew or not when he was a child. But he definitely knew after 1939 when his father died, and his mother went into hiding. She might be the reason why he joined the resistance."

Q didn't answer. A sick feeling of betrayal spread across his body. He and Leopold had known each other for more than twenty years, had even been good friends, and yet his friend had never seen fit to tell him the truth. Not about his parents. Not about his opposition to the government.

*It's not as if I was completely honest with him either.* Q realized that both of them had kept secrets they didn't want anyone else to know. He chuckled at the irony. *It's funny. We've been friends for more than half of our lives, and yet we never knew the other one was working for the same cause.*

The lawyer remained quiet as well, and after a while, the tension became unbearable.

"You have other news," Q stated matter-of-factly.

"Yes. Shall we find a place to sit?"

"No. Just tell me." Q increased his pace to get away from the prying ears of the guards.

"Very well. Hitler and Goebbels are still very indignant about your assassination plan."

Q drew a breath and clasped his hands together. "That doesn't sound like it bodes well for me."

"It doesn't. I received word that they are planning to publicly hang you in front of the Loewe factory."

The blood froze in his veins. *They want to make an example of me.*

# CHAPTER 38

H ilde sat in her cell, fingering the tranquilizers her mother had given her. Despite the aggravating circumstances, Annie's gesture moved her to tears. It probably was the nicest thing anyone had done for her in a while.

She vowed to work on a better relationship with her mother if she ever returned to freedom.

Several days later, Hilde seized the opportunity to buy paper for a secret message to her stepmother. Volker hadn't been able to travel for the scheduled visit, but she could at least write him.

*Dear Mother Emma,*

*You cannot mention this letter because it is not an official one. Send me your answer with the second sentence starting with "yes, my dear Hilde." This will be my clue that you received the letter.*

*My sincerest thanks for your last letter and for the nice pictures. You can't imagine my joy! Little Peter looks so cute standing beside his bigger brother, and I can see how he crumples his nose. It warms my heart. This is the first picture where you and Pappa are photographed as well. Now I have all four of you here with me in my prison cell.*

*I yearn to see my children again and am waiting for permission to at least see Volker. Mother Annie has promised me to ask, but we must wait until she comes back from her trip to the Baltic Sea.*

*As soon as I have held my dear little Volker in my arms again, I will be patient until I can see you and Pappa again. I hope that I will still be alive in half a year and maybe, just maybe, the war will be over by then. Wouldn't that be a joyous day?*

*Since yesterday, I am more confident because I have heard, already for the second time, that women are not executed anymore. I have also heard about three women who we thought had been killed, but no, they are still alive.*

*Following the advice of my lawyer, I have written an addition to my plea for clemency, and now wish to hope again – to hope for a little bit of life. I do not want to live for myself because I am not suitable for this world anymore. It is for the sake of my children that I hope.*

*At least I know that my children are in the very best hands with you, and of course, you shall decide fully about them. If I do not stay alive, the children can go and live with Q's cousin Fanny in America after the war. They would have a good life overseas. And you wouldn't have the burden of raising two more children now that your own are grown up. Please do not worry about the future.*

*How is your health? You never write about yourself, and you have all the work with the children. What about your legs and your heart, and can you sleep enough? Do you often have anxiety?*

*I always smile when you write me about them, how Pappa takes them with him to his clients, and what they like. Now in these warm summer days, I think even more about my sons. How we bathed in the lake. Had a picnic on the grass. We had plans to take them to the lake or the Baltic Sea this summer, if this horrible fate hadn't come over us.*

*Regarding your concern about sending Volker to Mother Annie, I don't think it will be bad for him, and it will bring you some relief. He is so much smarter than I was when I first came to you so many years ago.*

*Mother Annie will spoil him, that is for sure. But he'll be with her just a few days, and once he's back with you, he will surely accept that, at your place, he has to behave.*

*I pray it will be the last time he comes to visit me here. My lawyer is confident that my plea for clemency will be approved. Then they will take me to another place. A normal prison is so much better than here, where everyone is waiting for the worst.*

*And if God is with us, then this war will soon be over, and we can all be together again. Therefore, please think of this visit as the last one. Who knows how everything will look after another six months?*

*Please receive my sincerest thanks for everything you're doing for me. The cookies were delicious. You cannot imagine how bad the food is here. And if you don't receive food from outside, then it is a horrible hunger. They have reduced our rations twice since I arrived here. Apparently, they think prisoners can subsist on love and air alone...and there's not much love in here.*

*Thank you so much for the books; they are the biggest help because I'm always bored.*

*And give both my sons a big kiss from me. Don't let them ever forget about their mother. I'm not forgetting them either. On the contrary, I think of them every waking minute of the day and dream of them at night. I will love them until my last breath and beyond.*

*Love,*

*Hilde*


She folded the two sheets of paper and squeezed them into an envelope, sealing it. Now she would have to wait until one of the nice guards was on duty, and pay her to deliver the letter to the next mail office.

Hilde hoped to have the verdict on her pleas for clemency by the time she received Emma's answer. Then she could – with God's help – send her stepmother positive news.

# CHAPTER 39

Q received a letter from his mother and read it for the umpteenth time.

*My dear Wilhelm,*

*I want to thank you so much for your long and detailed letter. I have read it several times, and it has given me a clearer picture of your state of mind and your fate.*

*But I also must tell you that my soul is sick after reading it. My moods are swinging up and down in a turbulent, even violent manner.*

*While I will always love you and send you strengthening thoughts, I wish you would show remorse for the great guilt you've loaded upon yourself.*

*Both Gunther and I telegraphed Kriminalkommissar Becker and asked for permission to visit you. Denied.*

Q looked up to where Werner sat at the table. "Becker denied my poor mother permission to visit again. She must be out of her mind," Q complained.

"You mustn't let despair take over." Werner tried to calm him down.

"With her seventy-seven years and frail health, she begged him to see me one last time. And that cruel son of a bitch denied her request." Q sighed, burying his head in his hands.

"You must hold out hope that *Kriminalkommissar* Becker will relent sometime soon."

"Sometime soon?" Q asked him, a hint of sarcasm in his voice. "How much time do I, do you, have left? Every day can be the last one."

Werner shook his head. "None of us knows that. We've been here much longer than most of the other prisoners."

"Why? Why hasn't my sentence been enforced yet?" Q surged to his feet and paced the tiny space.

"I don't know the answer to that question. No one in this prison knows the answer. Those things are decided higher up the ranks."

"Nobody tells me or my family. We can only speculate. It might be because I'm sharing my research with the government. They might wait and see if they can get anything useful out of me."

"That is a good thing, correct?" Werner asked.

"Yes and no." Q ran a hand through his tousled hair. Since he was in prison, he didn't wear it short anymore, and his curls gave him a tight cloud around his head.

"Gunther visited Becker and asked what my chances were in case they petitioned for mercy on my behalf."

"What was his answer?"

Instead of a response, Q read from the letter:

*Kriminalkommissar Becker told your brother that, of course, every family is free to petition for mercy. Then Gunther contacted your public defendant but received the same answer.*

Werner scoffed. "What else would they say? Those Nazis have their mind made up; there's no backing up."

"At least the public defendant promised to discuss the subject with the responsible people at the *Reichskriegsgericht.*"

"You know that he probably won't follow through with his promise?"

"Yes, I know that." Q nodded and silence settled in the cell.

After reading his mother's letter again, Q said, "I will ask her not to file a plea of mercy."

Werner's head snapped around. "Why not?"

"It would be ineffectual."

"You can't give up hope. You have to be strong and believe that somehow this situation will right itself."

"I'm not giving up, but my spirit is already beyond the confines of this world. I'm not afraid of the end anymore. What I'm afraid of is changing my sentence to lifelong imprisonment. I don't want to put that burden on anyone. I have no place and no use in this world any longer."

"That is not true," Werner insisted.

"It is. And my mother will understand. Maybe she'll even be proud of me. One day," Q said, hoping that one day in the future his mother would come to understand why he had chosen to break the laws and work on the demise of this government.

"The end is near, my friend," Werner said. "The Russians are pushing the Wehrmacht farther West every day."

Q nodded, and the men lapsed into silence, leaving Q to think of the past.

It all started with the remilitarization after the Great War. Hitler explained it was to rectify the treaty of Versailles. And nothing would have happened if he'd stopped there. But the very moment he started his aggression against his former ally, Russia, things went down the drain.

Even without opening the Eastern front and going to war with Russia, it was a very risky undertaking to fight against the Allies.

All those sacrifices in vain again. Soldiers dying for nothing.

Some countries like Sweden and Switzerland knew that of those who came out of any war the happiest was the one who never went in.

# CHAPTER 40

Time was slipping away, and as July dwindled and headed into August, the news coming from the outside was terror-filled for Hilde. On July twenty-fifth, the Allies had begun daily raids on Hamburg in an operation called Gomorrha. Every day the death toll rose, quickly approaching thirty thousand.

Hilde fretted and cried, and Margit had given up trying to console her until a letter from Emma arrived.

*Dearest Hilde,*

*You have probably heard about the horrible bombings over Hamburg. The boys and I left the city immediately after the government advised all citizens to evacuate. We are now with my cousin who lives in the countryside.*

*Your father and Sophie remained behind because they are needed in the war effort.*

*I will send you a longer letter as soon as I find the time,*

*Your mother, Emma*

. . .

Hilde gave a long sigh. "Margit, good news! Emma and my sons are safe in the countryside."

"See, I told you they would be fine." Margit beamed as she climbed down from the top bunk.

"I'm so thankful she took them away from Hamburg, but how hard must it be for my father and Sophie to be alone in these hard times? She should reunite with them as soon as possible. Who is more important, her husband and daughter or her grandsons?"

"That question can only be answered by higher powers than we are," Margit answered.

"Bloody Hitler! Without him and his stupid war, none of us would be suffering now," Hilde exclaimed.

"Shush." Margit placed a finger over her lips. "Be careful, you never know who is listening."

Hilde rolled her eyes. "I'm already sentenced to death, remember? There's no need to be careful anymore."

Both women burst into a fit of giggles at the irony of the situation. When Hilde was able to breathe again, she said, "Anyway, Emma should be with her family. It is important during these times."

Margit frowned. "I disagree. I wouldn't want to be with my Nazi family."

Hilde looked at her friend with empathy. If you didn't have a family you loved, what was worth living in your life? "Maybe I should ask Emma not to travel with Volker to Berlin, although I really, really want to see him."

"Berlin is a horrible place right now with the constant shelling and firebombs. The Blonde Angel told me that the government might order an evacuation of the city soon."

"I'll bet they don't extend that to the prisoners." Hilde scoffed.

"Probably not. So far, the Propaganda Ministry has asked all non-working women and children to evacuate Berlin on a voluntary basis."

"What would the guards say if we volunteered to leave the city?" Hilde giggled.

Margit joined her giggles, and for a short moment, they forgot the reality, but then Hilde sobered. "I wonder if Q's mother has left the city. The last time she wrote me a letter, she told me that half of her one-bedroom apartment had been seized to house others whose living quarters had been bombed."

"I can't imagine living in such close quarters with people you don't know." Margit sighed theatrically, and Hilde burst into another fit of laughter.

"You mean like you and I do?" she asked her cellmate.

Margit furrowed her brows as if she had to think about the situation. Then she slowly nodded her head. "That's different, though. Anyhow, things in Berlin are bad, and I believe they're only going to get worse."

～

A few days later, Hilde received a letter stamped with the Imperial Eagle carrying the Swastika.

"Oh my God, Margit, it's from the *Reichskriegsgericht*," Hilde said and held the letter in her trembling fingers. "I can't open it."

"Shall I help you?" Margit asked, trying to snatch the envelope from Hilde's hands.

"No. Don't you dare." Hilde sat down on her bed and fumbled the letter from the court open.

In big red letters, the word *Abgelehnt* stared at her, and her eyes filled with tears. The sheet of paper sailed to the floor, where Margit gathered it and read it.

"Oh, Hilde, I'm so sorry. Your appeal for clemency appeal has been denied. By Hitler himself. There's no explanation as to why. It just says this decision is final." Margit sat down beside Hilde and wrapped her in her arms, where she cried like a baby.

"It's dated July 21, 1943," Hilde whispered between sobs. "It's taken them more than a week to notify me."

Margit held Hilde for a long time without uttering a word. She knew nothing could console her friend, whose hopes for a future had been shattered with one single word. *Abgelehnt*.

～

515

Three days later, two guards entered their cell, and Hilde jumped with terror. *They have come for me.*

"Gather your things," one of them said, pointing at Margit; "you are released."

"I'm released?" Margit almost fell from the upper bunk bed in her haste to get out of the cell before the guards changed their mind.

"Yes. Hurry."

"I'm getting out," Margit whispered as she hastily grabbed her few possessions. On her way out, she hugged Hilde tightly. "Don't give up hope. Remember that the Blonde Angel said that women aren't executed anymore."

"Thank you for being such a good friend. Live a good life." Hilde clung to her friend, sadness sweeping over her. How would she stay sane in here without Margit's cheerful companionship?

The guard cleared her throat.

Hilde knew Margit's father had arranged for her release because she'd finally agreed to put on a good face and fake remorse. She'd apologized to him for the error of her ways even while she'd discussed with her fellow prisoners how to best work in the underground to oppose the regime and help those less fortunate than she was.

"I need to leave," Margit whispered and turned around. In the door, she squared her shoulders and walked out of the cell, out of the prison.

Freedom was hers once more.

At least one of them might survive.

# CHAPTER 41

Q looked up from his research with surprise. *Pfarrer* Bernau stood in front of the small table. If Q wasn't mistaken, his weekly visit wasn't due for another two days.

"What brings you here, *Pfarrer*?" Q asked.

"I'm afraid nothing good. My colleague at your wife's prison has told me that her clemency appeal was denied."

Q slumped into his chair and buried his face in his palms. "This is all my fault."

"You must stop blaming yourself. It is not your fault, and you know this." The priest tried to console him, but Q wouldn't listen.

"Her birthday is three weeks from now. She'll turn thirty-one, and I won't be with her." It took all his self-control not to break down into tears.

The priest laid a hand on his shoulder. "Your wife knows your spirit is with her."

"It's not the same." Q's voice broke, and he had to breathe several times to gain control again. "If I had known what would happen...that I would be the reason for Hilde's condemnation...that I would kill the one person in this world I love the most...I would have done things differently."

"You wouldn't have fought against the Nazis?"

Q shook his head and tried to find the right words. "No. Of course I would still have pursued this mission, but I would have taken greater measures to protect her. Leave her. Disappear." He paused and then questioned his last statement. "I wonder what would have been worse... breaking her heart or ending her life?"

"None of us knows what the future will hold, and we have to put our faith in God that He knows where to put us on this earth," *Pfarrer* Bernau said with a solemn face.

"I was so careful and successfully kept secret the extent to which I despise the Nazis. My little talk against National Socialism here and there was nothing compared to what I really feel. But that I would destroy my most loyal friends..." Q shook his head. "I should have stopped all contacts with fellow scientists and engineers."

"Why them?" the priest wondered.

"There's not an engineer out there who doesn't know some military secrets. How do you think it was so easy for me to gather intelligence? Was it possible for me to anticipate this?" Q's chest fell with despair, and he looked at *Pfarrer* Bernau as if he could, by some miracle, redeem him from his guilt.

"We will never know this. God's ways are inscrutable."

"But these are the questions that weigh heavily on my conscience. And I'm afraid for everyone who is truly innocent even in the sense of the court. Whose only mistake has been to know me. Maybe even the good director of the Biological Reichs Institute, who let me work for the institution?" Q grew more desperate by the minute.

"You cannot burden yourself with guilt for the injustices the current regime commits. It is not your fault, and rest assured that every person has to step in front of the Last Judgment when his time has come."

"If only the earthly court would let me testify before my death, then I would energetically and without a shadow of a doubt tell them that nobody has helped me except for my good friend and boss at Loewe, Erhard. Then my life would still be useful if I could rescue someone else with my testimony."

"What makes you think the court would believe you this time? Haven't the judges shown time and again that truth does not matter to them?" the priest asked and folded his hands.

"Erhard, my conscious and active helper, is already dead. My wife will undoubtedly follow his path," Q growled like a wounded animal.

"That, we do not know. Just because her appeal for clemency has been denied doesn't mean she'll be executed. I haven't had to accompany a woman in a long time."

Q closed his eyes, trying to conjure up pictures of happier times. Times when he and Hilde had been together. Happy.

Her unconstrained laughter had mesmerized him before he'd even seen her for the first time. But that was history now. Q had no idea how long he'd indulged in reminiscences when the sound of someone clearing his throat brought him back to the present.

"*Pfarrer* Bernau, while I wished to dedicate my life to the pursuit of spiritual, cultural, and intellectual development, I had to fulfill the mundane necessity of earning money."

The priest smiled. "I know very well that feeling."

"At the same time, I decided early in my career to find ways to strengthen my Russian friends and weaken their enemies."

"If we can believe the news coming from the East, Stalin is betraying the ideals that made him great." *Pfarrer* Bernau furrowed his brows. "But I still tend to believe he's the lesser of two evils. How is your experience with the Russians?"

"They were always respectful and polite. My contacts never once urged me to change my profession and pursue a career that might be of more value for them. They respected the individual, me, which is a very high good."

"You liked these agents?"

Q nodded. "I did. The agents I met were fine people I simply had no choice but to like. We shared the same ideals and worked together for a good cause..." Q grew quiet and thought of the double agent who'd betrayed him. Even after eight months, this vicious deed stabbed at his heart. He had trusted this man – with his life. And now, not only would he pay, but so many others would too.

# CHAPTER 42

On the morning of August 5, 1943, Hilde was transferred to Plötzensee. This could only mean one thing: her time on this earth had come to an end.

"You can write as many goodbye letters as you wish," the guard said not unkindly as he gave her paper, pen, and ink. Then he left the cell and bolted the door.

Hilde stared at the door and then down at the paper. So many times she'd been afraid of this exact moment, but now that it had come, she was calm, even numb.

She sighed and fingered the tranquilizers her mother Annie had given her. She would use them later, after writing her letters. Because for those she needed a clear and sharp mind.

Her relationship with her mother had been complicated, but with the Grim Reaper waiting for Hilde, none of their quarrels mattered anymore. Despite all her shortcomings, Annie loved her daughter and had shown that she cared. It was time to make peace.

*My beloved mother,*
*It is the most terrible of all things that I have to give you this heartache. I have a few hours left and am calm and composed.*

*Please take solace in my sweet little boys, and you also have your son. If Klaus survives this cruel war, I'm sure he will bring you only joy. My best wishes for him. He should not get involved in politics; let him take on a harmless profession like a musician or something similar.*

*What else shall I say? I cannot allow myself to become too soft in these hours. But how can I say something comforting?*

*Do not take it so heavy. I tell myself that one shouldn't take oneself and one's fate as important. How many must die in this war, be it at the front, or at home due to air attacks?*

*I count myself as one more victim of this war.*

*With my estate, do as you believe best. I put all decisions into your hands.*

*Give to those whom I liked and who liked me, and those who have been nice to us, with full hands. Give to the Dremmers for their caring for the children.*

*It's so good that I have all of you who love the children so much and will care for them. I want that you see them often. That they visit you and that maybe you can go on vacations with them. Don't spoil them too much, though.*

*If they could live with cousin Fanny in America later on, that would be a nice comfort for my soul.*

*My dearest mother, I want to thank you for everything, especially for the life you gave me. It was wonderful, and I have lived it to the fullest and enjoyed it. Please forgive me all the sorrow I caused you.*

*Please see that my children will never forget both of their parents. We still love them, even when we're dead.*

*Goodbye. Forget all the pain and start enjoying life again – I implore you. I leave you now; you have to live on for my children. I have adored them more than anything in the world. Give them your and my whole love.*

*I will die thinking about my beloved Q, whose fate I share until my last breath.*

*Your daughter*
*Hilde*
*PS: Please greet all my good acquaintances again. I have thought*

*about each one of them often. My best wishes to everyone. Be brave and look at life with clear, courageous eyes.*

Hilde wiped a few tears from her cheeks as she signed the letter. She leaned back in her chair and thought about whom to write next. While her heart ached to tell Q how much she loved him, she would leave his letter for the last one.

She weighed the pen in her hand and stared at the grey wall in front of her. This cell was the size of a pantry and was equipped with a single chair and a table. Nothing else.

And what else could a person need who was about to cross into the beyond?

Her father and stepmother had been her pillars of support during those last eight months. They'd selflessly taken in both of her children and would now have to raise them as their own. Her heart was bleeding as she wrote her letter to them.

*My beloved father and dear good mother,*

*Today, I must give my beloved sons into your caring hands forever. This is the hardest part for me, to have to leave my children. At least I know they are in good hands with you. I thank you so much for your help and your love for my children.*

*It would be wonderful if they could live with cousin Fanny after the war; it is Q's and my biggest wish. If this does not work out for whatever reason, then I still wish that the two of them always stay together.*

*Please do not let them forget their parents and always keep us in good memory. Let them enjoy every moment of their lives.*

*For myself, I can easily leave the earthly life because I have enjoyed my life to the fullest, and I don't have regrets for things I have done.*

*I go calm and composed, almost happy into my death. It shall be a consolation for you to know it will be fast and painless. Not many people can say that for themselves. We fall in this war like so many others, and you have the burden and the sorrow about our boys, but I'm sure they will bring you much happiness.*

*You also have two daughters who will make you happy, more than I did. Please don't take my fate to heart, and for the sake of the children, please look with confidence into the future.*

*Please keep my beloved Q and me in good memory and forget the things you didn't like about us.*

*I have always loved Pappa and you, Mother. Even so, I have not always been able to show it.*

*Goodbye, my dear parents, Julia, and Sophie.*

*I'm your deeply thankful daughter.*

*Hilde*

*To my sweet little Volker and Peter. Your mother kisses you in her mind and while taking her last breath.*


Tears spilled down her cheeks as the cute little faces of her two boys appeared in her mind. Exhausted by raw emotions, Hilde had to take a break before tackling her last letter. When writing it, she stumbled over her words, and tears dropped onto the paper, resulting in blurs.

Her heart was torn apart with every sentence she wrote, and yet she somehow felt the absolute confidence that their souls were interwoven for eternity and she would meet Q again – on the other side.

When she finished her letter, she called for the guard. He collected her last greetings, promised to bring her a meal, and asked if she wanted to talk to a priest.

Half an hour later, the Catholic priest entered the holding cell and introduced himself as *Pfarrer* Bernau.

"Frau Quedlin, is there anything I can do to ease your mind?" the priest asked her, seeing how hard this was for her.

"No, no. I'm prepared to leave this world behind, but..." she had to swallow back her tears before she could continue, "it's the fate of my children that weighs heavily on my spirit. I'm going to repeat history and do the one thing I vowed I would never do – abandon my children to be raised by their grandmother."

He placed a kind hand on her shoulder. "Don't burden yourself with guilt. Instead, be grateful your children have family who loves them and will keep your memory alive."

"I am grateful. I just hope that, one day, they will forgive me and understand my reasons for helping the resistance."

"I'm sure they will, one day." The priest looked towards the door and then lowered his voice. "Frau Quedlin, I'm in contact with your husband and will give him a message for you."

Hilde nodded, tears filling her eyes. "Tell him I love him and death cannot change that. I will be waiting for him…" She broke off as sobs tore at her.

*Pfarrer* Bernau attempted to console her, but there was nothing he could say to make this any easier. He gave her the last rites and then left.

With trembling fingers, Hilde retrieved the tranquilizers her mother had given her from her pocket and swallowed them down. Her head fell on the table as she waited for them to take hold of her.

The executioners arrived some time later, after she was blessedly numb from the pills, and she followed them to the death chambers. Condemned prisoners were kept in a large cellblock building, designated House III, directly adjacent to the execution building.

She spent her final hour in shackles on the ground floor of the building known as the "house of the dead" before she was led across a small courtyard to the execution chamber, which was located in a separate two-roomed brick building.

By then, the tranquilizers had done their job, and Hilde was barely aware of her surroundings and was having trouble keeping her feet beneath her. As they laid her down on the wooden slab, she closed her eyes, bringing up the image of Q and her two boys the last time they'd all been together.

It was that thought, and the memory of Q's voice and Volker's laughter, that drowned out the sound of the guillotine blade as it dropped.

Hilde left this life, a half smile on her face. The Nazis might have taken her life, but they hadn't been able to take her soul or the memories of the joy she'd found in her family.

# CHAPTER 43

Q finished another report for the War Ministry about inventions in the technical flight area, which, in reality, were only variations on inventions that had already been made. He looked up as he heard the sound of the bolt and watched *Pfarrer* Bernau enter his cell. Given the late hour and the priest's serene face, something terrible must have happened

"*Pfarrer...*" Q said.

"I bring bad news, Doctor Quedlin. The worst. Your wife was beheaded this afternoon." The priest rested a hand on Q's shoulder as tears rolled down his cheeks. "This information isn't official yet, so you cannot show your sadness to anyone. But I had to come tell you."

"This is all my fault." Q felt as if a huge millstone was crushing him to shreds. Despite his knowing it might happen, the reality of her death took him by surprise.

"We've talked about this multiple times. Your wife knew what she was doing and made a conscious choice to fight by your side. She wouldn't have wanted it any different."

"No, my lack of quick-wittedness was the real reason for Hilde's death. She was condemned because of me. It remains my hardest burden and biggest guilt that I carry around with me every single second of the day and night."

"Your wife has forgiven you, and you should do the same," *Pfarrer* Bernau said.

Q buried his face in his hands and murmured, "How can I forgive myself for killing what I loved most?"

"I accompanied your wife today, and she asked me to give you the message that she loves you and even death cannot change that." The priest folded his hands in prayer. "Her soul is now with Him, and she suffers no more."

Silent tears ran down Q's cheeks. "If only I hadn't let her type the letters–"

"There is no use wallowing in what-ifs. We don't know what would have happened. They might have arrested her on something else; the fact of being your wife might have been enough. The court was out for revenge and not for justice. We both know this. Loving you was crime enough to receive capital punishment."

Q nodded, knowing the priest was doing his best to offer him comfort, but his guilt threatened to eat him alive. "At least I find consolation in the fact that I will pay with my own life for this mistake."

*Pfarrer* Bernau said nothing and simply sat with him for a while. When the priest left, Q slumped onto his cot, hoping to find the mercy of oblivion in his sleep.

Q spent an entire week in hellfire, grieving for his beloved Hilde, but forbidden to show any signs of sadness. Not even Werner knew.

On the seventh day, Q received Hilde's last letter. He held it in his hands for long moments, inhaling the lingering smell of his late wife. He caressed the paper as if it was her soft skin, and the tears started to fall as he began reading.

*My dearest Q,*
   *The time is here, and they have come for me.*
   *My life started the moment I met you – do you remember the film?*

Going Bye-Bye *by Stan Laurel and Oliver Hardy. I remember you and Leopold as if it was yesterday.*

*Your love and devotion to me has changed everything. During those nine years with you, I enjoyed every single moment of my life. I love you with every fiber of my being, and my only regret is that we didn't have more time together. I die content because I had you and our boys.*

*Don't feel guilty for my death. It was my conscious decision to stand by you, in good times and in bad times. We never took our wedding vows in front of a priest, but I always believed in the words "until death do us part."*

Q touched the paper where Hilde's teardrops had blurred the words. Memories of their wedding appeared in his mind. The matter-of-fact ceremony at the registry office. Misleading the waiting photographers with grimaces. The party with their friends and plenty of Hungarian wine.

He smiled through his tears.

*I absolve you, forgive you for every action or imprudence that might have caused my fate. We were in this together. And without you, my life wouldn't be the same. So, in some aspect, I'm happy that I'm the first one to leave.*

*I wanted to live for the benefit of our boys, not for my own sake anymore. They will now have to grow up without their mother. At least I know that Emma, Annie, Ingrid, and our entire family will love them and do the best to raise them into good men. I can believe nothing else.*

*And I pray that by some miracle you might still find a way to survive this war to be with them.*

*Sometimes, I wonder what might have been if we'd received the visas for America. But it wasn't meant to be. There was no easy way out for us, and I still believe we did the right thing.*

*This is goodbye, my beloved Q, but not forever. I will be waiting for you on the other side with open arms.*

*I love you.*

Violent sobs racked Q's body by the time he finished reading the letter. He crushed it to his chest and rolled onto his side on the cot, crying for the loss of his wife and their future together as a family.

A curious Werner turned around from the table where he'd been working on his novel, and one look into Q's face told him the contents of the letter.

He walked the two steps to Q's bed and sat on the edge. "I'm so sorry, my friend."

# CHAPTER 44

Q fell into a frenzy of activity in the following days. With Hilde gone, he felt the sudden urge to tie up loose ends and organize his affairs.

The first secret letter went to his cousin Fanny in America.

*Dear Cousin,*

*I assume you have already heard about our memorable fate.*

*Also that we recommend our children to you if the aging grandparents cannot cope with them anymore, and the circumstances in Germany become too dire, and if my friends in the USSR are not available to care for them for some reason.*

*Because my wife's and my main motive has been enmity to National Socialism, you might be able to get help from your government to help you care for our children.*

*If one day you feel that the burden of caring for them is too much for you, please think about the fact that their parents died in their fight against an insane, inhuman anti-Semitism.*

*Live well! And if my sons make it through the war healthy and alive, please help them to become good citizens of a leading world empire, where they can use their abilities to the fullest.*

*Thank you from the bottom of my heart, and know that I will be forever in your debt for any kindness you show my children.*

*Your cousin, Q*

He retrieved some of the money and stamps Annie had given him and waited for the shift of one of the guards who was known to smuggle secret messages out of prison.

It was a dangerous undertaking because the guards could get into trouble for doing so, and they required a fee for their services. Q could have asked *Pfarrer* Bernau, but he had vowed not to compromise another one of his friends – ever.

~

Q picked up his pen and started to write a letter to his mother. She had explicitly told him not to send any more secret messages, but today he just had to share the horrific news.

But he only got as far as "Dearest." For nine months now, it had been Hilde's name that followed. Now his Hilde was gone. Pictures of her took over, and he folded his hands and indulged in daydreams of a better time. It took him many minutes before he returned to the gloomy reality.

*Dearest Mother,*

*Thank you so much for doing so much for me; I feel guilty accepting all your gifts. Also, my companion Werner Krauss shares his warm meal with me every evening. I ask you not to send me more food because you need it yourself.*

*Please do not send me more than a tiny piece of cake once or twice a week. With the simple food here, just some oat flakes, sugar, and a piece of apple make a true feast. I have learned to appreciate the simple things in life since my arrival in prison.*

*As long as there's enough dry bread and potatoes, and they always taste good, then any sweet is a sensation.*

*I fully understand if you or Hilde's parents don't want to write me anymore, now that my beloved Hilde had to leave this world.*

*Officially, you're not allowed to know it. The official enforcement notice has been sent to the closest relative, which is Hilde's mother, Annie Klein. I imagine you are not talking to her anymore?*

*Anyhow, I received her goodbye letter on August 12, but the fateful day was August 5. A good soul gave me the notice that very evening, and I had to live the whole week as if I didn't know anything. But I will write you an official letter with the announcement as soon as I'm allowed.*

*Please let me know if my two little sons are well and happy.*

*How did they and the Dremmer family survive the horrible air raids over Hamburg? We have heard worrying news, but I have faith that those two innocent souls will survive this awful war.*

*For my part, I'm prepared for anything. Anything at all.*

*I'm numb to the dangers and the horrors around me. My only consolation is the knowledge that I will soon follow my beloved wife from this world.*

*All the atrocities happening around us, those that I couldn't prevent, don't frighten me anymore because I won't be around long enough to experience them.*

*But you, my dear mother, wouldn't it be better if you fled Berlin and tried to find a secure place in the countryside? Perhaps with your sister?*

*I ask this for a very selfish reason. I want you to stay alive for a very long time to help take care of my two innocent sons.*

*With the utmost gratitude, I heard the news that my brother and his wife have offered to care for them, if worst comes to worst. They have enough on their hands with their own four children. Therefore I am doubly thankful for the offer. Please give Gunther and Käthe my dearest wishes and all my love. They are such good people.*

*Can you let me know if poor Otto was imprisoned as well? He was a dear friend of mine, and I always thought the world of him, but I never let him in on my secret, so I hope with all my soul that he was not doomed because of my actions.*

*Otto and I had opposing political views, and he never agreed with my opinions about the Fatherland, treason, my fondness for Russia, and the communist idea. Nevertheless, I liked him very much, and I respected* him as a scientist and wouldn't want to cause him to choose between our friendship and his political opinions.

It was a hardship to hide my inner conviction from everyone around me, except for Hilde and Erhard. But I could not risk anyone's getting caught in the maze of the powers just because I wanted someone to confide in and lighten my own burden.

I will tell you, my dear mother, that day in and day out, I feel horrible guilt for being the cause and reason of the death of my wife. I have thought hundreds and thousands of times that I should have protected her better.

Please tell my in-laws that I suggested this very thing to Hilde (leaving her after a feigned fight), but she wouldn't let me. On the contrary, she told me she would stick with me in good times and bad times during life and until death do us part.

Her death has parted us, but I know that my death will reunite us forever.

My – our – life had become resignation and hardships, and therefore we decided to emigrate to America. My Russian friends never tried to talk me out of it, even though it was against their own best interest.

The war is now turning cruel, even on the careless Germans, who thought we were invincible. It is the difference in the experience whether you bomb the historic city of London with, at that time, superior weapons, or if you are now on the receiving end, enduring the tenfold of destruction by the now superior methods of the enemy.

In this country, the pain of others has never been important. There was no sympathy for their suffering. But true compassion has to be learned through our own pain.

This feeling of superiority and the arrogance of Germany is coming back with a vengeance,

But I do not expect a rebellion of our people against the futile war. No, it seems that at this time in history, the gods have decided that what has begun has to be ended. Our country has to drain the cup of sorrow. Until the bitter and complete defeat, when everything in our beautiful country has been bombed to ashes. Only then may we arise again to become a better nation.

I do not envy those of you who will be there. No, I believe my situa-

*tion is much more comfortable. A fast and painless end. The situation will get much worse before it gets any better.*

*Later, you will be able to calculate how little time was missing for my beloved Hilde and myself to survive.*

*Even our Hitler, always thinking of his ridiculous ideas, will not want to survive a capitulation. He will not want to witness the formerly enthusiastic masses turning against him. He will search and find death on the battlefield, maybe even this year. In three months? In six months?*

*But you, my beloved and strong mother. Don't be a coward. Stay alive courageously and learn from events. Stay alive for many years to come and enjoy your grandsons. Help them with emotional support should the harsh fate of their parents tear them down.*

*About my financial affairs, please talk to Gunther. I am the owner of several patents together with Otto. I hope that the Reich, during the short time it will still exist, doesn't confiscate my part of them.*

*It is my wish that my children will inherit the rights and the royalties.*

*As soon as you have officially received the announcement of my death, please go to the patent office and try to put the names of my sons in there.*

*If this isn't possible, don't worry. I do not believe that this Reich of a Thousand Years will exist for more than a few more months, and as soon as everything has crumbled to dust, an indemnification of the verdict against Hilde and me will be issued.*

*Then I'm sure Gunther will be able to receive what rightfully belongs to my children.*

*For you, my dear mother, it is my explicit wish that whatever money remains from my means and what you might still possess from the envelope I gave you, shall be used for your needs as well. This letter is my testament; please keep it dear and safe.*

*If worst comes to worst I'm sure my Russian friends will help you out.*

*You have never stopped loving me, even when my opinions didn't match yours. I'm grateful for your generosity because I wouldn't want to leave this world knowing the woman who gave birth and raised me had stopped loving me. You have no idea how much this means to me.*

*One day, you might receive an invoice for about ten or twenty*

*Reichsmark. It will say "for wine." Please pay it; these are debts of mine that I couldn't take care of due to the circumstances. And I wouldn't want such a minor thing as death to hinder me from paying my debt.*

*I am in the process of tying up all loose ends, which I know can be agonizing for those remaining. If you want to know anything, please ask me. I hope I will still have some days of sanity left to answer your questions.*

*My moods are constantly changing. They are pretty accurately described in my last official letter. As you know, official letters must be much more careful than this one. We wouldn't want to cause too much work for the censors, would we?*

*As of now, I am well prepared for the "miracle of death" and not very vulnerable anymore to earthly sufferings. My suffering nerves are benumbed.*

*This is why I can eat and enjoy. At times, I feel an almost mystic union with this world. Almost religiously, like you.*

*My beloved little mother. The one thing I ask you is to always remember me honorably.*

*This is another goodbye. I don't know of anything else to write at the moment. I have been writing this letter from eight in the morning to four in the afternoon.*

*Your – cursed by fate – son*
*Wilhelm*

# CHAPTER 45

On August twenty-third, Hilde's birthday, Q received permission to write his monthly letter. For a moment, he stared at the guard with disbelief at this inhumane cruelty, but then nodded and took pen, ink, and paper. The guard couldn't know.

He decided to write to the one person he had loved for all his life, and let her officially know about Hilde's death.

Werner seemed to notice Q's miserable mood and asked, "How are you holding up, my friend?"

"I couldn't be better," Q laughed sarcastically, "My sons are in the best hands with my in-laws, and I'm allowed to write down my research in the area of plant protection. What else could I ask for?"

"Freedom?" Werner asked with a shrug.

"Ha. Freedom is highly overrated. In here we have everything we need. No tedious household chores, no grocery shopping, and the – admittedly bad – meals are always punctual."

Werner laughed out loud. "Well, if you see it from that point of view…we get enough sleep, have good books to read, and even get to do some manual labor."

"See? The work they give us is even pleasurable."

"Well, I wouldn't classify labeling signs in a fancy type as *pleasurable*, but you're right, it could be much worse." Werner chuckled.

Q grew serious and fixed his eyes on Werner. Without his good comrade, he would have lost his mind months ago.

"I fully accept the right of my enemies to kill me, after the *chuzpe* I showed in my actions against them. And I die like so many others in this war, but I can say with pride that I have always been fighting against National Socialism and for a military defeat of Germany. My bad luck was being caught before the imminent end of war."

"At least you have the satisfaction to be in good company. In the best." Werner smirked and patted his chest.

"We all have to suffer the consequences of our actions, and I do it with pride. By now, I have had so much time to think about dying and how it will happen that it has lost its dread. Not many people in times like ours are allowed to die so quickly and without pain." Q sighed. It was true.

Every day at noon, except on Saturday and Sunday, he waited for the executioners to come for him, to be killed later that evening. But while, in the beginning, he'd waited in deadly terror, this had transformed into angst, curiosity, and finally acceptance. Since Hilde's death, it was like waiting to board the tram to reach his destination.

"By the way, my lawyer has told me that Hitler's idea of my public hanging in front of the Loewe factory has been canceled. I would have hated that."

"I guess you can thank our Russian friends for that. Rumor has it the government doesn't want to compromise their radio deception efforts with Moscow," Werner said, crossing his arms over his chest.

"Our goal was to make an end of this regime in 1942, but it wasn't meant to be." Q stood and paced the room, running a hand through his longish curls. "Not for me, not for you, and not for millions of innocent people on both sides who will continue to be sacrificed until some pigheads are finally smashed against the concrete wall."

Werner nodded. "At least we have the satisfaction that more and more people turn away from the praised ideals, despite the harshest sanctions and threats, leading up to the unhappy end of this whole lunatic undertaking."

"Operation successful...patient and doctor dead." Q laughed hysterically and started shouting, "I do not regret anything! Everything I see and hear fortifies me in my conviction! This government has to tumble! The Nazi bastards must be defeated!"

Worried, Werner approached him and laid a hand on his shoulder. "Hilde has forgiven you. You know that."

Q looked into the sad eyes of his friend. "I know, but..." Q sobbed and fell onto his cot. "Today is her birthday...I miss her so much."

# CHAPTER 46

In the following week, he all but stopped doing his research work, and instead thought of ways to help those who had helped him by sending him money, food, or other necessities while he was in prison.

He intended to say goodbye to the world, and at the same time do a little good with his last actions. His situation didn't allow him to offer any material help, but the one thing he had left was his conviction against Hitler and everything Nazi. This he would offer.

Germany would lose the war sooner or later, and he hoped that after the ultimate capitulation, his status as a traitor to the regime might benefit those he cared for even after his death.

Q made a list of those to whom he would write a secret message.

From his three closest friends, only Otto was – hopefully – at liberty. Jakob had died during the *Reichskristallnacht*, and Leopold, a traitor of the regime himself, had been sent to a concentration camp.

Gunther made it onto the list, as did Hilde's parents in Hamburg. They would have to shoulder the main burden of raising two orphaned boys. Q's heart grew heavy at that thought, but he shook it away. Now wasn't the time to get sentimental.

His mother. Hilde's mother. At the thought of Annie, he hesitated. His emotions toward her were mixed. But he would write one of his "recommendation letters" for her as well, for the sake of his boys.

The good director at the Biological Reichs Institute and several of his ex-colleagues. Martin, his partner-in-crime at Loewe. Q smiled at the memory of how Martin had proved his loyalty. He'd saved Q from being discovered by spilling a cup of coffee over the classified material Q had been copying.

Then he set out to write the first of those letters.


*Dear Friend,*

*My adored wife has been executed already, and I am eager to follow her. My two boys are well cared for with my in-laws.*

*And now world history seems to agree with the opinion of my adored wife and myself about the Third Reich and its cataclysmic ado in the garden of God.*

*We die fighting National Socialism. We hope all of you will survive the bad times that will get all the survivors into hot water, even though not without your own (passive) fault.*

*In the joyful certainty that this day is not far and that my wife and myself belong to the martyrs of the victorious side, I am greeting you.*

*Keeping this letter is dangerous. Please do so only far away from your own house, far away from Berlin, to be recovered only when Germany has lost the war.*

*I want to write down my plea to my friends in the Soviet Union, but also the other Allies, to give you and your family their benevolence, because of your good nature and your goodwill to me.*

*To whomever it may concern, I recommend the person presenting this letter as a technical expert, a good person, able to help in rebuilding this country, meant to work for the good of the nation in the future.*

*Prison Plötzensee, Cell 140*

*2. September 1943*

*Wilhelm "Q" Quedlin*


After sending at least a dozen similar secret messages, he leaned back, pondering what to do next. Life seemed so distant that he did not even find pleasure in his research work. Since the prison didn't have blackout curtains, there was a strict no-light rule in place from dusk to dawn. In early September, the sunlight faded into darkness shortly after dinner.

The next night, Q went to sleep with a satisfied feeling of someone who had organized his legacy, only to be awakened by the shrill noise of the air raid sirens.

Werner jumped down from the upper bunk bed at the same time Q heard panicked yelling from the guards and the other prisoners. He and Werner huddled beneath the table, pulling one of the mattresses around them in an effort to avoid being hit by pieces of falling plaster and concrete.

The hours passed, and the attack became worse. It was the most awful bombing they had ever experienced. A deafening noise indicated that several shells must have landed directly on the prison structure. Q coughed from the dust filling the tiny cell. The thick old prison walls shook like autumn leaves in the wind.

Another direct hit exploded somewhere nearby. Q ducked beneath the mattress and covered his ears until the smell of smoke made him look up. Torn open by the force of the explosion, the unhinged metal cell door swung back and forth.

"Look!" Q hissed. In the hallway rampaged a fire.

"We have to get out, or we'll burn alive," Werner yelled.

Heat and smoke filled the hallway as Q and Werner fled their cell. Many of the cell doors had cracked open, but others were still locked. Q heard the spine-chilling cries of agony from his fellow prisoners, begging for someone to rescue them, as the deadly smoke seeped beneath the doors of the cells.

But the guards had fled the cell block and sought shelter many hours earlier. There was no way to unlock the doors. Q cast a last glance backward as Werner dragged him down the stairs into the courtyard.

Shell after shell detonated in a blinding explosion and rocked not only the building but also the very foundations the prison was built on. The entire city of Berlin glowed with fire.

The Apocalypse had arrived.

Many prisoners in different states of shock gathered in the courtyard. Q ducked against the treacherous security of the wall, hoping – no, praying – that the dropping shells would stop.

It wasn't until the morning light arrived that his wish became reality. When the smoke settled, Q saw nothing but ashes and debris where buildings once stood. A huge part of the cellblock in House III, including the adjacent execution building, had been destroyed.

Half of Berlin had been destroyed.

When the guards returned, they did their best to control the chaos and crammed groups of prisoners into the remaining cells. Q and Werner shared a cell the size of their own with four other prisoners. After counting and re-counting everyone, it became clear that four prisoners sentenced to death had seized the opportunity and escaped.

As the guards took stock, it turned out the prison had sustained massive damage. The death chamber was missing its roof, and the guillotine was damaged by fire, torn out of its underpinnings, its operability questionable.

In the following days, repairs were carried out, and Q and Werner were relocated to their original cell, as only the door had been damaged.

Q couldn't have said what it was, but since the airstrike, a clammy tension had taken hold of everyone in the prison. The guards looked miserable, talking in hushed whispers while the prisoners waited in numb shock for things to come.

On the fourth day, Q noticed bustling activity in the courtyard. At least eight officials had arrived and were preparing – something. Leisure hour had been canceled for the day, and Q heard noises of construction work. He pushed the chair beneath the window to have a better view but couldn't see what they were doing. He supposed they were working on the destroyed House III.

As soon as night fell on September seventh, all prisoners were ordered outside for roll call.

"They're counting us *again*?" Werner tried to joke, but Q wasn't in the mood for joking. A sense of foreboding twisted his stomach.

It was cold that night, and the sky above the capital was pitch black, with the exception of the odd enemy firebomb detonating in the distance. Despite the blackout rule, spotlights lit the prison courtyard and their rays danced across the sky.

All prisoners were ordered to stand in file. Q took his place and then watched the spectacle in wonder, unsure what to expect from this highly unusual roll call. The tension was palpable, as everyone waited to be told what would happen next.

When the first eight men were called by name and led to the makeshift repaired executions building, a murmur went through the ranks. Several minutes later, eight more men were called out. The remaining men, including Q, stood in a stupor. Not a sound was heard.

Q closed his eyes. His time had come. He searched for Werner's hand and squeezed it for a moment. "That's it, my friend," he whispered.

Q stood there for a long time, while row after row of men were led away. He wasn't afraid or even nervous. The inevitable end was nothing to be afraid of. He even sensed a small relief that the waiting was over.

Once, the hangmen had to interrupt their work because several shells crashed into a building nearby. The spotlights went out, and only the half-moon cast the scenery into an eerie light.

The horrible murder continued until eight in the morning. When everyone was ordered back into their cells, Q didn't know whether he should be relieved or disappointed. He looked around, into exhausted familiar faces, and nodded a greeting. A night standing still in the cold, waiting for death to come, had taken its toll on everyone.

Q and Werner had both survived and fell on their cots to sleep the entire day. In the evening, the same spectacle was repeated – for five long nights.

At the end of the sixth night, Q and Werner were still alive. Q shrugged as neither joy nor relief settled in. After that many false alarms, his entire being was numb. All emotions had been extinguished like a candle.

In the evening, a visibly battered *Pfarrer* Bernau slipped into their cell.

"This…has been the most horrendous experience in my entire life," the priest said in a grave voice.

Q nodded. The priest was a good man. Having to watch hundreds of men being murdered must have been a lot to take in.

"Two weeks ago, Hitler complained that over three hundred prisoners were awaiting the outcome of their clemency proceedings and the Ministry of Justice promised to speed up the appeals. Which they did. In nearly every case, the sentence was ordered to be carried out immediately." The priest sighed and shook his head.

Q kept silent for lack of words.

"*Pfarrer*, you can't let those bloody nights destroy you. You need to stay strong and do good. The remaining prisoners need you." Werner had the ability to always find the right words, and after a few moments in silence, the priest showed something like a smile.

"I will. I will. I pray to God to give me the strength to continue."

"How did they manage to repair the guillotine this quickly?" Q couldn't resist asking.

"They didn't."

"They didn't?" Werner raised a brow.

"No. The initial plan was to transfer prisoners to a remote location to face a firing squad, but the logistics involved were too difficult. Instead, they installed a beam with eight ropes in the execution shed…" *Pfarrer* Bernau's voice trailed off.

"Hanging?" Q grabbed his throat. According to his research, hanging was slow and painful.

The priest looked out the window into the sky as he recounted with a shaky voice, "The prisoners had their hands tied behind them and were forced to climb the two-tiered stool. The executioner followed them and placed the thin cord slipknot around their neck before pulling the stool from under their feet. The next prisoners in line, who were neither hooded nor blindfolded, had to witness the struggles of the others as they waited for their turn. In total, two hundred and forty-six prisoners were murdered during the last six nights."

Q stared at the priest, wishing he could unhear that terrible news.

# CHAPTER 47

W hen the mass killings came to a stop, there was an eerie feeling of emptiness. Of the original three hundred prisoners on death row, only fifty remained.

The guards seemed as shaken as the prisoners. None of them had witnessed mass executions before, and rumor had it that more than one of them had to be carried away unconscious and were later seen vomiting their guts out.

Since the mass killings had ended, prisoners were allowed their daily hour of leisure time again. A week ago, the courtyard had been crowded and noisy, now it was deserted and quiet.

Q sensed a different kind of tension in the air, and soon enough knew why. Word came that Italy had unconditionally surrendered on September eleventh.

"Now the tide is turning," Q said.

"It was to be expected; Italy never had the military strength to oppose the Allies," Werner explained. "After Mussolini was deposed, the new leaders did the only rational thing." He always had more information than most of the prisoners, thanks to his influential contacts on the outside.

One of the guards overheard them and joined their discussion. "On the contrary, Germany has lost a lot of deadwood by losing Italy."

"Those *Itaker* have always been more burden than help," another guard said. "We really shouldn't have offered them the role of our allies."

Q kept silent, but he was positive that Italy's surrender was the beginning of the end to this horrible war.

The discussion turned to the horrific situation in Berlin. The air raids seemed to grow in intensity every night.

"Those child-murdering Tommies have reduced half of Berlin to ashes," one guard said.

"I heard that the most valued cultural possessions have been destroyed. Only a few precious pieces of art could be rescued in time and are now stored in underground mining facilities."

"To be honest, I'm sick and tired of this war. My two boys are fighting somewhere in Russia and my wife is a bundle of nerves."

"Our entire quarter doesn't have gas for cooking anymore," another guard complained.

"At least the city officials are providing meals for everyone three times a day. It's a bit of an inconvenience to go to the distribution centers, but our government cares for us. I'll bet the *Itaker* don't get that."

Q motioned for Werner to walk out of earshot of the guards. "Even when the entire country lies in rubble, the administration will still work, and they will still make one list or another."

"It's as much a virtue as it is a curse," Werner replied.

As they returned to their cells, the news of Italy's capitulation still occupied Q's mind, and he couldn't help but feel sorry for all of the poor soldiers out there. They were just men, or boys even. They shouldn't be out fighting each other.

"I often wonder what being in the trenches makes of a man. Gunther was in the Great War but refused to talk abut it," Q murmured more to himself than to anyone else. "Now his oldest son is a prisoner of war in Russia. His parents have no idea whether he's wounded or not. They are worried sick about him."

"There are rumors about the way Stalin treats the prisoners of war. Awful atrocities are happening on both sides," Werner said as he sat on the sole chair to continue writing his novel.

"I never thought humans could stoop so low," Q admitted. "Maybe Marx was right."

Werner looked up from his papers. "In what respect?"

"There is no good in humans. They are inherently bad." Q stretched out on his cot and looked at the ceiling. The damage of the awful air raids was still visible.

"Why would you say that?" Werner wanted to know.

"Think of all the things humans have done to one another in the course of this war. Our kind has behaved worse than wild animals. We're no better than barbarians, and it seems the human race hasn't evolved at all in the last few thousand years."

"I agree that there's a lot that is bad happening, but that doesn't mean all humans are bad." Werner furrowed his brows and smirked at Q. "There's you and me."

Q chuckled. "You're right, but we won't be around for long."

"Come on. If more good news like Italy's defeat trickles in, the war will be over in no time at all."

"God, no!" Q opened his eyes wide, as the meaning of Werner's words registered in his brain. "I hope the war doesn't end soon enough for me to survive."

"You would be the only person afraid to miss your own execution," Werner chuckled and turned to work on his novel.

# CHAPTER 48

The year 1944 had begun, and Q was still in prison. He'd spent thirteen months incarcerated and barely remembered how it was outside.

Hilde's death had left a huge hole in his heart and soul. Five months had passed, and he still woke every morning with insupportable pain and went to sleep with tears in his eyes. Only in his dreams was he happy, because he was with her.

Not even Werner's attempts to cheer him up worked, and day after day, Q's mind became more troubled. Like anyone else, he wanted to live, but not without Hilde.

*It's my fault she had to die.*

He'd had that same thought so many times that he had honestly started to believe that his rightful punishment was to die as well. Only then could he assuage his guilt.

Every day, he waited for his execution – and every day passed, and he was still alive. Deep down, he knew he didn't want any more. Despite his jokes about it, this awful limbo between life and death took a toll on his sanity, and he wished the waiting would finally end.

Sometimes he whispered the words without wanting to: "Please, God, let it end."

~

Q received a letter from his sister-in-law Julia with a picture of the boys. He stared at the picture, trying to manufacture the joy he'd always found in his children, but nothing happened.

The photograph had been taken on Volker's fourth birthday, and those two children didn't resemble the two boys that lived in his memory. It had been so long. Peter had been a baby – and now he was a boy. Try as he might, he couldn't reconcile his memory of them with the persons in the picture.

Q glanced one last time at the picture before he stashed it away. He consoled himself with the fact that they looked happy. *They are fine.* Then he locked up all feelings for them deep inside. *It's better that way.*

Several days later, a guard announced that he was allowed to write a letter, but it had to be written today.

The man wouldn't meet his eyes, so Q nodded and sat down to write…

*My dear beloved Dremmer family,*

*By now, I am experienced enough to throttle down my emotions to a small flame. But this isn't the reason for my bad handwriting. It's caused by the old quill pen and not by my dwindling mind.*

*This morning, I was surprised by the announcement that I'm allowed a letter today and have to use it. Otherwise, the next possibility of sending a letter would be in six weeks from now. But that is too far away to even consider it.*

*This is the reason I cannot wait for my dear mother's letter to answer it, but will take the opportunity to assure you of my love for you all.*

*While I'm still alive, Gunther has been made the custodian for my two little boys. I'm thankful that now two families, yours and his, are taking care of them.*

*Please tell my mother that I won't be able to write as often or as extensively as before, but that I'm longing for her letters and wish to know all the mundane details that you experience out there in freedom, and especially stories about the children.*

*There is an indifference settling into my mind, and the longer I must live with death as my constant partner, the more it loses its hold over me, and I fall deeper into numbness.*

*We humans will never be able to fully fathom the wonder and miracle of coming to life every morning and leaving the conscious mind behind every night when falling asleep, and finally when closing our eyes forever. The same way, we will never be able to fathom the vastness of the universe. But what we can do is to take away the mysticism and get used to it.*

*And I, for my part, have had enough time, and I can say with some satisfaction, "I'm done with it."*

*All the little things, all the thoughts you're sending me, are making it easier for me.*

*I've had several false alarms that gave me the assurance that I am not afraid to die anymore.*

*But this peace of mind is bought at the high price of indifference to human suffering out there. Nevertheless, I think of all of you in soft and distant love from far away over the clouds.*

*If you think of me and remember me in the years to come, be assured that I didn't suffer during this last part of my life. Know that I was bored.*

*For a long time now, I haven't felt hunger or thirst. As I said before, my life has been reduced to a tiny flame. I'm fully aware that outside, this life is not all sunshine. It is similarly constricted and unsatisfactory, surrounded by death.*

*The future is still a closed curtain, and as impatient as one may be, it won't be opened to anyone before the time is right.*

*Please take this letter as what it is. I have, in reality, not been there for you in a long time. Give my greetings to everyone, and especially my children, from a good friend who wasn't meant to be there for them.*

*I wish for my wonderful sons to be able to participate in rebuilding the world into a better place – albeit without their parents.*

*Yours, Q*


Q sent the letter off with a worrisome indifference. Nothing, not even his research, interested him anymore and he waited to join his beloved wife.

Several days later, the guard arrived with news for Werner.

"Pack your things, you're being transferred," the older man said.

"My clemency appeal has been approved?" Werner asked with a hopeful smile.

"Yes, to five years of prison, but don't rejoice too soon." The guard grimaced before he continued, "You're transferred to the Wehrmacht Prison Torgau Forst Zinn."

"A military prison?" Werner muttered, "But I'm not a soldier!"

"Every promoter of a seditious attitude can be interned there, including conscientious objectors, insubordinate personnel, deserters, those who aided the enemy, and spies, as well as prisoners of war and members of the resistance," the guard explained.

Q looked at his friend. Happy and sad at the same time. He wouldn't be executed, but what would await him in Torgau? A place where few men survived the harsh conditions and illness that so often affected those incarcerated there.

"Well, this is goodbye," Werner said, putting on a brave face.

"Yes, goodbye." Q shook his friend's hand and then found himself engulfed in a tight hug.

When Werner released him and met his eyes, unshed tears made them glisten. "Be strong, my friend. The war is almost over."

"Take care of yourself, and one day, we will meet again in another world."

"Time to go," the guard called from outside the cell.

It was with both a sad and hopeful heart that Q watched his friend walk away.

# CHAPTER 49

*January 27, 1944*

One month before his forty-first birthday, Q received news he would be transferred to the prison in Halle, a town about three hours from Berlin.

Everyone knew why people were transferred there.

"Is it time?" Q asked and looked around his cell, meeting the eyes of *Pfarrer* Bernau and the prison director, who had arrived to bid their farewell.

"Yes. It is time." The director stood in the doorway to the cell and nodded with a sad face.

Q shrugged.

"Doctor Quedlin, I want you to know how sorry I am about this. If there was anything I could do…"

Q shook his head. "No, this is how it has to be. How it needs to be."

The director nodded, then turned and walked away, allowing the priest to enter for a final few words.

"My friend, are you ready for what is to come?"

"*Pfarrer*, I am. I am done with this life and ready for what comes next. I'm waiting to be with my Hilde once again."

"I will say a prayer for you."

Q shook his head. "Save your prayers for someone who needs them, *Pfarrer*. My soul is at rest knowing that I will soon receive the judgment I deserve and my Hilde will no longer be alone. Goodbye."

The priest placed a hand on his shoulder and then left. Q and several other prisoners were escorted out to the small van. A few minutes later, he was on his way to his final home on earth.

Q arrived in Halle midafternoon and was put in a cell on the death row. It looked very similar to the one in Plötzensee but without any furniture. Just a mattress on the floor and a blanket provided some comfort.

He raised a brow as one of the guards shackled his arms and legs, but his soul was too far away to feel humiliation or anger. Despite the further-reduced ration, he wasn't hungry or thirsty. It was as if his body had ceased to function already. It was merely a shell holding his soul in place.

The minutes became hours, then days. A pasty mass of haze. Q lost all sense of time and place, the light and darkness of day and night the only indicator of passing time. He crouched motionless in the corner and waited.

Waited.

Waited.

On the eighth day, they came for him. In shackles, they led him to a room where pen, ink, and paper waited for him.

Q eyed the blank paper. He had said farewell to everyone he cared for a long time ago, and now only two letters were due.

*Dear family Dremmer,*

*Today I follow my beloved Hilde.*

*I'm glad that the time of waiting is over and I will soon rest in peace.*

*The outside doesn't have any promises left for me; so much is broken. To think of a better future and long for it, is too far away and too foggy in my imagination.*

*Please make my sons' lives easy and happy. Today, the sacrifices are made so that tomorrow, life will be innocent and relaxed again. One generation had the bad luck to drown in the cooking kettle of our era, to give the next generation a happy life without problems.*

*At least we, Hilde and I, have seen the best of our time. When will it ever be so enjoyable as we found it in the short years of living together?*

*I don't have sorrows anymore about what I leave here on earth. Everything is in order. My help in rebuilding this destroyed world has not been wished for by the higher powers of fate.*

*It will have to be done without me; there are plenty of others, maybe not as understanding as I would have been as a mediator between hostile worlds. But who am I to decide, now without me?*

*Q*

*February 4, 1944*

*PS: When you receive my belongings, please send a letter to Gunther. It's already stamped and includes a collection of spoonerisms. They may brighten the day of the ones coming after me.*


Q paused for a moment and then took another sheet of white paper to write to his mother.


*My dearest beloved mother,*

*This is my final goodbye.*

*Everything you need to know about how and why everything happened is explained in my previous letters to you.*

*Please do not mourn for me. I am resigned to what must now happen, and I will leave this world with my head held high. Soon I will be where I want to be – reunited with my adored wife.*

*Give my best regards to Gunther and tell him to live a good life once the war is over. May he care for you as I would have.*

*Know that I love you and cannot express my gratitude for all the love and strength you gave me, despite our disagreements over politics. With time, you will see how right I was.*

*Your loving son,*

*Wilhelm*

. . .

Q sealed both letters and left them lying on the small table. The guard returned with his final meal. Q drank the soda and ate the small piece of bread, chewing slowly and with great care. All too soon, he finished his meal, and the guard came to take him away.

The executioner was already waiting for him by the guillotine, and on steady legs, Q walked his way. Q caught the twinkling reflection of a ray of sunshine on the sharp metal blade and turned his thoughts to his wife.

*I'm coming, my love!*

Thank you for taking the time to read LOVE AND RESISTANCE. If you enjoyed it, please consider telling your friends or posting a short review. Word of mouth is an author's best friend.

I'm working on series set in Berlin 1943. The protagonists are three sisters, each of them facing her own challenges and struggles. To introduce the series, every person on my mailing list will receive Downed over Germany , the prequel to the War Girl series for free.

Tom Westlake is a Britsh RAF pilot. His struggle to survive starts the moment his fighter-bomber is shot down over Germany in 1943. Follow his adventures and find out if he manages to stay alive despite Gestapo hunting him down.

Sign up to my newsletter to receive a free copy of the short story Downed over Germany or buy it on the retailer of your choice.

War Girl Ursula, the first book in the series is available. Click here to buy.

# AUTHOR'S NOTES

Dear Reader,

Thank you for accompanying me on this emotional journey through my grandparents' lives.

Most of what I know comes from letters that Q (Hansheinrich in real life) and Hilde (Ingeborg) sent to their family members. I have scanned two letters at the end of this chapter, one as original in handwriting from Ingeborg to her family, the other one as transcription from Q's letter to his in-laws. Both are in German, but I've included them to show you these persons were real and as much as I would have wanted to write a different ending to the story, that's the way it was.

Unfortunately, the letters the two of them exchanged during their time in prison were never recovered.

The letter to Q's cousin Fanny in America (in Chapter 44) didn't make it across the ocean and was later found at the prison Plötzensee.

I took some artistic liberty with the person of Werner Krauss. He is a real person who survived the war and was indeed Hansheinrich's cellmate, but only for a few months. Krauss wrote a 33-page report about his involvement with the Schulze-Boysen group, which included several pages about his time in Plötzensee, sharing a cell with my grandfather.

From this report, I have reconstructed their friendship to the best of my ability.

*Pfarrer* Bernau, the priest, was modeled after the Catholic priest Buchholz and his Protestant colleague Harald Poelchau, who worked both in Plötzensee and belonged to the resistance.

The *Plötzenseer Blutnächte*, when the mass executions were carried out, happened between September 7 and 12th 1943 after a large portion of the prison was destroyed. Apparently, Hitler had complained about the slow clemency appeal process shortly before the air raids, and the destruction of many holding cells might have been the perfect excuse to speed up the killings.

It is not known why Hansheinrich Kummerow and Werner Krauss were among the few who were spared during those terrible five nights.

Not everyone in my family sympathized with the resistance. In fact, Hansheinrich's mother wrote in several of her letters to Ingeborg's family in Hamburg, *"I am not sad about Hans' death; he was lost to a diligent and civil life. Even after one year of imprisonment, he lived in such an illusion that he did not acknowledge the heavy guilt he had committed against his country. Our grandsons wouldn't have become good people with those parents."*

While Ingeborg's mother blamed him for the death of her daughter (and told him so), his mother blamed Ingeborg for the fate of her son. But she never said so openly to the two of them, only in her letters to Ingeborg's family in Hamburg.

This is what she wrote in one of the letters in the possession of my family: *"Inge has endured the hard penitence, but Hans is still purging. One thing both my oldest son and I know very clearly now by the happenings in combination with remarks of Hans to me in the year '42: Inge bears the bigger guilt at this tragic end to two lives. She bears the bigger guilt about the final sliding onto the wrong path."*

I believe after more than seventy years, history has decided that they hadn't taken the wrong path in life. But it would take many decades to acknowledge their sacrifice.

After the war, the family was further torn apart by politics. Some of them lived in the part of Berlin that belonged to the German Democratic Republic, the rest in West Berlin, and the Federal Republic of Germany.

Hilde's and Q's good name wasn't completely reinstated for decades in the Western world because they had the "wrong" political reasons in their fight against the Nazis.

During the Cold War, it was unthinkable to commemorate someone who had believed in the ideals of communism and had worked together with the archenemy, the Soviet Union. This changed only with the reunification of Germany in 1989.

In 1995 a student of political science visited my parents' house to write a bachelor thesis about my grandfather. This was the seed for me to start challenging old beliefs, and stoked the desire to learn what had really happened.

Thankfully, my uncle had collected all the letters from that era, and I was able to reconstruct much of their lives and their personalities from those letters and other material.

Volker and Peter (those are not their real names) grew up with their grandparents in Hamburg, and both of them followed in Q's footsteps, as they went to university and became scientists. Each of them married and had two children. Me, my sister, and my two cousins.

This trilogy is a story dear to my heart, and I've wanted to write it for many years. But somehow I never found the time – or the courage – to look deep into the past and dig up the truth.

My grandparents Ingeborg and Hansheinrich Kummerow were two remarkable people I unfortunately didn't have the opportunity to meet, because they died long before I was born. But their story – one of courage and unrelenting spirit – intrigued me and captured me until I gave in to the overwhelming need to write it down.

UNRELENTING is for them, to remember their sacrifice and the difficult choices they – along with many others in war-ridden Europe – had to make. Research on World War II showed me how heroic even the slightest act of resistance was during those dark times, and my admiration for my grandparents, and all the brave persons in the German resistance, has grown beyond imagination.

From a prison cell, my grandfather wrote in one of his many letters…

*"Ich lege durchaus Wert darauf, dass mein Andenken ehrenhaft ist."*
"I want to be remembered honorably."

~Hansheinrich Kummerow

With this book, I hope to honor my grandfather's wish. Honor his and my grandmother's unrelenting spirit. Their love. Their legacy.

# ACKNOWLEDGEMENTS

Writing this book was a long and rewarding journey, and I couldn't have done it without help. First of all I want to thank my terrific cover designer Daniela from www.stunningbookcovers.com. She has made a wonderful cover for me, while putting up with my endless change requests and a process that took more than a month to finalize the cover.

Then I want to thank my awesome editor Lynette, who was the first person to read the rough outline of this novel and who loved it from the first moment. Without her encouragement I might have abandoned the unfinished work.

Many thanks also to JJ Toner, who thoroughly checked and proofread my manuscript.

Thanks to A.Z. Foreman of http://poemsintranslation.blogspot.de/ for allowing me to use his translation of the poem of Lorelei:

*The fairest of maidens is sitting*
*So marvelous up there,*
*Her golden jewels are shining,*
*She's combing her golden hair.*

*She combs with a comb also golden,*
*And sings a song as well*

*Whose melody binds a wondrous*
*And overpowering spell.*

*In his little boat, the boatman*
    *Is seized with a savage woe,*
    *He'd rather look up at the mountain*
    *Than down at the rocks below.*

*I think that the waves will devour*
    *The boatman and boat as one;*
    *And this by her song's sheer power*
    *Fair Lorelei has done.*

# CONTACT ME

I truly appreciate you taking the time to read (and enjoy) my books. And I'd be thrilled to hear from you!
If you'd like to get in touch with me you can do so via

Twitter:
http://twitter.com/MarionKummerow

Facebook:
http://www.facebook.com/AutorinKummerow

Website
http://www.kummerow.info

# ALSO BY MARION KUMMEROW

**Love and Resistance in WW2 Germany**

Unrelenting

Unyielding

Unwavering

Turning Point (Spin-off)

**War Girl Series**

Downed over Germany (Prequel)

War Girl Ursula (Book 1)

War Girl Lotte (Book 2)

War Girl Anna (Book 3)

Reluctant Informer (Book 4)

Trouble Brewing (Book 5)

Fatal Encounter (Book 6)

Uncommon Sacrifice (Book 7)

Bitter Tears (Book 8)

Secrets Revealed (Book 9)

Together at Last (Book 10)

Endless Ordeal (Book 11)

**Berlin Fractured**

From the Ashes (Book 1)

On the Brink (Book 2)

In the Skies (Book 3)

**Historical Romance**

Second Chance at First Love

Find all my books here:

http://www.kummerow.info